THE PAPER

DAUGHTERS

OF

CHINATOWN

THE PAPER

DAUGHTERS

OF

CHINATOWN

HEATHER B. MOORE

SHADOW
MOUNTAIN

For Heidi and Lisa.

Thank you for introducing me to Donaldina Cameron.

Interior images by lisheng2121/Shutterstock

Visit us at shadowmountain.com

Library of Congress Cataloging-in-Publication Data
Names: Moore, Heather B., author.
Title: The paper daughters of Chinatown / Heather B. Moore.
Description: Salt Lake City : Shadow Mountain, [2020] | Summary: "A fictionalized account
    of the early years of Donaldina Cameron's work with the Occidental Mission Home for
    Girls in San Francisco, California, which worked to rescue Chinese girls and women from
    slavery conditions in the late 1800s through the early 1900s"—Provided by publisher.
Identifiers: LCCN 2020009531 | ISBN 9781629727820 (hardback)
Subjects: LCSH: Cameron, Donaldina MacKenzie, 1869-1968—Fiction. | Women social re-
    formers—California—San Francisco—Fiction. | Chinese—California—San Francisco—
    Fiction. | Chinatown (San Francisco, Calif.)—Fiction. | LCGFT: Biographical fiction.
Classification: LCC PS3613.05589 P37 2020 | DDC 813/.6—dc23
LC record available at https://lccn.loc.gov/2020009531

Printed in the United States of America
Lake Book Manufacturing, Inc., Melrose Park, IL

10 9 8 7 6 5 4 3 2 1

AUTHOR'S NOTE

The Paper Daughters of Chinatown is not intended to be a repetition of or addition to the already wonderful books published on Donaldina Cameron and the Occidental Mission Home for Girls. In late 2018, about three days into my research, I knew that in order to create a full-bodied historical work on Donaldina Cameron's life, I could easily write three or four volumes. Therefore, I've selected a period of approximately her first decade at the Occidental Mission Home to develop into a historical novel format. The intention of this work of historical fiction is to illuminate the life and service of Miss Cameron, as well as to bring attention to the continued work and diligence it takes to combat depravity and greed.

That said, this novel begins in the year 1895 on the day of Donaldina Cameron's arrival at 920 Sacramento Street in San Francisco, where she has agreed to teach a sewing class for one year at the Occidental Mission Home. We then follow her journey for just the next thirteen years, when, in fact, she spent the rest of her life serving, mentoring, rescuing, testifying, mothering, and loving the Chinese slave girls and many others she came in contact with.

Her story does not begin with chapter one of this novel, nor does it end with the last page. Miss Cameron retired in 1934 but continued aiding the mission home in one capacity or another until her death. Please see my recommended reading list at the end of this book, as well as ways you can aid in moving forward the work of Donaldina Cameron—and those she served with—to end human trafficking, which still continues today in myriad forms.

Throughout this novel, epigraphs appear at the beginnings of the chapters. Most of them are excerpts from published pieces depicting both the harsh reality of this era and the injustices that take place when human rights are either not granted, not enforced, or not respected. Our history can be a hard pill to swallow. And whether we are American, Chinese, or any other nationality, this plight is part of all our histories because we are all members of the human race.

The research for this book was immense and sometimes emotionally taxing. As an author, a woman, and a mother, I am forever tied to this heartrending story of a woman who proudly took on the title of *Fahn Quai,* or the "white devil," as slave owners and corrupt city officials called Donaldina Cameron. With her team of police officers, Chinese interpreters, and other concerned helpers, she swept into the darkest corners of Chinatown and helped to rescue the broken, the downtrodden, and the abused. They worked day and night to stop the abominable slave and prostitution trades that continued long after laws had been passed to abolish them.

Each chapter has accompanying chapter notes found at the end of the novel. But going into a story such as this, many questions will arise, so I'll attempt to answer a few of them here.

After China was defeated in the Opium Wars (1839–1842; 1856–1860), 2.5 million Chinese traveled overseas in the latter half of the nineteenth century to find jobs. Due to increased taxes, the impossibility of competing against imported goods, loss of land, overpopulation, and other calamities, including devastation from rebellions and uprisings, many Chinese turned to working in the gold mines or the railroad system in California as a way to feed a destitute people.

Chinese men mostly immigrated alone. Those who were married sent money home to their families, since the conditions of labor camps were harsh, and nicer accommodations were too expensive. In the 1850s, Chinese women made up less than five percent of the total Chinese population in America. Traditionally, Chinese women remained at home, caring for the household and children as well as aging parents, in order to adhere to the Confucian teaching: "A woman's duty is to care for the household, and she should have no desire to go abroad" (Yung, *Unbound Feet,* 20). Thus, the men arrived in America without their wives, creating a void in which women were not part of the fiber of the Chinatown culture in San Francisco. An opportunity was presented with this void, and organizations formed, such as the criminal tong, to provide women for the men—in the form of paid prostitution.

This played into the patriarchal culture of the Chinese, in which marriages were arranged and women "had no right to divorce or remarry," while men were "permitted to commit adultery, divorce, remarry, practice polygyny, and discipline their spouses as they saw fit" (Yung, *Unbound Feet,* 19).

Chinese women were up against anti-immigration laws from both sides of the Pacific. Chinese law forbade the emigration of women until 1911, and the 1852 Foreign Miners' Tax affected Chinese miners, along with taxes "levied on Chinese fishermen, laundry men, and brothel owners" (Yung, *Unbound Feet,* 21), making it even more expensive to support a family. Besides passing punitive ordinances aimed specifically at the Chinese, the California legislature denied them basic civil rights, including immigration rights, employment in public works, intermarriage with whites, ability to give testimony in court, and the right to own land.

Then came the Chinese Exclusion Act of 1882, in which Congress suspended Chinese laborers from immigrating for ten years. The Act was renewed in 1892, then again in 1904, and so on, until it was finally repealed in 1943. "In the interest of diplomatic and trade relations between China and the United States, Chinese officials, students, teachers, merchants, and travelers were exempted by treaty provisions—and therein lay the loophole through which Chinese, including women, were able to continue coming after 1882" (Yung, *Unbound Feet,* 22).

This was the open door that allowed slave owners or members of the criminal tong to bring Chinese women into the country under false identities supported by forged paperwork. By virtue of this forged paperwork system, in which the Chinese woman would memorize her new family's heritage and claim to be married or otherwise related to a Chinese man already living and working in California, the *paper daughter* was allowed into the country. "Upon arrival in San Francisco many such Chinese women, usually between the ages of sixteen and twenty-five, were taken to a barracoon, where they were either turned over to their owners or stripped for inspection and sold to the highest bidder" (Yung, *Unbound Feet,* 27).

It wasn't until the early 1870s that women's missionary societies discovered the need to provide a safe place for Chinese women fleeing slavery. Despite facing opposition herself for helping the Chinese women, Mrs. Samantha Condit, wife of a Presbyterian missionary assigned to Chinatown, advocated for their cause until she established the California branch of the Women's Foreign Missionary Society. Not only was she up against a myriad of anti-Chinese city ordinances, but finding donors proved to be difficult, with many refusing to donate to a cause that supported supposedly depraved women (*New Era Magazine,* 137).

Condit prevailed. In 1874, she and her board rented a small apartment just below Nob Hill in San Francisco, officially founding the Occidental Mission Home for Girls. This was the beginning of establishing a place of refuge, healing, education, and Christian religious instruction for the destitute women of Chinatown. Although Bible study and attending church on Sundays were part of the curriculum at the mission home, Donaldina Cameron and her staff incorporated the girls' heritage and culture as well throughout their education. The mission home didn't necessarily expect the girls to convert to Christianity, but some of them did (Martin, *Chinatown's Angry Angel,* 153). By the time Donaldina Cameron retired as the mission home's superintendent in 1934, the number of slaves she and her staff had rescued had reached three thousand.

HISTORICAL TIMELINE

1869: Donaldina Cameron is born in Clydevale on the Molyneux, New Zealand.

1872: The Cameron family moves to California, arriving in San Francisco.

1873: The California Branch of the Women's Foreign Mission Society is formed.

1874: The Women's Foreign Mission Society opens the Occidental Mission Home for Girls.

1882: The Chinese Exclusion Act is approved by Congress.

1894: The Occidental Mission Home relocates to 920 Sacramento Street.

1894: Tien Fu Wu is rescued and brought to the mission home.

1895: Donaldina Cameron takes train to San Francisco in April, arrives at mission home to teach sewing classes.

1897: Mission home superintendent, Margaret Culbertson, dies. Mary H. Field becomes new superintendent.

1900: Mary H. Field resigns, and Donaldina Cameron accepts the position as superintendent.

1900: Chinatown is scoured because of bubonic plague.

1906: An enormous earthquake devastates San Francisco.

1907: Cornerstone for new mission home is laid at 920 Sacramento Street.

1908: Miss Cameron and girls return to 920 Sacramento Street.

1908: The newly built mission home is dedicated.

1910: The Angel Island Immigration Station opens.

1912: Women are allowed to vote in San Francisco.

1934: Donaldina Cameron retires.

1935: Trafficked women testify in the Broken Blossoms court case.

1942: The mission home is renamed the "Cameron House."

1943: The Chinese Exclusion Act is repealed.

1968: Donaldina Cameron dies, with Tien Fu Wu by her side.

CHARACTER CHART

HISTORICAL CHARACTERS

(in order of their mention in this book)

Donaldina Cameron (Dolly)

Mary Ann Browne

Evelyn Browne

Margaret Culbertson

DONALDINA'S SISTERS:
  Annie
  Jessie
  Katherine
  Helen

Eleanor Olney

Tien Fu Wu

Yoke Lon Lee (Lonnie)

Dong Ho

Anna Culbertson
  (niece of Margaret)

Ah Cheng

Yuen Qui

CHINATOWN POLICE SQUAD:
  Jesse Cook
  John Green
  George Riordan
  James Farrell
  George Patrick O'Connor

Hong Leen

Woo Hip

Sing Leen

Charlie Bailey, Donaldina's
  brother-in-law

Mary H. Field

Ah-Peen Oie

Jean Ying

LAWYERS:
  Abe Ruef
  Henry E. Monroe
  Weigle
  Herrington

Kum Quai

Chung Bow

Wong Fong

Paul Dinsmore

Colonel Whitton

Dr. John Endicott Gardner

Leung Kum Ching

Ben Bazatas

Frances P. Thompson

President William McKinley and
his wife, Mrs. Ida McKinley

Caroline Bailey, Donaldina's
niece

Mrs. Bazatas, Ben's mother

Charles Bazatas

Wilmina Wheeler

Isabella Cameron
(lives in Scotland)

Aunt Catherine
(lives in Scotland)

Governor Pardee

Minnie Ferree

Yuen Kum

Hung Mui

Henry Lai

Sai Mui

FICTIONAL CHARACTERS

Mei Lien

Auntie Nuwa

Uncle Bo Wei

Wang Foo

Kang and Jiao, children
of Hong Leen

Zhang Wei

Huan Sun

Jun Ling, husband of
Ah Cheng

Li Na

CHAPTER ONE

*"From a woman, and she a pretty, fair-spoken Scotch maiden,
this slave trade took its hardest blow—playing her desperate
lone hand, she reduced the traffic by about one-half."*

—WILL IRVIN, SAN FRANCISCO CHRONICLE, 1907

APRIL 1895

Donaldina Cameron leaned her head against the cool glass of the window as the train slowed to a stop, its whistle mimicking the call of a mournful dove—deep and melancholy—a fitting echo of her life over the past few years. With no husband, no employment, and no parents to watch over, she felt as stagnant as a warm pond on a lazy summer day.

Death and loss had been a repeated pattern, and she'd been forced to piece together quilt squares of her life that didn't quite match. Since the death of her father, and then her failed engagement to George Sargent, Donaldina—or Dolly, as most people called her—didn't fit in with life at her family's ranch. Not anymore, not with her siblings all marrying, raising children, and moving on with their lives.

And now, here she sat, the lone passenger in a train compartment.

She refocused her gaze outside the series of square windows as the landscape came into view. Gone were the curved green hills and budding trees of her home in the San Gabriel Valley, now replaced by the ghostly outlines of buildings as the San Francisco fog clung to its final moments before giving way to the midday sun.

Donaldina tucked her stitching sampler into the small carpetbag next to her on the velvet-covered bench, then smoothed her hands over her black voile skirt. She was ready. Perhaps she could do this. Maybe.

She had agreed to teach for one year at a Presbyterian mission home, and she was not a woman to go back on her word, especially after what Mrs. Mary Ann Browne had shared with her. Mrs. Browne, the mother of one of Dolly's dear school friends, Evelyn, served as the president of the board of the mission home. Dolly and Evelyn had lost touch the past couple of years, but Mrs. Browne had unexpectedly visited the Cameron family that month. She'd described in great detail her life in San Francisco as she and Dolly rode together in a buggy from church to the Cameron ranch.

Dolly hadn't admitted her desperation to do something, to be someone, at the time. Instead, her curiosity only grew. What *did* she want to do with her life? At twenty-five years old, Donaldina Mackenzie Cameron had passable talents, enjoyed her family, and loved the peaceful life on the ranch where she'd been raised. But she couldn't very well live on charity with one of her married sisters. So where was her place in the world?

Mrs. Browne told Dolly about a woman named Margaret Culbertson who worked at the mission home, teaching and caring for young Chinese girls who had been rescued.

"Rescued?" Dolly had questioned.

"Yes," Mrs. Browne said, lowering her voice, although only the birds and sunshine were within earshot, "from the brothels of Chinatown."

The words sent a rash of bumps across Dolly's arms, as if she'd stepped into an underground cellar. Of course, she knew that women of the night existed—not that she'd seen any, in her recollection, but she wasn't completely naive. Still, she tried not to look so shocked at the subject matter. "And . . . Miss Culbertson helps these women? How?"

"Women *and* girls," Mrs. Browne corrected. "Some of the girls are as young as eight or nine. They're brought over from China by highbinders, promised a good life and marriage in America, yet the promises are lies. These young girls are sold as domestic slaves or forced into prostitution."

Dolly held very still, her mind trying to process what Mrs. Browne was saying. The warm sun and fragrance of apple blossoms seemed incongruent with the woman's words.

"When the girls are brought to the mission home, they're often sick and afraid," Mrs. Browne continued, seemingly oblivious to Dolly's mounting dismay. "They come with scars and bruises, and they know little of kindness. They cower at sudden noises or swift movements. But they are hungry to learn. Miss Culbertson teaches them English, along with how to cook, how to sew, how to pray, and how to hope."

"Hope," Dolly echoed in a whisper.

Mrs. Browne's nod was emphatic. "I saw the beautiful cushions you embroidered, Dolly. You're a natural seamstress. And you are outgoing, friendly, resourceful . . . come to San Francisco. Teach sewing to the Chinese girls in the mission home. We desperately need help from capable women like you."

Would Dolly be successful in teaching? Could she truly make a difference in the lives of motherless girls? Her gaze shifted to the soft gray outside the train window as they pulled into the station. Dolly's mother had died before she had turned six, and her childhood memories had long since faded. Raised by her older sisters—Annie, Jessie, Katherine, and Helen—Dolly hadn't lacked love and affection in her life. Yet . . . she missed her mother— not with tangible memories, but with something deeper, as if her mother's death had left a hollow spot in her heart.

The passengers already outside the train collected their luggage and greeted family members. Dolly felt removed from the warm welcomes. Her welcome would be of a different sort. Once she stepped off this train, her life would never be the same.

The voices and commotion in the train corridor faded, and Dolly released a shaky breath. She could do this; she would do this. She had committed to one year. It wasn't so long in the scheme of things—and besides, she would enjoy exploring San Francisco, seeing new sights, and meeting new people.

Dolly rose from the bench, picked up her carpetbag, and took a final look about the tidy compartment. Then she eased into the corridor and joined the last few passengers leaving the train.

The porter was waiting with her trunk by the time she stepped off the train into the late-morning fog. She didn't need to look at the written address in her notebook to remember the location of 920 Sacramento Street. The address had been etched in her mind for weeks. The porter, a burly man with a curling mustache, cheerfully pointed her in the direction of where she could hail a buggy.

Once the buggy driver had loaded her trunk, Dolly sank onto the thin seat cushion. She peered out the side as the buggy rattled along the cobblestones behind the draft horse. The streets were laced with fog, and Dolly's heart mirrored the grayness of the day. She pushed back the homesickness that threatened, and instead gazed at the sights as they left the warehouse district and its burly dock workers with arms the size of their necks, their wagons and carts pulled by the largest draft horses she'd ever seen.

As the buggy turned away from the train station, the landscape changed once again, and they drove through downtown. Dolly peered up at the tall buildings, counting multiple stories rising from the sidewalks. The Baldwin Hotel, with its five towering floors, was topped by domes and spires. It looked like an opulent castle, something out of a storybook. In front of the tall buildings, trees had been planted in a neat line, joined by hitching posts, not only to hitch horses or wagons but to prevent passing carriages from bumping into buildings.

She counted up to twelve levels on one building. Storefronts were lit with electric lights on Grant Street, glowing in the lifting fog, making the place look ethereal. Such beauty made it hard to reconcile that San Francisco was also such an underbelly of human slavery. Dolly's attention was caught by a woman exiting a shop on the arm of a gentleman. Her full skirt and frilly blouse were made complete with a short jacket and a hat trimmed in ribbons. The man at her side wore gloves and an elegant black suit coat with pinstripe trousers, his cane clicking along the cobblestones as he strolled.

The sights of the sophisticated shops and stylish men and women faded as they crossed Bush Street. It was as if they had driven straight into another country on Dupont Street. The elegant buildings were replaced with tall pagodas and narrow shops. Shop signs scaled the buildings, covered in red and yellow Chinese characters. A woman dressed all in black, her hair pulled into a severe bun, swept furiously at the boardwalk in front of her shop. She looked up at the passing buggy, and her mouth formed a grim line, her face mapped with deep lines.

Two Chinese men stood on the corner, sharing a long pipe, the trail of smoke dissipating into the fog. They both wore loose, black clothing and single long pigtails down their backs. The woodsy scent of their pipe reached Dolly, mingling with other sweeter scents of baking. The two men followed the passing cab with their gazes, and Dolly wondered if they saw her as an anomaly in this part of the city.

Then the cab turned off Dupont, and the driver urged the horse as they moved up a steep hill. They passed square, brick homes, some of them with multiple floors and windows scaling up the sides. Dolly wondered about the lives lived behind the closed curtains. She shifted in her seat to look down the hill. The city of San Francisco, still swathed in fog, had begun to take shape. With the lengthening rays of sun, the shadowed buildings warmed to yellows and golds. Smoke puffed from many chimneys, dispelling the cold morning, and beyond, the bay's murky gray water sharpened to a deep blue.

Excitement replaced any misgivings or threads of melancholy that Dolly felt, and moments later, the driver slowed in front of a five-story, red brick building. Her gaze followed the lines of the sturdy structure, and she was impressed with its size.

The driver made quick work of unloading her trunk and carrying it to the front door. Then he paused before climbing back onto the buggy. "Are you sure this is your destination?"

The 920 address left no doubt. "Yes," Dolly said.

His gaze darted past her. "Take care around this area, ma'am."

Dolly thanked him, then walked toward the square, stalwart building, reading the sign: *Occidental Board Presbyterian Mission Home.* The brickwork curved gracefully over the entrance, giving Dolly both a sense of grace and a feeling of security. The main-level windows stretched along the street, reflecting the early morning light. But the lower bank of windows told another story. Covered by grates, these windows were dark and appeared nearly impenetrable. They were certainly not built for gazing out upon the street or letting in light.

She walked up the flight of stairs leading to the heavy double doors, which were polished a warm brown. The chill in the air had softened. Raising the knocker, she let it fall, and the sound reverberated through the wood. What Dolly hadn't expected was the person who answered: a young Chinese girl. Her dark hair was parted straight down the middle, the ends woven into short braids. She wore a long white tunic over white pants, and her little golden feet were bare. The girl's deep-brown eyes seemed to have no end to their depth.

"Hello," Dolly said.

"Who?" the young girl asked, her small fingers wrapped tightly around the edge of the door. She couldn't have been more than seven or eight. Why had such a young girl been given door duty?

"I'm Miss Donaldina Cameron, and what's your name?"

The girl didn't answer, but she grasped Dolly's skirt, giving it a tug as if inviting her inside. Did the girl not speak English?

Dolly smiled and shifted her trunk inside the doorway. After she had set it inside the entrance, the young girl shut and bolted the door. Then, before Dolly could ask another question, the girl dashed off, disappearing into the depths of the house.

Dolly looked about the entryway and the staircase beyond. The dark paneled wood on the walls gave the home a graceful atmosphere, and the scent of cleaning oil told her it was well cared for.

Her attention was caught by a noise on the landing at the top of the staircase. Another young Chinese girl was crouched in front of the banister, her dark eyes peering through the slats. The girl had a deep scar along her jaw and more scars mapping her thin arms. Dolly guessed her to be about nine or ten. "Hello? What's your name?"

The girl gasped, and her eyes widened in what seemed to be fear. She scrambled to her feet and fled, her two pigtails bouncing against her narrow shoulders.

"Well," Dolly murmured, "a fine welcome to me."

Footsteps sounded on one of the upper floors, and the distant sounds of kitchen preparations from somewhere in the back of the house told Dolly that perhaps normal domesticity was a part of the mission home after all. Would either of the young Chinese girls alert a staff member she was here? As Dolly wondered if she should shed her hat and jacket quite yet, a door opened beyond the wide staircase.

"Dolly," a voice exclaimed. Eleanor Olney strode toward her, arms outstretched.

Dolly had gone to school with Eleanor years ago; she was now one of the staff members that Mrs. Browne had mentioned volunteered here. The two women embraced. Eleanor drew back and said, "It's been ages since I've seen you. I'm so glad you agreed to come."

"When Mrs. Browne told me about the work here, I was intrigued," Dolly said.

Eleanor flashed a smile. She always did have pretty teeth. "Last I heard, you were getting married to George Sargent. Whatever happened?"

"It's an old story now," Dolly said. George was five years in the past and not something she wanted to rehash with a mere acquaintance. "I'm more interested in the tour."

"Of course," Eleanor said. "Come, let me show you around."

They walked into the adjoining parlor, a pretty room by all accounts. The furniture was elegant but worn, as if it had been donated and not purchased new. A couple of bookcases lined the walls, and Dolly was curious about the learning that took place at the mission home, but Eleanor didn't pause. She continued to lead her into the next room.

"This is the Chinese Room," Eleanor said in a pleased tone. "Most of the items are gifts from the Chinese Legation and other merchants. We are fortunate to have such a place for the girls to feel connected to their heritage."

The space had a stillness to it, as if history had been lived here. Intricately carved teak furniture pieces stood in small groupings atop thick rugs. Various scrolls of Chinese watercolors hung on the walls—scenes of China painted in soft blues, greens, and pinks. Painted ceramic vases and bowls, depicting tiny figures and even smaller flowers and trees, were positioned around the room, demanding closer inspection later.

A beautiful room, and it was absolutely empty.

"Where is everyone?" Dolly asked.

"The younger girls are in classes," Eleanor said. "The older girls are doing their chores right now, working in the kitchen, doing laundry, or sewing."

"Where did the girl who answered the door disappear to?" Dolly asked. "And another one at the top of the stairs seemed afraid of me. She had terrible scars on her face and arms."

"Tien Fu Wu," Eleanor said with a sigh. "She should be in class with the others. Too curious for her own good." She paused. "How much did Mrs. Browne tell you about the girls?"

"She said they've been rescued from dismal situations," Dolly answered.

Eleanor lowered her voice. "Most of the girls have been severely abused. Sometimes the trauma they experience takes a long time to work itself out of their souls. Eventually, they learn to trust us. But when someone new arrives, their lives are once again interrupted, reshuffled, and the process starts all over again."

"So those scars on Tien's face and arms were not because of an accident?"

"No." Eleanor's gaze was steady. "The girls in your sewing class have deep, dark histories. Some can be . . . very difficult . . . like Tien. But please know that we are all here to help you and work together."

Dolly's throat had grown tight. It was one thing to know that a girl had been abused; it was another to see the permanent proof on her skin. How could she look past the scars and teach simple and mundane things like choosing the color of thread, or how large to cut a pillowcase, knowing the awful things these girls had experienced?

Eleanor touched Dolly's arm. "The girls will come to love you, you'll see. Now, if I haven't scared you off, come and I'll show you your room."

Dolly exhaled slowly and smiled, although her heart throbbed with a dull ache. "All right."

Eleanor returned her smile and led Dolly back to the staircase.

When they reached the third landing, they continued along a corridor. There, Eleanor entered a plain bedroom furnished only with a corner table, chair, and twin bed.

"You can leave your outer things here," Eleanor said, "and then I'll take you to meet the director."

Dolly quickly removed her hat, gloves, and jacket. She didn't mind the plain and simple surroundings, she really didn't. If anything, she felt humbled that Mrs. Browne had thought that Dolly could contribute in a situation like this.

She then followed Eleanor downstairs. On the second landing, she caught a glimpse of another Chinese girl whose black eyes gazed at her like a frightened animal. But the girl ducked out of sight, limping as she went, before Dolly could say anything friendly. Why was the girl limping? Dolly really needed to learn some Chinese.

Her thoughts were interrupted by an older woman's voice greeting her.

"Miss Cameron?" A woman walked toward her, the dimness of the hallway revealing an aged face, erect posture, and hair pulled into an immaculate pompadour, almost entirely gray. The woman's brown eyes seemed to reflect the wood paneling along the wall, and although her dress was elegant enough, it was clear that it was a poor fit—as if the woman had lost weight after being measured. "I'm Miss Culbertson, the director of the mission home." Frown lines pulled at her forehead. "Welcome."

The greeting was far from enthusiastic, and Miss Culbertson made no secret of thoroughly studying Dolly.

"Thank you," Dolly said. "Eleanor showed me around, although I've yet to meet anyone else save for one of the girls who let me in. It seems every girl who sees me disappears."

Miss Culbertson's brown eyes warmed. "Yes, well, making themselves scarce is a prized skill among our girls." She hesitated, as if she were battling what to say next.

Eleanor murmured that she needed to check on the progress in the kitchen.

The director nodded at Eleanor, then looked at Dolly. "Come into my office, Miss Cameron, where we can speak in private."

Something in the tone of Miss Culbertson's voice put Dolly on alert. If the present circumstances weren't unusual enough, she now sensed something was amiss with her arrival.

Dolly followed the director along the corridor. The woman walked slowly, and once in a while, she used the wall for a bit of support. Was the woman unwell? Now that Dolly was with the director, shouldn't she feel more relaxed? But her unease only tightened her stomach like a too-taut sewing stitch.

Miss Culbertson led the way down the stairs, then into her office. She indicated for Dolly to sit in a faded brocade chair. The director stepped to the window with a view of the street beyond and gazed outside for a long moment.

A cart clattered by, pulled by a horse.

Should Dolly be asking questions? The back of her neck prickled in anticipation, but she didn't know if Miss Culbertson's reluctance was a good thing or a bad one.

Finally, the director's brown eyes swung to Dolly. "Are you sure you will not be afraid of this work?"

Dolly thought she'd been clear in her letter of application. She had committed to teach for one year. Besides, Mrs. Browne had practically begged for her help. "I have come ready to work," she said, hoping to reassure the woman.

"Mrs. Browne was quite enthusiastic in her recommendation of you," Miss Culbertson continued, studying Dolly.

Perhaps Dolly had worn clothing that was too nice, thereby giving the impression of having certain airs and expectations. Eleanor's and Miss Culbertson's clothes were plain and serviceable.

"Mrs. Browne also says you're an excellent seamstress," Miss Culbertson said, "which is all well and good, but working here takes a bit of fortitude. Things in the city are quite different from life in the smaller towns."

Dolly didn't know how to respond. She supposed she had fortitude. Losing both parents, getting an education, keeping up with whatever needed to be done on the ranch . . . should she mention any of this?

"I am not a young girl recently out of the schoolhouse," Dolly said at last. "Both Mrs. Browne and Eleanor told me about the circumstances these girls come from. I am sure I have a lot to learn, but I'm looking forward to the work and will help with whatever is needed." Although this thought worried her a little. Beyond teaching, what else would be required of her? Possible discipline problems?

Miss Culbertson's frown returned. "There are dangers, you know."

Mrs. Browne had never mentioned this. "What sort of dangers?" Dolly asked, wondering if the girls got into fights. Pulled each other's hair?

Miss Culbertson crossed to the desk and placed a hand on the edge. There was another long pause, as if she were reluctant to speak. "This morning, we had an incident."

Dolly's stomach did a slow turn.

"We've had plenty of threats before, of course," the director said, "but this one was *inside* the mission home."

"Threats?" Dolly echoed.

Miss Culbertson seemed to peer straight into Dolly's soul as she said, "One of the girls found a long stick in the hallway. We called for the police to investigate, and they declared that it was dynamite."

"Oh." Dolly's thoughts raced. "An explosive?"

"Yes." Miss Culbertson rested both her hands on the desk as if she needed to support herself. "Our latest rescued girl was worth a lot of money to her owner. Thousands of dollars. We have many enemies, you see, Miss Cameron. Enemies who want their slaves back and would like nothing more than to see our work destroyed, both figuratively and literally. The dynamite was strong enough to blow up this entire city block."

Questions collided in Dolly's mind. She thought of the young girls she'd seen: their scars, their thin bodies, their dark, haunted eyes. Their fear of *her*—a white woman who had come to teach sewing skills. She blinked away the sudden burning in her eyes and refocused on Miss Culbertson.

The director's next words were spoken in a quiet, even tone. "You're tall, Miss Cameron, your eyes are green, and your hair a deep bronze. You will stand out, you must realize, in Chinatown. Not only that, but your Scottish accent will attract attention."

Dolly swallowed against the sudden rawness of her throat. "Is my accent a problem?"

"Not inherently," Miss Culbertson said. "But it will certainly draw notice from those who wish us to fail in our mission."

The breath in Dolly's lungs deflated. "I cannot help my appearance," she said, lifting her chin, "and I've never judged others for theirs."

Miss Culbertson eyed her for a long moment. Faint sounds reached through the closed door. Singing? "You will stay then," the director said at last, her tone softer than it had been, "despite all that I've told you?"

Dolly held the older woman's gaze. She'd thought that stepping off the train had been the turning point in her life. But she'd been wrong. This mo-ment was. The director was more than twice Dolly's age, and yet, she was liv-ing and working here. "Are *you* staying, Miss Culbertson?"

Miss Culbertson's brown eyes glimmered with surprise, but she gave a small, determined nod. "Of course."

Dolly muffled the rest of her questions. There would be time for them later. "Then I will stay too."

CHAPTER TWO

"Although as a race the Chinese are characterized for their love of domestic life, few family circles have been formed among them in San Francisco. Woman, the important link in the sacred chain, is not here; or if she is here she has been forced to engage in that infamous pursuit that is the destroyer of homes. Of the whole number of Chinese women in San Francisco, there are, perhaps less than a hundred who are lawful wives, or keepers of the home."

—B. E. Lloyd, Lights and Shades in San Francisco, 1876

1895

"Miss Cameron," seven-year-old Yoke Lon Lee cried. "Kicking!"

The young girl whom everyone called Lonnie was prone to hysterics. She was deathly afraid of fire and couldn't work in the kitchens. The burn marks on her arms were a testament to the reason behind her fear.

There was no fire in the sewing room, but Dolly couldn't brush off Lonnie's panicked voice.

Dolly had heard the sound of the kick.

"Kicking. Stop her!" Lonnie cried again.

"I saw her," Dong Ho confirmed, another scrap of a girl who had two moods: sweet or feisty.

Dolly knew it was only seconds before an all-out fight began. That was something she had witnessed more than once now.

Dolly turned to face another Chinese girl of about ten years old with horrifying scars along her jaw and arms: Tien Fu Wu. The young girl who'd been frightened of her on that first day at the mission home and who, since then, had shown nothing but defiance. Tien had made no secret of disliking Dolly, although she seemed to tolerate Miss Culbertson.

"Tien," Dolly said in a soft tone, "we must keep our hands and feet to ourselves."

Tien didn't make eye contact, but Dolly knew she'd heard because the honey color of her face had flushed.

"I'm not kicking," Tien said in surprisingly good English.

Dolly exhaled. Should she argue with the girl or just ask her to behave from here on out?

One week had passed since Dolly's arrival at the mission home. The Chinese girls didn't run from her anymore, and she'd learned everyone's names. The younger ones were more apt to display unimpeded affection, and Dolly often received hugs from a few of them. Their sweet affection melted her heart more with each passing day.

Anna, Miss Culbertson's niece, had whispered tidbits of the girls' stories until Dolly could hardly bear to hear any more. The younger girls were more prone to tantrums and arguing, whereas the older girls struggled with seeing the light through all the darkness they'd been through. Some of them didn't even emerge from their rooms for days at a time.

With Tien, the label *precocious* was too mild. Dolly could see the girl's mind working through her lovely dark eyes. She was intelligent and a quick learner. Despite her pretty features of rosy cheeks and pale gold complexion, the scar on Tien's jaw told a darker history. Yet she knew exactly what she was doing and the effect it would have. She didn't seem to care about consequences, though; in fact, she welcomed them.

Still, Dolly treaded carefully with Tien. Dolly had read the girl's record in the ledger and discovered that Tien had been sold by her father to settle gambling debts. Her new owner had unbound Tien's bound feet, then soaked them in saltwater over a period of several days so that she'd have the stability to work harder. But she was sold again to a cruel mistress and forced to work day and night or suffer abuse for laziness.

Dolly approached the ten-year-old girl now, telling herself that with some girls, gaining their confidence would take longer. Months, perhaps. All Dolly could do was extend compassion by speaking in soft tones to her students, smiling often, and pretending not to be ruffled or shocked by outbursts or scuffles. But Tien could not be allowed to get away with cruelty.

Dolly spoke quietly so the other girls wouldn't overhear. "Do you know what lying is, Tien?"

The girl didn't answer for a moment. Then her eyes flicked to Dolly's briefly. In a barely audible voice, Tien said, "Not telling the truth."

"Correct," Dolly said. "When we lie, we lose the trust of another person. Do you know what trust is?"

"I don't trust anyone," Tien said, her tone hard.

It hurt Dolly to hear this young girl make such a pronouncement. "What about Miss Culbertson? Do you trust her?"

When Tien didn't answer, Dolly continued, "When you don't lie, other people will trust you. Don't you want your teachers to trust you?"

The girl still didn't answer, but Dolly knew she had heard and understood. Tien returned to the quilt squares she was piecing together in a neat line. But while Dolly watched, Tien's stitches became uneven and sloppy, and Dolly knew the girl was doing it on purpose.

"Your sewing is beautiful, Tien," Dolly said. "The first rows of stitches are very nice."

The girl didn't react, and Dolly gazed down at her dark hair, parted neatly in the middle and braided. The only break in her composure was the slightest tremble of her slim fingers. Dolly crouched beside her. "If you keep progressing, and keep telling the truth, someday, you could teach this class."

Tien's dark gaze lifted, and Dolly felt physically slapped by the disdain she saw in the girl's eyes.

"I don't want to live here," Tien said in a sharp tone. "No." She ripped out a row of stitches.

Dolly had pushed too far. Not every girl in the home considered this place a sanctuary, and Tien's actions were a testimony of that.

Anna appeared in the doorway then, and her gaze took in the whole of the situation in an instant. Her brown eyes were the same color as her aunt's, but Anna's contained the liveliness of youth and expectation. It was refreshing to have such an ally, especially since Miss Culbertson had been feeling poorly for a couple of days.

Relief sang through Dolly, and she straightened and crossed to Anna.

"Miss Culbertson is asking for you," Anna said in a quiet voice, avoiding further attention from the girls who had their heads bent over their sewing.

"Is she feeling better?" Dolly asked.

"Not much, but she's working in her office," Anna said. "I'll oversee your class while you go speak to her."

Dolly nodded. "Just a warning, Tien is not happy with me." Perhaps it would be good for Dolly to leave the classroom for a bit. Tien could go back to her pretty stitching.

"All right," Anna said. "I'll keep a special eye on her."

"Thank you." Dolly strode to the office where she'd first been challenged about her loyalty to this position. Before knocking, she adjusted a pin to affix a piece of hair that had come loose. When she knocked lightly on the closed door, a voice called her inside.

Dolly stepped into the office to find that Miss Culbertson stood by the window, a small scrap of paper and a red cloth in hand. No lamps were turned on, and the early evening had left the office in shadow. The director turned, her expression graver than usual.

Without any preamble, the director said, "In two weeks, I leave for New Orleans to take one of the Chinese women to begin her married life. Some of these girls find love after their horrific experiences, but only after the potential groom is vetted by me. We also require that the men are Christians and hold to Christian values."

Dolly nodded. Some of the other staff members had said as much.

"I've been paying attention to you this past week, Miss Cameron," Miss Culbertson said. "I've watched your interaction with the girls, and I'm sensing a genuine affinity."

The director wasn't wrong. In only a short time, Dolly had grown fond of many of the girls. "I grew up in a large family," she said. "And having lost my mother when I was five, I guess I can relate to these motherless girls."

Miss Culbertson looked thoughtful as she scanned Dolly's face. "The girls are growing fond of you as well, although I understand Tien continues to give you trouble."

"She's young yet, and I gather she hasn't been here long."

"A year," Miss Culbertson said. "Long enough, but some girls have faced things that we may never know."

Dolly's chest felt heavy. Was Tien one of those girls?

"Since I'll be gone for a few weeks," Miss Culbertson continued, "I want to make sure that someone is trained in my stead." She raised a hand. "Not as director, since all the administration details can wait, but the rescue work cannot wait. In my absence, the work must go on. Which means I need your help tonight so that you can begin your training."

Dolly's brows pulled together. "Training for what?"

"We're going on a raid to rescue a girl kept prisoner in Spafford Alley," Miss Culbertson said. She set the paper on her desk. "This note details the name and location of the girl who is begging for rescue." Next she held up the red cloth. "This torn cloth belongs to the girl, and she will have the other half."

"So we can identify her?"

"Correct," Miss Culbertson said. "We need to get in and out of the place as quickly as possible. We'll leave at midnight. Ah Cheng will translate for us. Yuen Qui is helping with something else tonight."

Dolly opened her mouth, then closed it. She had many questions, but she also needed time to let this request sink in. There was no doubt she would accept, yet she felt as if she were running toward a cliff in the dark with no idea where the drop-off began. Would the rescued slave be sweet like Lonnie, or full of bitterness like Tien? "What should I wear?"

"Dark colors, and shoes you can run in." Miss Culbertson's gaze traveled the length of Dolly. "You must be very sure about this, Miss Cameron. You may be seen by members of the tong, and they will begin to associate you with the work at the mission home. From this point on, you will no longer be an anonymous Christian woman in San Francisco."

Air left Dolly's chest. Anna had told Dolly stories of the criminal tong— slave owners who would do almost anything to hide and protect their human property, including planting dynamite at the mission home. These criminal tong also had a history of trying to bribe, threaten, or intimidate those who helped Miss Culbertson. By agreeing to help in a rescue, Dolly would indeed become known to the tong. Fear pulsed through her at the thought of being anyone's target. But these men were cruel and abusive to young girls, ripping them from their homes and forcing them into slavery. If Dolly didn't stand up for the helpless, who would? The other volunteers were part-time workers. Here she stood across from a woman who had dedicated her very life to this cause. How could Dolly say no? She lifted her chin. "I will be ready."

By the time Dolly returned to her bedroom, the initial shock of the director's request had dissipated. She shut the door behind her and drew in a shaky breath. Going on a rescue was a far cry from teaching a sewing class inside the safe walls of the mission home. The staff members had spoken of rescues in hushed tones, raids in which police officers broke down doors and Miss Culbertson searched basements for pitiful slaves.

Dolly closed her eyes for a moment, wondering what sort of conditions

Tien had been discovered in. Surely she'd been too small to send a note on her own.

And now Dolly was being trusted with a rescue. She knew no Chinese, and although Miss Culbertson took an interpreter with her, could Dolly do what Miss Culbertson did? Go into cribs and opium dens and find slave girls clutching scraps of red cloth?

Dolly gazed about her neat and sparse bedroom. The white roses Anna had given her soon after her arrival sat in a vase on the table. Their blooms had peaked over the past two days, and now their sweet scent had become stifling instead of comforting.

Although Dolly had gone to the shops of San Francisco a handful of times now, she'd never felt she was in danger. She'd never been a target. Perhaps it had been naive of her to think so.

But now, after she had accompanied Miss Culbertson on a raid, that would change. The dinner hour was only a short time away, but Dolly wouldn't be able to eat. Not with the way her stomach felt as tight as a drum with the fear growing inside her. She paced her small bedroom, and her gaze landed on the letter she'd begun to write her sister Helen that morning. She'd received letters from all her siblings in the past week, and each one of her sisters—Annie, Jessie, Katherine, and Helen—had brought up how she might jeopardize her marriage prospects being so far away in a city like San Francisco.

The irony of it was that her broken engagement had been over five years ago, and in that time, she hadn't found anyone else. So what did it matter where she lived? Was she to put any potential accomplishment on hold in her life, hoping to cross paths with a suitable partner?

In the letter to Helen, Dolly had ignored her sister's worries about finding a beau. Instead, Dolly related the unique details of Chinatown just a few streets from 920 Sacramento Street, such as her first walk through the area with its bustling crowds of people and its street stalls where melons, Chinese cabbage, fresh and dried fish, sugared ginger, and incense were sold. She'd described the beautiful satin cheongsam gowns, the intricate porcelain vases and dishes, and the highly polished teakwood furniture almost too dainty to use. Dolly had loved the decorative lanterns that glowed in the evening, and the colorful red and gold signs that drew the eye toward the pagoda rooftops.

But now, Dolly would see the underbelly of Chinatown. She would witness firsthand where the darkness originated, where these girls at the mission home had lived and worked. By agreeing to help Miss Culbertson in this rescue, Dolly knew she was agreeing to much more than simply teaching sewing classes. The invitation alone told her that the director trusted her, for whatever reason. Dolly closed her eyes and released her breath in a slow exhale. She'd led a privileged life compared to so many out there. Yes, she'd had her sorrows and losses and disappointments. But she'd never been sold, her body had never been abused, she'd never been mistreated.

What if tonight she helped rescue a girl from a horrible life? What if because of Dolly's actions, a life was made free?

She opened her eyes. Nothing in her bedroom had changed, but inside, desire had sprouted. Teaching sewing skills was commendable, yet bringing another girl or woman to the point where she could support herself with sewing skills was a different matter altogether.

There was no use delaying. Dolly crossed to her closet and pulled out a navy print blouse. In the dark, it would appear black. She unfastened her underskirt and slipped it off, leaving only the main skirt. Next, she picked up the boots that she wore around the ranch back home. Why she had even brought them, she hadn't known at the time. Now it seemed providential that she had.

Dressed hours before midnight, Dolly picked up her pacing again, not even bothering to turn on the lamp. As darkness completely engulfed her bedroom, she grew more and more anxious. She wanted to leave now, no matter the outcome.

When a light tap sounded at her door, Dolly was more than ready. She opened it to see Miss Culbertson dressed in dark colors as well. The director made a quick scan of Dolly, then nodded with approval.

Without a word, Miss Culbertson turned, and Dolly followed her. They joined Ah Cheng, one of the Chinese interpreters, at the bottom of the stairs. They left by the front door, and Anna, grim-faced, locked it after them. The night was cool, and the breeze made Dolly grateful she'd brought her shawl.

Dolly followed the two women down the hill to Stockton Street at a brisk pace. She was glad that she'd been told to wear sturdy shoes. Her breath had been stolen by the time they reached the corner where three police officers waited. Miss Culbertson made quick introductions to the officers: Jesse Cook, John Green, and George Riordan. Their mustaches, bowler hats, and dark suits made it hard to tell the men apart in the dark. Dolly tried not to stare, especially since two of them carried sledgehammers, and one an axe. Where were they going that required such tools?

The police officers took Dolly's presence in stride, as if they already had confidence in her. The officers set off at a brisk pace. Her long legs had no trouble keeping up, though her pulse raced as if she had run for miles. They turned one corner and then another, walking through Chinatown. The other women traveled with two of the officers up ahead, and Officer Jesse Cook, the one with a cigarette, stayed a step or two behind Dolly as if he were keeping a lookout.

"Where are you from, Miss Cameron?" he asked, his voice low.

"San Gabriel Valley," she said.

A raspy chuckle came from the officer. "A mite different from Chinatown. What about your accent?"

"My family is from Scotland, although we lived in New Zealand for many years," Dolly answered. "And you?"

She was only being polite, but she realized she was quite curious about the life of a policeman, especially one who broke into places to rescue girls.

"I barely remember my previous life, miss," Cook said, taking another pull on his cigarette. "Sometimes it's better to forget and move forward."

His answer felt like it had more layers than the earth. "Is that why you go on these rescues?"

Cook didn't answer for a moment as the group up ahead hurried around the next corner. He took a look behind him, then motioned Dolly to follow as well. "The helpless have no chance for justice in this city. I couldn't sleep at night if I didn't do what I could."

His words settled deep into Dolly's heart.

"There's Bartlett Alley, up ahead," Cook continued. "If I could burn it down, I would." As if to demonstrate, he tossed his half-smoked cigarette into the gutter.

Dolly was about to question him, when up ahead Miss Culbertson turned and waved for her to join her. Dolly moved quickly to her side, and Miss Culbertson grasped her hand. "The men will get us inside, and then we must be fast and persuasive."

As they headed down the alley, Dolly was surprised how dark and quiet it was. Yet she sensed they were not alone. She kept her breath shallow so as to not inhale the scents of rotting vegetables and the sickly sweet of opium. Officer Cook stopped in front of a heavy door. His size and presence seemed to fill the dilapidated alley. Wasting no time, he knocked firmly on the rough wood.

Dolly nearly jumped. She must calm down. They weren't even to the hard part yet.

No one answered; the only sounds were the *drip drip drip* of water nearby. Cook glanced over his shoulder at Dolly and Miss Culbertson. The director nodded, and Cook pounded again, calling out in a gruff voice, "Open the door!"

No response. Unless Dolly counted the furious beating of her heart.

Officer Green moved to a covered window only a few feet away and rattled the metal grating. The sound pinged against the cobblestone road, and Dolly's heart jumped at the rhythm. "Open up!"

Dolly tried to imagine what must be going on inside the dark building. Were people hiding? Fleeing?

"Stand back," Cook growled as he lifted his sledgehammer and brought it down on the door latch.

Officer Green took hold of the metal grate over the window and wrested it free.

There was no way anyone within a hundred yards of the place didn't know that police officers were breaking into this building. Dolly wrapped her arms about her torso to steady her nerves as Officer Riordan shattered the window with an axe. Then he climbed in through the opening.

"It's our turn," Miss Culbertson said.

And somehow Dolly moved to the window, ready to help. She crouched, her heart thundering in her ears. Whatever room was beyond, it was nearly all dark save for the flicker of a guttered candle. Perhaps this building had no electricity. Dolly gathered in the fullness of her skirt and climbed through the window, following after Miss Culbertson and Ah Cheng.

It was the smell that hit Dolly first. Her throat squeezed, and she clamped her mouth shut to avoid breathing in any more of the rancid air. Despite the broken window, the small room was stifling. A ratty bed stood against the wall, its blanket soiled, and a basin sat in one corner next to a single, lopsided chair missing one leg. A cracked bucket served as a latrine. Someone huddled against the far wall of the room on the dirt-packed floor. At first glance, Dolly thought it was a small child.

But when she stood, the girl looked to be around fifteen, although it was hard to be certain because the young woman was very thin. Her too-large dress hung limply around her body, doing very little to conceal a bruise on her shoulder and scratches along her arms.

Miss Culbertson approached her with careful steps. "We're from the mission home. You sent for us?"

Ah Cheng translated, and the Chinese girl looked from Officer Riordan to Dolly and Miss Culbertson. Slowly the girl uncurled her clenched fist to reveal a scrap of red cloth.

"She will come," Ah Cheng announced, her voice triumphant.

24

Miss Culbertson extended her hand, but the Chinese girl didn't move. Instead she rattled off several phrases in Chinese.

Ah Cheng translated quickly. "She has valuables with her mistress. Some jewelry. She wants to bring them."

Dolly wanted to tell the young woman no. Shouldn't they hurry out of this dank place? She could hear the other two officers pacing outside, and someone shouted in the distance. What if the Chinese mistress retaliated?

Dolly was doing everything she could not to gag, not to flee this horrible room. She already wanted to scrub her hands with soap and rub these images of filth from her eyes.

"All right," Miss Culbertson said in a soft tone. "Tell her we will go with her to get her belongings."

Once Ah Cheng had translated, the young woman shook her head vigorously. "My mistress has them, and—"

They were interrupted by a man unlocking the door to the room from the outside. He burst through the doorway. He was Chinese, and evidently the owner of the place, if the angry flush on his face was any indication. "You cannot be here," he barked, glowering at Miss Culbertson. He glanced at Riordan, but didn't seem to care about the broken window. Instead, he turned to the young woman and issued a sharp reprimand in Chinese.

The young woman replied in a meek tone, and the Chinese master stepped toward Miss Culbertson, who didn't shy away from his aggressive stance. "She cannot prove she has jewelry," he said in clipped English. "These *mui tsai* lie. She no good. Look at her. Pitiful prostitute."

Even if the young woman didn't understand all the harsh words said about her, the words felt like a slap to Dolly. Who was this man to call the girl names?

Miss Culbertson only tilted her head, keeping her gaze steady on the man. "*You* are the one who took away her dignity, sir. You care only about the money she can bring you, no matter the cost to her life."

The man's face darkened another shade of red. His mouth worked, and his glance darted to Riordan. At that moment, the other two officers crouched at the broken window, making their presence known. The Chinese man glowered at them, then turned to the trembling girl and began berating her in Chinese. Ah Cheng did not translate his words.

"That's enough," Miss Culbertson said, her tone steely.

The owner grabbed the girl's arm and shoved her against the wall, then pointed a finger at Miss Culbertson. "*You* stop talking, woman. You will pay for this."

Officer Cook was through the window in a flash. He backed up the Chinese man against the wall without even touching him. His towering demeanor was enough.

Green joined them too and stood between the women and the Chinese owner.

The Chinese man lifted his hands in surrender and moved toward the open door, his expression twisted in rage.

Dolly was rooted to the ground, her stomach ready to heave, either from the awful smell, or in anticipation of someone getting hurt.

But nothing in Miss Culbertson's demeanor shifted. It was as if she hadn't been fazed at all. She simply told the young Chinese woman, through the interpreter, "Come with us now, before he tries to stop you. We will inquire about your property later."

The young woman's wide, dark eyes shifted from her owner to Miss Culbertson. Then she nodded, moved to her bed, and scrambled for something beneath the soiled scrap of a blanket. She brought out a round picture frame and clutched it to her chest. Her nod told them she was ready to go. One item was all she would take to begin her new life. Sounds erupted from within the depths of the house—someone shouting and someone else crying. But the Chinese girl didn't seem interested in turning around, and she climbed out the window with the help of Ah Cheng.

The cool night air was a godsend after the foulness of the basement room.

The police officers abandoned the mess they'd made, and their group moved quickly. Miss Culbertson held one arm of the young woman while Ah Cheng held her other arm. The poor girl was trembling, and she kept mumbling something in Chinese.

Dolly's heart felt like it had been ripped in half.

"Are you all right, miss?" Cook asked in a low tone after they'd cleared Bartlett Alley.

"I think so," she said, although she was pretty sure the shaking in her voice gave her away.

"It will get easier," Cook said. "Not that it's something you want to be easy, by any means."

"I understand." And she did. She was also grateful that this police officer cared about her well-being.

"You did fine in there, Miss Cameron," Cook continued. "I've known the director for many years, and she wouldn't have brought you along if she didn't think you would be an asset."

Dolly glanced over at him beneath the light of the moon. He walked with sure steps, his sledgehammer casually swinging at his side, as if he hadn't just beaten down a door a short time ago. "I did nothing, though," Dolly said.

"You observed," Cook said. "Don't worry, you will have plenty of chances to do more. This war is not over yet."

His words sent a shiver along Dolly's neck. "Will they not come after us for what we have done?" she asked.

"Not openly," Cook said. "These men work in secret, in shadowed corners and beyond prying eyes. Miss Culbertson keeps the girls under watch at all times."

How many slave girls had been rescued by Miss Culbertson and her team, and how many others were still out there, living in misery and filth? She marveled at how the Chinese girl they had rescued tonight was walking resolutely between the two women up ahead. Her entire life had changed tonight, and Dolly could only hope she would flourish at the mission home.

When they reached the base of Sacramento Street, Officer Green said,

"We'll wait here to make sure you get up the hill. Lock things up tight. One of us will be around every hour or so to make sure no one is trying to get her back."

His words made Dolly's stomach tighten with worry, but there was nothing she could do except move forward with the women. After they separated from the officers, the Chinese slave started quietly crying. Ah Cheng said a few soothing words to her, but the crying continued.

By the time they reached the mission home and were safely inside, with the door bolted once again by Anna, who had let them in, the Chinese girl was shaking so hard that Dolly wondered if she would become sick.

Anna took one look at her and said, "Can you help me, Dolly? We need to get her in a warm bath."

For the next hour, Dolly learned what it was to care intimately for another human, one who was scarred and soiled in ways that made Dolly's eyes scald with tears. She and Anna bathed the young woman while she sat in the bathtub and cried. Dolly was gentle with the soap and washcloth. The slave was thin enough that Dolly could have counted her ribs on her back.

Next, they washed her hair. At first the young woman was afraid to dunk her head, but Anna explained in broken Chinese that it would make her feel better. After the bath, the young woman trembled as she stood in a clean robe, her hair twisted into a towel. Her eyes were swollen from her crying, but in their depths was gratitude.

When the girl asked Anna how to say "thank you" in English, Dolly felt her heart would burst with both pain and relief.

Only when they had the young woman tucked between fresh, clean sheets, with a pot of hot tea beside her bed, did Dolly allow herself to absorb the events of the evening. Anna would be staying in the Chinese girl's room to offer her comfort and soothe any possible hysterics.

When Dolly left the new charge to Anna, she stood in the dimness of the hallway for a few moments, trying to comprehend the squalor and degradation she'd witnessed in Bartlett Alley. Tonight had not been what she'd expected. It had been both worse than she'd imagined and more rewarding. She'd never witnessed such grime, seen such desperation, or aided someone in such dire distress. The small acts of bathing and feeding the young woman had been simple, yet significant as well. And to think that this girl was sleeping in a clean and safe bed tonight because of the initiative of Miss Culbertson. . . .

Yes, Dolly had helped, but mostly she'd been an observer.

This war is not over, Officer Cook had said. His words wouldn't leave her mind.

How long had things like this been going on, and Dolly had been oblivious to them? She had been an observer most of her life. She'd been diligent, cheerful, hardworking, but she'd attended church each week and listened to sermons that she then ignored. *Feed my sheep,* the Lord had said. Sure, Dolly had served others in small ways. She believed she was a good aunt to her nieces and nephews. She'd been a good daughter to her father when he was alive.

Yet tonight had been the first time in her life that she felt like she'd accomplished something with eternal consequences. She had literally helped change a life for the better. She'd assisted in pulling out a young woman from the darkest, deepest, most vile pit of despair, and in doing so, Dolly had not only helped rescue another's soul, she'd rescued her own.

Her tears were not of sorrow, or pain, but gratitude.

A small cry caught Dolly's attention. She walked down the hall that led to some of the bedrooms. Someone sat huddled at the end of the hallway.

"Tien," Dolly whispered. "Why are you out of bed?"

The girl scooted farther into the corner, pulling her knees tightly to her chest.

Dolly saw the faint sheen of tears on the girl's face, even though Tien quickly tucked her head against her knees.

"Did you see the new woman we brought in tonight?"

Tien didn't move, didn't respond.

"She'll be all right," Dolly said. "She was very hungry and very dirty, but she took a bath and we gave her food, and now she is safe."

Tien's small shoulders trembled.

Dolly could only imagine that whatever horrible memories Tien had about her former life in slavery, they were now haunting her anew.

"Come, I'll sit with you in your room until you fall asleep," Dolly said, touching the girl's shoulder, hoping to give some comfort.

But Tien's head shot up, and she shoved Dolly's arm away, scratching her in the process with surprisingly sharp fingernails. Then Tien bolted past her, running down the hall, and disappeared into one of the bedrooms. The door slammed shut.

Dolly braced a hand against the wall, wondering what had just happened. She rubbed at the scratch on her arm. The sting of the scrape was nothing, she knew, compared to the pain that Tien must be feeling. Was this something she should report? Would punishing Tien make things worse?

Dolly waited in the dark hallway for a long moment, but no other sounds came from Tien's bedroom. Eventually, Dolly headed for the stairs and went up to the third floor to her own bedroom—to find Miss Culbertson waiting.

"Is everything with the new rescue all right?" Miss Culbertson said in a quiet voice, her face shadowed from where she sat by the single lamp.

"She seemed very grateful, and now she's resting, with Anna watching over her." Dolly rubbed at her stinging arm. "Tien was in the hallway, crying. I tried to speak with her, but she lashed out."

Miss Culbertson frowned and rose to her feet. "Let me see your arm."

Dolly showed the director her scrape.

"I'll speak to Tien in the morning," Miss Culbertson said. "Sometimes these girls reenact the things that have been done to them. But we need to reinforce proper behavior and respect."

Dolly felt like she should have been more upset, but after going on the rescue, she found she could harbor no ill feelings against a child like Tien. "Be gentle with her. She is hurting too."

Miss Culbertson studied Dolly. "You are generous, Donaldina. And to-night you helped when needed and stayed out of the way when required. I hope you haven't been scared off from the mission work."

"No." Dolly's throat pulled tight. "I'm honored that you invited me to help. I didn't know the living conditions would be so . . . depraved. And I didn't know a person could be so . . . abused."

Miss Culbertson's nod was grave. "We are lucky she came willingly. Her owner cursed her, and sometimes that's enough to change a girl's mind."

"What did he say?" Dolly asked.

Miss Culbertson returned to the single chair and sat down, then folded her hands in her lap. "He told her if she came with us, all her ancestors would curse her, and she would become a turtle."

Dolly frowned. "What does that mean?"

"Slave owners call women without virtue turtles."

"A prostitute, then." Dolly hated the word, but there was no help for that. She was no longer living a protected life at her family's ranch. Over the past couple of hours, everything had changed. She'd seen for herself the result of pure corruption. And she'd found herself in the middle of the war that Officer Cook had referred to.

"Ironic that the slave owner threatens a slave with what he has already made her, yes?" Miss Culbertson sighed. "Most of these girls have no idea what lies ahead of them in America. Their families are promised that their daughters will be married to wealthy men. And because of the Chinese anti-immigration laws, the agents train the girls on a new identity and produce false papers."

Dolly sat on the edge of her bed, trying to soak in all this information.

"Some of the girls are kidnapped by the highbinders, and their families have no idea that their daughters are alive," Miss Culbertson continued. "The girls take on new identities in America, and their lives are controlled in every way. They've been reduced to what we call paper daughters. Without a home. Without care or love."

"Paper daughters," Dolly whispered. These girls had become no more than documents with false names; they had given up not only their identities but their dignity.

Miss Culbertson clasped her hands together. "We were also fortunate that we had little interference transporting her to the mission home. Not all cases will be this easy."

This easy? Dolly didn't know if she could process any more atrocities tonight. Her mind was already reeling with all that she had seen and experienced. And right now, her heart was bleeding for a young woman one floor below who had spent most of her life living no better than a rat—and for the girl whose wounds had been reopened and who now huddled alone in her bedroom.

Dolly had no words. If she tried to form them, she knew she would only cry.

Miss Culbertson seemed to understand and rose to her feet, then crossed to Dolly and squeezed her shoulder. "Good night, Donaldina. Tomorrow is a new day. The sun will shine through the darkness you've experienced tonight. We must always be grateful for the blessings we *do* have. Tonight, one more Chinese girl is safe."

Dolly nodded. After the director left, she switched off the lamp. She was afraid to see her reflection in the mirror and remember what her eyes had seen. As she shed her outer clothing in the dark, tears slipped down her cheeks as she wondered how many other abused women and girls were out there beyond the walls of the mission home. Needing to be rescued.

CHAPTER THREE

1903

"You will be a beautiful bride." Mei Lien's mother held up her silk wedding dress, once red in color, now faded with age and wrinkled beyond description.

The fierce pride in her mother's eyes kept Mei Lien's opinions silent. The wrinkles could be pressed out and the discoloring concealed with a scarf.

On the other side of the wall, the Chinese emigration representative, Nuwa, waited. Mother and daughter had only a few more moments together, and each knew it was likely the last time they would ever see each other in this life.

Mei Lien had long dreamed of her wedding day. Her marriage had been arranged to another man from when they were both children. But he had become mad in his mind and abandoned the village, disgracing his family. Mei Lien knew it had been the opium. He had not been the same for the past year. Until that time, Mei Lien had thought her wedding day would be one surrounded by family, good wishes, and many gifts.

But now, she would marry a man she had yet to meet, and neither of her parents would be present. Her father had been dead these past three years, and her mother was unable to travel to the Gold Mountain due to anti-immigration laws. Only wives or daughters of men already working in America were allowed to immigrate.

Nuwa, the waiting agent, had promised that by the time they arrived in San Francisco, Mei Lien would be well trained on her adopted parentage. The white lies would be a small price to pay for Mei Lien's future. And her mother would receive four hundred Hong Kong dollars the moment Mei Lien signed the contract.

"Take this, daughter," her mother said in a trembling voice as she passed over the wedding dress. "May you never live another day hungry, and may your stomach always be too full to swallow down any sorrow. Always remember, you are my beautiful lotus. Any man would be proud to have you as his wife. Please your husband and have healthy babies."

The words were like a weight on Mei Lien's heart. Her mother had lost two sons in infancy, brothers she never knew because Mei Lien was born last. Her mother had always complained that the god of creation had closed up her womb after Mei Lien was born. She took the dress from her mother, the smooth fabric like water in her hands. Then she folded the dress and placed it carefully in her small wooden trunk.

"It is time." Her mother's dark-as-night eyes filled with tears. She quickly brushed at them with her field-callused fingers, her cheeks flushing with embarrassment. Not typically an emotional woman, she prided herself, Mei Lien knew, in being stoic at all times.

Mei Lien knew also that she was blessed, despite not having a father or a brother. Her mother had been loving and kind. And now, she was willing to sacrifice her only living child in order to provide a better life for Mei Lien.

"Thank you, *Ah Ma*," Mei Lien said, reverence in her voice.

Her mother's face crumpled with emotion, and the two embraced, one woman at the sunset of her life, the other not yet sixteen, with a horizon of opportunity stretching before her.

Mei Lien drew away, leaving part of her heart with her mother.

Tears dripped down both of their faces, and her mother said, "Now, go, my lotus. Don't look back. The goddesses will take care of me, and I will burn incense every week for your soul."

It wasn't an idle promise—that Mei Lien knew.

Her mother moved past her, and, in her last act of service, she latched the trunk, then handed it to Mei Lien.

"It is time," her mother repeated, her tears starting again. "Good-bye, my beautiful lotus."

Mei Lien dabbed at her own tears and moved toward the curtain that separated the tiny bedroom from the rest of the house, which amounted to only one other room. She gazed a final time at her mother, seeing the petite woman's work-worn hands, callused from long days harvesting. The deep circles beneath her eyes, which contrasted with the love and warmth emanating from her. The threadbare dress, which had once been a deep green, now faded white. The bare feet that had walked many miles and would carry her body for many more.

"Good-bye, *Ah Ma*," Mei Lien said softly.

Then, with her throat feeling like she'd swallowed a burning rock, she shifted aside the drape and stepped into the dim interior of the main room. On the bamboo table, the remnants of a steamed sponge cake remained, to be cleared later by her mother. Nuwa stood expectantly, her long, elegant fingers clasped in front of her. The eagerness in Nuwa's eyes only made Mei Lien want to return to her mother, poverty or not. They would survive together. They had so far.

Nuwa then pulled out the contract from a square satchel, along with the money promised to Mei Lien's mother. Seeing them on the bamboo table next to the chipped porcelain plate, Mei Lien knew she couldn't back out of her commitment. Her life was no longer here, and in leaving Hong Kong, Mei Lien would be providing for her mother for many years to come.

Mei Lien forbade any more tears from forming. She didn't want Nuwa to think she wasn't grateful, and she didn't want her mother to hear her crying. It was time to shed her childhood and become the new Mei Lien. No longer the poor girl living in an even poorer village. She was to be married to a wealthy man. She would have sons and daughters, and she would manage a beautiful home. Perhaps one day her husband would send for her mother.

Mei Lien stepped forward, bent, and signed the contract with an X to represent her name.

There was no turning back now.

Following Nuwa out of the house of her youth, Mei Lien noticed details that she had always taken for granted. The flower bed her mother took immense pride in. The neat pen she'd repaired only a few days ago. Their three chickens. Mei Lien expected the chickens to dash toward the far end of the pen, but they watched in muted silence as she crossed the dirt yard for the final time.

She followed Nuwa along the winding dirt road to where a rickshaw waited at the edge of the village. Although the morning had yet to bloom with the sunrise, plenty of people witnessed her leaving. A few even waved. Mei Lien's heart felt full of gratitude and ready to break at the same time.

Uncle Bo Wei climbed out of the rickshaw and motioned for Mei Lien and Nuwa to climb in. No, Bo Wei wasn't her uncle, and Nuwa wasn't her auntie. But that was what she would be calling them until they arrived in San Francisco.

The journey to the Hong Kong harbor took several hours, and Mei Lien indulged in a nap, only to awake to Nuwa speaking in rapid tones to Bo Wei. Both of their faces were painted with worry.

Mei Lien immediately straightened and looked about her. The rice fields and rows of shacks had turned into close-quartered buildings and narrow alleys, with dozens of rickshaws and crowds of people everywhere she looked. "Is something wrong?" Mei Lien asked.

Nuwa's brown eyes settled on Mei Lien. Strain lines appeared about her mouth. "We are blessed that Uncle bought our passage a week ago. There is a crowd trying to get on the ship."

Mei Lien followed Nuwa's gaze and saw a couple of dozen men in a tightly knit group, not looking too happy as one of them argued with a pale-faced ship captain.

Uncle commanded the rickshaw driver to stop; then he swung down from the seat and started unloading their trunks. "We must hurry," he said in a clipped tone, his glance darting to the crowd of men. "Women are usually the last ones allowed onto a ship."

"We have tickets," Mei Lien protested, but Nuwa's long fingers clamped down on her upper arm.

Mei Lien almost yelped at the sudden pain from the woman's surprisingly strong grip.

"Do not speak to anyone," Nuwa commanded in a fierce whisper. "Do not *look* at anyone."

Mei Lien immediately lowered her eyes and nodded. She walked with Nuwa and Uncle toward the waiting ship, her ears burning with the complaints, jeers, and foul language that caused her steps to falter more than once. *Mui tsai!* The men continued in their insults. A livid heat coiled in Mei Lien's stomach. She did not work in a brothel. She had never known a man. Hadn't even been kissed. She would never live in the way these vile names suggested.

Nuwa had been right. Mei Lien should not look at anyone. It was the only way to disconnect the words from the images of those who spoke them. She would forget quicker that way. Only a few more steps, and finally they were on the ship. Mei Lien breathed out, relieved to have made it this far.

As if reading her mind, Nuwa's fierce whisper came again. "Don't turn around."

Mei Lien obeyed and pressed forward with Uncle and Nuwa as they moved through the people on the upper deck of the ship. Mei Lien didn't even have time to appreciate the fact that she was on a ship for the first time in her life before Nuwa steered her down a narrow flight of stairs into the darkness below.

By the time Mei Lien's eyes adjusted to the below-deck dimness, she was positive that Nuwa's fingerprints would be left on her arm in the form of five rounded bruises. Did she have to continue gripping Mei Lien so hard? Had she not been obedient?

Around the next bend of the narrow corridor, they stepped into a large space filled with bunk beds bolted to the wooden floor. The rest of the floor space was taken up by lumpy mattresses. Mei Lien was taken aback. Though she had not come from a life of luxury, even in her poor state, she and her mother had always had pride in their living standards.

"This is yours." Nuwa released Mei Lien's arm at last.

Mei Lien wanted to sit on the bunk bed that Nuwa had indicated, but something told her now wasn't the time to relax.

"Here is your trunk, and inside you'll find papers." Nuwa pointed her long finger. "These false papers will be the only thing to prove who you are to immigration. Do not forget the details that Uncle told you. The immigration officers cannot know your true identity. They might ask you many details, down to the number of chickens in the courtyard of the home you are now from."

Mei Lien opened her mouth to ask a question, but Nuwa's eyes had narrowed. How had Mei Lien thought Nuwa was a sweet, pleasant woman? The woman staring at her now looked like she could strangle an entire nest of snakes. Mei Lien lowered her gaze and nodded.

"Stay near the bunk, and don't talk to anyone," Nuwa hissed.

After the woman left, the bunks slowly filled with other passengers, including a few women and girls. Mei Lien opened the trunk and pulled out the papers that Nuwa had slipped inside. They were sewn together along one edge, like a bound pamphlet.

Slowly, Mei Lien turned the pages. She couldn't read, but she thought over what Uncle had told her. Her new identity placed her at age eighteen and called her the youngest daughter of a man named Wang Foo, who lived in a valley near San Francisco. Mei Lien had memorized the siblings' names and ages. She was traveling with her auntie and uncle and would be working in her father's clothing shop. Nothing was mentioned about marriage.

Judging by the sounds and movements of the ship, Mei Lien was sure they'd left port.

Mei Lien tried to think of her future instead of what she'd left behind. Tears tracked along her cheeks despite her resolve. She could pretend she was someone else for a short while; then surely her life would become wonderful with her new husband.

She still hadn't seen Nuwa or Uncle, so Mei Lien placed the papers back in her trunk, slid it under the bunk, then headed up the stairs. Sure enough, the ship was in open water.

Mei Lien joined the people standing at the rail and watched the city of Hong Kong grow smaller and smaller. The air was brisk, almost cold, and the salty breeze stung her eyes.

"You must get below," Nuwa's voice sounded sharply in her ear. "You are not safe up here."

Mei Lien flinched, and Uncle appeared on her other side. She wanted to ask why it was unsafe, but she didn't. She went with Nuwa below deck again. This time, Uncle followed. They sat next to her on the bunk and, in low tones, questioned her about what they had already drilled her on.

She answered what she had learned so far, then mentioned, "Do I not tell them about my marriage?"

"The immigration officers do not like Chinese, and they don't like our customs," Uncle said. "If they think you are coming into the country to marry and have Chinese babies, they might turn you away. They will only let you come if your father already lives there and you are going to work."

Mei Lien supposed that made sense. "But I will marry, right?"

Nuwa glanced at Uncle, then said, "Perhaps. If you can pay off your contract."

Mei Lien tried not to look surprised. After all, Nuwa had given Mei Lien's mother the contract, and she had approved. Mei Lien had signed it, trusting that it was about marriage. "What do I have to pay off?" she asked, her heart fluttering like a bird with a broken wing.

"Discuss the contract later," Nuwa snapped. "Time to practice now."

Uncle's voice was far calmer. "I will quiz you again now on your new family. You must know every detail and date better than your natural family."

Mei Lien nodded, but she had one more question. "Can I go above deck tomorrow?"

"No," Nuwa said immediately. "Others will see you, and we can't protect you up there."

"Protect me from what?" Mei Lien asked, even as the shouts and jeers of the men at the dock returned to her mind.

Nuwa's gaze shifted to Uncle. "From those who have not paid for you," he said. "You must assume your new identity without error. If you make a mistake, you will be deported, and there will be nothing we can do. Your mother will have to pay back the money we gave her. Do you want that to happen?"

"No," Mei Lien whispered. The amount her mother had received could never be paid back on laborer's wages in their village even if they both worked their entire lives.

Nuwa leaned close, clamped a strong hand on the girl's wrist, and twisted. "No mistakes, Mei Lien. This is your last warning. Your very life depends on your obedience."

CHAPTER FOUR

"Aug. 15/92. With the assistance of two police officers and Ah Cheng we
went to Bartlett Alley and rescued the girl of above name. She is very
small stature—looks like a midget—has an old and peculiar face—give
her age as 22 years. Sing Ho says her mother died in San Francisco and
her father returned to China—that her parents owed money and that
she entered upon a life of sin to pay their indebtedness. Sing Ho was
a victim of the opium habit and after spending a night in the Home
decided to return to the brothel—she could neither eat nor sleep."

—MARGARET CULBERTSON, MISSION HOME RECORD, 1892

1895

The day Miss Culbertson left for New Orleans to deliver a bride to her
new husband, Dolly felt the director's absence keenly. It wasn't that she didn't
think she could manage the household for a few short weeks, but what if a call
for a rescue came?

Since the night Tien had scratched Dolly, the girl hadn't spoken a word to
her. In sewing class, she kept her head down, her eyes on the shirts they were
making. Dolly's scratch had healed quickly, but the memory of the frightened,
crying girl huddled at the end of the hallway hadn't faded at all. So it was with
more compassion that Dolly viewed Tien, and not as a troublemaker.

Now Dolly walked by Tien as she routinely checked on each girl's progress. With around thirty girls and women in the house, sewing and repairing clothing was an unending task. Tien had returned to her neat, even stitching, her nimble fingers working quickly and efficiently.

"Very nice, Tien," Dolly said in a soft tone.

The girl flinched and hunched her shoulders, but she didn't slow her pace or make deliberately sloppy stitches. Was this progress between them? Dolly could only hope.

Next she checked on the other girls, and most of them beamed under her praise. The younger girls were missing their "mama"—Miss Culbertson, who had become the mother that many of these girls had either lost or never had.

When Dolly helped Lonnie with her sewing, Lonnie promptly threw her arms about Dolly's legs and said, "You're a nice mama."

Dolly smiled and hugged her back. "Well, thank you." She never took affection for granted. She only wished Tien would be more receptive. The girl's pain seemed to be a living thing that kept her in a shell of loneliness.

Just then, Anna rushed into the classroom and motioned for Dolly to come out. The woman was out of breath, and the urgency on her face told Dolly that something serious had happened. She excused herself from her students as calmly as she could and met Anna outside the room.

"Officer Cook is downstairs," Anna said. "He's brought word about a Chinese woman who used to live at the mission home. She married and moved to China, but now she has returned to San Francisco with her two children. Hong Leen is very ill and is asking for us, but the authorities won't let her out of the immigration station unless we vouch for her. We need to go speak to the immigration officers."

Dolly wasn't sure who Hong Leen was, but the name was familiar. Regardless, she grabbed her cloak to protect her from the potential rain and hurried out of the house with Anna.

Officer Cook waited on the porch and greeted Dolly with a tip of his hat. The scent of his cigarette reminded Dolly of the last time she'd seen him—on the rescue with Miss Culbertson.

His smile beneath his mustache was brief, but his eyes remained warm. "Are you doing well, Miss Cameron?"

"I am," she said. "Thank you. I see that you are in one piece as well." Officer Cook seemed much less imposing in the light of day, even though the day was a gray one. That might also have had to do with the fact that he wasn't carrying a sledgehammer.

"Things have been quiet lately," Cook said, as they continued toward the docks.

"I suppose that's good news," Dolly said.

"We've had these calm spaces before." Cook touched the brim of his hat to acknowledge a passerby. "It only means that messages are being intercepted."

This didn't sound good at all. "Is there a way to find out if someone needs help without a note?"

"All types of messages, on paper or in person, are equally dangerous." Cook pointed his chin toward a storefront they were passing. "Notice how the shop owners disappear into their shops as we approach."

Dolly looked down the street they were walking on. Things had suddenly gone quiet. "You're recognized."

"*We're* recognized," Cook corrected. "Word is already out about the tall white woman from the mission home."

It was a strange thing to consider, even though Miss Culbertson had warned her.

"Don't worry, Miss Cameron," he said. "You can call upon the Chinatown police squad anytime."

"Thank you, sir," Dolly said.

He lit another cigarette, but stamped it out when it was only half smoked. As they neared the docks, Dolly asked how long ago Hong Leen had lived at the mission home.

"Oh, many years ago," Anna answered. "She was rescued by my aunt, and eventually she married Woo Hip. They returned to China together to build a new life."

"Where is her husband now?"

"I don't know," Anna said. She slowed her step as they passed by a long, warehouse-type building sitting on piles over the bay. "I hope she's not in there."

Dolly studied the low building. "What is that place?"

"The detention shed," Officer Cook said. "They keep the foreigners inside while they wait for their hearings. No latrine facilities, and they're fed only the very minimum. Most of them are deported. A rough place."

Dolly wanted to pry open the door and let out the poor people locked inside.

Passing the detention shed, they reached the pier, where they paused in front of the immigration office. "I'll wait for you ladies out here," Cook said, "in case you need an escort back to the mission home."

Dolly thanked him, and she and Anna walked into the office, where they were greeted by an immigration officer. He led them to the back room, where a Chinese woman waited with two young children. Hong Leen's face brightened at the sight of them, but the pallor of her complexion told Dolly she wasn't well.

Anna hurried to Hong Leen's bench and embraced the woman. While Hong Leen communicated with Anna in a combination of English and Chinese, Dolly soon discovered that the woman had been ill the entire voyage over. She had also lost her husband to plague a couple of years ago.

Dolly focused on the two young children, a four- or five-year-old girl and her younger brother, who couldn't have been more than two. They watched Dolly with open curiosity as the other women talked.

Dolly smiled, and when they smiled in return, she crouched before them and asked them their names in what little Chinese she had picked up. The girl broke into a giggle at a white woman's jarring attempt to speak Chinese.

They exchanged names, and Dolly learned the boy was Kang and the girl, Jiao.

"Would you like to come to the mission home?" Dolly asked in English.

"Yes, we will come with you," the little girl answered, speaking English herself, to Dolly's surprise. "Our father died," Jiao said matter-of-factly.

Kang leaned his head against his sister's shoulder and popped his thumb into his mouth.

"I'm sorry to hear that," Dolly told the children.

The conversation between Anna and Hong Leen continued, with the Chinese woman explaining how her husband had come down with the plague when they had arrived in Hong Kong, and by the time they had reached his family's home, he had gone mad with the disease. Her husband's passing had left an irreversible void, especially since Hong Leen's in-laws had blamed her for their son's death.

Hong Leen had continued to live with her in-laws, but they had found small ways to persecute and disparage her.

When Hong Leen finished her story, Anna asked Dolly to go speak to the immigration officer and vouch for the little family. Dolly straightened and left the back room, sensing she would repeat these types of requests to immigration officers many more times.

Taking a deep breath, she offered a small smile to the officer. The worn lines about his eyes told her that he'd already had a long day, and the morning was still young.

"We are willing to care for Hong Leen in her illness and take on her children as well," Dolly said.

The officer nodded. "You'll need to sign paperwork that you have her in custody until we decide on her legal rights to remain here."

"Of course." Dolly's heart thumped as he produced a form for her to sign. Hong Leen and her children were able to come to the mission home. Every part of Dolly flooded with relief.

After signing, she hurried back to the room and shared the news.

The children hugged Dolly, and her heart brimmed as she squeezed them back. These children were so innocent, so trusting. Now, she could only hope that their mother would recover her health soon.

Officer Cook was waiting for the small group as they left the immigration office. True to his word, he escorted them all the way back to the mission home—except he hired a carriage for Hong Leen so she wouldn't have to walk. There was only room for Anna to accompany the small family, so Dolly elected to walk. Along the way, Cook asked Dolly how the young woman they had rescued the other night was doing.

"She's very quiet," Dolly said. "But she's getting along with the other women and seems to have found her place. She also has a beautiful singing voice."

"I'm glad to hear she's doing well," Cook said. "Not everyone can make the adjustment."

Dolly thought of Tien, and how her animosity still ruled over her, even after a year in the mission home. "Do you know Tien Fu Wu?"

Cook frowned. "How old is she?"

"About ten," Dolly said. "She's been at the mission home for about a year. No one at the mission knows her true age. I guess she was sold or kidnapped quite young."

"Ah, I do remember her," Cook said.

"Were you part of her rescue?"

"I guess you could say that," he said. "I'd seen her more than once, and each time, I noticed fresh signs of abuse."

"Oh," Dolly breathed. "That's awful."

"I questioned her owner once, but then after that, Tien Fu Wu disappeared from the little neighborhood where I had first spotted her." Cook adjusted his hat. "It was one of those times I knew that her 'mother' wasn't who she said she was. So, when providence brought us in contact once again, I simply picked up the child and brought her to the mission home."

Dolly stopped walking and turned to Cook. "You what?"

His gaze slid past hers, and he exhaled. "I guess you could say we snatched her from the streets."

Dolly opened her mouth, then closed it. "Is that legal?" she finally asked. "I mean, you are an officer of the law."

Cook drew off his hat and scrubbed his fingers through his graying hair. Replacing his hat, he said, "Sometimes, Miss Cameron, war hurts the innocent children the most. I believe we were given the chance to rescue her, and if we didn't do it then and there, worse things would happen to the little girl."

Dolly nodded, then started walking again, her steps slower this time, her thoughts tumbling together.

"How is Tien Fu Wu doing now?" Cook asked.

That was a complicated question to answer. "She's very bright, but she doesn't like me much. Miss Culbertson says some girls take a longer time to heal."

Cook nodded. "Years of abuse can't be erased in a few months."

His comment took root in Dolly's mind. A life couldn't truly change in a short time.

Once she had returned to the mission home, Dolly found Anna and the children in the kitchen, where they were eating.

"How is Hong Leen doing?" Dolly asked.

Anna motioned for her to step out of the kitchen. "I've sent for a physician," she said. "He should be here soon, but I don't have much hope for Hong Leen. She's very ill. It's not good, Dolly, not good at all."

"What will happen with her children?" Dolly asked.

"Provided the immigration office allows them to stay, we will raise them," Anna said immediately.

Dolly saw the determination in the woman's eyes. "Of course. And I will help in any way I can."

Now, all they could do was wait for the physician to arrive. Dolly returned to the kitchen, and when she sat down, little Jiao climbed onto her lap. She wrapped her arms around the child. Dolly couldn't explain the overwhelming sense of protection she already felt for these two young children, and knowing that their mother might not survive made her want to shield them even more. When Kang finished eating the rice and chicken, he joined his sister on Dolly's lap, and she put her arms about them both.

Just then, Tien appeared at the doorway of the kitchen. She gazed at the two children on Dolly's lap.

"Are you hungry?" Dolly asked, even though the residents weren't supposed to eat between meals.

Tien turned immediately and left. Dolly couldn't very well go after her, but she wondered what was going through the young girl's mind. And what Tien had thought when Officer Cook had snatched her from the streets and brought her to the mission home.

When the physician arrived, Dolly stayed with the children in one of the bedrooms, which was shared with a couple of older girls who were sweet to the new arrivals. She waited until the children had fallen asleep before she went to find Anna and hear the report.

She came upon Anna in her aunt's office with the door open. Dolly paused in her step. Anna sat at the desk, her shoulders slumped while she propped her chin with her hands, gaze downcast.

Dolly entered quietly and sat in the chair opposite.

Anna slowly lifted her eyes. "It's cancer," she said in a rasp. "The physician found signs of internal bleeding and doesn't think she'll last more than a few days. The hospital would just want to run painful tests. He advised us to make her comfortable here until she passes."

Sorrow rippled through Dolly. "What will we tell the children?"

"I don't know yet." Anna traced a small circle on the desk with her finger. "We will have them visit their mother in the morning. Perhaps she'll tell them."

Dolly's throat felt as if it had turned to sandpaper.

"Hong Leen gave me her final wishes," Anna continued. "She wants her daughter to become a medical missionary and her son to become a minister."

"Hong Leen is Christian?" It shouldn't have surprised Dolly, because Bible study was part of the curriculum at the mission home. The residents all attended church on Sundays, but that didn't mean everyone converted or kept with the faith after moving out.

The edge of Anna's mouth lifted, and her brown eyes warmed. "Hong Leen became a devout Christian while living here the first time. Her husband converted as well. Sadly, that would have been another complication in her relationship with her in-laws."

Long after Anna left, Dolly sat in the empty office with the changing shadows of the afternoon shifting through the room. Distractions would come soon enough, and the busyness of the day would consume her time, but for a few moments, she contemplated how the lives of these children were about to change once again. She knew firsthand what it was like to lose a mother at such a young age. But her father and older sisters had been there for her, had continued to raise her.

And now, Dolly would be there for someone else.

Two days later, Miss Culbertson returned from her travels.

Three days after that, Hong Leen died.

Dolly did her best to soothe the orphaned children's fears and sorrows. She held them, she fed them, and now she sat with the children, distracting them with picture books while Anna directed the funeral preparations. Anna had taken over the arrangements, since Miss Culbertson had been ill since her return. The director was thinner than ever and depleted of energy.

Hong Lee was to be buried at the Six Companies cemetery in Colma.

The youngest child, Kang, didn't seem to fully understand the loss of his mother. But he followed Dolly about the mission home like a shadow, frequently tugging on her skirt so that she would pick him up. Jiao had cried and cried the day of her mother's death, but now she sat very still, listening to the story with all her attention.

Although Dolly's heart was heavy with the tragedy, she read story after story in a cheerful tone, exaggerating the character parts and earning a few smiles from the little children. More children gathered about them to listen, including Lonnie and Dong Ho, and Dolly marveled that all these orphans or sold children were now starting to feel like family. With no husband or children of her own, Dolly believed she now had a taste of what it was to love completely and fully. She could not deny the attachment she had to each child, which only grew deeper the more time she spent teaching them and serving them.

As she turned the page of the picture book, she scanned the young, eager faces, their deep brown eyes, golden skin, and black hair. She knew everyone's names now, along with their personality quirks, and she loved seeing their eyes light up when she spoke to them. Kang had claimed his usual place on her lap, and the other children crowded about her knees.

Ever so silently, Tien crept into the room. Dolly pretended not to see her because she knew if the girl was acknowledged, she would flee. Dolly held back a smile as Tien sat cross-legged by an end table.

"I want to read!" Lonnie cried out. As usual, she shouted her demands, unlike most of the other young girls, who had more demure personalities.

"*May I please?*" Dolly corrected.

Lonnie looked far from repentant, yet said in her same volume, "May I please read the story?"

"Do we all agree that we should let Lonnie read to us next?" Dolly asked the group.

The dark heads bobbed. Dolly glanced at Tien. She was now leaning forward, seeming intent to hear the story. Dolly shifted over on the settee to allow more room for Lonnie to sit on her other side. The children became equally entranced with Lonnie's rendition, and after she finished, another little girl wanted to read next. Dolly obliged, wondering how many more times she would hear the story read before the dinner hour. Then Anna arrived in the doorway.

Dolly extracted herself from the children and went to meet Anna in the hall, passing by Tien, who merely watched her walk out.

"We've had a message," Anna said in a hushed voice as she handed over a folded piece of paper.

Dolly's heart dropped like a stone to her stomach as she read the scrawled address on the piece of paper. It was a street several neighborhoods away in the heart of Chinatown.

"This came with it." Anna handed over a torn piece of red fabric.

Dolly grasped the fabric remnant. It might once have been a scarf or handkerchief.

"The girl you need to rescue will have the other half of this cloth," Anna whispered. "Ah Cheng will go with you, and I've already notified the Chinatown squad. They'll meet you at the bottom of the hill in a few hours."

"Tonight?" Dolly said. "Is Officer Cook coming too?" The rescue couldn't wait—she knew it couldn't. Miss Culbertson was still ill, so this rescue would be up to Dolly.

"I don't know which officers will be there," Anna said.

Dolly returned to the children and the storybooks, but her mind was no longer engaged in the entertainment. Thankfully, dinner was ready soon, and Dolly ushered the young ones to their places at one of the dining tables to eat dumplings and stew. Tien never had a problem eating, so she sped past Dolly to join others at the table.

During the meal, Dolly took small glances at Tien, then the other rescued girls. All of them had been in deplorable situations before. If it weren't for Miss Culbertson, who knows what their fate might have been? Confidence renewed, Dolly returned to her bedroom to quickly change. Then she headed downstairs to find Miss Culbertson and Ah Cheng waiting for her.

"Thank you for doing this," Miss Culbertson said. Her complexion was wan, and she was wearing a thick shawl, as if she were cold. "I wish I could—"

Dolly placed a hand on the woman's arm. "We will be fine. Ah Cheng will be of great help. Just give me the directions."

The director's relief was palpable, and she showed the note to Dolly that contained the number of the place. "The girl is at the end of Bartlett Alley in one of the cribs."

When Dolly had gone with the director on that first rescue, they had gone to Bartlett Alley as well. But they had not ventured as far as the cribs: a place of the vilest depravity where girls and women were kept in cagelike rooms and forced to peddle their services. Dolly's stomach felt leaden at the thought of facing such a place without the guidance of the director, but the wan pallor of the director's face told Dolly that she was needed more than ever. "We will return as soon as possible."

Dolly and Ah Cheng left 920 and met Officers Cook and Riordan at the bottom of the hill. Dolly was relieved to be accompanied by men she knew already, but needles of anticipation pricked the back of her neck at the sight of their sledgehammers and crowbars. Hardly a breeze stirred the trees above, and the air felt warm, nearly stifling. The brightness of the moon, and the thought of saving another woman from her life of abuse, sent a shiver through Dolly.

She could do this, taking over Miss Culbertson's duty yet again.

"You'll be fine," Officer Cook told Dolly, moving by her side as they strode toward Bartlett Alley.

"Is my nervousness that obvious?" Dolly asked.

"I've never seen you walk so fast."

She was too anxious to laugh. "Are these rescue missions why you smoke?"

Cook glanced at the cigarette in his hand. "One of many reasons."

Once they entered the alley, they continued past the area where Dolly's first rescue outing had been. The window grate had been repaired and replaced. The scents of rotting vegetables and urine, combined with the now recognizable sickly-sweet smell of opium, made Dolly want to cover her nose and breathe through her fingers. But she continued, ignoring her rebelling senses and cramping stomach as best as she could.

The sound of desperate crying came from a second-story window. In the darkness, Dolly couldn't make out the exact location, but the crying felt like nails scraping her skin. She wanted to change course, find out what was going on in the building above her. But the squad pushed forward deeper into the alley.

When the officers finally slowed their progress, Dolly scanned the rows of shacks that were no more than twelve by fourteen feet in size. The wicket windows were the only thing separating the street from the women inside. The structures looked like human cages. Her throat burned, and bile threatened as she watched the officers rattle one of them.

"Sing Leen," Cook called out. "Are you in there?"

A voice so quiet it sounded like a wisp of wind said, "I am here."

"Stand back," Cook said, then used his crowbar to pry off the grate.

Ah Cheng linked arms with Dolly, and together they backed up.

Riordan set the grate aside, and Cook climbed into the square hole.

"Let's go," Ah Cheng whispered, then followed Cook through the window while Riordan kept watch on the alley.

Before Dolly could follow, she heard Ah Cheng's quiet Chinese.

Dolly knew that Ah Cheng would first verify if Sing Leen was the one who had sent the message.

With shaking hands, Dolly gripped the edge of the crude wooden opening and stepped down into a room not much larger than a closet. It contained only a washbowl, a single bamboo chair, and a bed covered with matting. The space was completely taken up with Cook, Ah Cheng, Dolly, and a woman who was the size of a child.

The young woman held up a torn piece of red fabric and began to cry.

"Come with us," Ah Cheng said in a gentle tone. "We'll take you to safety. This is Miss Cameron from the mission home."

Dolly tried not to blanch at the foul, cell-like room. She smiled at the Chinese woman. "We are here to help you."

Ah Cheng translated, and Sing Leen unfolded herself from her crouched position. She wore the uniform of her trade, a blue silk blouse with embroidered green piping. With the help of both Ah Cheng and Dolly, she climbed out of the crib.

The woman clung to Dolly's arm as she stepped into the alleyway, as if she were petrified. Dolly grasped her around her waist to make her feel secure. Sing Leen's hold was so desperate, so fierce, that Dolly wished they had a buggy to whisk her away in to get her to the mission home faster. Sing Leen's face in the glow of the moonlight showed a woman who was perhaps twenty, despite her birdlike limbs. Her frailness was only accentuated by her bare feet.

As they walked through the alley, Dolly expected someone to chase after them, or, at the very least, for the woman's owner to confront them. But the alley was eerily silent and empty. Even the police officers were quiet, their expressions wary, alert.

By the time they reached 920 Sacramento, the adrenaline running through Dolly had left her emotionally exhausted. Thankfully, the moment they crossed the threshold of the mission home, Miss Culbertson had hot tea ready in the kitchen.

Sing Leen allowed herself to be taken to the kitchen, although she was trembling like an autumn leaf in a windstorm. Ah Cheng went to fetch the woman a shawl while Dolly and Miss Culbertson sat with Sing Leen.

Sing Leen's hand shook as she reached for the tea. Her eyes closed as she sipped the hot liquid, and Dolly couldn't help but notice the bruising along her neck.

"Eat something," Miss Culbertson said in a soft voice as she slid over a dessert plate with a leftover pastry from dinner.

Sing Leen eyed the food, then gingerly broke off a corner. She ate a single bite, but strangely, she didn't seem interested in the food. She picked at another piece but didn't put it in her mouth. Then she pushed the plate away.

Miss Culbertson didn't seem bothered by the action, but a knot of worry curled in Dolly's stomach. Surely this woman was hungry. Why wouldn't she eat more? When Ah Cheng returned with a shawl, Sing Leen snapped her gaze to the interpreter. She said something in rapid Chinese, refusing the shawl.

Ah Cheng's thin brows pulled together, and she replied, her words urgent.

Dolly looked over at Miss Culbertson, but the director made no move to intervene. Suddenly, Sing Leen stood and backed away from the table.

"Wait," Miss Culbertson said in English. She moved to the Chinese woman's side and took her arm, but Sing Leen twisted out of the older woman's grasp.

"What's wrong with her?" Dolly asked.

"She wants to leave," Miss Culbertson said. "She's addicted to opium, and she needs another dose."

Sing Leen continued to twist away until Ah Cheng wrapped an arm about her shoulders.

"I will take her upstairs," Ah Cheng broke in. "She'll stay with me tonight. I don't trust her on her own. Help me, Miss Cameron."

Dolly followed, walking behind the pair as Ah Cheng kept a firm hold on Sing Leen, who had begun to wail in Chinese.

"Hush!" Ah Cheng said over and over, but the woman continued to wail, oblivious to anyone who might be sleeping in the home.

They made it to Ah Cheng's bedroom, where Sing Leen immediately went to the window and opened it. There was no escape though, not through the secure grate.

"Can I do something?" Dolly didn't think she should leave Ah Cheng alone with the upset woman. "Should I stay too?"

"No," Ah Cheng was quick to say. "There's no reason for us both to miss a night's sleep. You have your classes in the morning. I'll sleep when Sing Leen does."

"I don't want to leave you alone with—"

"It is better this way." Ah Cheng practically pushed Dolly out of the bedroom. "I speak her language, and I'll get her to calm down. Having you here will only put her more on edge."

"All right." Dolly was still hesitant, but she trusted Ah Cheng's logic. Dolly left the women. Regardless, she spent the rest of the night listening to Sing Leen's wails and Ah Cheng's replies, soothing words alternating with reprimands.

Perhaps she slept; perhaps she didn't. The night became a haze of passing time. When the approaching dawn finally shifted the purple twilight outside Dolly's bedroom window to a warm yellow, she heard footsteps pounding down the staircase.

On instinct, Dolly flew out of her room to see what the commotion was. Ah Cheng was following after Sing Leen.

"Help me stop her!" Ah Cheng cried out when she saw Dolly. "She wants to return to the cribs where the opium is."

Miss Culbertson and Anna stood at the front door waiting, as if they had known Sing Leen would try to flee the mission home.

Dolly reached the bottom of the stairs as the women faced off, Sing Leen's flushed face streaked with tears, her breathing coming in gasps. Ah Cheng's face was equally flushed, her gaze desperate.

When Ah Cheng latched onto Sing Leen's arm with a tight grip, Miss Culbertson moved toward the pair. "We cannot force her to remain or to change," she said in a calm, firm voice.

"She's going through withdrawals," Ah Cheng protested, keeping her grip on the Chinese woman. "Once they pass, she will feel better."

But Miss Culbertson continued in a perfectly calm tone, "Let her go, Ah Cheng. This must be *her* decision."

Dolly stared as Miss Culbertson opened the front door. It was as if a barrier had burst. Sing Leen wrenched from Ah Cheng's failing grasp and bolted out the double doors. She nearly tripped going down the porch steps, then ran, fleeing down the hill into the early morning light.

No one spoke. Dolly's eyes pricked with heat. There was no doubt that each person watching Sing Leen's departure knew what she had in store for her if she returned to the cribs. She would return to her depraved life, going back to where she would live out what few months or years she had left as a slave to the darkness that had become her one and only mistress.

CHAPTER FIVE

*"SEC. 11. That any person who shall knowingly bring into or cause
to be brought into the United States by land, or who shall knowingly
aid or abet the same, or aid or abet the landing in the United States
from any vessel of any Chinese person not lawfully entitled to enter the
United States, shall be deemed guilty of a misdemeanor. . . .*

*"SEC. 14. That hereafter no State court or court of the United States
shall admit Chinese to citizenship; and all laws in conflict with this
act are hereby repealed."*

—Chinese Exclusion Act, approved May 6, 1882, US Congress

1903

Mei Lien stood with the other travelers on the steamship's deck as the shores of San Francisco grew closer. She hadn't been above deck in the daylight since leaving Hong Kong. Uncle and Auntie had allowed her only short visits when it was dark—in order to protect her from others, they had claimed.

The first thing that Mei Lien noticed about her spotting of San Francisco was that there was no gold mountain. The grays and greens of the approaching land seemed ordinary enough, yet Mei Lien's pulse felt like it was on fire. She was almost to America, a fabled land of opportunity, where poor Chinese women like her could secure their futures, marry, and raise children who would never face starvation or poverty.

The smaller fishing boats they passed shimmered orange in the late summer sun, and Mei Lien studied the fishermen with interest. She had never seen a white man until she'd stepped on the ship and seen the captain and his officers. Now she would be in a land of many colors, many religions, and many opportunities. If only her mother could be here with her; they could share the experience together.

The ocean breeze cut a chill across her skin, but Mei Lien didn't mind. Auntie had told her to wear the finest cheongsam they'd brought in order to impress upon the immigration agents that she came from a wealthy family and would not be a burden upon society.

Mei Lien was mindful of any ocean spray so as not to damage the silk she wore. The handful of other young women on the ship had also come above deck to watch the approaching land. Mei Lien had been obedient to Auntie's request to not speak to any of them.

"They'll tell you lies," Auntie had whispered. "Or they will try to involve you in their deceit. Chinese women are not allowed to enter America unless they are the daughter or wife of a man already living there."

Mei Lien kept to herself, but here on the deck, she wanted to talk to someone about what she was seeing, about what things to expect.

She wasn't given the chance.

"Remember all that you've learned," Uncle said, breathing close to her ear as he took his place next to her at the railing.

Without turning to look at him, Mei Lien nodded.

"We will all be separated and questioned." His hands gripped the railing next to her. "Our stories must be identical."

"Yes, I am ready." And she was, although her heart raced and her palms felt hot when she thought about being interrogated.

Soon it would all be over. Soon she would be presented to her new husband and her future would begin.

The excitement and chaos of disembarking echoed in Mei Lien's rapid heartbeat. She found herself in a line herded by immigration agents. Uncle and Auntie were with her one moment, then separated the next, just as Uncle had warned.

Mei Lien was led into an airless room with a high window. She sat on a bench with three other girls. None of them spoke to each other, but Mei Lien was by far the best dressed among the group. When her name was called by a white immigration officer with a thick mustache, she followed him into a second room. There at a table sat a Chinese man who Mei Lien guessed was the interpreter.

For the next several minutes, she was asked all kinds of questions, and some of them more than once. The immigration officer watched her closely, his deep green eyes seeming to pierce right through her. But Mei Lien had been well trained. Although her palms sweated and she felt prickly all over her body, she didn't lose her composure. She kept her voice calm, even, and innocent.

Even as she answered the questions, she thought of her new life. If she could only get through this interview, she would be free. That thought kept her focused on each and every question. Finally, she was ushered out of the room and told to sit again on the bench. The other young women were gone, and Mei Lien didn't know what that meant. Had they passed their interviews? Would they be sent back to Hong Kong?

Then the immigration officer returned with the interpreter. "You may join your family now," he said. "Your answers have matched with those of your aunt and uncle."

Mei Lien felt like she might melt with joy. She rose on shaky limbs and bowed to the interpreter. He gave a brief nod and nothing else.

When she came out of the building, Uncle and Auntie were waiting for her. Mei Lien couldn't help but smile, and Auntie gave her a half smile and a nod of approval. The small acknowledgment only compounded Mei Lien's relief. She was *here,* in America. Her life would be nothing but wonderful.

"We'll hire a buggy to take us to our destination," Uncle said, his tone light and cheerful. It seemed he was happy to have made it this far.

Mei Lien was eager to keep pace with Uncle and Auntie as they walked along the harbor to where Uncle hired a cab. Hunger cramped her stomach, and her legs still felt wobbly from the ship, but neither mattered. She couldn't wait to meet the man she would marry.

The three of them crowded inside the cab, but Mei Lien didn't mind. There was much to see outside the windows. She gazed at the children with their white skin and Western clothing. Girls and women strolled about, the girls wearing short dresses with frilly hems, the women clothed in long skirts, blouses, hats, and gloves. These women and girls walked like men, with their flat feet and long strides.

In Hong Kong, proper women didn't walk the streets; only their servants did. Proper women had bound feet, and they ran their homes and raised their children. Mei Lien had not grown up in a wealthy home. Her feet had never been bound, which Auntie had been very pleased about during their first interview, since she wouldn't be limited to stay inside a house in America.

Mei Lien took in the sights and wondered if she'd ever be able to tell her mother about all that she was seeing. She imagined her mother's exclamations, especially about the tall buildings and the different-colored people. "Japanese are here too?" Mei Lien said when she saw two men who were at least a head shorter than the average Chinese man.

"Some Japanese are here," Uncle said. "But they keep to themselves. You will see, once we get to Chinatown, that most of us are Chinese."

The change in architecture and scenery was a sharp contrast once they arrived at the so-called Chinatown. Nostalgia twisted hard inside Mei Lien. The people, the smells of food, the shop displays, all made her miss her mother even more. Most of the people she saw were Chinese men wearing loose, dark clothing, long queues braided down their backs, their dark eyes following the buggy as if they wanted to see inside. The lack of women on the narrow streets told her the women were properly settled in their homes raising their babies and running their households.

"How long until I meet my husband?" Mei Lien asked, her nerves buzzing along her skin. Would he be handsome? Young? Old?

"Not long," Uncle said.

Auntie pressed her lips together and exchanged glances with Uncle.

Mei Lien wanted to ask what *not long* meant, but it seemed the elation of having cleared immigration had already worn off of Auntie, and she was back to her glowering self.

The buggy jolted to a stop, and Uncle climbed out.

Mei Lien made to rise, but Auntie shoved her back into her seat. "We're not there yet. Stay seated."

Mei Lien didn't move after that. Not when Uncle got back in and said that the buggy driver hadn't wanted to take them past a certain point, so Uncle had given him a tip. Now, the buggy rumbled forward again, and, after a couple more turns, it stopped again.

Uncle climbed out, then held open the door for Auntie. Mei Lien was the last one to step down. They had stopped in front of a three-story building. The outside lettering scaling up the brick wall proclaimed that it was a hotel. Mei Lien had thought Uncle owned a house in the area, but perhaps they were meeting her husband here?

She didn't have time to ask, because Auntie's clawlike fingers propelled her forward. They stepped into the dim interior of the building, and the smoky atmosphere made Mei Lien's throat tickle. The sickly-sweet smell was familiar, and she immediately knew it had to be opium or some form of it. But here it was stronger than she had ever smelled, less bitter, sweeter.

The tickle in her throat turned to a burning, and she started to cough.

"Enough coughing," Auntie hissed, tightening her grip. "You don't want them to think you're sick."

Mei Lien tried to keep her coughing to a minimum, which only made her eyes water and her throat burn more. She had never been inside a hotel before, and she didn't know what to expect. The lobby was lovely, with tall plants, velvet drapes, a deep burgundy rug, and teak furniture.

A man who was tall for Chinese stepped through a set of velvet drapes and walked toward them. Was this her husband? He was dressed in an elegant silk suit, and his hair was smoothed back from his high forehead so tightly that it made his eyebrows arch into peaks. His braid down his back told her that he was traditional. He nodded to Auntie and Uncle; then his gaze landed on Mei Lien. The man studied her for a moment, and no one spoke, as if they were waiting for him to make some kind of pronouncement. That he approved of his new bride? The man was older than she had thought, perhaps late forties, and Mei Lien sensed that she wouldn't be his first wife. Hopefully she would be second wife then, and still have status in his household.

When the man nodded, Auntie's grip on her arm lessened a fraction.

Mei Lien wanted to know what the nod meant.

"This way," the man said. "The others will be here soon."

Others? Were they witnesses, and she was to marry tonight? Was his family coming, and the ceremony would be in this hotel? Mei Lien thought of her mother's wedding dress, crushed and wrinkled in her small trunk. Would she have time to press it?

They followed the man through the hanging drapes, and the sweet smoke intensified. Mei Lien covered her mouth to suppress another cough, and Auntie increased her grip once again. As they headed up a flight of narrow stairs, mercifully, the smoke lessened. At the top of the corridor was a long hallway, the walls covered in a patterned paper, connecting with the dusty wooden floor below. Mei Lien breathed freer as they walked down the hallway.

The man opened a door at the end of the hallway, and they all walked inside a bedroom. This room was absolutely opulent, with silk hangings, jade statues, and landscape art. Then Mei Lien noticed they weren't alone. Three young women, close to Mei Lien's age, stood along one wall, opposite the large bed. Another Chinese man, in his late fifties or early sixties, with shoulders as broad as an ox, perched on the edge of the bed, smoking.

The girls' painted faces and expensive satin clothing sent a shiver of warning through Mei Lien, and she remembered the foul names she'd been called at the harbor in Hong Kong. Were these women daughters of the night? Did her husband want concubines, too?

Mei Lien's eyes watered, but she miraculously held back her cough. Was she to be married to the old man? Her heart sank at the prospect. She didn't want to be a widow in a few years, kicked to the street to fend for herself. If her husband died, she wouldn't be able to marry again, and unless she had a grown son, there would be no one to care for her, no extra money to send to her mother.

Mei Lien knew she couldn't ask any questions now, not with so many strangers staring at her. The other women didn't look too pleased that she had come. Mei Lien finally identified her unease about the women: the eyes of each had that same glassy look that reminded her of Li Qiang, her betrothed, who had become addicted to opium.

Then the door opened again, and three more people entered. All men.

Uncle crossed to the men and bowed as if the new arrivals were of some importance. Their words were fast and whispered. Mei Lien caught only a small part of their discussion, which sounded like they were bartering over something. Discussing prices.

Mei Lien glanced again at the women against the wall. One appeared about to faint. The other two met her gaze, then quickly looked away.

The man with the pipe spoke for all to hear and ordered the three women to stand on chairs. It was then that Mei Lien noticed four chairs had been lined up in front of the wardrobe. The women moved to the chairs and obediently climbed up on them.

Auntie turned toward Mei Lien and hissed, "Are you stupid? Did you not hear the man? Get on a chair!"

Mei Lien opened her mouth to protest. What was going on? Where was her husband? Who were all these people? But Auntie pinched the top of her hip. Hard.

Mei Lien nearly yelped. Her eyes watered from the sharp sting, and she moved to the last chair and climbed up on it.

The men were still talking to Uncle, and now the man with the pipe had joined in. Their conversation became heated, rising whispers. When Uncle and the man with the pipe quieted and stood aside, Mei Lien watched the three men advance toward the chairs.

One of them stepped close to Mei Lien. He leaned forward and drew in a deep breath.

Mei Lien wanted to slap him away. What was he doing? Why was he smelling her? Then he lifted his head and met her gaze.

His eyes were very dark, like two pools with no end to their depths, and a slow chill spread across her skin. She supposed he was handsome, but his sharp features and cold eyes were disconcerting. Then he snapped his fingers.

The sound was unexpected, and Mei Lien flinched.

A bright flush spread across Auntie's face. "Take off your dress now."

Heat prickled Mei Lien's neck. "What?" Her voice sounded foreign to her ears.

Auntie advanced toward her, her cheeks enflaming. "The man wants to see you without clothes. Take off your robe now so that he will know exactly what he is buying."

CHAPTER SIX

"Jan. 17/94. Tai Choie alias Teen Fook was rescued by Miss Houseworth, Miss Florence Worley and some police officers from her inhuman mistress who lived on Jackson St. near Stockton St. The child had been very cruelly treated—her flesh pinched and twisted till her face was scarred. Another method of torture was to dip lighted candlewicking in oil and burn her arms with it. Teen Fook is a pretty child of about ten years old, rosy cheeked and fair complexion."

—MARGARET CULBERTSON, DIRECTOR OF THE MISSION HOME,
WRITING ABOUT TIEN FU WU, 1894

JULY 1897

"The apples are all gone," Ah Cheng said, coming into the office where Dolly had been working because Miss Culbertson was still faring poorly.

Dolly rose to her feet, alarm shooting through her. Apples were a delicacy—to have them go missing was no small matter. "What do you mean? Maybe someone moved them? Did you ask any of the girls?"

Ah Cheng folded her hands in that patient way of hers. "I've questioned several of the girls, but will you come with me to Bible study and we'll ask them as a group? I don't want Miss Culbertson hearing of this and worrying over it."

"Of course," Dolly said. The mountains of paperwork would have to wait, as usual. If only she could do one or the other—manage the girls, or do paperwork. The superintendent's job was overwhelming.

She followed Ah Cheng to the parlor where the girls were gathered for Bible study and singing. Evelyn Browne was volunteering today, and she always had a sweet way with the girls and women.

Evelyn paused when she saw the two women, and Dolly walked to the front of the room. "We need to talk about something important. The apples from the kitchen are missing, and we know that apples are a special treat. It's not fair if someone keeps them all to herself. Remember how we learned about the Ten Commandments in the Bible, and how stealing is a sin?"

"Lying is a sin too!" Lonnie announced.

"You're correct," Dolly said, scanning the faces before her. It was good to see Jiao and her brother, Kang, sitting next to Lonnie—the girl had taken them under her wing like a big sister. Dolly had been able to secure guardianship papers for the children, and as soon as Kang was old enough for school, he would be transferring to a mission home for boys. "After Bible study, I hope that the person who knows what happened to the apples will visit me in the office." She was just about to find a seat when Tien spoke up.

"I took the apples."

Dolly froze, then slowly turned her gaze to Tien. At nearly twelve now, her legs and arms had lengthened and her thin face had become more rounded. Dolly couldn't say she was entirely surprised that Tien had been behind the missing apples, but she was surprised at the public confession. Dolly knew she had to tread carefully. Her relationship with Tien had never warmed, something that she wished she could change. "Why did you take them?"

"So that I wouldn't be hungry."

The idea wasn't logical to Dolly, since they had three meals a day at the mission home. But she had seen enough of what these girls and women went through to know that the fear of starvation didn't just disappear.

"Don't you want the others in this room to enjoy the apples too?" Dolly continued.

Tien blinked, then looked at a few of the other girls—girls she had been living with for three years now. When her gaze returned to Dolly, Tien said, "I didn't want to lie, either, because I want Miss Culbertson to trust me."

Dolly remembered one of their first conversations from when she had started teaching sewing. Miss Culbertson's illness was another complication. The girls worried about her.

"Thank you for being honest, Tien," Dolly said.

"I'll go get the apples right now." Tien ran out of the room, and her footsteps could be heard pounding up the stairs.

This is good, Dolly decided. Tien could make recompense by returning the apples. It seemed that even when Dolly wasn't sure if she was getting through to the girl, she in fact had made some progress.

The next day, Miss Culbertson took a turn for the worse, with violent fits of coughing. Dolly spent the morning at the director's bedside as her body shuddered with the aftermath of a coughing spasm.

When she could take a normal breath, Miss Culbertson said, "I've decided to retire."

The news shouldn't have surprised Dolly, but the reality of it still shocked her.

"I'll move back east to be with my siblings and their families," Miss Culbertson said. "Then perhaps I can recover my health."

"Does the board know?" Dolly asked in a quiet voice. The board meeting would take place that day, and Dolly had planned to give the reports in the director's stead.

Miss Culbertson rested her frail hand on Dolly's wrist. "I sent them word yesterday. And now, today, you must go hear what the board has to say." The crack in her voice only testified of the pain she endured. "You are the only staff member who has the capacity to fill my shoes, Donaldina. You've been fearless in the rescues, and you're not afraid to say what you think. You've been a leader, and the Chinese women look up to you."

But Dolly didn't want to attend the board meeting that started in an hour. She knew what the board members would propose: that she, Donaldina Cameron, take over the directorship of the mission home. Dolly had been teaching for only a little over two years, and yes, she had gladly helped with plenty of rescues. But balancing the needs of the residents and teaching classes, along with overseeing the donations, handling the legal matters, hosting visiting sponsors, and preparing reports for the board all seemed way beyond her scope of capabilities.

"I will go," Dolly assured Miss Culbertson, because what else could she say to a dying woman who had devoted her life to rescuing hundreds of enslaved women and children? Dolly knew she wasn't ready to take on the full responsibility of running the mission home, but she hoped to continue as a teacher.

When her first year of teaching had ended, the board had asked Dolly to stay for another year. For some reason, the decision had weighed on her more heavily than she would have imagined. *Yes* was the short answer, but she also knew what the commitment entailed: long days, sleepless nights, participating in raids that were dangerous even with the presence of police, taking care of the physical needs of the younger girls and the emotional needs of the older ones, helping to facilitate weddings between the Chinese women and eligible and approved Chinese Christian men.

Dolly's heart had broken more than once when she had watched young women who had pleaded for rescue change their minds and reject a warm, clean home. Dolly had learned some Chinese, as well as some Japanese, in order to communicate better with the rescued women. But Ah Cheng and Yuen Qui were needed for interpreting.

Dolly had asked to take two weeks off while she made her decision whether to commit to another year of teaching. She had traveled back to the San Gabriel Valley with her brother-in-law Charlie Bailey, husband of her sister Jessie. In La Puente, she'd spent two glorious weeks enjoying her family, the scent of orange groves, the sun on her face, the sweet-smelling breeze, and the lazy days filled with love and laughter. Yet even during her moments of absolute happiness with her family, her heart ached for the plight of the women she had left behind. When she closed her eyes, she could see Dong Ho's dimple on her honey-colored cheek, Jiao's shy smile, Lonnie's sturdy legs as she ran down the stairs whenever someone knocked on the door, and even Tien's dark gaze flashing with annoyance.

Before the first night at Jessie's home had passed, Dolly had known she would accept the board's invitation and stay on for another year. Even though it meant her salary would be only twenty-five dollars a month, and she would still have to pay for her room and board. . . .

"Miss Cameron," Miss Culbertson said, using her formal address to cut into Dolly's scattered thoughts. "You have been well prepared, and you have a gift with the women and children. They rely on you. They respect and love you." She brought her handkerchief to her mouth and coughed. Her eyes squeezed shut for a moment. When she spoke, her voice was faint, raspy. "You are needed. Desperately."

Dolly blinked back the tears threatening to give away the depths of her heart. She nodded because her throat was too tight and she knew any words she tried to utter would only be choked off.

Less than an hour later, she took her seat in front of the members of the board as they were all seated in the chapel. All eyes were upon Dolly, as she'd expected. She had worn her best outfit, one she'd brought with her when she'd first traveled to San Francisco two years before: a full voile skirt in black over an orange-brown petticoat, along with a purple shirtwaist with leg-o-mutton sleeves. Dolly had pinned her hair into her usual pompadour. She'd noticed more gray strands than usual threading through its deep auburn.

The president of the board, Mrs. Mary Ann Browne, greeted Dolly warmly, then called the meeting to order. Dolly looked about the room at the other board members, which included Mrs. E. V. Robbins, who was one of the original founders. Mrs. Robbins had faced plenty of persecution and hatred when she first rented quarters for the Chinese girls in 1874. She'd even been spat upon by the landlady. Other board members included Mrs. Sara B. Cooper and Mrs. Phoebe Apperson Hearst.

When Mrs. Browne turned to Dolly and began to address her, she knew what was coming.

"Miss Culbertson can no longer continue in her role," Mrs. Browne said. "She has devoted many years to this work, but now it is time to assign a new director. And by all accounts and purposes, the board would like to invite you to take the position."

The warmth of everyone's eyes upon her should have given Dolly more confidence. She felt too hot, and her neck prickled beneath her high collar. She wanted to say yes, but she knew she could not. Her throat suddenly parched, she said, "I am twenty-seven, and even though I have been mentored by Miss Culbertson for two years, I don't have the capacity or training to take on such a role. I belong at the ground level. Teaching the girls. Caring for their needs. Protecting them."

Her job had become much more than that, and Dolly was sure that everyone in the room knew this, but if she agreed to assume the directorship, her life would forevermore be at the mission home. Her future would never leave 920 Sacramento Street. As much as she loved the girls and didn't want to be anywhere else in the world at this moment, she wasn't ready to commit more than was possible.

Mrs. Browne's mouth straightened into a tight line, and the other women nodded their understanding. Yet Dolly witnessed the disappointment on their faces.

"Very well," Mrs. Browne said in a decisive voice. "We have prepared for this possibility and have researched a second candidate." She looked at the other women in the room. "I propose we offer Mrs. Mary H. Field the position of superintendent. You should have all been apprised of her credentials."

Dolly sat in silence as the board voted unanimously to hire Mrs. Field.

Dolly should have been elated, but she only felt more burdened. She didn't know Mrs. Field, and there would be a new routine to learn with the departure of Miss Culbertson. As stern and businesslike as Miss Culbertson had been in the beginning, Dolly had grown to love the woman like a family member.

When Dolly returned to Miss Culbertson's room later that evening, the older woman had already heard the news. Instead of any sort of reprimand or expression of disappointment, Miss Culbertson lifted a hand and motioned for Dolly to sit near her bedside.

"Mrs. Field will be a fine superintendent," Miss Culbertson said in a gentle tone. "And you may continue in what you are already good at."

Dolly released a soft sigh. "I'm sorry."

Miss Culbertson's mouth lifted into a faint smile. "There is nothing to apologize for. You are young, and you have your entire life before you."

Dolly nodded, but still her heart was heavy—not with regret, but with the feeling that she'd disappointed Miss Culbertson all the same.

The two women didn't speak for a few moments as the sounds of nightly preparations from the women and girls echoed through the hallways outside the bedroom door.

"I heard Dong Ho call you mama," Miss Culbertson said after a while.

Unable to hold back her smile, Dolly said, "Yes. A few of the younger girls do. Even Jiao, although she still misses her mother, Hong Leen, so much."

Miss Culbertson reached over and patted Dolly's knee. "For many of them, you are the only mother they'll know. Even Tien."

Dolly exhaled at this. "Do you think Tien will ever see me as someone not to resent?"

"I heard about the apples," Miss Culbertson said. "I think you're going in the right direction with her. Be patient. These girls have lost so much, and they know you understand what it's like to lose a mother at a young age."

Nothing could replace a mother's love, that Dolly well knew. And no, she had not borne a child from her body, but the girls she served day and night felt as if they had become her own flesh and blood.

"Dong Ho is as sweet as they come," Dolly said. "I'll never forget the day she showed up on our doorstep, that tiny bundle of her earthly possessions gripped in her skinny arms."

Miss Culbertson chuckled softy. "I believe she could have fought off two dragons if needed. She didn't want anyone to touch her things."

Dolly nodded at the fond memory. "Ah Cheng and I helped her into the bath, and still she kept an eagle eye on that bundle."

"It took a week before she allowed you to peek inside."

"Yes," Dolly said. "Imagine having your most prized possessions be two chopsticks, a broken comb, and a couple of soiled garments."

"Garbage to some people," Miss Culbertson mused.

"Yet priceless as pearls to Dong Ho." Dolly leaned back in the chair and smiled over at Miss Culbertson. "They will miss you."

Tears gleamed in Miss Culbertson's eyes. "I could not leave them to anyone else but you. Director or not, you will be their mama, and that is all that matters."

"Do you ever wonder how your life might have turned out if you hadn't come here to work?" Dolly asked.

"I stopped wondering that many years ago," Miss Culbertson said. "I discovered that although my life is not conventional, I've been happy."

Dolly considered this. Working so many hours and in the capacity that she did left little opportunity for socializing or finding a beau. Miss Culbertson had never married, likely because the director's role at the mission home was all consuming, mentally, physically, and emotionally. But the mission work had its own rewards.

Somehow Dolly slept that night even though she knew Miss Culbertson would be leaving soon with her niece Anna. Dolly would dearly miss both women.

Mrs. Field arrived at the mission home the day after Miss Culbertson's departure, so it was up to Dolly to show her around. The woman wore all black, as if she were in mourning, and the severity of her bun drawn back from her face made her eyes pull tight. Dolly guessed her to be in her early forties.

"Welcome," Dolly said, leading Mrs. Field into the foyer. Dolly decided not to go by her first impression, but to stay open-minded.

"This place is so dark," Mrs. Field said right away. "Why are the windows so high up?"

Dolly clasped her hands together. "The dark paneling creates a soothing atmosphere, and the high windows make the mission home more secure."

Mrs. Field's brows pulled together, deepening the lines on her forehead. Dolly continued the tour and made introductions. Mrs. Field asked a few questions, but mostly her expression gave away very little emotion. She didn't even smile when a group of the younger girls sang a hymn for her.

Dolly accompanied her to the office where Miss Culbertson had first told Dolly about the many layers of work at the mission home.

Mrs. Field took a cursory look about the place. "This will do. If I have questions, I will seek you out." And then Mrs. Field promptly shut the office door.

Dolly stared at the door for a moment, wondering if Mrs. Field just needed time to warm up. The woman had been recommended by the board, and she had accepted the position. Things didn't have to always be done exactly as Miss Culbertson had done them. Dolly headed to the parlor, where she stood in the middle of the room for a few minutes as the sun's rays dappled the furniture and rug.

A movement behind the chair caught Dolly's attention, and Tien rose from where she'd been hiding. The girl could make herself so small and unnoticeable, Dolly didn't doubt that Tien was very well informed of the goings-on at the mission home.

"I don't like her," Tien said.

It was perhaps the first time that Tien had started a conversation with her.

"We need to help the new director all we can," Dolly said. "She's new here and has a lot of responsibility."

Tien's mouth flattened, and the displeased look in her eyes was well familiar to Dolly. "She doesn't like Chinese girls."

"Heavens, what makes you say that?" Dolly asked, although the growing knot in her stomach told her that there might be some truth to Tien's observation.

"The Chinese don't like Mrs. Field."

This was out of line. "Remember we need to speak the truth. Mrs. Field is our new director, and she's devoted to the cause of the mission home."

But Tien didn't relent. "I heard Yuen Qui say that the tong is glad Miss Culbertson left."

Yuen Qui was one of the Chinese residents who had assisted on a few rescues when Ah Cheng couldn't go. She was a pretty young woman whom Tien seemed to follow around frequently. Before Dolly could reply, someone knocked at the front door, and the sound echoed into the parlor.

Tien startled like a rabbit, then steeled herself, as if talking herself into not reacting to the sudden noise. This made Dolly wonder if Tien always reacted this way to someone knocking on the door.

"I'll answer it," Dolly said, heading out of the parlor. She didn't think Tien would attempt to answer the door. In the last several months, Miss Culbertson had put a rule into place that only a staff member could answer a door, especially after night fell.

Dolly unlocked the door and drew it open. A young man stood there; Dolly recognized him as the errand boy who delivered telegrams. Now, he held out a telegram toward Dolly. She gave him a small tip, and he scampered off.

Dolly shut the door and was about to take the telegram to the new director, but then the sender's name gave her pause. It was from Anna Culbertson, and it was addressed to Donaldina Cameron.

Tien had emerged from the doorway of the parlor. Well, perhaps there was happy news from Anna's travels that Dolly could share with Tien. And maybe this change in the mission home director could be a new beginning between Dolly and Tien.

Dolly opened the telegram and began to read.

The printed words were no report of good news or safe travels. Miss Culbertson had taken a turn for the worse and passed away before reaching her destination. Dolly was stunned. She didn't know how long she stood in the entryway of the mission home, not moving and not speaking.

Tien must have alerted Ah Cheng, because she came running, and when Dolly shared the terrible news, the two women fell into an embrace. Then Yuen Qui arrived and wrapped an arm about Dolly.

"Let us sit down," Yuen Qui said in a quiet voice.

The two interpreters led Dolly back to the parlor, where they sat on the settee together. All Dolly could think about was poor Miss Culbertson wanting to travel to see her family and to spend her retirement in peace, but her body had given out. How would they deliver the news to the girls who had loved her so much?

"I will call everyone together," Ah Cheng said. "And we will put together a memorial service so the girls can share their feelings."

Dolly gave a numb nod. "And Mrs. Field. She must know."

"Yes, I will speak with her," Yuen Qui said.

Yuen Qui and Ah Cheng kept discussing how they would help the girls, but Dolly's mind was on Tien. Where had she gone?

"I need to find Tien," Dolly said. Her heart was tight with stunned grief, but she could not wait on this. She found the girl in her bedroom, sitting on the corner of her bed and staring at the window.

Everything about the tenseness of Tien's body told Dolly not to touch her. So Dolly remained in the doorway and spoke softly. "Miss Culbertson is no longer in pain, and she'll be happy in heaven. From there, she can watch over all of us."

Tien didn't respond.

"She loved you and trusted you, Tien," Dolly continued. "I know that if she could tell you one more thing, it would be to help the younger girls. They look up to you as someone wiser than they are. You can help the other girls because you understand what they are feeling."

Tien's shoulders sagged, but she still didn't move.

"We'll be gathering downstairs to tell everyone." Dolly waited another moment, then she finally left the forlorn girl whose life had changed yet again today.

As Dolly began the slow walk back to the parlor, she knew the Chinese girls would depend on her more than ever. It was up to her to be the comforter at this time, since Mrs. Field hadn't yet forged any personal relationships.

After the staff delivered the news of Miss Culbertson's passing, the quiet that settled over the mission home was one of mourning and memories. Mrs. Field stayed in the office for hours at a time, and Dolly canceled classes and spent time with the women and girls. Most of them had called Miss Culbertson their "mama," and this loss was deeply felt. Dolly wasn't even sure she had slept a full night in many days, as she was awakened over and over by someone knocking on her door in tears. Dolly could not turn away the brokenhearted, no matter how exhausted she was. She would invite whoever had knocked into her room and offer hugs and soothing words.

Just when it seemed a new routine had finally taken root, with Mrs. Field in charge, Yuen Qui returned from the marketplace one afternoon with purchases for dinner. Instead of ordering the dinner preparations to begin, she sought Dolly where she was teaching Bible study. One look at Yuen Qui's pretty face clouded with worry told Dolly that she needed to excuse herself from class. She asked Lonnie to be in charge in her absence, then followed Yuen Qui out of the room.

Tien came after them, always Yuen Qui's little shadow. Dolly didn't have the heart to chastise Tien for leaving class. Besides, whatever was distressing Yuen Qui, Tien would find out soon enough anyway.

"There are rumors going around Chinatown," Yuen Qui said once they were in the hallway.

"Should we report to Mrs. Field then?" Dolly immediately suggested.

"No," Yuen Qui said. "This is about *you*. We already know the tong members celebrated Miss Culbertson's departure."

Dolly glanced over at Tien, who had told her as much. The girl was watching them with open curiosity.

"But now, the tong plans to enact their revenge on *you,* Miss Cameron," Yuen Qui said. "They plan to stop you at all costs. They've hired lawyers to issue warrants that will accuse our girls of theft so the police will have to return the girls to their owners."

Dolly's breath stalled. The issuing of warrants wasn't new. It was one of the reasons Miss Culbertson allowed only a staff member to answer the mission home door.

She felt Tien's gaze on her, and Yuen Qui's fear was palpable. "We will find a way," Dolly said at last, lifting her chin. "None of these girls would be here if it weren't for Miss Culbertson. If she were still alive, she wouldn't let a few rumors stop her. She faced threats every day, and so will I. As Miss Culbertson did, we will continue to put our faith in the Lord."

Dolly stepped past Tien and Yuen Qui and reentered the classroom to resume the Bible study. One day at a time, sometimes one moment at a time, would be the way to move the work forward. Threats would not stop her. The words of Officer Cook would not leave her mind. This was truly a war, and the tong were only raising the stakes by issuing warrants. So Dolly would raise the stakes too.

No, not every rescue had gone smoothly. A few months ago, one of the young Chinese women had been returned to her owner due to a fictitious search warrant that claimed the woman had stolen jewelry. The woman had been taken away sobbing, and when her court date had come, Miss Culbertson had come back to the mission home saying that the girl had not shown up. They could only conclude that the owner had taken her and fled.

As Dolly stood in front of the classroom again, she clapped her hands for full attention. "We will memorize the words of Paul. Repeat after me: *I can do all things through Christ which strengtheneth me.*"

The dark-eyed girls, sitting in their rows, clasped hands resting on their white outfits, repeated the phrase back to Dolly.

"Again," Dolly said. As the girls repeated the holy words, she let the cadence of their feminine voices wash over her.

Tien joined the back row and repeated each word along with the others, her eyes fierce and intent on Dolly. In that moment, Dolly knew Tien was slowly becoming her ally. At last.

Shortly after the dinner hour, Dolly received a note delivered anonymously to the mission home. This in and of itself wasn't unusual, but Dolly was wary as she read the address from the girl begging to be rescued. Right in the heart of Chinatown. She approached Mrs. Field with the note, and the woman waved it off. "Go do your rescues. I'll not walk among the filth of Chinatown."

So Dolly sent word to Officer Cook, and she and Ah Cheng met Cook and Riordan at the bottom of the Sacramento Street hill just as twilight deepened the sky to black.

Cook fell into step beside her as Dolly led the small group with her long strides straight to the address. "You've heard the news about the tong's increased determination," he said.

"I have," Dolly said.

"And you're not going to back down like they wish?"

Dolly cast him a sideways glance. "What do you think I should do, Officer Cook?"

"I think you should carry on, Miss Cameron," he said. "You're the new general of the missionary army now."

A smile curved her mouth. "I like that title."

"I thought you would," he said in a warm tone.

She wasn't looking at him, but she could feel his smile. A moment later, the scent of cigarette smoke ebbed around her.

Threats or no threats, she would keep putting one foot in front of the other.

They had little trouble entering the building. Cook and Riordan didn't have to use their sledgehammers to break down doors or smash windows. The place seemed quiet, which told Dolly there might have been some warning of the raid. Slave owners sometimes had watchmen in place, and tonight might be such a case. Dolly had been in this building before with Miss Culbertson, so she was familiar with the layout. She led the squad up the back staircase to the second floor.

She stopped before the numbered door with its faded Chinese lettering. It matched the information in the note. First, Dolly knocked, and predictably, there was no answer. Then she tried the doorknob. When the door opened with no trouble, Cook said, "I'll go in first. Stay back."

He moved in front of her, but Dolly quickly followed. Sometimes the girl would be hidden, and if Dolly could get inside fast enough, she would glimpse the closing of a secret panel.

But there was no one in the room—at least no living person.

Hanging from the ceiling was a human form, an effigy. The long skirt, the bronze hair, and the green-painted eyes left little doubt of whom the hanging effigy represented. The swaying body might be fake, but the dagger plunged into the center of the look-alike's chest was not.

The message was clear: this was no game or joke. Other threats to the mission home had seemed less personal, but Dolly couldn't deny, watching the slow swing of the effigy in the garish light, that she was staring death in the face.

She drew in a shaky breath, closed her eyes, exhaled. Then she turned from the room and walked out. She had already committed herself to this work, so putting her future into the Lord's hands was all she could do now. Come what may. Her work would go forward, threats and all, as long as she was able.

CHAPTER SEVEN

*"The only entrance to the crib was a narrow door, in which
was set a small barred window. Occupants of the den took
turns standing behind the bars and striving to attract the
attention of passing men."*

—HERBERT ASBURY, BARBARY COAST, 1933

1903

Mei Lien could not move, and she wasn't even sure if she was breathing. Every part of her body trembled as she huddled against the wall of the hotel room she had come to loathe. She'd been told to dress again, and the other women with their painted faces had been escorted out by the man with the pipe.

But the three men who'd inspected her body as if she were a skinned chicken at the market were still in the room speaking to Uncle. Their voices were no longer fierce whispers; now they were openly arguing about her . . . *price.*

Mei Lien's stomach tumbled with nausea, both from lack of food and water and from the knowledge that not once had the word *husband* been uttered.

Auntie stood between Mei Lien and the men as if she were some sort of guard or sentinel, and the look on her face told Mei Lien that there was no use asking any questions.

"*Three thousand,*" Uncle growled. "You saw for yourself she is prettier than any girl in Chinatown. The men will pay double the price of a white woman."

What was Uncle talking about? Why were they speaking of the price of women as if they were something to be bought and sold?

One of the men offered two thousand, eight hundred.

Uncle raised his hands. "Enough. We will take her elsewhere. There are others—"

"All right," the man said. "Three thousand. And I want her right now. No delay."

Uncle nodded, then motioned toward Auntie. "Come and witness Wang Foo's counting."

Mei Lien wondered if she were dreaming, or, more accurately, in the middle of a nightmare. Perhaps she was still below deck on the ship, and when she awoke, she would discover that they had yet to land in San Francisco. But no, Auntie stood next to Uncle and the remaining man as he counted out bills reaching three thousand dollars.

Auntie nodded after the money was counted, then she loaded the bills into Uncle's trunk.

Wang Foo smiled, stretching his wide face even more, then bowed before Uncle. "On your way out, send in my procuress."

What did he mean, *procuress*? Was Mei Lien to be a wife or not? And why had there been such a large money exchange?

Uncle opened the door of the hotel room. He cast a glance toward Mei Lien, his expression hooded and unreadable.

Auntie crossed to Mei Lien. "Your trunk will be left downstairs. Do not cause trouble. If you do, your ancestors will curse you, and your mother will be left to starve in the streets. One bad word about you, and she'll be tossed out of her home and shamed. Do you want that?"

Mei Lien fought against the bile stinging her throat. "No."

"Good." Auntie turned away.

Panic raced through Mei Lien's veins. "Auntie," she cried. "Is this man to be my husband, then?"

Auntie stilled but didn't turn around. "No, Mei Lien. You are to keep Wang Foo happy, though. Your life and your mother's life depend upon it."

The door opened then, and a woman stepped through. She was tall for a Chinese woman, and although she was years past her youth, she was beautiful, with creamy skin, perfect rosebud lips, and dark, soulful eyes.

The woman nodded a greeting to Auntie, but neither of them spoke. When the door shut behind Auntie, the woman looked over at Wang Foo. "Is this the girl?" she asked in a lilting tone that reminded Mei Lien of a cooing dove.

"Yes," Wang Foo said. "She is yours now. We paid three thousand for her, and I expect every bit of that back as soon as possible."

The woman smiled, and it completely transformed her face. Her beauty had been noticeable before, but now it was breathtaking. She advanced toward Mei Lien. The woman's walk was just as lilting as her speech, due to her bound feet.

When the woman stopped before her, she was still smiling her beautiful smile, yet Mei Lien didn't see any warmth in her eyes. Her gaze was sharp, assessing, and despite Mei Lien's being fully clothed, she felt as if this woman could see past every layer and stitch.

"What is your name?" she asked, her lilting voice like a musical bird, entrancing.

Mei Lien opened her mouth and found her own voice scratchy. "Mei Lien."

"Mei Lien," the woman repeated. "I am Ah-Peen Oie Kum, and you now belong to me. You will do as I say. You will not speak unless you have permission. And you will earn back every cent of that three thousand Wang Foo paid for you."

"Will he be my husband?"

Ah-Peen Oie lifted her hand and struck Mei Lien.

The resounding slap echoed in the room, and it took several moments for Mei Lien to comprehend that the sharp cry had been her own.

Mei Lien's cheek throbbed, and her eyes watered. Not even her own mother had ever struck her. Mei Lien covered her burning cheek with her hand and straightened from the wall. She didn't know what she was going to do, but it wasn't remaining *here*, with these people.

"You've already forgotten the rules?" Ah-Peen Oie mocked. "Such a foolish girl. *Do not speak unless you have permission.*" The woman's hand clamped down on Mei Lien's wrist and began to twist, slowly and painfully. "Perhaps this will help you remember."

Mei Lien gasped as Ah-Peen Oie continued to twist until she was sure the small bones in her wrist would break.

"Have you had enough?" Ah-Peen Oie asked, her smile broad on her face.

The smile was no longer beautiful to Mei Lien, but reminded her of a painting she'd once seen of an evil goddess.

Mei Lien nodded vigorously, too afraid to speak a single word.

"Very well." Ah-Peen Oie released her wrist and stepped back. "Now we will prepare you for your initiation."

Mei Lien's wrist burned. And even though she couldn't ask what the woman meant by *initiation*, her expression conveyed her confusion.

"You are more foolish than I thought," Ah-Peen Oie said with an artful lift of her brow. "Did your emigration agents not tell you anything?"

Mei Lien shook her head.

Ah-Peen Oie folded her deceitfully delicate arms that were in truth remarkably strong. "We have one week to prepare before your introduction banquet. Men from the city will come and meet you, and you will charm them into bidding for the privilege of winning your first night. Mystery surrounding you and competition among the men will bring in the money. After your night with the highest bidder, you'll become a regular prostitute, and we'll be less picky. In fact, we'll turn no one away. You, dear Mei Lien, are a beauty who will bring us great profit."

Mei Lien's knees became water, and her stomach turned to rock. She could not stop herself from sliding to the ground. From somewhere deep inside, she felt herself breaking completely in half.

She couldn't decipher what Ah-Peen Oie had started yelling at her, joined by the deeper cadence of Wang Foo. Both of them were shouting, and Mei Lien wasn't sure if it was at her or at each other.

"Mama," Mei Lien whispered. "Help me."

Strong hands gripped her upper arms and roughly hauled her to her feet. But Mei Lien could not put any weight on her feet. Nothing in her body cooperated. It was as if all her limbs were anchors pulling her deeper toward the depths of the ocean.

Someone picked her up, and Mei Lien struggled to free herself. Another person slapped her other cheek. The pain was nothing compared to the downward spiral of her hope. She only wished she were strong enough to wrest away and to run. Where she would run, she didn't know, but anyplace would be better than in the clutches of this mistress and master.

Then, Wang Foo grasped her jaw between his thick fingers and forced her mouth open. A bitter powder burst upon her tongue, and she tried to spit out the vile taste. But it was too late; Wang Foo had clamped her jaw shut again. Mei Lien's eyes and nasal passages burned as the powder dominated her senses.

She had never tried opium before, but she instinctively knew she'd been given an opium dose. Despite the revulsion, it didn't take long for Mei Lien's body to relax against her will. Then she was being carried out of the bedroom with its silk hangings and thick rug. She tried to memorize the turns and passages through the hotel, but the walls seemed to tilt, and her thoughts jumped around no matter how hard she tried to focus.

Maybe when they fell asleep, she would find a way out of this place.

Would they leave her alone? Especially after paying three thousand dollars for her? The amount of money was beyond anything she or her mother could earn in both their lifetimes. This told Mei Lien that escape would be difficult. No person would let a three-thousand-dollar investment out of their sight.

Mei Lien's thoughts began to scatter, and she couldn't remember the last turn that Wang Foo had taken, or if he was going up the stairs or down the stairs. *Down,* she decided. The air grew cold, a sharp cold that scattered goose bumps along her arms. And now her vision was blurry. Laughter bubbled in her chest for no reason.

A breeze hit her face. They were outside now, and somehow the sun must have already set because stars glittered between the clouds above. Wang Foo settled her into a buggy, and it lurched forward, bouncing over cobblestones. Mei Lien tried to stay awake enough to peer out the windows at the passing buildings, but it was so hard to keep her eyes open. She dimly registered that they were passing shops, and people, and dogs, and other buggies.

Outside, everyone went about their lives as if no one knew she existed.

And perhaps that would soon be true. Mei Lien's life as she knew it was ending.

She was tired, so tired, and she decided she could close her eyes for a few minutes. Then escape later. When she wasn't exhausted.

"Mei Lien." The woman's voice sounded familiar.

But no matter how hard Mei Lien tried to remember, she wasn't sure where she knew this voice from.

Something shook Mei Lien's shoulder, and it made her teeth rattle.

The woman spoke again, this time more quietly but also with more force. "Mei Lien. You must wake up now. It's time to get out. We are here."

Here? Mei Lien was still tired and knew she could sleep for hours and hours more. But she opened her eyes to see that they'd arrived at an elegant building that was much fancier than the hotel where Uncle and Auntie had taken her. This building towered three stories high, or maybe four. The windows were long and narrow, fitted with red-painted balconies.

And she could smell delicious food. Not rotting vegetables or stinging opium smoke.

She pushed off the bench, her legs feeling wobbly, but Ah-Peen Oie helped her down out of the buggy almost gently. What had happened to cause the woman's kindness? Even Wang Foo was gazing at her with approval as he stood by the front door, holding it wide for the women.

"Come inside." The music in Ah-Peen Oie's tone returned. "We will bathe you, and you'll wear beautiful clothing. I have a pretty jade comb I'd like you to try on. It will bring out the sparkle in your eyes."

Mei Lien wanted to laugh at this woman's words. Was she speaking in jest? One part of Mei Lien's mind wanted to climb back into the buggy, but the other part propelled her forward. It seemed that her legs and feet agreed with following Ah-Peen Oie wherever she commanded.

The interior of the nice hotel was brightly lit with what must have been electricity—something that wasn't available in Mei Lien's village back in Hong Kong. She slowly looked around at the rich furnishings, and at the men who sat among the low tables, many of them smoking pipes of opium mixed with tobacco.

This time, Mei Lien knew better than to cough.

The men noticed the new arrivals, and a few smiled at Ah-Peen Oie. Mei Lien looked at her mistress to see the woman blushing and giving small smiles to the men as if she were able to share wordless signals with them.

The admiration in the men's gazes caused Mei Lien's thoughts to jumble. What was this place? And who was Ah-Peen Oie to these men? As they walked through the lobby, the men bowed in turn, and Ah-Peen Oie murmured honeyed greetings.

Mei Lien followed, because Ah-Peen Oie's grasp was still firm, but Mei Lien's actions felt as if they were two steps behind her thought processes. By the time she realized this place wasn't a traditional hotel, she had already been ushered up a flight of stairs. They passed a series of closed doors. At the end of the hallway, a young servant girl with two braids waited, her eyes lowered.

She opened a door, and Ah-Peen Oie led Mei Lien through it. They stepped into a small, dark bedroom, lit only by a single lamp, casting the rest of the room in shadows.

Another bedroom. Another hotel. Would she be asked to undress again?

Panic lanced through her stomach, and she twisted away from Ah-Peen Oie's grasp. Futile, Mei Lien knew, but this time it wasn't because she dared flee but because she was about to be sick.

"Get her a bowl," Ah-Peen Oie commanded.

The servant girl produced that bowl, and as Mei Lien retched, Ah-Peen Oie kept her upright, preventing her from collapsing onto the rug and seeking the oblivion she craved.

"You will not be ready tonight," Ah-Peen Oie said, gripping her shoulders. "By tomorrow, you'd better be cooperative. Or you'll not taste a morsel of food again."

Mei Lien heard the words but hadn't fully processed them until Ah-Peen Oie shook her shoulders. "Did you hear me? Answer."

"I heard you." Mei Lien's voice sounded far away, even to her own ears.

Mercifully, she was led to the bed and told to lie down. This she could do. *Sleep.* She closed her eyes with a sigh, and even though her stomach felt as if it had been turned inside out, she hoped the ache would ease soon. Yet the bitterness in her mouth and parched state of her throat caused her to risk speaking again. "May I have water?"

The room was so silent that Mei Lien wondered if the mistress had left. Then the sound of trickling water caused her to crack an eye open to see Ah-Peen Oie pouring water from a pitcher into a glass. Only half a glass, but at least Mei Lien would get something.

Her mouth salivated as Ah-Peen Oie crossed to the bed.

Mei Lien tried to reach for the glass of water, only to find that her hands had been buckled to the bedposts. When had that happened? She tugged, but the effort did little more than chafe her wrist.

Ah-Peen Oie's beautiful eyes shone with amusement. "Ah, you poor bird.

That opium must have been a stronger dose than intended." The woman didn't look apologetic at all.

For a moment, Mei Lien wondered where Wang Foo had gone. Had he come up the stairs with them in the first place? If not, who had tied her in straps? But that didn't matter much now; what mattered was the water that was only a couple of handspans from her mouth.

Was Ah-Peen Oie going to help her drink?

Mei Lien opened her mouth, and Ah-Peen Oie smiled, then tilted the water glass. It was too far away, though, and the water spilled in a thin drizzle upon the bed. Mei Lien lurched for the stream of water, trying to get close enough to drink. Ah-Peen Oie continued to pour, keeping it out of Mei Lien's reach.

Mei Lien didn't even realize she was crying until she felt the hot tears slide down her cheeks and pool at her neck.

"Tomorrow," Ah-Peen Oie said in her smooth lilt. "Tomorrow, you will have water if you're an obedient *mui tsai.*"

Mui tsai. It was what the men at the Hong Kong harbor had called her. Mei Lien's eyes slid shut as more tears escaped. Was there no other choice? She didn't want to see Ah-Peen Oie's face again. Or her beautiful, cruel smile. Or those captivating eyes that were evil themselves.

It was better for Mei Lien to fall into a dream, then wake anew to find that none of this had been real. *Sleep. Dream. Sleep. Dream.*

Even when the cool fingers of Ah-Peen Oie grasped Mei Lien's jaw and slipped in another powdery dose of opium, she didn't react. Her soul had already slipped into her dream of nothingness.

CHAPTER EIGHT

"We do not always walk crowned with laurel. . . . 'Tis not enough to help the feeble brother rise; but to comfort him after. This we find the greatest responsibility of our Mission work. . . . With simple faithfulness, therefore, let us go forward looking to God for our pattern, then weave it into human life; thus will the world become better."

—Donaldina Cameron, mission home report

1899

Dolly looked up from the dining table where she sat with the other staff members as Mrs. Field walked in. The director wore dark colors, as usual, and her hair was fashioned into a severe bun. Mrs. Field's reserve had driven the girls to become closer to Dolly, which she didn't mind at all. Yet, Dolly did wish that the director would make more of an effort in cultivating relationships.

Mrs. Field smiled a rare smile as she crossed to her place at the head of the table. It was unusual for her to be late for a staff meeting, and Dolly decided there must be a good reason for it.

"Good morning, everyone." Mrs. Field's pale blue eyes surveyed the staff. "I've brought Kipling's new poem. I think you'll find it very applicable as well as fascinating."

It wasn't unusual for a staff member to share a tidbit of inspiration in their meetings, but typically it was a scripture that had taken on extra meaning during the previous week.

"The poem is entitled 'The White Man's Burden,'" Mrs. Field said. "As you can see, the title alone aligns with our work here at the mission home."

Dolly raised her brows to keep them from dipping into a frown. What was the director getting at? Surely she didn't mean that the work of rescuing Chinese slaves was a burden to the staff?

"Listen carefully." Mrs. Field cleared her throat. "'To wait in heavy harness / On fluttered folk and wild— / Your new-caught, sullen peoples, / Half devil and half child.'" She lifted her gaze, her pale blue eyes gleaming in the morning light.

Dolly couldn't meet Ah Cheng's or Yuen Qui's eyes. Despite English being their second language, there was no doubt they had understood Kipling's words perfectly.

Mrs. Field had no trouble looking directly into the face of each staff member around the table. She set the poem on the table before her, then folded her hands atop it. "I know I haven't been here as long as most of you, but we cannot deny that these rescued girls have vulgar habits, some of which cannot be broken."

Dolly exhaled as her neck prickled with heat.

"The women from the brothels have no integrity," Mrs. Field continued, "and I'm sorry if that's difficult to hear. We are all doing our best and acting as true disciples of Christ, but let's not ignore the fact that some souls are too depraved to change or to be saved."

The anger kindling in Dolly's chest burned hotter, and she gripped the edges of the table in order to keep from saying something she would later regret.

"These low-grade Mongolian women are a bad influence on the other, more innocent girls." Mrs. Field's gaze finally landed on Dolly. "Their spirits are turbulent, and allowing them to live among the more innocent girls is lowering everyone's morale and decency."

Ah Cheng and Yuen Qui were both looking down at the table. Now, things that Dolly had overlooked over the past months about the way Mrs. Field reprimanded and ordered punishments made sense. If she believed the abused women they rescued were beyond saving and had become, in fact, half devil, her actions were consistent with that belief. The volunteer staff members were perhaps as flabbergasted as Dolly, yet she couldn't stay silent any longer.

"I disagree, Mrs. Field." Dolly clasped her trembling hands on her lap. "The work we are doing is *not* a 'white man's burden.' Each woman we help is her own person, and each woman is capable of living a full and joyful life. We are here to offer light to all the souls who come to us for rescue, no matter their race. Like a crop of wildflowers, the women will grow and develop with our sunshine and water."

Mrs. Field pursed her lips and looked about the table. Her frown deepened when no one took the opportunity to agree with her. "I believe time will prove me right, and I daresay that many *will* agree with me. Maybe not here, among the staff who's devoted to *you,* Miss Cameron, but others who have been dealing with these types of depraved people year after year and have seen no improvement as a whole."

Dolly exhaled slowly. "Many of the rescued women find employment or marry and raise families, becoming productive members of society."

"I guess it depends on how you define *productive,*" Mrs. Field said. "I don't count the type of progress you are suggesting, and I don't think it's possible with the type of coddling you do with these girls. You've allowed them to stay in their beds when suffering from melancholy, and the ones who are pregnant . . . well. They should not even be allowed residence here."

Dolly was stunned. She could only imagine how the other staff members felt.

From beyond the kitchen, Dolly heard a tumble of footsteps. Someone was coming. She sorely wanted to excuse herself to answer, if only to take a break from the hateful words and icy composure of the director. But a moment later, Tien appeared in the dining room and produced a note.

Mrs. Field snatched it from Tien, while the Chinese girl cast a guilty glance at the staff members, and Dolly suspected the girl might have been eavesdropping. Dolly was sorry that Tien, as difficult as she could be to manage, had overheard such hateful words from the director.

Dolly watched Tien exchange glances with Yuen Qui, a woman whom she idolized, and saw the girl's expression soften. Dolly was glad that Tien was fond of at least one staff member since the departure of Miss Culbertson, because the relationship between Dolly and Tien was still tenuous at best.

Tien was a stubborn girl, sometimes to her credit, and sometimes to her detriment. In this case, she remained in the dining room as Mrs. Field read the note.

Mrs. Field's mouth pressed tight as she read; then she snapped her narrow gaze to Dolly. "Well, it looks like you've been summoned once again, Miss Cameron, to go save the world."

Dolly's face burned hot, but she rose from her chair and took the note. Ignoring Mrs. Field's disapproval, Dolly read through the lines quickly. The immigration office had requested her presence. Ironically, the summons was a relief—an excuse to leave the mission home for a while and clear her head. She wished she could take both interpreters with her, but with Mrs. Field's negativity, Dolly didn't want to leave the girls abandoned, so she invited only one.

"Yuen Qui, will you come with me?"

The young woman rose quickly, nodding a farewell to the others at the table.

Dolly wished she could speak to the staff members without the director and explain that she didn't have the same feelings. Yet she knew Ah Cheng could handle herself around Mrs. Field.

Tien followed Dolly and Yuen Qui to the front door, where Dolly told the girl, "Stay out of trouble while we're gone. Help Ah Cheng if needed."

Tien nodded like an obedient child.

The fall day was cool, but the sun felt lovely on Dolly's face. They walked to the corner, where they hailed a buggy. As Yuen Qui settled next to her, Dolly couldn't help but say, "I'm sorry about Mrs. Field."

"I know who you are, Miss Cameron," Yuen Qui said in her accented English. "You are not Mrs. Field."

This was perhaps the nicest compliment Dolly had ever received. She hoped she was nothing like the director, but she still didn't understand how the woman could be so cold toward other humans in desperate need.

When they arrived at the harbor and climbed out of the buggy, Dolly took a few deliberate, calming breaths. She never knew what to expect on this type of errand, so she silently prayed that whatever the situation was, she would be able to help.

Moments later, she and Yuen Qui stepped into the immigration office.

The immigration officer on duty adjusted his spectacles and greeted her, then nodded to Yuen Qui. "We've a young woman in custody. She's about fifteen, is my guess, and that's what she told us as well. But her story has many holes, and she's already broken down more than once, becoming nearly hysterical. I think it would help her to speak to a woman, and maybe you can find out if she's speaking the truth." He continued to relay brief details about the young woman and why he didn't think she was telling the truth.

Dolly didn't hesitate. "Show us to the girl."

The immigration officer led Dolly and Yuen Qui past two doors, then stopped at the third. He turned the knob, and Dolly entered the room to find a young Chinese woman sitting alone on a bench. She clutched a small satchel against her as if she were afraid someone would take it away. Her gaze met Dolly's, but there was no emotion or interest in her eyes.

Dolly crossed to the young woman and sat next to her, with Yuen Qui hovering close. Dolly smiled and said, "I'm Donaldina Cameron, and I'm from the mission home. What's your name?"

The young woman's gaze darted to Yuen Qui as she translated Dolly's words. Then the young woman looked back at Dolly, who smiled again and pointed to her own chest. "Donaldina Cameron." Then she pointed to the young woman.

"Jean Ying," she said at last.

"And where are you from?" Dolly asked.

Another darted glance at Yuen Qui as she translated, then Jean Ying said, "I am from Canton."

Dolly nodded. "Wonderful. Are you here with your family?"

Jean Ying's story came out in a halting tone, and it was what she had also told the immigration officer. Jean Ying was adamant that she had a job and a family in the area, and that they were expecting her.

Finally, after asking all the leading questions she could think of, Dolly placed a steady hand on Jean Ying's petite ones. "We wish you all the best in San Francisco. But should you ever need any help, please send word to 920 Sacramento Street."

Jean Ying lifted her chin and nodded with a confidence that wasn't reflected in her dark brown eyes.

Dolly sensed that the immigration officer was right to have doubts. Jean Ying was holding back information. At this point, however, there was nothing else Dolly could do. Perhaps this mission had been a failure from the start. Only time would tell.

After Dolly and Yuen Qui left the office, they returned to the mission home wrapped up in their own thoughts. Just before they reached the front steps leading to the porch, Dolly stopped Yuen Qui. "Your people are not a burden," Dolly said quietly. "All humans need a helping hand now and then on this earth. Right now is the time that your people are in need, and providence had given me the opportunity to help."

Yuen Qui nodded, moisture welling in her eyes. She clasped Dolly's hand. "Thank you, Miss Cameron. You are good to us."

The women both smiled at each other through their tears. Walking back into the mission home, Dolly kept her head held high. She knew that, as the director, Mrs. Field dealt with many burdens and stresses of the business side of the mission, but no one could ever tell Dolly that whatever service she could render to another woman was ill-conceived. And no one could ever tell her that another soul wasn't worth trying to heal, no matter how broken that soul was.

Over the next few weeks, Dolly went about teaching her classes, following leads sent to her by informants to rescue slaves, and mostly avoiding Mrs. Field. Dolly supposed that they would have to talk things out eventually and smooth things over. But for now, she was filled with resentment, both toward Mrs. Field's negativity and toward herself for being the one who couldn't take over the directorship when she had been asked by her beloved Miss Culbertson.

One night, after everyone in the house had settled to sleep, Dolly was summoned by Ah Cheng. "There is a man to see you at the front door," she told Dolly.

Dolly knew instinctively that the news couldn't be good. No good news came late at night. She didn't recognize the Chinese man waiting for her, and although Ah Cheng translated his words, no translation was needed for Dolly to comprehend the man's desperation. His deep brown eyes kept glancing toward the front door as if he expected a member of the tong to catch him in the act of patronizing 920.

He held out half of a red handkerchief, which reminded her of the very first time Miss Culbertson had used this method to make sure she was fetching the correct slave. "Can you help?" the man asked. "There is a young woman who was sold to a very bad house. She says that you will come get her. But watch for the tong, they are watching for you. Now they have their own lawyers."

Dolly wondered exactly which woman this man was referring to. But this was no time to guess. She took the handkerchief from the man.

"We will come," she said. "Tonight."

The man nodded when Ah Cheng translated the English to Chinese, then he bowed and took a step toward the door. He paused before leaving. "The highbinders call you *Fahn Quai*," he said quietly.

"What is he saying?" Dolly asked Ah Cheng.

"*Fahn Quai* means white devil."

The man continued, "They tell the paper daughters on the ships that you will capture them and force them to eat poison. They make the girls afraid of you before they even arrive in San Francisco. They tell them to run and hide if they see you coming with the policemen."

Dolly's breath stilled. "And what do you think, sir?"

A shout came from somewhere outside the building, and the man flinched. Then he whispered, "I think you are an avenging angel. You are the light among the darkness of Chinatown. And I am honored to meet you, if only once in my life."

Another shout sounded outside, and the man acted like he wanted to disappear beneath the floor. "I was never here, and I never spoke to you." He opened the door and disappeared into the black night, leaving Dolly to stare after him.

Ah Cheng didn't say anything.

Shouts continued outside from the street, and Dolly moved to the high window and peered out. In the darkness, she could see a group of dim figures confronting the man who had just left the mission home. In a flash, a fight broke out.

And then—a gunshot stopped all the commotion.

The men scattered like litter tumbling with the wind, abandoning the crumpled form of a single body.

Dolly pressed a hand to her stomach. She had no doubt that the messenger had just sacrificed his life to deliver his message.

"Call the Chinatown squad," Dolly told Ah Cheng in a strained voice. "There has been a murder on our street. We will also need help for our rescue."

Ah Cheng joined her at the window and gasped. "We cannot go out tonight."

"We must go out tonight," Dolly said. "The tong will not stop at any cost, and neither will we. Tell Officer Cook we'll need as many men as he can spare. And we'll need a search warrant if the tong now have their own lawyers."

Ah Cheng drew in a deep breath and went to make the call.

Dolly looked down at the grungy red handkerchief and wondered again which woman knew her enough to send specifically for her. Which woman had been desperate enough to send for the white devil?

A small sound from the landing caught Dolly's attention. She saw a flash of white clothing disappear into the corridor. *Tien.* She was sure of it.

She hurried up the stairs and went directly to the girl's bedroom. Predictably, the door was locked. Luckily it was late enough that the other residents were in bed. She would leave a note for Mrs. Field on her desk; otherwise, Dolly would be completely on her own with Ah Cheng. But what had Tien seen and heard tonight?

"Tien," Dolly called softly. "Ah Cheng and I are going on a rescue. You will be safe here. I promise. A man sacrificed his life tonight to help us save another girl. He has brought the mission home honor."

The door cracked open, and Dolly found herself gazing down at Tien's tear-stained face. The girl said nothing, but she didn't draw away when Dolly placed a hand on her shoulder. "Do you want to stay with Yuen Qui?" Dolly asked.

Tien nodded, and she walked with Dolly to Yuen Qui's bedroom. After explaining the circumstances, Dolly was able to leave the two of them together. Her heart hurt for Tien, but Dolly was also grateful for the girl's growing trust in her.

An hour later, Dolly and Ah Cheng left the mission home and headed down the hill in the deep of night to meet the police officers. As they walked past the location of the murder, Dolly blinked back hot tears.

Three officers waited at the bottom of the hill: Cook, Riordan, and James Farrell.

Cook's expression was grim, and he confirmed that the murdered man was the one who had delivered the message. "You can turn down a rescue request, Miss Cameron," he said. "Or take a break for a while. One man has already died tonight."

And that man had told her that the highbinders were warning the paper daughters about her far in advance of any rescue efforts. She knew she should probably let things cool off, but her heart wouldn't let her. Instead she said, "Do you have the search warrant?"

"Yes, but that house will be heavily guarded." Cook's thick brows pulled together. "We will meet with resistance."

Dolly eyed the other two officers. Farrell carried an axe, and Riordan and Cook had sledgehammers. "If you're willing to accompany us, then I don't want to back out."

All three officers nodded, their stoic gazes telling Dolly that they wanted the same results as she.

It was nearly midnight by the time they wound their way through the streets of Chinatown and reached the narrow, three-story house. The dim glow of lights came from inside, and Dolly suspected their raid wouldn't be a surprise, just as Cook had said.

"We should divide up," Cook said. "I'll knock, and the rest of you find the back entrance. I'll give you a signal."

Cook approached the front door while Dolly and Ah Cheng slipped around the back of the house with Farrell and Riordan.

No lights glowed from the back of the house, and Dolly paused with Ah Cheng, catching her breath in the inky darkness. They waited for Cook's high-pitched whistle to signal he was inside the front door, but no sound came.

After several moments, Dolly whispered to Ah Cheng and the officers, "We need to go inside the back door. It's been too long."

Farrell nodded, then tried the back door. It was locked, so he used his axe to hack at the door latch. Two strikes later, the door swung open, and with only a glimmer of moonlight to show the way, Dolly rushed into the house and up the set of back stairs. Scuffling feet and muffled voices sounded from the floor above.

"They're going to hide her," Dolly hissed as they reached the second floor.

Farrell followed, and Dolly started opening doors as they moved down the hall, but all the rooms were empty.

She stepped into one of the rooms, sensing it had recently been vacated. Spying a long crack in the far wall, she crossed the room. The crack turned out to be a secret panel. Dolly swung the panel open to find a ladder that led up a narrow chute to the roof. "They've gone up here," she said with a confidence that she couldn't explain. With one hand grasping her skirts, she started up the ladder.

The two officers and Ah Cheng followed, but Dolly was the first to the rooftop. Two buildings over, three dark forms crouched and were moving toward a third building. Still grasping her skirt to give her feet and legs more freedom, Dolly leapt the few feet from one rooftop to another. Farrell made the leap as well, but Ah Cheng stayed rooted in place on the roof of the first building.

Dolly moved as fast as she could, the moon throwing hopeful light across the rooftops as she determined to reach the fleeing party.

A piercing scream split the night, and Dolly stumbled to a stop. Two of the people up ahead were forcing the third person off the roof.

"Stop!" Dolly yelled, running straight at them. Perhaps it was because they hadn't expected her to keep running, or because the girl they had between them somehow wrenched herself away from her captors, but Dolly was able to grasp onto the girl and pull her free.

By then, Farrell had caught up, and he produced the warrant as Dolly held onto the trembling, crying girl. The girl opened her closed fist and revealed the other half of the handkerchief. She said something in Chinese that Dolly didn't understand, but she didn't need any more clarification that she had found the right girl.

Her captors had been two women, and they backed away, their gazes furious. One of the women spat toward the girl and cursed her. "You are dead to all Chinese if you go with *Fahn Quai*."

Dolly didn't need Ah Cheng to translate the meaning of *Fahn Quai*— *white devil*. If these slave owners considered *her* a devil for demanding freedom, then so be it. Dolly tightened her grip around the girl's thin shoulders and led her away from the cursing women.

By the time they found their way back to street level and rejoined Ah Cheng and Officer Cook, Dolly realized this young woman was Jean Ying, the fifteen-year-old she'd spoken with at the immigration office a few weeks before. Another paper daughter, then. Dolly could only hope that the warrant wouldn't be contested.

At the mission home, Dolly and Ah Cheng helped Jean Ying bathe and dress as she trembled uncontrollably. Dolly knew she should have been used to witnessing abuse marks on those she rescued, but it added another crack to her heart each time. She was gratified when Jean Ying ate everything they placed before her at the kitchen table. The young Chinese woman might be exhausted, but she also needed nourishment.

"I am sorry I lied to you," Jean Ying told Dolly in a faint voice.

Jean Ying's entire story came out through Ah Cheng's interpreting. Her father was a wealthy manufacturer in Canton, and she was kidnapped one day when walking to meet some friends. She was taken to Hong Kong and sold to an agent who paid 175 Hong Kong dollars. On the steamship across the Pacific, she was forced to memorize details of a false identity.

Dolly held Jean Ying's hands as she listened to the tearful tale. When she finished, Dolly said, "We will write to your family and let them know of your safety."

Jean Ying's shoulders shook with sobs, and several moments passed before Dolly could get her to calm down. When the girl looked again at Dolly, she said, "What if they don't want me back? I am a soiled dove now."

Dolly blinked back her own tears. "You have done nothing wrong, dear Jean Ying. Your family will be overjoyed to know that you are still alive. That is all that matters."

CHAPTER NINE

*"Quite a number of Chinese prostitutes have been brought to
this country by unprincipled Chinamen, but these, at first, were
brought from China at the instigation and for the gratification of
white men. And even at the present time, it is commonly reported
that part of the proceeds of this villainous traffic goes to enrich a
certain class of men belonging to this Honorable nation."*

Letter to President Ulysses S. Grant, from the Six Companies, 1876

1903

The weeks slipped by, day blending with night. The only indication that
the sun had risen was the thin frame of light surrounding the dark drapes in
Mei Lien's bedroom. She had always been slender, but now her ribs could be
counted by merely a glance. Water had to be earned. And food was a privilege.

But it didn't matter to Mei Lien. She would rather die than attend any of
Ah-Peen Oie's banquets where the men flirted with courtesans. It was only a
precursor to what happened next, when the highest bidders were invited into
the courtesans' bedrooms for the night.

Mei Lien had long held a vague idea of what would happen on her wedding night should she marry. And she knew that wealthy Chinese men had
more than one wife, at least in China. With arranged marriages, love and
devotion were rarely a part of a Chinese marriage, yet Mei Lien had seen love

between her mother and father. A rare occurrence, to be sure, but Mei Lien had thought that if she married, she could find happiness with her own husband through devotion and mutual values.

This would never happen now. Even if, by some miracle, Ah-Peen Oie decided Mei Lien could be a kitchen worker or other type of servant, Mei Lien knew that she had no value in the eyes of a man looking for a wife.

Mei Lien turned over on her soft bed and watched as the frame of light around the single window brightened with the rising sun. On her second day here, she'd pulled aside the heavy drapes only to find the window barred. And when Ah-Peen Oie came next into her room and discovered that the drapes had been moved, the woman had beat her with a fire poker.

Those bruises had now faded, but other bruises soon appeared from other beatings. Most of the time, Mei Lien didn't even know why she was being beaten. At least she was no longer tied to her bed. And it had now been eight days since the last beating, or maybe nine or ten, since the days and nights seemed to blend into a vast nothingness. The passage of time with no incidents made her nervous. Had Ah-Peen Oie decided that Mei Lien was no use after all? Would she be dumped in the street to live like a rat?

Mei Lien laughed a dry, raspy laugh that tasted bitter in her throat. She was a rat *now*. A rat addicted to opium. Despite the three thousand dollars Ah-Peen Oie had paid, she kept spending money on keeping Mei Lien drugged. As the window brightened with the day, her body began to shiver, a sure indication that her next opium dose was due. Despite her aversion to opium and her self-loathing that her body and mind could betray her, her thoughts focused on the sounds of the house, seeking out any signs of imminent relief.

She listened for footfalls that might indicate Ah-Peen Oie, or one of the servant girls, would soon arrive with the bitter powder. And not make her beg, as she had yesterday. But no footsteps approached her bedroom door. Mei Lien climbed out of her bed and reached for the satin robe draped over the single chair in the room. All her old clothing had been taken and burned, replaced by luxurious clothing befitting a woman of high status . . . or a courtesan. Once she had clothed herself more securely, she padded to the door and listened. She knew better than to open the door and look into the corridor. She'd done that on day three, and Ah-Peen Oie had seen fit to enact her special discipline.

No sounds save for the usual creaking of the household in the lazy early mornings. Mei Lien closed her eyes and inhaled, then exhaled. Her head was starting to hurt, and she knew it would only intensify if she didn't get her next dose, and soon. Mei Lien turned to look at the window. The soft yellow light was now a hot orange. It was at least two hours past when Ah-Peen Oie should have arrived.

The headache that had been a warning screamed through her temples now, and Mei Lien sank to her knees and rubbed at the sides of her head. The pain wouldn't abate, and there was no food or water inside the bedroom to help anything.

Goose bumps raced across her skin, and she started to tremble violently. She curled up in the robe and shivered, gripping the silk close. Maybe if she didn't move, didn't think, her body would relax, and the withdrawal wouldn't be so bad.

But the pain in her head only intensified, and Mei Lien gripped her hair, feeling as if pulling her hair out might relieve the pressure. She moaned, but even that was soundless. She tried to rise to her feet and make it to the door. Perhaps begging would bring mercy. But she didn't have the strength to lift her head, let alone cry for help if she wanted to.

A faint click of the door opening sent a rush of gratitude through her, and she dragged her eyes open.

Beautiful and exquisite Ah-Peen Oie stood above her, the blessed packet of opium in her hand. "It is time," she said, her voice soft.

The words took a moment to filter into Mei Lien's comprehension. And then she scrambled to her knees and reached for the packet. But Ah-Peen Oie drew away, out of reach. Mei Lien dropped to her hands. Beg, she would beg. But her headache pressed harder, and her breathing turned shaky.

"Tonight," Ah-Peen Oie continued, "you will attend the banquet. You will accept your destiny. And you will pay back every cent you owe me."

The woman's words might have been daggers a few weeks ago, but now they were simply a statement of truth—a truth that Mei Lien had to not only accept but take ownership in. She wanted to live now. Live for the next dose of opium. "Yes." Her voice came out a rasp.

"Yes, what?"

"Yes, I will work to pay you back the money." Producing the entire sentence had been taxing, and Mei Lien fought for a full breath.

The scent of jasmine surrounded her as Ah-Peen Oie bent and administered the powder. Mei Lien sank to the floor and leaned against the bed, the bitter taste like nectar on her tongue. The powder took only moments to calm her trembling and quiet her headache. Mei Lien had entered another existence—one in which she could clearly see that this was her life now, that it was prudent to accept her destiny, just as Ah-Peen Oie said.

The next hours were spent in preparation as Ah-Peen Oie directed one of her servants to help Mei Lien. After she'd bathed and scented her body, Mei Lien dressed in a pale peach cheongsam. The servant drew Mei Lien's hair into an elegant twist, then applied careful makeup.

When Mei Lien was led to a mirror in another bedroom, she stared at her own transformation. Gone was the girl from the Hong Kong countryside. Mei Lien looked like the women she had been warned about, the women who had no other choices in life. In her reflection, she might see the shape of her mother's eyes, but Mei Lien also saw a young woman who had no future. No hope for a different situation. But she would pay back her contract, if only to protect her mother.

"I'm sorry, *Ah Ma*," Mei Lien whispered to her mother's eyes.

Then she turned away from the mirror and took the dose of opium offered by the servant.

Mei Lien was ready. The girl from the country was gone, replaced by a woman who would forget herself and focus only on what it would take to protect her mother.

When the hour of the banquet arrived, Mei Lien walked with the other courtesans into the dining room. Silk hangings adorned the walls. Elegant sofas sat next to teakwood furniture holding painted vases. The women were to take their places before the guests arrived. None of the other courtesans spoke to her, but their gazes told Mei Lien that she was not a welcome addition. She supposed it was because she might give them competition.

But whichever man chose her tonight would not be getting Mei Lien, the young woman from Hong Kong. He would be getting an alternate version. She was a ghost now. Just like her ancestors.

The first two men entered and greeted the courtesans with surprising grace and courtesy. Mei Lien gave a shy smile as she'd been instructed to, and although she'd told herself to show no reaction, her pulse raced despite her resolve. She didn't want to be in this room. She didn't want the eyes of these men to peruse her.

Mother, she thought. *You are the only thing important to me. Nothing else matters.*

Mei Lien didn't know what she said, or how she managed to laugh and titter at the men's stories and compliments, but the hours somehow passed as each course was served. The compliments directed toward her were many, and each time a man paid her special attention, Ah-Peen Oie's eyes flashed with approval.

When the dessert was served, one by one the courtesans began to leave the room. They were soon followed by the men who had arranged with Ah-Peen Oie for the night's payment.

"You are from Hong Kong?" a male voice asked, and Mei Lien looked over to see who had spoken.

The Chinese man was younger than most of the other men in the room;

Mei Lien guessed him to be only ten years her senior. His face was handsome in a boyish way, and he was nicely dressed, although not in a flashy fashion.

Mei Lien knew better than to give out too much information. She simply said, "Yes." Then she quickly lowered her gaze, as if she were bashful. This was not a hard part to play. Until tonight, Mei Lien had never flirted with a man.

"I am from Hong Kong too." His voice was warm, genuine, unlike the other men's leering tones. "Although it has been many years since I've been there."

At this, Mei Lien raised her eyes. "How many years?" Was the question too personal? She cast a glance in Ah-Peen Oie's direction, who was watching them while she flirted with an older man named Zhang Wei. Mei Lien had heard whispers about him being a very wealthy leader of the tong.

"Fifteen years," the man next to her said.

Mei Lien met his gaze again. His eyes had faint lines about the edges as if he smiled a lot, although he wasn't smiling now. He was looking at her with an interest that some of the other men had, but this man's interest seemed more genuine.

"Do you . . . do you miss it?" Mei Lien asked in a quiet voice, not wanting to be overheard by anyone else.

His nod was brief.

"I miss it too," Mei Lien said, and to her horror her voice cracked and her eyes filled with tears.

She looked down, blinking rapidly. Had he noticed her tears? Would he laugh? Would he say something to Ah-Peen Oie? But he said nothing.

Mei Lien worked hard to compose herself, to think of something else to say. But before she could come up with anything, he had moved away and begun speaking to one of the other men. They laughed about something, and Mei Lien's cheeks burned. She didn't even dare look in Ah-Peen Oie's direction.

Mei Lien still had another couple of hours before an opium dose, but she suddenly craved one. Even breathing hurt. She lifted her gaze and found Ah-Peen Oie had moved on to another patron.

The older man Ah-Peen Oie had been speaking to was now sitting by himself, smoking. His eyes connected with Mei Lien's, and embarrassment jolted through her. She had been explicitly commanded not to make any advances. But the curved edges of his mouth told her it was too late; he'd seen the longing in her eyes for a hit of the opium pipe.

He crooked his finger, and, like a spider spinning a web, drew Mei Lien toward him, her feet moving of their own accord.

He patted the chair next to him, and she sat obediently. Without a word, he handed over the pipe. She had never tried smoking before, but she was willing to experiment. The first inhale burned her nose and throat, and she barely managed to hold back a cough. The second inhale sent a pleasant buzz through her.

"Are you friends with Huan Sun?" Zhang Wei asked.

"Who?" Mei Lien asked before she could stop herself. Surely her cheeks were red now.

But Zhang Wei didn't seem bothered. He only chuckled, which of course drew Ah-Peen Oie's notice. "The man you spoke to."

"Oh." Mei Lien exhaled and handed the pipe over. She had gone too far. She shouldn't have shared the pipe, and she should know the names of the men in attendance. "I have only just met him."

Zhang Wei chuckled again, and Mei Lien was surprised by the man's good humor, considering that he was one of the most feared of the tong in all of Chinatown. "I am glad I came tonight, Mei Lien."

He knew her name?

"Ah-Peen Oie was right," he continued.

"I'm always right," Ah-Peen Oie said in a lilting tone as she appeared and rested her hand on Zhang Wei's shoulder. "Can I get you any refreshment?"

Zhang Wei lifted his pipe. "I have everything I need right here." His gaze shifted to Mei Lien, causing her temperature to rise.

She quickly lowered her eyes, if only to avoid Ah-Peen Oie's sharp observations. It would not do to be caught blushing in front of the man the mistress considered her private client. Mei Lien had also heard from the chattering courtesans that Ah-Peen Oie didn't share her personal clients with anyone.

"See to refilling Huan Sun's glass," Ah-Peen Oie said.

Mei Lien obediently rose and nodded at Zhang Wei without meeting his gaze directly. Then she moved away from the pair, feeling both of their gazes upon her back. She found a wine bottle and made her way to Huan Sun, where he was still speaking to two men.

"More drink?" she asked when there was a break in the conversation.

The men all turned and smiled at her. Mei Lien ended up refilling all their glasses. She warmed under Huan Sun's kind gaze. He was different from the other men, and she wondered who he would be if she had met him in another place, another time. When she returned the wine bottle, Zhang Wei was no longer in his chair smoking. She didn't dare look about the room for him because she was sure Ah-Peen Oie was watching her every movement.

The next hour passed slowly, and another courtesan left. Now only four remained. Soon, the evening came to an end, and Mei Lien knew that one of the lingering men would speak for her. There had been too many glances her way, too many pretty compliments handed over.

What she didn't expect was Ah-Peen Oie's clawed grip on her upper arm, and the fiercely whispered words, "Zhang Wei has requested you for the night. But Huan Sun has bought a three-month exclusive. Return to your bedroom now and wait for his arrival."

Mei Lien couldn't help but stare at her mistress. Zhang Wei was *her* client. He was off-limits. A whoosh of panic expanded in Mei Lien's chest, rising in her throat. What would her punishment be tomorrow? For Ah-Peen Oie's expression was one of controlled fury.

"All right," Mei Lien whispered.

Ah-Peen Oie dropped her grip and turned back to the banquet with her benign smile, and Mei Lien slipped from the room.

She passed the corridor that led to the front of the hotel. What if she continued down that corridor and simply walked out into the street? Took her chances?

Would they track down her mother? Make her pay?

Mei Lien's breathing was shaky, and her hands trembled. It would do no good to greet Huan Sun in her current state. She had to gain control of her hysterics, and fast. Mei Lien detoured to Ah-Peen Oie's bedroom. The place had always been forbidden, but surely the woman had opium stashed somewhere.

Mei Lien cracked open the door. Even in the dimness, she could see the opulence of the fine furnishings, the plush rugs, the glowing Chinese lanterns, and embroidered silk wall hangings. She moved quickly, and, as quietly as possible, she opened drawers until she located pouches of opium. Mei Lien took three small ones, hoping they wouldn't be missed.

By the time she slipped out of her mistress's bedroom and made it undetected to her own, Mei Lien had wasted valuable time. She lit several candles, as instructed in her training; then she waited for her first client.

Tonight, she would begin to earn back the money paid upon her contract. Tonight, she would take another step in securing her mother's safety and future. Tonight, the former Mei Lien would cease to exist.

CHAPTER TEN

"We do remember her as we first saw her, sitting by the fireside
awaiting our return from church. As we drew near and spoke
to her, she shrank away frightened, while tears and sobs were
her only response. An hour later we saw her quietly sleeping on
her pillow, her hand tightly clasping a bit of candy, that sweet
comforter of childhood's sorrows. As she grew up to womanhood,
she learned English and became our interpreter."

—MARGARET CULBERTSON, WRITING ABOUT SIX-YEAR-OLD CHUN FAH, 1878

MARCH 1900

Evening's shadows stretched across the office space as Dolly flipped through the record book in which Miss Culbertson had carefully recorded the comings and goings of the Chinese girls, how they were rescued, and when they left the mission home.

Mrs. Field had pleaded a headache and was spending the rest of the day in her bedroom, which she seemed to do earlier and earlier of late, and that gave Dolly precious hours in the office by herself. Her hand paused on the more recent pages—pages that detailed the rescues she'd been a part of—details she had recorded herself. Each entry brought memories into sharp focus.

The names were growing in number, and the success stories were frequent, although every so often a rescue was botched for one reason or another.

The tong relocated the girl, or the girl refused to come, or the tong's lawyers served a warrant for her arrest from the mission home.

A knock sounded at the front door; judging by the lateness of the hour, it could very well be a message about another rescue. Dolly rose from the desk, bustled to the door, and called out, "Who is it?"

When a male voice answered that he had come to serve a warrant, Dolly rang the brass gong by the door. Sounding the gong in the daylight hours would have been the girls' first alert to stop lessons, drop their sewing projects, and put away brooms. Then the papered girls could gather in the chapel while the unpapered ones would go down the back stairs to hide in the basement. Would the signal work at night?

She stalled as long as she could by turning the multiple deadbolts one by one, as slowly as she could, giving the girls more time to prepare or hide. Then she opened the door a crack. Three men stood on the porch.

A tall man with slicked-back hair, wearing a double-breasted suit, said, "We have a search warrant for Chan Juan."

She knew the man in the suit, a lawyer by the name of Abe Ruef. He used to work with Miss Culbertson, but recently he had sold out to the tong, and now he did their dirty work.

Dolly glanced at the Chinese man behind the lawyer. His cold gaze could have frozen an entire Chinese banquet. Ruef shoved the warrant toward Dolly, and she took it, but not before glancing at Officer Cook. His expression was closed, his eyes shuttered. Dolly knew he hated this as much as she did, yet he'd been called upon to see this warrant served and executed.

Panic stung her throat. Applying for guardianship had become a crucial part of every rescue, but sometimes the paperwork was slow to process. And the name on the warrant was Chan Juan, a girl who'd only been with them for three days. She had just begun interacting with the other girls, and color had slowly returned to her cheeks.

After stalling as long as she could by reading every word of the warrant, Dolly drew open the door to let the men in, hoping beyond hope that she'd given the unpapered girls enough time to make it to the basement and hide under the rice bags by the gas meter. "You're welcome to look for Chan Juan," Dolly said. "I don't think she is here, though. These girls come and go."

Tension vibrated from Cook as he entered and moved past her. She could very well guess his thoughts. They had both been witnesses to girls being returned to their owners. Better-case scenarios were when the judges placed them with Chinese families or allowed them to stay in the mission home, where Dolly adopted them as wards. Not-so-favorable judgments included the deportation of Chinese girls back to China, or the girls being released as wives to the Chinese husbands who claimed there had been a legal marriage. Which usually meant the girl was returned to a life of slavery or prostitution.

"Please take care to respect our property while you look." Dolly lifted a brow at Abe Ruef. "Translate for your client, please."

Ruef translated, but the Chinese owner didn't seem fazed, and he barreled into the kitchen, banging through cupboards. Dolly followed. The owner was thorough, checking each cupboard and shifting through the rice bags in the pantry. Finding no one, he moved to the dining room and checked behind the folding doors.

Next, he headed upstairs, and Dolly accompanied him as he looked into the bedrooms, scouted under beds, and opened closets.

Mrs. Field came out of her bedroom and stood like a sentinel at the top of the landing, watching the men go in and out of the other rooms.

Chan Juan was not among any of the faces. Dolly could not relax, though—not until these men were gone. She hoped that Chan Juan was smart enough to stay in the basement and not try to escape through the underground tunnel. Her owner might have a guard watching outside.

Dolly accompanied the owner down the stairs, followed by Mrs. Field, who was quite pale.

The owner paused at the front double doors. His face red with frustration, he cursed Dolly in Chinese. She didn't need an interpreter to recognize when he called her the *Fahn Quai*. If that was what the tong chose to call her, then so be it. Dolly would wear the title with pride.

The Chinese owner and his lawyer left the house, promising to return the next day, and possibly the next. When Cook paused on the threshold before leaving, he turned to Dolly and said in a quiet voice, "Secure those guardianship papers as soon as possible, Miss Cameron. Mr. Wang Foo is a top member of the tong. He will not let this rest. My hands are tied on this one."

"I understand," Dolly said.

Cook leaned closer. "You need to understand he paid five thousand for her."

A chill raced through her. Dolly knew the sums of money paid for the paper daughters could be extravagant, but five thousand was the highest she'd ever heard of. In 1870, the highest amount paid for a Chinese girl once she arrived in San Francisco was one thousand. Now, that number had inflated.

"I'll speak to my attorney tomorrow," Dolly said. Her attorney, Henry E. Monroe, had replaced Abe Ruef when he had switched to aiding the Chinese tong. Monroe had helped the mission home secure the legal guardianship papers needed to protect the girls.

"Good." Cook left with a shake of his head, and Dolly shut the door. The scent of Cook's cigarette smoke lingered in the entryway, both a comfort and a warning somehow.

"We can't have this kind of trouble brought upon the mission home," Mrs. Field said from behind Dolly. "We need to draw the line at harboring criminals. They might bring harm to the other girls."

Dolly spun toward the woman, trying to hold back words she might regret. She swallowed her anger and said as calmly as possible, "Each girl is valuable here. And we will do whatever it takes to protect them."

Without waiting for the director to reply, Dolly turned to the door and slid each lock into place. When the last bolt clicked with finality, she discovered that Mrs. Field had gone back up the stairs, and the other women and girls had collected on the landing.

Dolly scanned their faces. "Where is Chan Juan?"

Lonnie pointed downward, a solemn expression on her face.

"I showed her where to hide in the basement," Tien said. "And I told her not to be afraid."

"Very good," Dolly said. She was proud of Chan Juan for her bravery and pleased that Tien had helped the frightened girl. The Chinese owner hadn't even dared go down there. It was a rare Chinese person who would venture into a dark sub-basement; most harbored a fear of lurking evil spirits. But Tien had an odd fascination with the dark place.

Dolly strode to the basement door, Ah Cheng following. Dolly called for Chan Juan as soon as she stepped into the darkness. "They are gone," she said in a soft voice. "Come out, dear, you are safe."

Ah Cheng walked with Dolly, translating into Chinese. Finally, Dolly heard a scuffling sound from the far corner, and the young woman appeared, clothed in her nightgown.

She trembled like a dead leaf in the wind. Dolly reached Chan Juan and wrapped an arm about her thin shoulders. "Come," she said. "We'll get you some hot tea."

Chan Juan nodded, then wiped at the tears on her cheeks. She had refused to share her story with anyone at the mission home. Perhaps someday she would, but for now, Dolly would show her the compassion and love that every girl deserved.

When Dolly brought Chan Juan out of the basement, the girls surrounded them, hugging Chan Juan. Some even wept with her. Dolly's heart swelled at the compassion the girls showed each other. That alone would make their rocky journey a bit smoother.

By the time Dolly returned to the office, her heart had been wrung dry.

She sat in the chair and lowered her head into her hands. What if Chan Juan's owner returned before they could get the guardianship papers? She hoped that Monroe would be able to work a miracle tomorrow.

"Miss Cameron?" Ah Cheng said from the open doorway.

Dolly lifted her head. The line drawn between Ah Cheng's brows didn't bode well. "This just came." She held up a rumpled piece of paper.

"Can it wait until morning?" Dolly asked.

Ah Cheng shook her head, apology shining in her eyes.

With strength Dolly didn't know she had left, she rose to her feet and crossed to Ah Cheng. After taking the paper and reading the few short words, Dolly knew her interpreter was right. "I'll be ready in a few moments."

The evening hour was late, but still early enough that Chinatown would be lively with night life. Going now would ensure Dolly and her rescue team an audience, and possible barriers, but that couldn't be helped. A slave girl on Baker Alley needed rescue. And the young man who'd brought the note was waiting at the bottom of the hill.

Dolly couldn't call Officer Cook because he was still likely with the men who had come to search the mission home. So the moment Dolly and Ah Cheng were ready, they headed outside. At the bottom of the hill, they found the young Chinese man waiting. He nodded and took off at a brisk walk. Dolly was curious about this man who was leading their rescue, but asking questions would only delay them. He led them along several streets, then cut into a narrow alley. The darkness permeated the alley like a living thing, although there were plenty of people on the sidewalks, most of them loitering. Both sides of the alley rose up two or three levels. Someone was crying in a second-level room. Two men were arguing with each other somewhere above. She couldn't see them, but she could feel their vehemence. Dolly's stomach felt like a lead weight.

Although the scent of sweet, burnt opium was well familiar to Dolly by now, it singed her throat. And memories returned of finding girls in deplorable conditions, desperation in their eyes like vast pools with no end. The young man wove in and out of the groups of Chinese on the sidewalk, and Dolly and Ah Cheng hurried to stay close to him.

When he stepped inside a building that was a known gambling den,

Dolly hesitated, but then he turned and motioned for her to follow. When Ah Cheng stepped forward too, the man waved her off.

"You must go without me," Ah Cheng whispered. "I will not be welcome."

"I don't want to leave you here alone," Dolly protested.

"Then hurry."

Dolly had no choice. She lifted her chin and walked in behind their informer. Her chest burned with the pungent smoke. Gambling tables were situated about the room, and in the smoky dimness, Dolly spotted several young women dressed in fine silk clothing, their painted faces garish in the yellow lamplight.

"*Fahn Quai*," someone hissed. Another laughed. A couple of men started to tap their gambling table with their fists in an eerie rhythm. The Chinese girls watched her as well, some of them turning away after looking; others gaped, then whispered fiercely to their companions.

Dolly kept her gaze focused on the informer, although she had recognized members of the tong, with their American clothing of stylish suits and hats giving away their identities. And now she was in the thick of them with no police escort. The informer was a brazen man to walk right into this gambling den, leading Dolly. He approached a girl near a back table. She was a very pretty girl, no more than seventeen. The informer leaned down and spoke into her ear.

The girl's beautifully decorated eyes connected with Dolly.

In a flash, Dolly saw the depth of pain this young woman must be experiencing. Dolly knew enough stories to know that whoever this girl was, her life was of more value than the amount of money a tong member had paid for her.

A few more steps and Dolly reached her side. "Do you know who I am?" she asked in her memorized Chinese.

The girl nodded.

"What is your name?"

"Kum Quai."

"Kum Quai," Dolly repeated. "I will take you to safety if you allow me."

The girl grasped Dolly's hand. Could it be this simple? The noise in the room had quieted as all eyes turned on them. Dolly knew they had only moments before someone tried to stop them. Whoever this girl's owner was, he was not here. Surely someone would be quick to alert him, though.

"Come." Dolly led the girl out, moving around the tables, past the heckling man. A few of them grabbed for Kum Quai, and she squealed. The other courtesans laughed as if it were a game. This would be no game once Kum Quai's owner discovered his missing slave.

Outside, Ah Cheng joined their little group. The young man who had first brought them had disappeared, and apparently the women were on their own. Ah Cheng grasped Kum Quai's other arm. Ah Cheng asked a few questions in Chinese, but the conversation was too rapid to understand. Besides, a crowd had gathered on the street, alerted by the appearance of *Fahn Quai*.

Dolly ignored them all, but her heart was racing faster than a train. Thankfully, Kum Quai was a willing traveler and moved quickly with them.

Once they had the Chinese girl inside the mission home, with the doors locked, Ah Cheng reported to Dolly that the gossipers on the street had said that Kum Quai's owner was in San Jose.

After they had helped Kum Quai bathe, the girl started to pull at her hair so hard that several strands came loose. Tears came to her eyes as she yanked. Dolly grasped Kum Quai's hands, but the girl only grabbed at her hair again.

"What is she doing?" Dolly asked Ah Cheng.

Ah Cheng questioned Kum Quai in Chinese, and the girl gave a tearful answer.

"She says she doesn't want to be beautiful anymore," Ah Cheng said. "If she pulls out her hair, maybe the tong won't want her back."

"But she's hurting herself." Dolly again grabbed the girl's hands. "Tell her we can cut it short if she'd like."

So, moments later, they had Kum Quai sitting on a chair while Dolly cut the girl's hair. When they finally got her settled in bed, with Ah Cheng watching over her, Dolly made her way to the office.

She wrote down the events of the night in the record book. Seeing Kum Quai's desperation to pull out her hair only testified of how afraid she was of her owner. How long of a reprieve would they have? Word would travel fast, and Dolly likely had only two or three days to secure guardianship of Kum Quai.

Finally, when Dolly went up the stairs to her bedroom, she saw Tien sitting at the top of the stairs. The girl didn't move as Dolly approached. Was this progress? Tien not running from her?

But when Dolly grew near, she found that Tien had fallen asleep. Had she been waiting up for their return? Had she been worried about more tong members coming to the mission home?

Dolly crouched and lifted the sleeping girl into her arms. She carried the girl to her bedroom, then carefully tucked her beneath a blanket. For several moments, Dolly gazed down at Tien. Her expression was so smooth and peaceful. What she'd seen in her young life might take a lifetime to erase, and Dolly could only pray that she would be able to help. Quietly she left the room, hoping that the residents of the mission home could all find their own peace.

The following week, the dreaded knock on the door came soon after the breakfast hour. When Dolly saw a Chinese man and a constable she didn't recognize on the front step, she immediately rang the warning gong. Since it was daytime, everyone would be alerted to stop lessons and assemble in the chapel room. There was no one to hide in the basement at this time.

Dolly knew very well that these men could be here for either Chan Juan or Kum Quai, both of whom Dolly had been able to secure guardianship papers for.

Still, her heart stuttered when the constable said, "We have a warrant issued by the San Jose court of law for Kum Quai's arrest."

Dolly took the official-looking paper and read through the warrant. Kum Quai was being charged with grand larceny by Chung Bow.

Dolly felt like the air around her had whooshed out of the house. Even if Dolly contacted their lawyer right now, Kum Quai would have to appear before a San Jose judge. Not even guardianship papers could protect the girl from a court date. Still, Dolly had to try. "There has been a mistake. This girl is not here."

The constable pushed the door open. "We are coming in. Chung Bow will identify the thief."

Dolly stood aside, helpless as the constable and Chung Bow followed the sounds of the gathered girls, ushered there by Mrs. Field, who was determined not to allow the men to search through the house again.

Dolly watched from the entryway as the constable and Chung Bow surveyed the gathered girls and women in the chapel. Kum Quai was among the group as well, her shorn hair not enough of a change to hide her identity. And no one had told her to flee to the basement because the guardianship papers should have made her safe.

Dolly's fingers curled into fists as Chung Bow shoved the warrant at Kum Quai and barked short words at her in Chinese.

Then the constable grasped Kum Quai's arm and led her out of the room. The other girls and women watched in horror, and many of them started to cry.

Helplessness and panic collided in Dolly's stomach like two boats ramming into each other. She couldn't bear watching Kum Quai's terror-stricken expression.

Dolly hurried after the trio, and just before the door shut, she grasped the edge. "I'm going with her," she called back to Ah Cheng. "Tell Mrs. Field, and send a message to Attorney Monroe. Tell him I'm going to need help in San Jose."

"No," Ah Cheng protested. "You will be—"

But Dolly was already out the door, and before the three had climbed into the buggy, she reached the constable. "I'm coming too," she said in a single breath. "I am the girl's guardian."

He frowned, but before he could reply, Dolly climbed into the buggy and settled herself right next to Kum Quai. Dolly grasped her hand, and the girl buried her face against Dolly's shoulder. As a courtesan, Kum Quai had been bold and striking, her clothing exquisite, her makeup perfection. As a mission home resident, her hair was short, her face free of makeup, her clothing simple, but her true light had begun to shine through.

The buggy started forward, and Dolly's heart drummed a staccato of fear. They were in for a long ride that would take the rest of the day and most of the night if they didn't stop to rest. There were fifty miles between San Francisco and San Jose. Dolly had no shawl, coat, or hat. Kum Quai wore only her lightweight clothing provided by the mission home.

The buggy stopped in Palo Alto to change horses when night had fallen. Despite the hope that Dolly had for a fair trial in San Jose, that hope was soon dashed when the constable announced that a judge in Palo Alto had agreed to hear the case.

They entered the courthouse after hours with the constable and Chung Bow. The smell of stale air and dust tickled Dolly's senses, but perhaps they could get this over with quickly and return to San Francisco. Both she and Kum Quai were tired from the journey and emotionally wrung out from the unknown.

The judge strode out of his office, looking none too happy to be bothered. He all but ignored Dolly as he spoke with the constable. When Dolly overheard him saying that they needed time to assemble a jury and witnesses, she protested.

"I am witness enough." She stepped forward, boldly interrupting the conversation. "We can hold a trial right now. There's no reason for all of us to be dragged to San Jose, since this girl's home is with me in San Francisco."

Annoyance crossed the judge's face. "My first decision stands. Kum Quai will spend the night in jail, and if tomorrow we have everything in place, we'll hold the trial."

Kum Quai couldn't understand the words of the judge, and Dolly couldn't leave the poor, frightened girl.

"I will stay with her, then," Dolly said.

The judge raised a single brow. "As you wish."

Dolly was on her way to jail.

CHAPTER ELEVEN

"It took only four years to set the negroes free throughout the whole of the South; for twenty-five years a few women have been wrestling with the Chinese slavery problem and it seems no nearer a solution now, than it did more than a quarter of a century ago when the rescue work was first organized."

—Donaldina Cameron, address to the mission home board, April 1902

1903

Click. The door opened.

Click. The door shut.

Mei Lien heard his footsteps brush the rug, then stop.

She needed to open her eyes; she *had* to open her eyes. This was only business, and she was a businesswoman now, determined to satisfy the demands of her contract, and then she would leave.

She would return to Hong Kong, and she'd find her mother.

Mei Lien would never think of San Francisco or California again. She would become the village girl again and let this new Mei Lien die.

"Mei Lien?" His voice made her flinch.

She hadn't taken the opium; instead she had stashed it in a hole on the other side of her mattress, knowing that there might come a time when she was desperate again.

Slowly, she opened her eyes. In the candlelight, Huan Sun smiled.

She tried to smile back, she really tried, but instead a tear spilled onto her cheek.

Huan Sun's dark eyes filled with questions. "Are you ill? Should I fetch Ah-Peen Oie?"

How could she be so careless? "No, I am overwhelmed by your generosity." She hoped he would believe her. If word got back to Ah-Peen Oie that she'd displeased one of the clients . . .

Huan Sun nodded, then moved closer and took her hand.

His touch wasn't too bad, she told herself. Huan Sun's hand was warm and gentle. His eyes were kind, and . . . another tear escaped. She brushed it away quickly.

Huan Sun released her hand and stepped back, concern replacing the interest in his eyes.

Dismay ebbed across Mei Lien's skin. She had already failed. He would report her to Ah-Peen Oie. "Please forgive me." She heard her own pleading in her voice. "I do not mean to—"

He held up his hand. "There are many layers to you, Mei Lien. One woman in the banquet, another woman sharing memories of her home, and one woman now. Tell me, who is the real one?"

Mei Lien bit her lip. None of the women were truly her. She didn't know who she was, and she didn't know which story would please Huan Sun. "I am not sure," she admitted.

He crossed to the chair in her room and took a seat.

He was not leaving, then?

She didn't know whether to be relieved or not.

"I think that is the most honest answer I've ever received." Huan Sun's expression was wistful, and Mei Lien had no idea what to hope. "When I first came into the banquet room, I knew you didn't want to be there."

Mei Lien inhaled sharply. Had Ah-Peen Oie noticed too? "I am still learning the protocol," she said.

Huan Sun nodded. "Then you smoked the opium with Zhang Wei, and I could see the desperation in your eyes."

Would he tell Ah-Peen Oie? "I—I was nervous."

Huan Sun leaned forward, and although he was sitting across the small room, Mei Lien was certain he could see right into the hidden corners of her soul. "Your nervousness is understandable. Tonight, we will only talk, blossom. Tell me of your home."

The endearment made her eyes sting with tears again. Did Huan Sun truly want to talk only? His demeanor remained calm, relaxed, and perhaps that was all the encouragement she needed. She began to tell him of her childhood. Her mother and father. Her small village.

Huan Sun listened intently, smiling at her stories. Then Huan Sun spoke of *his* family, his brother who still lived near Hong Kong, his father who had died the year before. His voice was low, mellow, and soothing.

Mei Lien was entranced, and she reclined on her bed as he continued with his stories. Some of them made her laugh; others made her marvel that of all the men she could have met tonight, Huan Sun had been the one to come to her bedroom.

His words washed over her with warmth, bringing up cherished memories of her own, memories she had never known she would want to hold onto and never let go. She closed her eyes, enjoying the rumble of his tone, the gentleness of his voice, the humor at the edges.

When Mei Lien opened her eyes, she realized two things immediately. First, she had fallen asleep listening to Huan Sun's stories. And second, he was no longer in the room.

She shot up in bed, then groaned at the sharp headache piercing her temples. The light around the window was a dull orange, and, judging by the dryness of her throat and the pinch in her stomach, Mei Lien guessed the hour to be midday.

When had Huan Sun left? Did Ah-Peen Oie know they had only talked? Would she be furious?

Something in her room was different. The chair Huan Sun had sat in hadn't been moved. Her clothing still hung in the wardrobe, untouched. She scanned the rest of the room. Then she saw the vase on the bureau.

She climbed out of bed and crossed to the bureau. Someone had left a vase of water. She took a long drink, then noticed a small clay bowl filled with water behind the vase. Floating in the center of the bowl was a white magnolia. Somehow she knew it was from Huan Sun. Who else would have left such a thing?

Footsteps sounded outside her bedroom door, and moments later, the door opened.

Mei Lien stared at Ah-Peen Oie, trying to gauge her mood. Was she supposed to drink the water? Had she broken some rule? When the woman smiled, Mei Lien's shoulders relaxed.

"Huan Sun was complimentary when he left," Ah-Peen Oie said. "Well done."

Mei Lien lowered her head, waiting for any other pronouncements by her mistress.

They came immediately. "Since Huan Sun has requested you for three months, you will no longer be needed at the banquets."

Mei Lien released a breath.

"The attentions Zhang Wei paid you last night should never happen again," Ah-Peen Oie continued. "Next time they do, you will pay dearly. Do you understand?"

"Yes," Mei Lien whispered.

Ah-Peen Oie gripped her chin and forced her face upward. "I cannot hear you."

"Yes," Mei Lien said in a louder voice.

Ah-Peen Oie's beautiful eyes were laced with malice. "The only reason you are bruise free right now is because of the amount Huan Sun paid for you. As long as you keep him happy, you will be spared punishment."

Mei Lien swallowed against the slow burn in her throat. "Thank you for your kindness."

Ah-Peen Oie nodded, then released Mei Lien's chin. Her gaze trailed to the bureau. "The water is from Huan Sun. Be sure that you show your deep gratitude when he returns tonight. I will not have a dissatisfied client in my house."

Mei Lien paced her room the rest of the day. She took only half the dose of opium offered, and she fought the threatening headache. But the extra water helped, and the floating white magnolia gave her renewed determination. She didn't want to be dependent on the opium. Mei Lien wanted to be stronger than her addiction so that when she left this house, her journey wouldn't be controlled by her physical dependency. She could do what was required to pay off her contract; she could survive and return to her mother.

Click. Click.

Mei Lien turned from the darkening window to see Huan Sun enter her bedroom. Her skin heated with expectation, and her pulse went from walking fast to running. She bowed and greeted him, and Huan Sun returned her greeting with a smile.

"I brought you something." In his hands, he carried a wide bowl painted with bonsai trees.

He approached Mei Lien, and her curious gaze fell to the contents. Inside the bowl, dirt had been layered with gravel. The top of a plant had emerged from the base, and Mei Lien knew immediately what it was. "A lotus?"

Huan Sun's expression was pleased. "Yes. Now we need to add water. And it requires sunlight."

This Mei Lien could not do. "I cannot open the drapes."

Huan Sun set the bowl atop the bureau, then moved past her to the window. He tugged the drapes aside. Through the grate, the gilt-edged mauve of twilight glowed. "I will speak to Ah-Peen Oie. The lotus is my gift to you, and if it's not cared for properly, it will die."

Mei Lien couldn't stop the hope that had slowly uncurled as a flower might after a cold rainstorm. "She might insist that it be kept in the dining room."

Huan Sun turned. "It belongs here. I will speak to her."

Mei Lien wanted to believe that Huan Sun could make such a request, and perhaps he could.

"Now." Huan Sun approached her. "You should add the water."

Mei Lien picked up the vase, which was nearly empty. She poured the remainder of the water into the bowl until the bud looked like it was floating, although it was still attached to its base.

Would the lotus really thrive and bloom in this small room with barely any light?

Huan Sun gave her a proud smile. "The lotus reminds me of you, blossom. Right now it's hiding in the dirt, but soon it will bloom."

Was this what it was like to be wooed? Except—that was impossible because Huan Sun was paying for her. Yet . . . "Thank you, it is beautiful already." And it was.

Huan Sun took his place in the chair where he had sat the previous night, and Mei Lien sat opposite him on the bed. The room seemed smaller than before, the distance between them much shorter, and she wondered when he was going to tire of that chair.

She didn't know if she should start the conversation, but she did anyway. "What did you do today?"

Huan Sun owned a tailoring shop, and he told her of the customers who had come in: from the servant of a very particular housewife to a member of the tong. Huan Sun's detailed stories captivated Mei Lien. She felt as if she'd been to the shop herself.

"There is an important banquet next week that Ah-Peen Oie is hosting for the tong," Huan Sun said. "I have many orders for making new clothing and repairing traditional costumes."

"The banquet is here?" She thought of the one member of the tong she had met—Zhang Wei. Having a whole host of them in the house would be disconcerting, but she wouldn't be at the banquet anyway.

"Ah-Peen Oie is a grand mistress of Chinatown," Huan Sun said. "I think everyone fears her a little."

Mei Lien pressed her lips together to let the urge of complaining about her mistress pass. "She has forbidden me from all banquets."

Huan Sun studied her, his gaze moving over her from head to foot. "You are very beautiful. Perhaps she doesn't want the attention drawn away from her."

Mei Lien straightened and frowned. "I am nothing compared to Ah-Peen Oie. She is a lovely, sophisticated woman."

"Not every man wants a sophisticated woman," Huan Sun said in a quiet voice.

Mei Lien had to look away then because her neck was heating up at the way he was looking at her. Would tonight be the night? How long would he wait?

"I hope I can please you," she whispered.

She heard him rise to his feet and walk toward the bed. When he stopped, he did not touch her as she expected. He only breathed out a sigh. The silence ticked like a clock between them, and finally Mei Lien looked up.

She couldn't read his expression, and she didn't know if she wanted to. Because when he leaned down and ran two fingers along the edge of her jaw, her heart seemed to expand two sizes. This wasn't supposed to happen. She wasn't supposed to *like* the men visiting her room. But Huan Sun was different.

"You look pale." His voice was gentle, laced with concern. "Do they feed you enough?"

It was mostly a teasing question, but tears welled in her eyes. Huan Sun sat next to her and drew her hand into his. "Tell me."

She exhaled a shaky breath. "I haven't eaten today. The water you sent was all that I was given. Ah-Peen Oie says that I must pay for my own food now that I have a patron, but she has not given me any money yet."

Huan Sun didn't move for a long moment; then he released her hand and left the room.

Mei Lien sank against the single pillow. She couldn't imagine where Huan Sun had gone or what he would do. She bolted upright when she heard an argument coming from somewhere down the hallway. Mei Lien crept to the door and listened as closely as she could. It was Huan Sun's voice, speaking to Ah-Peen Oie. He was berating the mistress for not feeding her.

Mei Lien brought a hand to her mouth to stifle her gasp. She had never heard anyone speak sharply to Ah-Peen Oie, and Mei Lien could only imagine the woman's horrified fury.

Then a door shut. Hard. Footsteps again. Mei Lien hurried to the far side of the bedroom and hovered near the window that was now dark.

When the door next opened, it was not Huan Sun or Ah-Peen Oie who stepped in, but a servant girl with a tray of food. It smelled delicious, even in its cold state. After the girl left, Mei Lien didn't move for several moments, waiting. When no one else came in, she finally crossed to the food and ate her fill of chow mein and dumplings.

She waited long into the night for Huan Sun to return, but he never did, and eventually she fell asleep.

Two days passed, two days of food and water delivered to her room, but no Huan Sun. Mei Lien paced her bedroom. She spent long moments staring at the lotus. She parted the drape and watched out the forbidden window, ignoring her half-completed embroidery work.

On the morning of the third day, Mei Lien woke early and checked on the lotus. The bud had yet to open, but the rest of the plant seemed to be thriving. She added a little more water, then drank some herself. Last night there had been a banquet, and Mei Lien had spent the evening in her room. Had Huan Sun come to the banquet but not visited her? She had no way of knowing. The other courtesans kept to themselves, and she doubted any of them would be awake until the afternoon.

A scratching sound drew her attention, and Mei Lien turned toward the window. A robin had landed on the outside sill. Mei Lien watched the small bird flinch and dip its head. She didn't move or make a sound. Envy heated her body. The creature could fly away at any moment, fly away to whatever its next destination would be. Its freedom.

If only Mei Lien were as small as a bird. She could leave the house, fly away, and soar above all that was her life.

Her door burst open, and Mei Lien turned with a gasp as Ah-Peen Oie stormed in, followed by two other girls.

"Have you been stealing money from me?" Ah-Peen Oie ground out, crossing the room to stand before her.

Mei Lien was so stunned it took her a moment to say, "No, of course not. Why would you—"

Ah-Peen Oie slapped the side of Mei Lien's jaw. "Stop talking. We will find out soon enough."

It was then that Mei Lien realized the two other girls were pulling her clothes from the bureau, inspecting every seam, every pocket. Next, they opened the drawers, going through the few items that had been given to Mei Lien. They turned to the bed, stripped it of the coverings, slit open the pillow and shoved their hands inside, searching.

They lifted the mattress, then looked under the bed. Mei Lien felt hands pat her down, and finally, one of the girls poked her fingers into the lotus bowl.

"No," Mei Lien cried out before she could stop herself.

Everyone in the room froze. Then Ah-Peen Oie's face formed a cruel smile. "Bring me the bowl."

With Mei Lien watching in horror, Ah-Peen Oie dumped the entirety of the contents onto the stripped mattress. Dirt, gravel, water, and the fragile plant landed in a clump.

There was no money to be found.

Ah-Peen Oie had the audacity to look disappointed, and she dropped the bowl onto the mattress next to the scattered dirt. "Next room."

Mei Lien didn't move after Ah-Peen Oie left her bedroom. Noises of yells and shrieks came from the next bedroom over; then another room was invaded, and another.

Someone screamed, and the sound pulled Mei Lien out of her numbness. The screams turned into begging cries. Mei Lien walked to her still-open door. With numb disbelief, she watched Ah-Peen Oie drag one of the courtesans out of her room. The young woman was half clothed, and the makeup on her face was streaked with tears.

Mei Lien didn't move, didn't try to stop anything, as Ah-Peen Oie forced the girl down the back stairs. Mei Lien leaned against the frame of her doorway as the screams continued to echo throughout the house and out onto the street.

The girl would be locked out. She was disgraced, and no one in Chinatown would take pity on a used-up woman from Ah-Peen Oie's house. She might survive if she begged for work at the cribs; otherwise, she would meet the fate of the outcast—left to beg for her food until a merciful death claimed her.

Mei Lien shut her door quietly, then crossed to her soiled mattress. With small pinches, she began to reassemble the destroyed lotus plant.

CHAPTER TWELVE

*"Seldom anywhere has a great audience made so wonderful
a demonstration of enthusiasm as when Miss Cameron
came forward in response to the introduction and told her
simple, straightforward story of the experience she had had
in attempting to protect her ward. . . . Although low, Miss
Cameron's voice was heard in all portions of the room."*

—SAN FRANCISCO CHRONICLE, APRIL 3, 1900

1900

Dolly didn't think she would ever sleep, not on the hard-packed dirt of the Palo Alto jail. She and Kum Quai had been forced into a locked cell inside a shack behind the court building. There was no bed or latrine. Even though Kum Quai had insisted that Dolly use the two boxes in the shack as a bed, she couldn't let the poor, trembling girl sleep on the ground. The place was more of a storage room than a jail cell. Bits of lumber and smaller boxes were scattered about. Judging by the soft breathing coming from Kum Quai, Dolly could at least be at ease in the fact that the Chinese girl had stopped crying and was getting some rest at last.

If only rest would come for Dolly. She stared at the high, horizontal window where the moonlight spilled through. A few stars also winked against the black of the night sky. Out there was the world, while inside the jail cell it was a different existence altogether. Only a few hours in, and it seemed the room grew smaller and smaller with every passing moment.

The coolness had turned to cold, and Dolly burrowed further into her short jacket. The single blanket covered Kum Quai, and Dolly didn't want it any other way. Witnessing the fear and desperation in Kum Quai's eyes had been heart-wrenching, despite all the other rescues Dolly had been exposed to. Tonight, while she shared unjust penance with Kum Quai, Dolly had never felt more protective or more like a mother in her life. She knew, without a doubt, that her mother would have done the same thing to protect any of her children.

Blood or not, Kum Quai deserved a mother's protection.

Dolly's gaze found the empty water pail. The water had been stagnant, but they had shared equal portions anyway, and now her stomach pinched with hunger. They'd had nothing to eat since the breakfast meal back at the mission home. She wrapped her arms about her drawn-up legs and rested her chin on her knees. Closing her eyes, she prayed for rest, for safety, for the lawmakers to release them in the morning.

Shuffling footsteps sounded outside the jail cell, and Dolly went immediately on the alert. "Who is it?" she called out.

The jailer's voice came through the door. "Someone is here to pay bail for the Chinese girl."

Dolly scrambled to her feet. "Who?" Miss Culbertson had told her of tricks played by Chinese owners and how they pretended to bail out their slaves, only to keep them in hiding, often under worse conditions than before.

"It is a friend of Kum Quai," the jailer said.

The whimper from the makeshift bed told Dolly that Kum Quai was awake. Dolly crossed to the door. "She has no friends. We will wait here for tomorrow's trial."

The scrape of a key turning the lock sent Dolly's pulse jumping. She grabbed one of the lumber scraps and propped it against the door, then lifted another lumber piece and did the same thing.

"Don't come in," Dolly called out. "We reject the bail money."

The door rattled as the jailer pushed against it. Dolly shoved the opposite way with all her weight. Moments later, Kum Quai joined her and helped push as well. Together, with the help of the lumber pieces, they could deter the jailer.

When he left in a huff, Dolly sagged against the door. She couldn't very well explain what was going on to Kum Quai, but the girl's wide eyes told Dolly that she knew enough.

"*Lo Mo*," Kum Quai whispered.

Those two small words said everything that Kum Quai couldn't express. *Lo Mo* meant "old mother," but it was an endearment full of respect. The affectionate title of *Lo Mo* had been bestowed on Miss Culbertson. Dolly reached for the girl's trembling hand.

Then, a terrific shudder ripped through the door.

The jailer had an axe.

Dolly grabbed Kum Quai and pulled her away from the door. The clung to each other as the jailer broke a hole through the door, then reached through and pushed aside the lumber.

Kum Quai screamed.

There was nowhere for the women to go. They were trapped.

The jailer had no qualms about crossing the room and wrenching Kum Quai from Dolly's grasp.

"Don't you touch her," Dolly yelled, but the jailer was already half dragging the girl out of the cell.

Dolly ran after the jailer, grabbing for Kum Quai, but the man seemed to have the power of an ox. He half carried, half dragged Kum Quai out of the shack and across the dirt yard beneath the moonlit night to where a buggy waited. The jailer loaded the crying Kum Quai into the buggy, handing her off to two other men. Dolly wasn't going to let her go alone, and she grabbed the edges and climbed in too.

One of the men inside struggled to keep Kum Quai's screams quiet. The only thing Dolly could decipher from the girl's Chinese was *"Lo Mo,"* cried over and over.

"Let her go!" Dolly reached for Kum Quai, but the closest man shoved Dolly hard. She grabbed for something to hold onto, anything, but just then the buggy lurched forward, and she tipped out. She tumbled onto the road, scraping her arms and bruising her hip.

"Stop!" Dolly scrambled to her feet, ignoring the aching and throbbing. Even if she ran, there was no way she could catch up to the buggy.

Slowly she spun, the darkness of the cold night unreal and eerie. The jailer had disappeared inside the jail, and Dolly had never felt so alone and unsure. She looked toward town. If the jailer wouldn't help her, surely someone in town had a reasonable head. There wasn't time to assess any injuries with the buggy getting farther away.

She began to walk, limping with the pain of one of her ankles. But she didn't care about any physical pain; she cared only about finding someone to track down a helpless girl.

Dolly's limping turned to a loping run as she picked up her skirts and headed for the nearest building, the girl's cries for *Lo Mo* still ringing through her head. The darkness from every window of the druggist shop was disconcerting, but someone had to help her. She pounded on the door, then the windows. "Help me!" she cried. "Someone please help!"

She could only guess that it was well after midnight. But she kept pounding and calling until an older man came out, rubbing at his face with one hand, spectacles in another.

"They've taken her." Dolly choked back the threatening sob. "They've kidnapped her."

The older man's brows dipped. *"Who* was kidnapped?"

His calm voice pulled Dolly back to semi-reason. "Kum Quai. She's a Chinese girl, and I'm her guardian." She explained the events at the mission home, the charges and the impending trial, how they'd been in the jail cell just down the road. All the while, the man listened.

"I'm Dr. Hall," he said. "Let's get you to the hotel, and I'll call the sheriff of San Jose and alert him about the traveling group."

Dolly walked along the silent, dark streets with Dr. Hall to Larkin's Hotel. Her head ached, her throat throbbed, and her body trembled. No matter. She had found someone who had listened to her and promised help.

Once they reached the hotel, the proprietor offered her a hotel room. On another day, or under other circumstances, she might have appreciated the room. But she couldn't relax her vigil at the front entrance; she needed to hear news the moment it was received.

"I won't be sleeping," Dolly said. "I need to know what's going on."

The proprietor nodded. "I'll fetch you a blanket, and you can wait on the sofa in the lobby."

Dolly clutched the blanket to her as she listened to Dr. Hall telephoning the sheriff's office. When the call was completed, Dr. Hall turned toward her. "The San Jose sheriff is sending a search party to recover your ward."

Dolly's knees nearly buckled. "Thank you. Thank you very much," she whispered.

Dr. Hall only nodded, then led her to the sofa. "Rest here, Miss Cameron. Hopefully we'll have news by the time the sun is up."

Dolly waited on the sofa, curled up with the blanket. She wanted to run out of the hotel and continue running toward San Jose until her tired body completely gave out. Thoughts of what Kum Quai was experiencing at this very moment felt like a hammer against her heart. Dolly watched the changing shadows of the lobby as the night softened to gray, and finally the sun rose. Surely, there would be news by now. How had Kum Quai fared? Where was she now?

Dawn had lit the sky a brilliant orange by the time Dr. Hall strode into the hotel with another man. By the somber look on Dr. Hall's face, she feared the worst.

"What is it?" she rasped. "Where is Kum Quai?"

Dr. Hall's jaw tightened. "Her group was stopped last night by the Palo Alto justice of the peace."

Wasn't this good news? Then why was Dr. Hall not looking pleased?

"The Chinese men demanded a trial then and there," Dr. Hall continued. "Right on the roadside."

Dolly blinked. "W-what?"

"The trial was granted, and Kum Quai waived the right to trial and counsel." Dr. Hall cleared his throat. "She pleaded guilty to the charge, and she was fined five dollars, which was paid by one of her . . . escorts."

Dolly reached for the wall, or a table, anything to steady her wobbling legs.

Dr. Hall grasped her upper arm.

"She doesn't even speak English," Dolly whispered.

Dr. Hall's expression remained grave. "One of the men with her interpreted."

"Of course he did," Dolly snapped, anger replacing her shock. "One of her abductors asked for a trial at two-thirty in the morning, was granted one, then she pled guilty to false charges, and now . . . now where is she? Abducted again!"

Dr. Hall released her arm and stepped back, nodding to the man next to him.

"We do not know, ma'am," the second man said. "I'm a police officer here in Palo Alto, and that is what we are trying to figure out before . . ."

He didn't need to finish, and perhaps the expression on Dolly's face told him to stop speaking. Slave girls had been killed for deserting their owners.

"How can we help you, Miss Cameron?" Dr. Hall asked in a gentle, respectful tone. "Do you need to telephone anyone? Do you need a meal? Do you need an attorney?"

"I have an attorney," Dolly said in a defeated tone. This could not be happening. If only this were a nightmare that she would soon awaken from. "I want every resource used," she said, mostly to herself. "I want to know who is behind all of this. Who filed the charges on behalf of the Chinese owner?"

The two men before her promised they would do everything they could to help, and Dolly had no choice but to believe them.

Dolly didn't have to wait long. By that afternoon, the newspapers had caught word of the situation, and nearby Stanford University students had circulated handbills calling for action:

ON TO PALO ALTO!
OUR REPUTATION IS AT STAKE.
BRING OWN ROPE.
NO. 3 HALL. 8:00 TONIGHT.

All the city officials invo d in the Kum Quai affair had been named and criticized, includi who had ordered Kum Quai to be thrown in jail, the jailer wh rag er out of the cell, the peace officer, the San Jose sheriff, and e law d filed the charges in the first place.

"Miss Came an d.

Dolly looked the newspaper she was reading in the lobby. She had finally consented to take one of the hotel rooms, but after a short nap, she was back in the lobby. Now she sat at a small table, waiting and watching for any more developments.

"I'm Attorney Weigle." He extended his hand. "I've been on the telephone with Monroe, and I'd like to represent you in this case."

Dolly shook Weigle's hand as she examined him, determining that he was of middle age, his eyes were intelligent, and his manner confident. He smelled faintly of pipe smoke. "What do you recommend?" she asked.

"May I sit?" He indicated the chair opposite her.

"Of course," Dolly murmured.

Weigle sat and adjusted his cuffs. His face danced with shadows in the lamplight surrounding them. "I recommend that you prepare an official statement. This thing is not going to be over quickly. The sooner you write the events down, the more accurate they will be. Tomorrow we will—"

Dolly heard the commotion outside the hotel at the same time as Weigle, and they both turned toward the window. A large group of people, most of them appearing to be college students, walked down the street together, shouting something.

Dolly rose to her feet. "What's going on?"

Weigle frowned; then his brows shot up. "They're protesting the wrongful treatment of your Chinese ward, Miss Cameron. I didn't know it would reach these proportions, though." He moved toward the front door, whe other hotel patrons were gathering to watch.

Dolly followed and stepped out of the hotel. The chanting was lou. now, and, up close, she felt the energy radiating from the college students. The night's atmosphere was like an electric charge. "Oh, my goodness," she murmured.

The end of the street revealed that not just a few dozen but hundreds of college students were marching together. Torches and lanterns in hand, their chants echoed through the night.

"To the jail!"

"Burn it up!"

"Tear it down!"

Dolly had lost track of where Weigle had gone, but she was transfixed as she watched the approaching mob. Their voices echoed off the buildings on University Avenue, and Dolly was reminded of an impending fierce thunderstorm.

"What's that?" she said to herself as she noticed a smaller group carrying an effigy.

"It's the justice of the peace who humiliated Palo Alto with a false trial," a young man next to her replied.

She turned to look at him, but he had disappeared into the crowd, joining the protesters. Then Dolly watched with mixed fascination and horror as the mob turned down the side streets leading to the jail. She brought a hand to her mouth, not even feeling the hot tears splashing onto her cheeks.

"You should go back inside." Weigle appeared at her side and grasped her elbow. "I don't know what will happen."

"No," Dolly said in a clear voice. She breathed in the cool evening air, the crackling excitement, and the sight of hundreds supporting her cause. "I want to watch."

She began to walk, following the mob at a good distance, and Weigle kept pace with her. He acted as if he would have to defend her at any moment, but Dolly wasn't worried in the least. These students from Stanford were after one thing only: *justice*. And whatever form that took, Dolly would support it.

The crowd of students didn't tear down the jail, nor did they burn it. Instead, they removed the contents from inside the jail cell—the filthy blanket, the boxes, and the wooden boards. They carried the items back to the street, where they lit them on fire.

Along with the effigy of the justice of the peace.

As the crackling orange flames reached toward the dark sky, the mob continued in their shouting and cursing, demanding reform. Promising change.

Dolly couldn't agree more.

CHAPTER THIRTEEN

BILL OF SALE

Loo Wong to Loo Chee

April 16—Rice, six mats, at $2 .... $12

April 18—Shrimps, 50 lbs., at 10c 5

April 20—Girl..................... 250

April 21—Salt Fish, 60 lbs., at 10c 6

Total: $273

Received Payment

Loo Chee

—Bill of sale for nine-year-old Chinese girl
printed in the San Francisco Call, 1898

1903

The birds were quiet this morning as Mei Lien unpicked the row of stitches she had just completed. Silence always unsettled her since she didn't know what was going on, what to anticipate. She relied on sound in this house. Footsteps told her that someone was coming. Voices clued her into the mood of Ah-Peen Oie. Clattering pots and plates told her everyone would eat that day.

Mei Lien's gaze cut to the recent gifts sent by Huan Sun. A small, framed watercolor of a pagoda. A set of lucky stone frogs. Another lotus plant, since the original one could not be rescued. Huan Sun had been kinder than Mei Lien had ever expected a man who was visiting a brothel to be. When they had finally shared a bed, his tenderness had made her wonder if he had sincere feelings for her. She had quickly dashed those thoughts away, though. If she couldn't protect her body or mind, then she could at least protect her heart.

Huan Sun would visit her tonight after the banquet. Ah-Peen Oie had forbidden Mei Lien from attending banquets when Zhang Wei was in town, which included tonight.

Mei Lien was grateful. She knew all men weren't kind as Huan Sun. She'd heard plenty through the walls and doors of the house over the past three months to understand that she had been somehow blessed with a reprieve. At least until tomorrow.

Huan Sun's contract would run out, and he would not be expected to renew. In fact, it would be highly unusual. Would another man contract long-term with Mei Lien, or would she serve as a one-night girl? The shudder that rippled through her body made her miss the next stitch. Mei Lien unpicked the stitch, then surveyed the embroidered pillowcase she was making for Huan Sun. A farewell gift.

The thought of saying good-bye to him should not make her cry, but despite her resolve, a tear slipped out. She was a woman of the night, and here she was, crying over a man who paid to spend time with her.

She did not love him. Could not love him. Mei Lien knew that the opium she took every day had altered any logical thoughts. She began each day resolving to not take any opium, but by the afternoon, she gave into the craving.

The knock at her door startled her, and Mei Lien set aside the embroidery. She crossed to the door and opened it only to find Huan Sun on the other side. It should have brought her happiness, but his eyes were somber, his mouth unsmiling.

"Oh. You are . . . here?" she said.

Huan Sun stepped inside the room with a nod, and Mei Lien shut and locked the door. When she turned to him, she found him standing before the grated window, pulling aside the drape. He gazed out at the fading light.

Mei Lien waited a few moments for him to speak, but when he said nothing, she asked, "Did you close your shop early?"

He shook his head. "Someone robbed the store last night. Took all my savings."

Mei Lien gasped. "All?"

"I can salvage the goods and the fabrics, at least." Huan Sun looked over at her. "But I have nothing . . . for you."

"I don't care," she said in a rush. "Take your gifts back. Perhaps you can sell them."

Huan Sun's brows shifted. "I don't want to take the gifts back."

"You don't?"

He crossed to her then and took her small hands in his larger ones. "I cannot pay for another quarter with you. Not even another night. Not until I can recover my business."

She looked deep into his eyes. That was what he was worried about? *Her?*

"You do not have to pay." She hadn't intended to make that offer, but she was more afraid of which man might claim her next.

His gaze showed only sadness. "Ah-Peen Oie would never allow that."

Mei Lien knew this. Of course she knew this. She looked away from Huan Sun because a crack had started growing in her heart, spreading fast.

"I am sorry," Huan Sun said in a tender voice.

Mei Lien nodded, unable to speak. Her throat burned with threatening emotion. Today might be the last time she ever saw Huan Sun.

"I am sorry too," she said at last.

Huan Sun's smile was gentle, sad. He cupped her face with both hands, then leaned forward and kissed her.

The kiss felt like a good-bye, and that was exactly what it was. When he released her, she felt as if the earth had opened beneath her. "I have made you something," she said, "although it's not quite finished yet." She moved to where she had set down the embroidery. "I can complete this, and when you come again—"

"I'm afraid it might be a while before I can afford luxuries such as visiting this house," he said. "I don't mind taking it unfinished."

She hesitated, then handed over the piece, trying to smile even though the crack in her heart had splintered.

Huan Sun examined the embroidery, running the tips of his fingers over the intricate stitching. "It's beautiful, Mei Lien." Then his gaze met hers, and he smiled that smile she had become fond of. "I must go. I cannot let Ah-Peen Oie think that I am able to renew any contract. But first, I have one more gift for you, my blossom."

Mei Lien wanted to tell him no, but she was also curious about what he could have possibly brought her. When he produced a bracelet of pearls, she brought her hands to her mouth. She had never owned jewelry this beautiful.

"This was my mother's," Huan Sun said.

As beautiful as the pearls were, she could not keep the bracelet. "I can't take your mother's pearls."

Huan Sun refused to take them back, though. "She told me to save them for someone special."

Mei Lien fought against the tears burning in her eyes. His mother had died many years ago in Hong Kong before he came to San Francisco. "Huan Sun . . ."

He closed her hand around the bracelet, then wrapped his fingers over hers. "I promised my mother I would, so they are yours."

She opened her palm and gazed for a long moment at the pearl bracelet. Then she slipped it on her wrist. "Thank you," she whispered.

Huan Sun leaned forward and pressed a soft kiss on her forehead. "Good-bye, Mei Lien."

When the door clicked shut behind him, Mei Lien didn't move for a long moment. The soft weight of the pearls on her wrist somehow made the pain of Huan Sun's departure more palpable.

She wished she could help him find his stolen savings. Another knock on the door sent darts of hope through her. Perhaps Huan Sun had returned after all. But the door opened before she could reach it.

Ah-Peen Oie swept into the room wearing an elegant silk dress. Her hair was pulled into a high twist, and she smelled like a garden of roses.

Mei Lien moved her hands behind her back to hide the pearl bracelet, then lowered her eyes so that her mistress wouldn't think her defiant.

"I sent Huan Sun on his way." Ah-Peen Oie crossed to the bureau. She sorted through the few things upon it, and Mei Lien tried not to bristle or complain. "He is no longer welcome in my house until he has recovered his fortune."

Mei Lien knew better than to speak, but listening without replying was like sitting on a jagged rock.

Ah-Peen Oie stopped in front of Mei Lien. With a long fingernail, the mistress lifted Mei Lien's chin. "Zhang Wei has requested your presence to-night at the banquet."

Mei Lien had no doubt that if Ah-Peen Oie had been a living dragon, smoke would be coming out of her nostrils right now.

"Do not encourage him," Ah-Peen Oie warned. "If he speaks to you, reply as little as possible." She leaned so close that Mei Lien could smell the cinnamon on her breath. "He is *mine*. Don't forget it."

Ah-Peen Oie lowered her fingernail, but not before scraping beneath Mei Lien's chin.

Her skin burned with the scratch.

When the mistress left, Mei Lien sank onto her bed. Squeezing her eyes shut, she curled up on her side and let the tears fall. Tears for the loss of Huan Sun. Tears for the changes coming into her life yet again. Tears for a mother she was slowly forgetting.

Time pulsed forward, and when darkness fell, Mei Lien reluctantly pre-pared herself for the banquet. Walking down the corridor felt like she was leaving a life she had reconciled herself to and stepping toward one she feared.

The cloying scent of smoke, rich perfume, powdered faces, and oiled hair was stifling, and Mei Lien wished that she could have stayed in her room tonight. But business came first. And Mei Lien had a long way to go to pay off her contract.

Zhang Wei sat in one of the high-backed chairs, puffing on his pipe, his eyes half-lidded as he watched Mei Lien. His gaze hadn't left her all night, and although he had yet to speak to her, she knew that Ah-Peen Oie was furious. The mistress flirted and chatted with all the other men, including Zhang Wei from time to time, but the red stain along her neck told Mei Lien enough.

She would not escape punishment for this.

And then it happened.

"Mei Lien," Zhang Wei said from across the room. Somehow his low voice cut through the din of conversation and laughter.

She turned from where she had been speaking to another courtesan.

The edges of his mouth lifted. "Tell me a story of your home."

It was a trick question, one in which she would be tested for her cleverness and quick wit. Zhang Wei didn't really want to hear about her widowed mother and the hours spent working in the fields. He wanted to be entertained.

A hush had fallen over the group, although no one seemed to be paying attention to them. Mei Lien was not fooled. The Chinese courtesans used both ears—one for the person they were speaking to, and one for the person they were spying on.

With no other choice, unless she wanted to embarrass everyone and bring down the reputation of the house, Mei Lien crossed to Zhang Wei.

He nodded at the nearby chair, and she sat, folding her hands in her lap. She had hidden the pearl bracelet beneath her mattress. There was no way she wanted the others to see such a precious gift.

Mei Lien sorted through many tales she had heard, some from her childhood, and others she'd heard recited by other courtesans. She settled for the girl on the moon—Chang E—and told how she was exiled from heaven with the Jade Emperor's son, Hou Yi, for displeasing the emperor. Chang E and Hou Yi worked together to find the elixir of life so they could regain their position in heaven. Chang E drank it all, and she became too buoyant for earth and instead floated up to the sky and landed on the moon.

"Chang E still lives on the moon," Mei Lien said. "And that is why we eat mooncake every autumn." As if to prove her point, Mei Lien lifted a mooncake from the silver tray in front of her and took a delicate bite.

A few of the men clapped lightly. The courtesans giggled behind their fans. Ah-Peen Oie said nothing. Then everyone waited for Zhang Wei's pronouncement. He smiled, then chuckled. It might have been a delayed reaction, but there was no doubt that he was showing his pleasure at the tale. Mei Lien had never seen the man smile, and she could see why Ah-Peen Oie was possessive of him.

"You are a dainty thing, aren't you?" Zhang Wei's gaze slid over her.

Mei Lien didn't know how to respond. Was he giving her his approval? She didn't dare look over where Ah-Peen Oie stood, likely pretending to be interested in another conversation.

Zhang Wei leaned forward slightly, but it was enough to catch Ah-Peen Oie's attention. Mei Lien found she was holding her breath. What would he do? What would he say?

"Do not accept any other offers tonight," he said. "I paid dearly to get rid of Huan Sun."

Mei Lien stared at the man. "What?" Her throat was suddenly bitter. "What did you do?" But she knew.

Zhang Wei was a powerful tong leader. He could do anything he wanted—including ruining another man's livelihood.

Zhang Wei's dark eyes narrowed. "I wanted you to myself."

One moment his eyes were on her; the next moment, he had risen from his chair. The knowledge of what Zhang Wei had done to Huan Sun for *her* shoved guilt into her heart like a dagger. She sat perfectly still while her stomach tried to rebel from the anger and disgust battling inside her. Anger at

Zhang Wei and disgust at herself. How had she become the cause of Huan Sun's downfall? This was her fault. She wanted to flee the room, wanted to scream out her agony. Instead, she barely breathed as she watched Zhang Wei cross to Ah-Peen Oie. The mistress graciously accepted a kiss on the cheek, then listened as he spoke into her ear. The woman's face pinked, and her gaze cut to Mei Lien.

The hatred in Ah-Peen Oie's eyes sliced through Mei Lien like lightning. When the mistress looked back at Zhang Wei, she smiled prettily, then nodded.

The transaction had been agreed upon.

CHAPTER FOURTEEN

"The citizens of San Jose in mass meeting assembled denounce the late outrage committed at Palo Alto by officers of Santa Clara county in the name of the law upon Miss Cameron of the Presbyterian Mission of San Francisco and the Chinese women in her charge.

"We admire the fearless, heroic, and womanly action of Miss Cameron in her efforts to prevent the abduction of her ward, which was accomplished under the guise of law."

—"Palo Alto Resolution," San Francisco Chronicle, April 3, 1900

APRIL 1900

"Are you ready?" Attorney Weigle asked Dolly as they stood outside Turn Verein Hall, where the hearing for the Palo Alto scandal would take place. And scandal it had become.

The lawyer for Chung Bow and Wong Fong had been identified and accused of hatching the abduction plot.

"The rumors are just rumors," Weigle told Dolly.

"The gang bosses are using their people to intimidate the judge," Dolly said. Word was that people had been recruited in support of Attorney Herrington, the lawyer who represented the Chinese owner.

"True," Weigle agreed. "But we have used our power as well to combat the supporters of Herrington."

She stared into the lawyer's eyes. "Such as?"

Weigle leaned close, the musty spice of pipe smoke about him, reminding her for an instant of Officer Cook. "Paul Dinsmore raised five hundred dollars to charter a train from Palo Alto. They filled it with Stanford students, and they're in the center section of the great Hall."

Dolly's pulse skipped. "They're here? Right now?"

Weigle grinned. "Yes."

She would not cry. She had to be strong and eloquent as she faced the judge. Clutching her hands in front of her in a tight grip, she said, "I am ready."

Weigle nodded and opened the door leading to the corridor that led to the Hall. As the pair of them stepped inside, the hushed murmurs of the gathered audience went silent. Hundreds of pairs of eyes watched Donaldina Cameron walk with Attorney Weigle to their places.

She knew her face had flushed, but she kept her chin lifted and focused on taking steady breaths. Weigle gave her a nod of approval and encouragement as they took their seats.

The chairman, Colonel Whitton, wasted no time in beginning his opening remarks, in which he explained that the meeting had been called to denounce the actions that had taken place in Palo Alto by the officers of the law.

His speech was frequently interrupted by applause and calls of agreement from the student body. Dolly's heart expanded at each utterance from the supportive audience. There was no secret as to which side of the issue they all supported. Whenever Whitton mentioned the Palo Alto justice, the audience groaned, bringing laughter to the inane situation they all found themselves in.

Then, Colonel Whitton called upon Miss Donaldina Cameron.

With her heart beating in her throat, Dolly rose. All eyes were on her again, and she knew that her words had never had such impact as they would now. With the eyes of her supporters on her, as well as those who wished her to disappear from the face of the earth, Dolly stood before the chairman and began to speak.

She started at the beginning.

Her words might have started out a bit hesitant, but soon her passion thundered in her chest, and she told the captive audience every detail of the journey, including the final moments of seeing Kum Quai dragged away by the jailer, then carted off with two Chinese men who thought they were above the law and God himself.

"*Lo Mo,*" Dolly said. "Those were the final words I heard Kum Quai say. *Lo Mo* is what a Chinese daughter calls a beloved mother, for I am Kum Quai's mother."

When Dolly returned to her seat, it was to the thunderous applause and foot stamping by those who had called for justice and change weeks before in the streets of Palo Alto while they had stoked the flames of the bonfire.

Chairman Brun of the Palo Alto investigation committee was next up on the docket, and he read the statement, which perfectly corroborated Dolly's story. Then Attorney Weigle took his turn conveying his agreement with Miss Donaldina Cameron and the need to find and liberate Kum Quai.

The doors at the back of the room banged open, and a tall man walked in. He might have been considered handsome, with his piercing eyes and determined jaw, but with his entrance, Dolly felt only a foreboding. Attorney Herrington had the gall to attend the meeting. It was as if she were facing a member of the leering tong—men and women who did not see Chinese girls as humans but as chattel, to be used for monetary profit.

Herrington grinned broadly at the hissing audience and those who were insulting him. He continued to stride up the aisle toward the chairman, who indicated that he could speak next.

Herrington turned toward the jeering audience. "I'm here to announce the marriage between Kum Quai and her new husband, Chung Bow."

Dolly couldn't hold back her gasp. She gripped Weigle's arm as they both stared at Herrington.

"The happy couple were married last Saturday on Pacific Street," Herrington continued. "Justice Dunn performed the honors, and Chung

Bow's friend Wong Fong was the witness. The marriage license was legally obtained by Attorney H. H. Lowenthal. There was no objection to the marriage, and the newly married couple are traveling to their new home to start their lives together."

Dolly had so many questions, but the horrific news had drained her body of all reaction. She could not believe for one moment that Kum Quai had been a willing participant in the marriage. Like many Chinese girls before her, she had been forced to enter into such a contract.

When Herrington triumphantly left the meeting, ignoring all the disparaging comments sent his way, Dolly felt as if she had fallen off a cliff and everything inside her was broken and useless.

"Miss Cameron," Weigle said in a gentle tone, "we'll find out where they are headed. We can still stop them. We can still free Kum Quai."

"It's too late," Dolly said, her voice cracking.

"It's never too late," Weigle said.

He was saying the words that *she* should have been saying, *had* been saying . . . yet the pompous image of Attorney Herrington had somehow weighed her down like a ship's anchor.

Weigle produced a handkerchief, and Dolly wiped at the tears on her cheeks. "Onward," she said in a whisper, but the word fell flat in her heart.

Shortly after returning to San Francisco, unable to shake the feeling of defeat, Dolly found out from informants through Ah Cheng that Kum Quai had been forced into marriage with death threats. The news didn't surprise Dolly, but the confirmation still stung.

She paced the street level of the house late at night. No rescues tonight, but Dolly still couldn't sleep. Kum Quai had been married after all, so of what use had been all the work they'd gone through? Not even a government could stop the Chinese slave owner.

The creak of the stairs caught her attention, and Dolly turned, wondering who else was awake in the middle of the night. Tien came down the stairs, her hand on the railing, her steps determined.

Dolly was about to tell her to go back to bed when Tien held out her hand. Dolly stepped forward to see the blossom of a lotus flower in Tien's palm. Some of the Chinese grew the flowers in their rooms in wide vases of water.

"What's this?" Dolly asked, unsure what Tien wanted her to do.

"For you." Tien wouldn't meet her gaze, but kept her dark head lowered.

Dolly took the blossom. "Thank you; it's beautiful." The gesture was so unexpected, especially coming from Tien.

Before Dolly could say anything else, Tien turned and fled up the stairs like a startled squirrel heading up a tree.

The reason for her haste became apparent when Mrs. Field appeared at the top of the stairs, wearing a dark robe over her long, white nightgown.

"That child should not be up at all hours," Mrs. Field said. "I've a mind to lock her in her room right after her evening chores."

Dolly released a slow breath. "She can't sleep when she worries."

Mrs. Field's hand tightened on the railing. "Are you still going on about Kum Quai's marriage?"

Dolly's mouth parted in surprise. "Going on? She's in a terrible situation, and we need to come up with a way to free her."

The director narrowed her eyes. "She is lost to us, and it's just as well. Too much trouble surrounded her. You went to jail, for heaven's sake. You can't be running off like that, soiling the reputation of the fine mission ladies who work here. We must be respectable women, and not get so involved in the Chinese girls' lives. If they aren't inside our walls, then they should be left to their own destinies."

The heat in Dolly's chest felt like it was going to burst into flames. "Kum Quai is one of *us,* ma'am. She was kidnapped and coerced. She was tricked and lied to. I will *not* abandon her. Just as the Lord left the ninety-nine sheep to rescue the one, I too will go after the one."

Mrs. Field waved a hand in dismissal. "Now look who's comparing the

Chinese to sheep. The residents here are in the middle of their education, and you cannot leave me to cover both my job and your job."

So this was what it had come to. "Ah Cheng and Yuen Qui are able to help out anytime."

Mrs. Field scoffed. "I can barely communicate with them."

Now Mrs. Field was being ridiculous. The interpreters spoke fine English.

Dolly was exhausted, and arguing in the middle of the night with Mrs. Field wasn't doing either of them any good. If Mrs. Field wanted to recommend to the board that Dolly be let go, then so be it. "I will continue to work toward Kum Quai's freedom with all of the resources I can muster. If you need more help, I can talk to one of the staff members for you."

Mrs. Field lifted her chin. "Don't overstep your authority, Miss Cameron." Then, without waiting for an answer, she turned and walked away, leaving behind only the echo of her brisk footsteps.

Dolly looked down at the lotus blossom in her hand, then brought it to her nose and inhaled the soft, sweet fragrance. She would count whatever blessings came her way, and the rest . . . well, the rest, she would turn over to the Lord. Somewhere out there, Kum Quai was trapped and desperate. And Dolly would not abandon her.

Over the next few days, Dolly continued reaching out to all her sources, trying to find a solution, although Mrs. Field refused to even speak of Kum Quai.

"Jun Ling says he is keeping his ears open," Ah Cheng told Dolly one morning over breakfast. Thankfully, Mrs. Field had already left the breakfast table, since she disapproved of using resources to continue their search.

Dolly reached across the table and clasped Ah Cheng's hand. "Jun Ling is a good man and a good friend to the mission home."

When Ah Cheng's face flushed a pretty red, Dolly tightened her hold. "What is this? Do you think of Jun Ling as more than a friend?"

Ah Cheng's blush deepened, but her smile was genuine.

"Tell me," Dolly said. "I want to hear everything."

Ah Cheng looked down at the table, then released a slow breath. When she next looked at Dolly, her dark eyes were beautiful with love and excitement. "He's asked me to marry him."

Dolly yelped. "Oh, my goodness. How wonderful!"

"I know," Ah Cheng whispered. "I never thought I'd . . . find so much happiness."

When she hesitated, Dolly guessed what would come next. "We will miss you," she said, speaking with more courage than she felt. She couldn't let Ah Cheng feel guilty about leaving to marry. It was something that Dolly supposed she might do herself one day if the right man came along. "But you can come visit anytime, my friend."

Ah Cheng nodded, her eyes filling with tears. "I know. It will be hard to leave, though. But I love him."

Tears stung Dolly's eyes, too. She rose and crossed to Ah Cheng, pulling the woman into a hug. "I am happy for you." And she was. Truly. Ah Cheng would be dearly missed, but Dolly's mind was already moving ahead. Yuen Qui had interpreted plenty of times, and she was the natural choice to fill Ah Cheng's shoes.

"Yuen Qui has agreed to help," Ah Cheng said.

"She already knows?"

Ah Cheng smiled. "You've been very busy lately. I didn't want to take away from your focus. Our marriage won't be for many months yet."

Dolly pulled Ah Cheng into another embrace. "How did I get so blessed in life?"

The women drew apart at the sound of someone knocking at the door.

"I'll get it," Ah Cheng offered.

"No, you finish your breakfast," Dolly insisted. She left the dining room and walked to the front door. The few moments to herself were much needed, because new tears burned her eyes now—ones born of the realization of how lonely she sometimes felt. Loneliness was an interesting animal of its own accord. Days and weeks would pass when Dolly hardly gave a thought to how a well of loneliness had taken up residence next to her heart. But then the quiet moments would come, the exhaustion would take over, and she would feel like she was missing something, or someone, she couldn't quite name.

The knock sounded again at the door. Dolly had delayed too long with her own thoughts. There was no time for wallowing. She drew in a breath and turned the locks, then opened the door.

On the other side was a messenger from the post office, a boy who was familiar to her.

"A note for you, Miss Cameron," the boy said.

She thanked him, then read through the note quickly. B. F. Hall, a telephone agent at Palo Alto, had written that one of the Chinese captors of Kum Quai was on his way to San Francisco.

Dolly lowered the note and closed her eyes. Wong Fong would be in San Francisco. She didn't know if Kum Quai or her husband, Chung Bow, would be with him, but right now it didn't matter.

"Ah Cheng," Dolly called out, and the woman came out of the dining room. "Get the police on the telephone. We're going to the train station to apprehend Wong Fong."

Ah Cheng didn't even hesitate; she only turned and hurried to the office to telephone the police.

Dolly waited by the door for Ah Cheng to return since she didn't want to face Mrs. Field's disapproval or questions. Within minutes, Dolly and Ah Cheng were heading to the train station, where they were met by Officers Jesse Cook and Patrick O'Connor.

"What's going on, Miss Cameron?" Cook asked the moment they were near enough to speak.

He wasn't openly carrying a sledgehammer or axe, but Dolly wouldn't be surprised if he had one hidden in his jacket. Cook hadn't been told the exact nature of the assignment, just that Donaldina Cameron needed his help. And that was enough.

When Dolly explained about the wire she had received informing her that Wong Fong was on the train from San Jose to San Francisco, Cook said, "When you see him, let us know."

Cook and O'Connor began to scan the crowds, keeping close to Dolly and Ah Cheng.

As the train finally came into view, Dolly's heart joined the rhythm of the sounds of the approaching train. People milled about, waiting to meet those on the train, but Dolly kept her eyes on the passengers filing out of the various doors.

When she saw him, she knew immediately it was Wong Fong. She could never forget the man from that night of the abduction. The shape of his face, the line of his jaw . . . his eyes might be downcast, his manner inconspicuous, but it was definitely him.

"There he is," she told Cook. "The man with the dark overcoat."

Cook and O'Connor strode to Wong Fong's side.

Dolly wanted to revel in the abductor's shocked expression as Cook grasped Wong Fong by the upper arm, then handcuffed him, while O'Connor told him he was under arrest. Dolly felt only regret that she hadn't been able to stop the sham marriage. Even now, understanding the complications of the law, she could only hope that the charges would stick.

Dolly was elated when she returned to the mission home, and not even the cold silence of Mrs. Field at the staff meal could cool her excitement. She sought out Tien as soon as possible, finding the girl sitting in the kitchen with Lonnie. Lonnie would never go near the stove, or anything hot, but at least she was in the kitchen. Tien was helping her make almond cookie dough. The scene was surprisingly tender and domestic.

"There you are," Dolly said to Tien.

Despite the things that had passed between them, Tien's sharp gaze was suspicious.

"I wanted to tell you that we caught Wong Fong today at the train station," Dolly said. "He was one of the men who kidnapped Kum Quai."

Lonnie immediately asked, "Did you find her?"

"Not yet," Dolly said. "But I'm not giving up."

Tien's mouth curved into the slightest smile, and she quickly looked down at the batter she'd been mixing.

"I hope the bad man will go to jail for a long time, Mama," Lonnie said.

"I do too," Dolly said.

Over the next weeks, more information came to Dolly about how Kum Quai had originally been part of a larger group of girls brought over from China under the pretense of working at the Omaha Exposition. But in reality, they had been sold into the San Francisco slave market. Dolly telephoned her lawyer when she found out the news. "I need to meet with the federal authorities. Kum Quai has no legal right to remain in the United States."

"Is that the argument you want to go with?" Monroe asked. "You know the risks."

"Yes," Dolly said. "Kum Quai needs to be freed from her sham marriage—whatever it takes."

"Very well." Monroe's tone was brisk. "I'll see you at Wong Fong's trial in Mayfield."

The day of the trial arrived a few weeks later. Another courtroom, another full house, due to the media attention and the ranting articles in the newspapers disparaging those behind the abduction of Kum Quai and the legal system that kept her in her abductors' possession. Dolly took courage from the editorials published in Kum Quai's favor. Dr. Hall was in attendance, the man who had originally helped her in Palo Alto, as well as Dr. John Endicott Gardner, who had been sent by Colonel Jackson, the Collector of the Port and Immigration Commissioner for San Francisco. She glanced only once in Wong Fong's direction. She hoped that, after today, she would never have to see the man again.

Watching the trial of Wong Fong was immensely satisfying, but she couldn't have been more surprised when Attorney Herrington announced, "I have brought Kum Quai today. She will be her own witness and testify of the advent of her marriage."

The courtroom erupted into speculation, and sure enough, moments later Kum Quai walked into the courtroom. She was escorted by another woman, who Dolly later learned was Herrington's sister. Kum Quai wore an American dress, but a veil covered both her short hair and her face, so Dolly couldn't see the young woman's eyes.

Dolly knew that if she could get a good look at Kum Quai, she could get a sense of what was going on in her mind.

"We need an interpreter," the justice of the peace said.

At that moment, Dr. Gardner, an official government interpreter, stood.

Dolly wanted to clap, since an interpreter would give Kum Quai a better understanding of what was truly happening at the court. Instead, Dolly clasped her hands together as Dr. Gardner offered his services.

"May I ask the witness Kum Quai a question?" Dr. Gardner asked the judge.

"You may," the judge replied.

Dr. Gardner turned to face Kum Quai, and, before the entire court, he asked, "Do you have a *chuck-jee?*"

A *chuck-jee* was a legal registration card, and Dolly leaned forward in her seat so that she wouldn't miss out on a single word from the veiled Kum Quai.

"I do not," Kum Quai said. "No *chuck-jee.*"

Perhaps not everyone in the courtroom understood the significance of this admission, but it was made clear when Dr. Gardner said, "Then I place you under arrest in the name of the United States government."

Protests rang out from the audience, but what they didn't know was that Kum Quai would now be protected under federal jurisdiction and separated from her captors.

Red in the face, Herrington leapt to his feet and raised his hands for quiet. When the courtroom had settled enough for Herrington to speak to the judge, he said, "My client needs to wait outside the courtroom. This is very distressing. My sister will stay with her, since they have become attached these past few weeks. The women can wait in the comfort and shade of the buggy."

"Motion granted," the judge said.

Dolly's pulse thudded as Kum Quai was once again led up the aisle. Dolly didn't like this turn of events at all. Her gaze caught Dr. Gardner's, and he rose, apparently thinking the same thing, along with Dr. Hall.

Soon, Dr. Gardner and Attorney Herrington returned to the courtroom to continue the trial proceedings. Dr. Hall remained with the women, guarding them. Dolly was itching to leave too, but she had to find out the final judgment against Wong Fong.

When Herrington left the courtroom unannounced, Dolly wondered where he could be going. The answer came moments later when Dr. Hall came running into the courtroom. "He's fleeing with the women!"

The courtroom erupted into action, and Dr. Gardner was out the door first. Dolly arrived in time to see Gardner and Hall pursuing the fleeing buggy in Hall's sulky.

More men untied horses and urged their buggies and hacks into pursuit. In his haste, Herrington took a side road that was blocked by a padlocked gate.

Dolly picked up her skirts and ran down the road with a crowd of people. She couldn't tell what exactly was going on until the crowd parted enough for her to see Herrington's buggy returning to the courthouse. Dr. Gardner rode at their side, his hand holding the reins of the horses, steering the party.

The crowd shifted, allowing Dr. Gardner to pull up to the courthouse. He alighted from the sulky and said, "Attorney Herrington and his sister are now under arrest. I'm placing Miss Kum Quai in custody of Donaldina Cameron under federal mandate."

Dolly gave up on holding back her tears, and as soon as Kum Quai alighted from the buggy, they embraced. Finally, Dolly had her daughter back. Finally, Kum Quai was free.

CHAPTER FIFTEEN

"In the summer of 1899, a ship sailing from Hong Kong to San Francisco had had two cases of plague on board. Because of this, although no passengers were ill when the ship reached San Francisco, it was to be quarantined on Angel Island. When the boat was searched, 11 stowaways were found—the next day two were missing. Their bodies were later found in the Bay, and autopsy showed they contained plague bacilli. Despite this scare, there was no immediate outbreak of disease. But rats from the ship probably had something to do with the epidemic that hit San Francisco nine months later."

—"Bubonic Plague Hits San Francisco: 1900–1909," PBS.org

1900

Dolly set the newspaper on the table and looked at the gathered staff members, which included the interpreters, part-time staff, and Mrs. Field. Everyone's expression was somber because they had all heard the rumors. "The rumors are true," Dolly said. "The bubonic plague has spread and taken root in Chinatown."

Yuen Qui gasped. "What will happen?"

Ah Cheng rose from the table. She walked to the kitchen window and gazed outside, her hands set firmly on her hips.

"More of what's been happening over the past year," Dolly said. "But full quarantine this time. Of the entire Chinatown."

"It's best for everyone," Mrs. Field said, her lips pulled into a thin line. "They have to stop the spread of the disease somehow."

Ah Cheng turned from the window. "They tried that in Hawaii, and what happened?"

"They burned homes and shops." Dolly folded her arms against the chill pricking her skin. "Yet it still didn't stop the plague from spreading."

"Until there is a better solution, this is the only choice." Mrs. Field clasped her hands atop the table. "And don't get any foolish notions of continuing rescues. You'll only put the rest of us at risk." With her gaze focused on Dolly, it was no secret whom Mrs. Field was addressing. She rose from her chair as if she were putting a stop to the conversation. No one spoke as she left the room.

Dolly watched the woman go. Yes, there would be more risk involved . . .

The mission home had already stopped all visits from sponsors and donors. Visits gave the chance for the girls to show off their talents, including singing and recitations. The donations were often generous following a performance. The quietness of the mission home had been unsettling.

"She might be right," Yuen Qui said in a tentative voice.

"Should we turn down pleas for help?" Ah Cheng asked.

This was not a question for Dolly, even if Mrs. Field might disagree. Dolly met the gazes of her two interpreters. "We will do as we've always done," she said in a firm tone. "We will find a way around any obstacles."

"I will go," a voice said from the kitchen doorway.

Dolly turned to see Tien. The girl had become a young woman now. Her legs were longer, her eyes bigger, her curves softer. But she was still much too young to go on rescues. There was too much potential risk that she would draw the attention of the tong in the wrong way.

Yuen Qui smiled at the girl. "Thank you for the offer, Tien. Right now, we don't know what kind of help we'll need. We don't know how the plague will affect us all."

Tien's face reddened, and Dolly worried that the girl felt affronted. But Yuen Qui had a way with Tien and brought out her softer side.

"But if we need you, we'd be happy for your help," Yuen Qui continued.

At this, Tien gave a satisfied nod, then left the doorway. Without a sound. As always.

Dolly exhaled. "Well, it appears that not everyone at the mission home is afraid of the plague."

Her own words haunted her a few days later when a young girl, no more than nine years old, arrived on their doorstep.

Dolly was preparing to scout the streets and find out which areas in Chinatown were in quarantine, when she opened the door to discover Leung Kum Ching. At least that's what Dolly deciphered through the girl's hysterical sobs.

Dolly drew the crying girl into the house and shut the door. Ah Cheng appeared almost immediately. Mrs. Field didn't even open her office door to investigate.

"You need to take deep breaths," Ah Cheng said, placing her hands on the girl's shoulders. "Tell me what is wrong."

In between broken sobs, Leung Kum Ching said, "My sister is dying. Our owners left her on the street to die. They say she has the plague, but she doesn't have all the symptoms."

Dolly met Ah Cheng's doubtful look over the girl's head. "Ask her how long her sister's been sick."

Ah Cheng asked the question, and Leung held up two fingers. "Two days. She will die if you do not come."

Dolly didn't need to know why Leung had come to the mission home for help. She could only assume that the Chinese healers were afraid the girl was sick with the plague, and therefore would have nothing to do with her.

Quarantines were in effect in most of Chinatown's neighborhoods. It broke Dolly's heart to know that anyone sick would be left outside to die.

Bodies had been reported hidden all over the city because people feared their homes being quarantined. Immunizations had been sent from the U.S. Surgeon General in Washington, D.C., but Chinese superstitions about being stuck with a needle they believed contained poison stopped most of them from getting immunized. Besides, some of the early vaccinations had caused several side effects, including fevers, pain, and even death.

Now, Dolly could see the hesitation in Ah Cheng's eyes.

"We must go," Dolly said in a quiet voice. "It doesn't sound like the plague, so maybe we can help her."

Ah Cheng pursed her lips, but she nodded all the same.

Dolly grasped the young girl's hand, then told Ah Cheng, "Ask her on which street we'll find her sister."

Dolly couldn't conceal her height, but she brought a cotton umbrella and dressed in dark colors to be less conspicuous as the late afternoon light settled over the city, throwing orange-gold patterns on the walls of the buildings.

With another staff member feeding Leung, Dolly and Ah Cheng headed down Sacramento Street and turned on Sutter. The location given to them was in the heart of Chinatown, and Dolly knew she would have to be creative to get around the barriers. But when she reached the next street, she stopped. New barricades had been set up, and guards were stationed in front of them.

Without clearance from the Board of Health, Dolly couldn't get past them, especially to fetch a sick girl. She turned to Ah Cheng, and the woman nodded, already knowing what Dolly was thinking.

The pair of them hurried in the opposite direction, not meeting anyone's eyes as they traveled, until they reached an herbal shop run by a man whom Dolly knew. His wife used to live at the mission home.

When the herbalist opened his door, Ah Cheng quickly explained what they needed.

He asked a few questions about the symptoms they'd been told about by

Leung. Then he waved them inside. "You can go up here." He pointed to an opening in the roof that let in light from the sky.

Dolly looked up at the skylight. It would have to do.

The herbalist brought over a stool, and, with a boost from Ah Cheng, Dolly climbed through the skylight and arrived on the roof. When Ah Cheng joined her, they thanked the herbalist and said they hoped to return soon.

He nodded, and then Dolly scanned the rooftops of Chinatown, determining where they needed to go. "Come," she told Ah Cheng.

The interpreter kept up as they scurried along the rooftops and leapt from one building to another. Fortunately, the housing was so congested that leaping from house to house wasn't too hard.

But as they neared the neighborhood, they would have to find a place to jump down. Dolly eyed their choices and finally settled on a narrow alley. Its walls were made of protruding bricks, and Dolly knew she could use them to scale down until she could jump to the ground. How would she return this way with a sick little girl, though?

"Over here." Ah Cheng pointed to a skylight on the next rooftop over.

Dolly followed. The women pried up the skylight and descended into a shop. No one was about, and they unlocked the door from the inside, then slipped into an alley.

The alley was bathed in twilight shadows, and Dolly had to ignore the hairs standing up on her neck. No place was safe for women after dark in Chinatown. But it was too late to seek the help of the police. Besides, not even the squad members most loyal to her cause wanted to risk exposure to the plague.

Without a word, Dolly led the way through the alley until they connected with Commercial Street. She used her cotton umbrella to keep her face hidden away from curious onlookers and, more importantly, the white guards or police officers. She was familiar enough with the street that she knew which tenement building Leung had been referring to.

When Dolly saw the young girl lying across three wooden chairs, curled up like a rag doll, she rushed to her side. Dolly knelt beside the girl and placed a hand on her shoulder. Her body was still warm. A good sign.

Ah Cheng knelt on the other side of the girl and leaned close. "We are here to help you," she said in soft Chinese.

The girl didn't stir. Dolly guessed her to be about eleven or twelve, although she was severely undersized. Dolly rested a hand on her forehead. Her skin felt cool to the touch, but still she didn't move or wake up.

"Let's take her to the mission home," Dolly said. "From there we can call the Board of Health." She scooped the little girl into her arms. They returned to the skylight, and with both Ah Cheng and Dolly working together, they were able to climb through it with the girl. Once they reached the herbalist's shop, night had fallen over Chinatown, pierced with glowing lights.

Leung was waiting just inside the door of the mission home when they arrived with her sister.

"Don't touch her until we know what's going on," Dolly immediately said, and Ah Cheng translated.

They settled her onto the couch in the parlor, and Tien took it upon herself to make sure everyone stayed away from the room.

"Mrs. Field wants to see you," Tien told Dolly.

For an instant their gazes connected, and Dolly knew Tien was not happy about the request.

Dolly needed to use the office telephone anyway, so if she had to deal with Mrs. Field at the same time, so be it.

"What are you doing?" Mrs. Field said the moment Dolly walked into the office. The woman's eyes seemed to be on fire. "If that girl is sick, you've just given the entire mission home a death sentence."

Dolly clasped her hands tightly in front of her. "I am calling the Board of Health right now, and I will follow their advice. No one needs to touch her except me."

Dolly could see the argument in the director's gaze, but Dolly wasn't about to back down.

"If the girl has the plague, I will see to it that you're dismissed," Mrs. Field said. "Are you ready to take that risk?"

"I am," Dolly said, keeping her voice steady.

Mrs. Field turned on her heel and strode out of the room, leaving silent disapproval in her wake.

Dolly crossed to the desk and telephoned the Board of Health. Thankfully, the doctor who answered the phone was much calmer than Dolly felt. "I'll send an ambulance to 920," he said. "You can come with the little girl, and we'll do our best to help her."

Dolly thanked him, then hung up and wiped at the new tears in her eyes. Next, she hurried into the parlor to tell Ah Cheng and Leung the good news.

Leung pleaded to come, but Dolly told her that she didn't want her around more sick people. Besides, Dolly knew there was a risk of Leung being taken away or quarantined. Dolly wrapped an arm about the girl's shoulders. "I'll be back as soon as I can."

Ah Cheng translated, and Leung threw her arms around Dolly's legs. She patted the girl's head, already feeling a great deal of affection toward this child.

When the ambulance showed up, Dolly bundled the sick little girl into it. The ride to the house at Jackson Street in the dark seemed agonizingly slow, but once they arrived, they were ushered inside without delay. The same doctor she had spoken to on the phone led her to one of the rooms set aside for examination.

As the lights cast a warm glow about the room, Dolly silently prayed, telling herself that everything would be fine. The doctor would know what to do. She gripped her hands together as she watched the doctor check for signs of bubonic plague, then press down on various areas of the girl's body. When the little girl cried out as the doctor pressed on the right side of her stomach, he lifted his hands, then looked over at Dolly.

"It appears that she has acute appendicitis," he said in a quiet tone.

Dolly's mouth went dry. Her mother had died from appendicitis. Perhaps medical science had advanced enough to treat this little girl. "What can be done? Will she need surgery?"

The doctor hesitated. "It's too far advanced, I'm afraid."

Dolly stepped away from the examination table and sank into a nearby chair. "No," she whispered.

"I'm very sorry." The doctor's voice held compassion and regret.

His kind words could not prevent the pain for the little girl waiting at the mission home for news of her sister. "What . . . can I do?" Dolly asked.

The doctor rubbed at his face, then sighed. "We'll move her to one of the other rooms with a more comfortable bed. I'm afraid she won't last more than a day or two. Perhaps bring her sister to say good-bye to her?"

"Yes," Dolly murmured, numbness spreading through her. "I will bring Leung."

The doctor nodded, then picked up the little girl and carried her to another room, where he laid her on a clean bed.

Dolly followed and helped to adjust the covers. "I'm very sorry," she whispered, resting a hand gently on the little girl's forehead. "I'll bring your sister so you can be together."

The child didn't respond.

"The ambulance can take you back," the doctor offered.

Dolly nodded and rose to her feet. Facing Leung with this news was going to break both of their hearts.

The ride back to the mission home in the dark felt oppressive, as the night seemed to not only surround her but press its way into her heart. When she knocked softly on the front door, she waited for Ah Cheng to unlock all the bolts.

Leung stood just inside.

One look at the girl's tear-stained face only made Dolly's task seem more monumental. "Did the doctor see her?" Leung asked through Ah Cheng's translation.

"Yes," Dolly said, clasping the girl's hand. "Let's go sit down."

Ah Cheng followed them into the parlor, and Dolly sat on the sofa with Leung, still holding her hand.

The nine-year-old's dark eyes were so trusting, it made the news even harder to deliver. "Your sister is very, very sick," Dolly said, and Ah Cheng translated.

"Will she die?" Leung asked, her chin trembling.

"Yes," Dolly whispered.

Tears filled the girl's eyes.

The lump in Dolly's throat turned painful. "But you still have time to tell her good-bye."

"I don't want to say good-bye."

"I know." Dolly pulled the little girl close, and Leung moved onto her lap. Dolly rested her chin atop her newly shampooed hair, which was still damp. "When I was a young girl of five years old, my mother got very sick too with the same disease as your sister."

Leung lifted her face, her eyes wide. "Did she die too?"

"She did," Dolly said, her throat hitching. "But she is in a very lovely place now called heaven. She will never be sick again, and she's always happy."

"Oh." Leung blinked slowly. "That sounds nice. My sister will like that. Are there flowers there? My sister loves flowers."

Tears burned in Dolly's own eyes. "Yes, I believe there are flowers in heaven. Your sister will be very happy, and she will miss you too. But you won't have to worry about her being sick anymore."

Leung tightened her hold on Dolly.

Dolly ran her hand over the little girl's back, hoping to soothe her as much as possible.

Leung's next words were mature beyond her years. "I will tell my sister where she's going. I will tell her how beautiful heaven is."

Dolly had to smile, although fresh tears had started. "Do you want me to come with you to say good-bye to your sister?"

Leung nodded emphatically.

"Then I will come," Dolly said.

Ah Cheng reached for Leung's hand. "I will come too."

CHAPTER SIXTEEN

"I was kidnapped in China and brought over here. The man who kidnapped me sold me for four hundred dollars to a San Francisco slave-dealer; and he sold me here for seventeen hundred dollars. I have been a brothel slave ever since. I saw the money paid down and am telling the truth. I was deceived by the promise I was going to marry a rich and good husband, or I should have never come here."

—Testimony of Paper Daughter, 1892

1903

Click.

The night was not yet over, but the tong leader Zhang Wei had already left Mei Lien's room. The sound of the door shutting behind him echoed in her mind. Had others in the house heard him leave? Had Ah-Peen Oie?

Mei Lien didn't know if she had pleased him. It had been different with Zhang Wei. There had been no caring, no gentleness, no tender words. In fact, he'd spoken very little. And when he left, tears slid down her cheeks. She was no innocent, not after Huan Sun. But the difference between the two men made her feel as if she'd betrayed Huan Sun. She had crossed an irreversible line, and she'd betrayed herself. Betrayed her soul.

From the deep purple outside her window, she guessed that dawn was still hours away. Sleep would not come, she knew. Climbing out of bed, she located the pearl bracelet, then slipped it on. Curling up on her side, she pulled on her blanket, then rested her cheek on the pearl beads. This was how she would sleep, remembering Huan Sun—the man who had cared about her. Who had seemed sorrowful to leave her.

Click.

Mei Lien opened her eyes, wondering if Zhang Wei was back. Perhaps he had merely gone to fetch food and water?

But the figure walking into her room was too small to be Zhang Wei.

"Ah-Peen Oie," Mei Lien murmured and rose from the bed.

She didn't get very far because Ah-Peen Oie brought a switch down on the side of her face.

Mei Lien fell back with a cry. Her cheek stung, and she wouldn't be surprised if blood had been drawn. But Ah-Peen Oie wasn't finished.

Mei Lien tried to ward off the blows from the switch, but Ah-Peen Oie's strength and ferocity were unmatchable.

Turning away from the violence, Mei Lien shielded her face. The blows kept coming, striking her arms, her shoulders, her torso, her hips.

"Stop," Mei Lien cried. "I did nothing wrong. He came to me."

Ah-Peen Oie screamed something in her fury, but Mei Lien couldn't understand the words through her seething pain.

So this was her punishment. And this was her life. Assault, opium, men, fading memories of her home and family.

When Ah-Peen Oie finished, Mei Lien didn't even hear her shut the door because her mind was numb. She felt nothing. Thought nothing. She was nothing.

Three days passed.

At least, she thought it had been three days. Mei Lien didn't move for hours, and when she finally did, it was to find that her water was mostly gone. No food had been left in her room. And her door was locked from the outside.

As that first day slipped into night, then morning again, no food or water was brought. And her door remained locked.

When Mei Lien heard voices in the corridor, she called out for answers, for help, for food, for drink. No one replied.

She used the hidden stash of opium to calm her headaches and shaking for a few hours. But the reprieve was much too short, and she huddled on the floor, unable to stand.

By the third morning, Mei Lien decided that it was better this way. Curled up on the floor, her stomach clenched tight, her headache screaming, she decided that death would be a better option than this . . . than any of this. She supposed she was lucky that Ah-Peen Oie hadn't kicked her out of the house onto the streets. Or perhaps that would have been merciful.

Mei Lien could only hope that her mother was doing well. It was all that Mei Lien could wish for right now. She knew she could never earn back her contract. Ah-Peen Oie would make certain of that. Mei Lien shouldn't have been surprised when Ah-Peen Oie entered her room and told her, "You will be sold to another owner. You have a quarter of an hour to make yourself presentable."

Someone else had entered the room behind the mistress—one of the kitchen girls—and set some water and rice on the bureau.

"No," Mei Lien croaked out, but Ah-Peen Oie had already left.

The door shut, and Mei Lien was left alone again. She could smell the rice, and her throat begged for water. Crawling, she reached the bureau, then pulled herself up on unsteady legs. She probably ate too fast, but she couldn't get enough. After drinking all the water, she was still hungry and thirsty, but she wasn't shaking as badly.

She couldn't be sold. She couldn't stay here, either. Time was running out. Would the owner come into her room? Or would she be forced into the banquet room?

Mei Lien sank onto the unkempt bed. What did it matter where she lived? Or worked? Huan Sun wasn't coming back. And she would never be able to put off a member of the tong such as Zhang Wei. Someone rapped on her door, and Mei Lien flinched.

"They are coming up," a soft voice said. The kitchen girl.

Was it time already?

Mei Lien rushed to change her clothing. A glance in the tiny mirror told her that she still had deep bruises showing from the switch. She combed through her hair, then twisted it back. Next, she put on a silk dress; then she straightened the coverlet on her bed. She wanted nothing from the bedroom except for the pearl bracelet. Everything else would be too hard to conceal.

She was ready when Ah-Peen Oie entered the room with another man. The Chinese man was thin, but his sharp eyes missed nothing. Would he find her bruising and thinness repulsive?

Moments after looking at her, he turned to Ah-Peen Oie. "I don't want a troublemaker."

"She has learned her lesson," Ah-Peen Oie said.

The Chinese man walked over to Mei Lien. She tried not to draw away. Getting out of this house was a must. And she didn't want to give this man any reason to leave without her. When he walked around her, Mei Lien didn't move.

Finally, he negotiated a price for Mei Lien, and moments later, she was walking out of the house with him. The morning sun was bright, and Mei Lien had to squint against the light as her new owner led her to a buggy. The smells and sounds of the busy street assailed her senses. It had been months since she had been outside, and she didn't know what to look at first.

The man ushered her into the buggy, and almost immediately it set off down the street.

Mei Lien peered out the window at the shops, the people, a dog running alongside a boy, the food stalls . . . all that she had been missing. And where would this new owner take her? Into another house? Or worse?

The buggy slowed at a corner, then passed a tailoring shop. The Chinese lettering was yellow, bold, and seemed to be shouting at her. She knew it wasn't Huan Sun's shop, but it reminded her of him. How was he doing? Had he recovered his money? Of course not. Zhang Wei would have made sure of that. He didn't want the competition. For *her*.

Another corner, another shop, more people, more sounds and smells . . . and life.

Mei Lien had no life. She was a slave of the worst kind. Her life was no longer her own to live, and if she never saw her mother again, what did anything else matter? She was now away from the clutches and control of Ah-Peen Oie, only to be thrust at a new owner.

Glancing over at the Chinese man, Mei Lien moved as close as she could to the door of the buggy. Only a single latch separated her from the streets. From freedom. She might die on the streets if she escaped, but perhaps that would be a better fate anyway. Or she could try to find Huan Sun's place. Beg him for mercy to hide her. Would he be able to get her back on a steamship to Hong Kong?

The buggy slowed to go around another corner, and Mei Lien's hand found its way to the door latch. She didn't think, didn't plan, she only acted. Pushing down the latch, she opened the door and jumped.

She landed hard on the cobblestones, and after rolling a couple of times with the momentum of the impact, she scrambled to her feet. Sure enough, the buggy had drawn to a halt, and she heard yelling from her new owner.

Mei Lien looked left, then right. She had no time to decide where to run. Nothing was familiar to her. She picked an alley across the street and headed for that.

"Stop her!" the man yelled after her.

Mei Lien didn't slow; she didn't look for any other options. She only ran toward the alley. Once between the buildings, she continued pounding along the street until she found herself in a courtyard filled with plants and statues. She saw a ladder leading up to the rooftop.

Her hands trembled against the rungs as she climbed the ladder, and she missed a step and almost fell. But finally she reached the top. Turning, she wrenched the ladder away from the wall and pushed it over. The owner came into the courtyard, saw her, and screamed, "You will pay twice for this."

Mei Lien ran across the rooftop. She jumped to another roof and kept running. Tears streaked her face, and her heart beat faster than a rabbit's, making her wonder if it would give out, but she didn't care. She had never felt this free in her life. If these were the last moments of her life, she would spend them running, leaping, and hoping.

When Mei Lien tripped, she tumbled against the rooftop. For a breathless moment, she didn't move. Everything throbbed, and her knees and hands stung. But there were no sounds of pursuit, no footsteps chasing, and no one screaming at her to stop. Only the sounds of the city below.

She pushed herself into a sitting position and looked about. The wind and the sun were her only companions. She was alone at last.

Remaining on the roof, she pulled her knees to her chest. With the sun upon her head, she closed her eyes and focused on catching her breath. The air was cool and moist and clean, and for a moment, she imagined herself back in her Hong Kong home. With her mother. Taking a break from their labors.

Perhaps she was having tea with her mother, and they were sharing stories of their day. They would laugh at something, they would reminisce about the past with smiles, they would know only happiness.

The clouds came hours later, and Mei Lien remained on the roof although she was so hungry, she could have eaten dirt. When the drops of rain started, slow at first, then increasing in tempo, she looked about for shelter. Nothing on the rooftop.

Curling tighter into herself, she tried to return her mind to the pleasant things of home. But the cold rain pinged against her neck, her cheeks, and her hair fell damp and lank about her shoulders. The shivering returned, both from the increasing cold and hunger, and from her having no supply of opium. At least the last three days of taking very small doses had helped the withdrawal symptoms.

When dark cloaked the city, Mei Lien moved to her feet. Her joints and limbs were stiff and aching, and she crept to the edge of the rooftop. Below, the number of people in the street had lessened, and some of the shops looked like they had closed. There was no sign of the slave owner's buggy. She watched a mangy dog trot along the street looking for scraps of food.

The hunger in the dog's eyes mirrored the hollow in Mei Lien's stomach. She felt completely empty. But she had no money and nothing to trade. Unless she wanted to go back into prostitution, she would have to find someone to take pity and hire her.

The rain continued, and Mei Lien found a place to climb off the roof. Huddling in an alley wasn't much warmer, but at least she wasn't getting rained on anymore. The cold only deepened. And then she had a thought. What if she sold one of the pearls from her bracelet?

With trembling fingers, she lifted her sleeve and slid the bracelet off. She was too exhausted to count the number of pearls, but one missing wouldn't make the piece any less beautiful.

She unclasped the bracelet, then worked the strand loose until she had disassembled the pearls. After slipping the rest of the pearls into her inner pocket of her damaged dress, she clutched a single pearl in her hand.

Walking out of the alley, she nearly bumped into a young boy.

He looked her up and down, then sneered a curse: "*Mui tsai!*"

Mei Lien felt singed to the core. The first time she had been called that on the wharf of Hong Kong, she'd been disgusted. This time, it was true.

"Where is the nearest boardinghouse?" she asked the boy.

He stared at her as if he hadn't understood her Chinese. Surely, he spoke some. When she asked again, he shook his head and took off running along the street. Trying to get away from her.

Mei Lien didn't dare call after him. Inky black had enveloped the street now. She would just have to follow any scents of cooking food. Putting one foot in front of the other, she walked along the edge of the street, keeping her eyes out for the slave owner, or even for Ah-Peen Oie.

Freedom so far was not what she had expected it to be. Freedom was full of fear. Freedom was riddled with hunger.

But Mei Lien had walked only a block when a hand grasped her and roughly pulled her inside a building.

CHAPTER SEVENTEEN

"The girls of the Presbyterian Mission have organized a Red Cross
Society. . . . We try to help the soldiers all we can by sewing for
them. And we always remember them in our prayers, because
we think that they are right and we know that God will help the
right. We are very glad that the American soldiers are not fighting
for land or money, but to make men free."

—Kum Yin, secretary of the Junior Red Cross Society, referring to the
Boxer Rebellion in China and the Spanish-American War

1900

The fog was little deterrent to Dolly as she and a few of the Chinese girls
boarded a streetcar on the morning of Ah Cheng's wedding. Dolly wanted
fresh flowers, and she was determined to get them at the wholesale market.
Mrs. Field had called it a waste, since the flowers would only die soon, but
Dolly said she would use her own salary to pay for them. Her relationship
with Mrs. Field was strained anyway, so at any complaint from the director,
Dolly would immediately find an alternate solution that Mrs. Field couldn't
object to.

Now, Leung and Jiao walked with her through the flower market, and
Dolly was gratified to see the smiles on their faces. With Jiao losing her
mother, Hong Leen, and saying good-bye to her brother, Kang, when he went

to a boys' school, then Leung losing her sister so recently, this outing was good for all of them. Soon, Dolly and her girls had armloads of white blooms, including roses, chrysanthemums, and dahlias.

After spending the rest of the morning decorating the chapel, their newly expanded meeting room, Dolly checked in the kitchen.

The wedding cake was cooling. Lonnie and the kitchen girls proudly showed off the Chinese pastries they had baked. Lonnie had been braver in the kitchen lately, and she had taken it upon herself to help Leung and Jiao learn how to bake. All was in place, and everything was turning out perfectly. So why did Dolly feel a sense of emptiness? Yes, she would miss Ah Cheng deeply, but Dolly was happy for her friend and fellow staff member.

Other rescued women had been married in the mission home, and the occasions had always brought Dolly joy and pride. But today . . . at over thirty years of age, she supposed that in most people's eyes she was too old to marry. She hadn't had much opportunity to meet men in social capacities, but she was truly fine with it. Mostly. She thought little of her first fiancé, and she didn't regret for a moment having come to San Francisco.

Yet . . . Dolly walked through the chapel alone while the others in the house were dressing or attending to preparations. She stopped by the vines and branches that arched into a bower where the bride and groom would soon stand and take their vows. The fragrant white flowers tucked into the greenery created a cocoon of lovely scents.

Dolly closed her eyes and breathed in the heavenly blooms. Alone for a few precious moments, she waited to feel the sorrow, the emptiness, and the loneliness grow bigger than her heart. After her first failed engagement, she had felt the solitude more acutely, especially when she saw young married couples. Their shared smiles and affection made her want to find a way to cut away her single status as if it were an inconvenient burr in her hair.

But now . . . she didn't feel the same way. There was no pressing weight on her chest. No burning ache of regret. What was different? Was it because she had so little time and energy to devote to her own contemplation? Or had *she* changed? Most nights she fell into bed too exhausted to think, let alone to dream, or to dwell on how she might never share a life with a husband. And on the nights that her sleep was interrupted with a call to another rescue, her hours were counted down until the next evening when she could catch up on sleep.

Yet, despite the unpredictability of her life and the many challenges she faced on a daily basis, her soul had been filled. The Lord had blessed her with happiness, and contentedness, peace, and love surrounded her at all turns. It brought her joy to see the Chinese girls and women blossom in the security and routine of the mission home. Even her relationship with Tien was moving forward to a greater light.

Laughter and the merriment of happy voices drifted down from the upper floors. The mission home was by no means a perfect place, but love existed between the walls, and peace was something within reach for all.

If the Lord wanted Dolly married, well, then, the man would have to come to her.

She was too busy to involve herself in situations that would take her long from the mission home. Of course, her sisters' letters continued to encourage her to keep looking, but they couldn't understand that Dolly was busy.

"A note for you," Lonnie said in her sweet voice, appearing at the doorway. She had already dressed in a new white outfit she had made herself. "From your sister Jessie."

Lonnie's proud expression told Dolly that she was happy to have been able to read the return address.

Dolly held out her hand, and Lonnie rushed forward, all eager smiles.

The letter was short and to the point, which only made Dolly laugh at the irony. Jessie had invited her to her home in Alhambra, near Pasadena, for a weekend visit. Her other sisters, Annie, Katherine, and Helen, frequently invited her to their homes, too. But in this letter, Jessie had made no secret that she thought the minister of their town congregation would be a great match for Dolly. Reverend Ben Bazatas was passionate about saving lives and souls—something Dolly could relate to. She had met the reverend on prior visits to Jessie's church, of course, but Jessie had never been so adamant before.

Dolly sighed and squeezed Lonnie's hand. "Thank you for bringing me the letter. I should go and check on Ah Cheng."

"Can I see the bride?" Lonnie asked in a hopeful tone. "Please, Mama?"

"If you are very well behaved," Dolly said.

Lonnie nodded her head so hard that her teeth snapped together.

"Come." Dolly led the way out of the room and up the stairs, wondering if Reverend Bazatas was even interested in her, or if the Lord just had a good sense of humor.

Whatever the case, Dolly's melancholy lifted by the time she reached Ah Cheng's room. The bride was beautiful in her white wedding gown.

"Look at you," Dolly said. "Jun Ling will be blushing before you reach him at the end of the aisle."

Ah Cheng's own face flushed at the comment. "Do you think I will please him?" Ever the modest Chinese woman, Ah Cheng still displayed some insecurities.

"He loves you," Dolly said. "You love him. Nothing else matters."

Ah Cheng nodded. Then her gaze dropped, and her mouth turned down.

"What is it?" Dolly asked in a quiet voice to prevent Lonnie from overhearing.

"Should I be wearing white?" Ah Cheng murmured.

Dolly's eyes burned. She knew Ah Cheng's question wasn't referring to the traditional red that Chinese women wore on their wedding days. The mission home provided white wedding gowns to its women in order to symbolize their purity. Whatever Chinese women had experienced during their captivity, their escape cleansed the old darkness and provided new life and new light.

"You, of all people, are the *purest* soul I know." Dolly pulled Ah Cheng close. "Jun Ling knows this, and *I* know this. You deserve to wear white as much as any other woman."

When Ah Cheng drew away, tears rimmed in her dark eyes. "Thank you."

"Now, a hundred guests are about to arrive," Dolly said with a watery smile. "And you will soon have an anxious groom downstairs who can't wait to see you. Where is your bouquet?"

Ah Cheng exhaled. "I think someone took it downstairs already. I left my bedroom for a few moments, and when I returned, it was gone."

Dolly frowned, looking about the room. "No one should have taken it. How long were you gone for?"

"Only a few minutes, but it's all right," Ah Cheng said. "If . . . if someone took it, I will go without."

Ah Cheng was an angel beyond anyone Dolly had ever known. She didn't want to think one of the girls had stolen the bride's bouquet, but a wedding day wasn't something that every woman and girl would celebrate. Some of them had deep wells of pain associated with their own weddings and the betrayal surrounding them. Or jealousy could also be a factor.

"I'll be right back," she told Ah Cheng.

"No, I'd rather you didn't reprimand anyone," Ah Cheng said. "Let it go."

Dolly paused. "I'll check one place, and if it's not there, I'll return immediately." She had a notion where the bouquet might be and who had taken it. She didn't want to be right, but if she was, she would rather deal with it now than have Ah Cheng face her wedding-aisle walk stripped of what was rightfully hers.

She hurried to Tien's bedroom and found the door locked. Dolly knocked softly, and when no one answered, she said through the door, "It's Miss Cameron, Tien. Can you open the door for a moment? I need to speak with you about something important."

A moment later, she heard a shuffling sound. Then the lock turned.

Tien opened the door a crack. "I'm sick."

And perhaps she was, but Dolly said, "We need your help with Ah Cheng's wedding."

Tien's eyes widened. "Why?"

"We need you to be in charge of the ledger where the guests will sign their names," Dolly said. "Not all the guests will sign their names because they might not know how to write. You can ask them their name, then write it down."

Tien's brows pulled together. "What if I spell something wrong?"

"I'll look at the names afterward with you and see if there should be corrections," Dolly said. "But you are the only one I can trust with this. Can you come now?"

Tien hesitated.

"You get ready, and I'll see you downstairs very soon." Dolly stepped back from the door, hoping that she had done the right thing, and that now Tien would do the right thing. "Oh, and if you've seen Ah Cheng's bouquet, can you make sure it gets back to her bedroom? We're nearly ready to start."

Tien wouldn't meet her gaze, but it didn't matter. Dolly had done what she could, and in the process perhaps they would all learn something today. Sometimes the most joyful moments for one person brought on deep pain for another.

Dolly made her way along the corridor, then paused before Kum Quai's door. Today, Dolly knew, the young woman would have troubled feelings about her own forced wedding. Dolly tapped on the door, and when Kum Quai answered, sure enough, tears stained her face.

"Oh, my dear," Dolly said as she pulled the young woman into her arms.

Kum Quai knew very little English, but there was no language barrier in an embrace.

Dolly held her for several moments until Kum Quai drew away, a smile on her face despite the tears. "Thank you, *Lo Mo*," she whispered.

Dolly kissed the top of her head; then, with assurance from Kum Quai, Dolly continued downstairs, where she waited with the others for Ah Cheng to appear. When she did, she was radiant. And she was carrying her bouquet.

The festivities were all that Dolly could hope for, and the guests loved the wedding. Dolly kept an eye on Tien, who took her task with the guest ledger very seriously. Although Tien wouldn't look at or acknowledge Dolly, likely due to her embarrassment, Dolly was pleased. She could see so much potential in Tien, and Dolly only hoped that one day, the girl blossoming into a young woman would see it too.

The next morning's staff meeting was delayed an hour so that everyone could get extra rest. It was strange not having Ah Cheng present, but Yuen Qui was a clever, bright woman who would fill Ah Cheng's shoes nicely.

All eyes turned on Mrs. Field as she entered the dining room. She was late, and Dolly found that unusual. She hadn't been part of the wedding cleanup, but had retired to her room early.

"I am finished," Mrs. Field said, standing at the head of the table.

Dolly furrowed her brows. "Finished with what?"

"I will be turning in my resignation within the hour." Mrs. Field then stepped back from the table and left the dining room.

Dolly stared after her. None of the staff members spoke.

Yuen Qui was the first to recover. "What happened?"

Dolly met the woman's deep brown eyes. "I have no idea. Should I go after her? Perhaps the wedding wore her out, and she's not thinking clearly."

The edges of Yuen Qui's mouth moved upward. "I think it is time, Miss Cameron."

"Time for what?"

Yuen Qui looked over at the other staff members, who nodded.

"Miss Culbertson wanted you to be the director here," Yuen Qui continued in a quiet voice. "We have all been patient under Mrs. Field for three years. Are *you* ready, Miss Cameron, to assume the position?"

Dolly could barely comprehend that Mrs. Field had notified them of her resignation. Mrs. Browne had recently resigned from the board as well. And now this? Dolly thought of the changes to her routine that would happen if she took on the directorship, the additional work and responsibility for much more.

Now, Dolly looked from Yuen Qui to the other staff members and saw only confidence in their gazes. Dolly took careful, measured breaths as her heart rhythm mimicked that of a fluttering bird's wings. "All right," she said. "If you're sure, then I'll speak to the board."

A half laugh escaped Yuen Qui, and she rose from her chair and hurried to embrace Dolly. Soon Dolly was embracing each of the staff members in turn.

"I've no doubt the board will approve." Yuen Qui wiped the tears from her face. "The girls will be delighted."

The scuff of footsteps coming from the far side of the dining room drew Dolly's attention, and she looked over to see Tien in the doorway. When their gazes connected, Tien gave her a hard stare, then turned away. Perhaps not everyone would be happy about her new commitment.

Dolly could hardly believe she was willing to take this step herself. She had been at the mission home almost six years, and each year, her feet became more firmly planted on this corner of 920 Sacramento Street. And each year, she forgot bit by bit whatever dreams she might have had before arriving on that foggy morning in 1895. At the mission home, she'd found a new path and a different family—both unexpected and lovely.

Yuen Qui broke up the circle. "Come, let's tell the girls in the kitchen. They will be over the moon."

Dolly touched Yuen Qui's arm. "I need to speak to the board first before we can make an announcement, but today, let's skip classes. I'll take a few of the girls on an outing so we can enjoy the weather."

Yuen Qui smiled. "Which girls?"

"Whoever is on kitchen duty today." Dolly knew that would include Tien, but who knew if the girl would agree to the outing if Yuen Qui wasn't involved?

When they reached the kitchen, several girls were working to prepare breakfast for all the residents, but Tien was nowhere to be found.

Yuen Qui clapped her hands together, and the girls in the kitchen turned to look. "Miss Cameron has an announcement, everyone."

Dolly met the gazes of the girls, her eyes landing on Lonnie, who was peeling fruit at the far table. "Today after breakfast, we'll take an excursion. Perhaps a ride on the ferry to Oakland. Who would like to go?"

Every hand shot up, and a couple of the girls giggled.

Lonnie rushed to Dolly, never one to hold back her emotions, and wrapped her arms about Dolly's waist. "Thank you, Mama."

As soon as breakfast preparations had been completed and the meal served, Dolly left the mission home with eight little girls in tow, including Leung, Jiao, and Dong Ho. Lonnie insisted on being one who held her hand as they headed for the ferry. Wispy white clouds meandered across the sky, and the sun provided the perfect amount of warmth.

The ferry was nearly full by the time Dolly embarked with her group, and there wasn't room for everyone to sit. She was happy to stand at the railing with a few of the girls, Lonnie among them. As they pulled away from the shore, Dolly watched the happenings of the busy city—the sea vessels coming and going, the dock workers, the tourists, the horses and buggies.

The breeze tugged at Dolly's hair beneath her hat as she inhaled the scent of salt and brine. Seagulls screeched nearby, and one of the girls giggled at a brave seagull that landed within a couple of feet of her. Dolly scanned the landscape as they passed it, thinking of her next steps in life. Was she truly prepared to become the director? Would she rise to the occasion and be able to keep everything in balance? Her sisters already told her she worked too hard, and at times Dolly agreed. But when one had a passion, it was hard to not delve in. And the work of the mission home had become a passion.

She thought of the director assignment from all angles, but it came down to two things: Miss Culbertson's belief in her before she died, and the warm assurance that kept pricking her skin. *Yes,* it said. *You are prepared.*

That assurance didn't mean she wasn't nervous or intimidated. It meant that she could put one step forward, followed by another. She could only do her best. And if the Lord wanted her to be an instrument in this work, then she would rely on Him to make up for her weaknesses.

She didn't know the exact number of girls who had been rescued by the mission home so far, but she knew in her heart that there were many more out there. Perhaps some were inside the very buildings she could see from the ferry. Those girls needed to be her focus, not money or other distracting things in life. She would forget herself and go to work.

"Mama." Lonnie tugged at Dolly's skirt. "What would the mission do without me?"

Dolly held back a laugh and gave the question serious consideration. "I don't know what the mission would do," she told the bright-eyed girl. Pulling Lonnie close, Dolly added, "But I know *I* couldn't do without you."

"It's my turn to stand by Mama," Jiao said.

Lonnie reluctantly moved over, and Dolly smiled. Jiao hadn't forgotten her mother, Hong Leen, but that didn't stop her from calling Dolly mama. Dolly wrapped an arm about Jiao's shoulders, and the girl leaned her sun-warmed head against Dolly's hip.

"How long until we get there, Mama?" Lonnie asked.

"Very soon," Dolly said for the benefit of all the girls.

Dolly felt the watchful eyes of the other passengers upon her and her little troupe, but she didn't mind. It might be unusual to see a white woman with a group of Chinese girls, all of whom called her mama, but Dolly only smiled when inquisitive glances were sent her way.

As they neared Oakland, Lonnie pointed to the harbor. Beyond, trees interspersed with buildings and homes followed the curve of the hills. "There it is."

"You remembered." Dolly ran her hand over Lonnie's braid. "What should we do first?"

"Excuse me, ma'am," someone said behind her.

Dolly turned to see a middle-aged woman wearing a lavender hat set upon her elaborate pompadour. Her clothing was cut in a stylish fashion that told Dolly she was likely a tourist from the East. The woman's blue eyes were curious. "Are all of these little girls yours?"

Her tone wasn't spiteful in the least, but Dolly was sure this question was on everyone's minds on the ferry, at least among those who were close enough to overhear the group.

"Yes, they are," Dolly said.

The woman glanced at the upturned faces of the girls, who had heard the interchange. The woman touched a hand to her throat. "All of them?" she asked in a quieter voice.

"All of them," Dolly clarified, and she shared a smile with Lonnie, who grasped her hand as if to claim her mama.

The woman's brows rose. "You . . . are so young to . . ." Her words cut off, and she gave Dolly a tremulous smile. "Well." She turned then and walked to her seat.

Dolly reclaimed her place at the rail, surrounded on both sides by her Chinese daughters. At that moment, she knew, despite blood or skin color, these girls were her own. And she was a mother after all.

The breeze dried her tears before they could spill, and her heart soared with the escaping seagulls as they neared Oakland.

Today would be a joyous day, and tonight, she would likely have an answer from the board about her future. Tomorrow, Dolly would begin the transition.

She didn't sleep that night—couldn't. The board had agreed to meet with her the following afternoon, and Dolly had gone through a list of names in her mind of people who could assume the majority of her current duties.

Frances P. Thompson was at the top of the list. As a frequent volunteer at the mission home, Frances had proved trustworthy, and the girls were fond of her.

By the time the birds were chattering outside her window with dawn's arrival, Dolly was already up and dressed. She had penned a note to Frances, and as Dolly opened her bedroom door, she was met with the sight of one of the girls curled up on the floor, sound asleep.

Dolly crouched down and tapped the girl's arm. "Lonnie," she whispered. "What are you doing on the floor?"

Lonnie opened her dark eyes. "I wanted to tell you something."

Dolly held back a chuckle. "Couldn't it have waited until the sun was up?"

At that moment, Lonnie yawned, then she rose and snuggled against Dolly. "We need to give you a Chinese name."

"Oh?" Dolly pulled the girl into her arms and breathed in Lonnie's sleepy warm scent.

Lonnie yawned again. "We will call you *Lo Mo.*"

Dolly tightened her hold. Kum Quai had called her *Lo Mo*, and now with Lonnie saying it too, Dolly had never been so honored in her life.

"Whatever you wish, Yoke Lon," Dolly said in a tremulous voice, using the girl's Chinese name.

Lonnie's smile was huge.

"Now, let's get you back to bed," Dolly said. "Today is an important day, and you need your rest."

"Why is it important?" Lonnie asked.

Dolly held back a secret smile and drew the girl up by her dainty hand. "You will find out this afternoon."

The day sped by, and Frances's reply came an hour before the board arrived. She would be pleased to take up the position of the new housekeeper. By the time Dolly joined the board, her nerves were buzzing with anticipation, but she felt a confidence that could only be explained as coming from the Creator.

They met in the chapel, and Dolly walked to the front of the room. Nerves danced along her skin as she stood in front of everyone, hands clasped together.

"You might have already guessed what I'm about to say," she began. "I wanted everyone to know that I haven't made this decision lightly, or just because Mrs. Field resigned. I've been thinking about it for years—truly, since Miss Culbertson asked me to consider it."

She scanned the faces smiling back at her. Several of the ladies nodded their encouragement. Dolly felt overwhelmed by the support and love in their eyes, especially coming from the women who had championed the mission home in all ways. These women had volunteered countless hours raising funds, petitioning lawmakers, spreading the message of tolerance, educating the deprived. "I've come to request the position of the director of the mission home, with your blessing, of course. If you've found another, I'll be happy to continue on as an assistant."

"There is no other," the president said immediately. "I move that we vote now. All in favor?"

The unanimous ayes that echoed through the room made Dolly feel as if her entire body had been infused with warmth and light. She was not alone in this position, and she would never be alone—not as long as she had the support of these good women and the Lord. And beyond the board meeting, there were fifty Chinese girls and women living in the mission home, many of them dealing with the aftereffects of traumatic events and abuse, yet Dolly didn't want to be anywhere else.

After everyone's votes had been officially recorded in favor of Dolly's new position, the president spoke of how more people than ever wanted to visit the mission home, considering it part of their Chinatown tour. Dolly's mind spun with new thoughts and ideas—both of how they could benefit from the interest and increased donations, and also of how she could protect the girls who were greatly struggling.

That night, she fell into a dreamless sleep, only to be awakened a couple of hours later by a knock on her door. Dolly mustered herself out of bed, drew on a shawl, and opened the door to see a wide-eyed Frances standing there.

"A note has been delivered."

Dolly was about to turn and begin dressing, assuming that another slave girl had requested rescue, but Frances's next words stopped her. "A distinguished guest is on his way."

Dolly stilled. "Right now?"

Frances held out the note. "The messenger is waiting on the porch."

Dolly read the words, then nodded. "We need to wake everyone up," she said. "And we need to give U.S. President William McKinley the warmest welcome possible."

CHAPTER EIGHTEEN

"For the consideration of [whatever sum has been agreed upon], paid into my hands this day, I, [name of girl], promise to prostitute my body for the term of _____ years. If, in that time, I am sick one day, two weeks shall be added to my time; and if more than one, my term of prostitution shall continue an additional month. But if I run away, or escape from the custody of my keeper, then I am to be held as a slave for life.

"(Signed)_____"

—CONSIGNMENT CONTRACT FOR SLAVE GIRLS ARRIVING FROM CHINA

1903

The man's breath was foul, his clothing tattered. He was much larger than Mei Lien, yet that didn't stop her from wrenching out of his grasp and fleeing toward the exit of the building. But the man had the advantage, knowing his way in the darkness. He lunged for her and caught her clothing, dragging her down.

Mei Lien had hardly eaten in three days, and she didn't know where her strength came from. But she rolled out from under the man and was once again on her feet. Half running, half limping, she made it to the door.

The man cursed, and she heard his labored breathing. He was coming for her. This was not how her life would end, she promised herself that. She ran into the dark, rainy night. She nearly slipped on the wet cobblestones, but she kept her balance and moved as quickly as she could. She didn't stop until she saw a café window with light spilling from it.

Hurrying inside, ignoring the stares of the handful of diners, she headed for the kitchen in the back. She approached the oldest person in the kitchen—a woman—and held out a single pearl. The older woman's eyes widened.

Mei Lien knew she looked like a drowned rat, but she didn't let her appearance dissuade her. "I will give you this in exchange for directions to Huan Sun's tailoring shop."

The woman reached quickly for the pearl. But Mei Lien was quicker. She snapped her fingers into a fist and withdrew her hand. "Do you know Huan Sun?"

"No," the woman said. "But I can find anything and anyone."

"This is true," a young man said as he stirred something in a sizzling skillet.

The woman harrumphed. Mei Lien was out of options. "All right." She opened her hand and placed the pearl in the woman's hand. Within seconds, the woman had hidden the pearl someplace within her clothing.

"Sit there." The woman pointed to a greasy stool in the corner of the kitchen. Then she disappeared.

Mei Lien kept her eyes lowered even though she knew the young man kept watching her. It seemed like hours before the older woman returned, but it couldn't have been more than a half hour.

"Three streets over," the woman said. "Next to the butcher shop."

"I can take you once we close," the young man said.

"No," Mei Lien was quick to say. She didn't trust him. She didn't trust any man other than Huan Sun. Their relationship might be over, but she believed him to be an honest and fair man. In her heart, she knew he would aid her if he could, or at least give her guidance about how to stay safe. "Draw me a map. I will find it."

A few minutes later, Mei Lien found herself outside in the dark again. The rain had ebbed, but the cold bit through her thin clothing. She hurried along the street, keeping her eyes and ears tuned to any danger in the silent alleys. Hoping that the woman and her son had given her the right information, she slowed when she reached the final turn.

And there it was. *Sun Tailoring.* Mei Lien's body slumped in relief. But she wasn't in the clear yet. All was dark inside, which made her wonder if he still owned the place. Since she didn't want to attract attention by knocking, she headed into the alley on the side of the shop and found a narrow door. She tried the knob but found it locked.

Tears came fast. What if Huan Sun was gone? For good? She sank onto the ground and huddled against the door. She was exhausted, hungry, wet, cold. She had come so far, yet she still felt lost.

She closed her eyes and bowed her head. She would wait until the morning and hope that Huan Sun would come and find her. If he wasn't here, then there was nowhere else for her to go. Ah-Peen Oie wouldn't take her back. Earning money for a passage back to Hong Kong would be futile because she didn't have any papers with her or money to buy false papers.

The rain stopped, but the dripping in the alley continued. The sound made her feel like it was her life that was dripping away. Bit by bit. Drip by drip.

"Oh, Mother," she whispered. "I hope you will never learn of my fate. I hope you have happiness all the remainder of your days."

"Mei Lien?" someone said.

It was a dream, only a dream. A nice dream. One in which Huan Sun had found her and brought her into his shop.

Then she realized she was truly being carried into a building. She could no longer hear the dripping rain, and the deep cold had eased somewhat.

His voice came again. "How did you get here?"

Now, that was a strange question. She had walked, of course. But that wasn't what he was asking.

Mei Lien dragged her eyes open. She was sitting on a cot inside some sort of storage room, if the stacked crates were any indication. Personal effects were scattered about. A cracked lamp on a small table. A chipped teacup. A closet door partway open. Was this his bedroom, too? And . . . Huan Sun was looking down at her. He looked both the same and different. His boyish face was achingly familiar, and those laugh lines were still about his eyes. Yet he had violet circles beneath his eyes, making him look tired. She felt a pressure on her hand, a warm pressure, and she realized that he was rubbing her hand.

Then he lifted her other hand and rubbed that one, too.

Pricks of warmth penetrated her cold hands, then moved slowly up her arms.

"You . . . you found me." Her words sounded strangely thick and slow.

Lines pulled between Huan Sun's brows. "I found you outside my shop."

It was then she noticed that he was wearing a simple garment—something he had slept in? Was he working around the clock? Searching for the thief?

"Zhang Wei," she said. "He stole your money."

Huan Sun stilled, pressing his lips together as if he were in deep thought. "Did he tell you this?"

"Yes."

By the knowledge that flashed in Huan Sun's eyes, she knew that her announcement told him many other things as well.

Huan Sun drew away. "You should change into this dry clothing. I will get you tea. Then you can tell me what happened."

Mei Lien rose from the cot to change into the robe Huan Sun had left. Her fingers trembled as she peeled off her wet clothing. She wondered if she would ever be truly warm again. She had settled beneath the blanket again when Huan Sun returned, carrying a cup of steaming tea.

"Drink this." He handed it to her, then moved away again. Sitting on the other side of the room, Huan Sun warily watched her.

Mei Lien sipped at the tea. She had never tasted anything so heavenly, and the warmth traveled throughout her, slowly warming her body. "Thank you," she whispered. "And I am sorry to cause you trouble."

Huan Sun's eyes flashed with something unreadable, but his brows remained furrowed in worry. "What happened to you? Why are you here?"

"I was sold . . ." Mei Lien whispered. "Zhang Wei visited my room, and after he left, Ah-Peen Oie beat me."

Huan Sun pressed his lips together as his gaze flitted over her covered form. "Did you displease Zhang Wei?"

"No," Mei Lien said. "Ah-Peen Oie was angry that he requested me. She did nothing about it until he left, then she locked me in my room for three days. When she finally returned, it was to bring a new owner."

Huan Sun said nothing as Mei Lien continued with her story. At last she said, "I could not continue living that way. I decided that if I couldn't find a way out, then I would rather die in the streets."

Huan Sun's mouth opened, then shut. He stood and paced the small room. "You should not be here. I have nothing to give you, no way to provide. My own shop has been robbed by Zhang Wei. Imagine what will happen if your owner finds out where you fled to."

Mei Lien buried her face in her hands. It was all too much, and now she had brought Huan Sun into the middle of her mess. He was in danger now too.

She took a shaky breath and moved into a sitting position. The night was still deep, and the pattering of rain had started up again, but she had to be long gone by morning. Pushing aside the blanket, she rose to her feet.

"What are you doing?" Huan Sun paused in his pacing.

"I should have never come." Her voice cracked. "I-I do not want to bring harm to you. I should not be your burden."

Huan Sun gazed at her, and it was like a battle was being fought in the depths of his brown eyes.

"Stay tonight," he said. "Perhaps no one saw you, and no one knows you're here, right?"

Mei Lien thought of the woman and her son at the café. They knew where she was going, as did whomever the woman had asked for directions. "There are some people I asked how to find your shop."

Huan Sun stilled. "Do they know your name?"

Mei Lien shook her head.

"Then we will rely on fortune and hope that your trail grows cold," he said. "Tomorrow I will try to find a place for you."

She couldn't have described the relief that coursed through her. One night. At least she had that.

CHAPTER NINETEEN

"I can do all things through Christ which strengtheneth me."

—DONALDINA CAMERON, QUOTING THE APOSTLE PAUL, PHILIPPIANS 4:13

1900

Dolly had a hard time believing she wasn't dreaming as President William McKinley and his wife walked into the mission home. Mrs. McKinley had lost two children and suffered from a nervous condition. Evidently, she had recovered from a rough afternoon and was able to make the late-night visit. If there was one thing to impress Dolly about the president, it was how greatly he cared for his wife's well-being and comfort.

Everyone in the household had been awakened, and now the girls, women, and even the babies were assembled in the chapel to welcome the president. He led his wife to a comfortable chair, and she encouraged some of the younger girls to sit by her. Her hair had been tightly curled about her head, and her dark clothing was formal, but her eyes were soft and warm.

The president took time to shake everyone's hands. He was an austere-looking man, with a square jaw and a commanding presence, though his smile was genuine and his manner friendly. Finally, he turned to Dolly. "I have heard of the remarkable work you've done for the people of San Francisco, Miss Cameron."

Dolly couldn't imagine where he'd heard that from, but she tried to smile demurely. "Thank you, Mr. President. It's an honor to have you in our home." They hadn't had much time to ready the house or the girls, but thankfully, they had kept up on chores, since sponsors frequented the house, asking for tours. Of course, if Dolly had had more notice, she might have bought out all the flowers from the market. And Frances would have had the girls baking sweets all day.

As it was, the girls performed songs in their sweet voices and offered recitations of poetry and scriptures. Dolly smiled at the girls she loved so much—Lonnie, Leung, Jiao, and Dong Ho. Tien stood in the very back, as if she didn't want to be noticed, but her curious peeks at the president and his wife gave away her interest.

Mrs. McKinley clapped in appreciation, her gaze wistful at the same time, and soon her husband joined in the clapping.

"How do you like living in the mission home?" Mrs. McKinley asked the girls.

"I love it," Lonnie said, throwing her hands in the air.

The president's wife laughed; then she turned to Dolly and asked, "They are in school, here, yes?"

"That's right," Dolly said. "We also teach them sewing skills, including darning socks and piecing quilts. The girls earn money as well by making buttonhole strips. We make clothing, comforters, and bed linens. With thirty-five to fifty girls in the house at any given time, we're making about one hundred and forty garments every four or five months."

"Goodness," Mrs. McKinley said. "There *is* a lot going on here. Do you make time for anything fun?"

Dolly smiled. "Of course. We take field trips to places like the Golden Gate Park. We love smelling the flowers and feeding the ducks."

Mrs. McKinley settled back in her chair, seeming pleased at Dolly's answer. President McKinley asked for another song.

When the McKinleys had left, and the children were all finally tucked into bed, Dolly realized that Yuen Qui hadn't stayed for the meeting. The interpreter had been coughing for a couple of days, but Dolly felt bad that Yuen Qui had left right after introductions had been made. Dolly headed toward the woman's bedroom. Sure enough, she heard Yuen Qui coughing.

Dolly knocked softly on the door, then turned the knob. "Can I come in?"

Yuen Qui only gave a quiet moan, alarming Dolly. She stepped into the bedroom to find Yuen Qui sitting on her bed, her shoulders hunched, as she held a handkerchief to her mouth. Dolly turned on a lamp and found the woman looking dreadfully pale. Dolly rested a hand on Yuen Qui's forehead—her skin was too warm, hot, even. Then Dolly saw the dark red stain on the handkerchief Yuen Qui held to her mouth.

"I'll call a doctor." Dolly tried to tamp down her worry, even though she knew something was terribly wrong.

But Yuen Qui shook her head, her eyes widening with fear. "Don't call the doctor," she rasped.

Dolly knew that many Chinese did not trust American doctors, preferring their old medicine and superstitions to modern methods. Often a Chinese apothecary would simply examine the patient's tongue and take her pulse, then make a diagnosis and create a prescription for a medicinal tea.

"I only need more tea," Yuen Qui insisted. She began coughing again, and her body tensed with the obvious pain. Dolly winced, feeling helpless as she watched her friend suffer. More blood had appeared on the handkerchief.

"I'll be right back with your tea," Dolly said when Yuen Qui relaxed again. "Lie down. You don't need to worry about anything else."

When Dolly stepped out of the bedroom, her heart was racing, and her own hands felt clammy with apprehension. She slowed when she saw Tien down the hallway, hovering. The worry lines on the girl's face only mirrored Dolly's heart.

Before Dolly could say a word or offer any comfort to the girl who idolized Yuen Qui, Tien disappeared down the hallway toward her bedroom.

Dolly exhaled and walked down the stairs to the kitchen, where she made tea in the quiet stillness of the night. Through the walls, she heard Yuen Qui struggle with another coughing fit. Soon, Dolly returned to Yuen Qui's bedroom, and thankfully, the tea seemed to soothe her enough that she fell asleep.

Dolly sat in Yuen Qui's room for another hour, until she could hardly keep her own eyes open. She finally made her way to her own bedroom, where she sank into a dreamless rest. But the hours somehow passed while she slept. And the moment dawn pierced the sky, Dolly awakened to a feeling of urgency. She needed to check on Yuen Qui.

When Dolly cracked open the woman's door, she was pleased to see that Yuen Qui still slept peacefully. A shape on the floor caught Dolly's attention, and she found Tien curled up on the rug, also sleeping.

Quietly, Dolly crossed to the bed. Upon closer inspection, she found another handkerchief spotted with blood. She couldn't delay any longer, and she left the bedroom to telephone the doctor to come immediately.

Two hours passed before the doctor could arrive and make his diagnosis. By that time, the rest of the household had risen, finished morning chores, eaten breakfast, attended devotional, and were now involved in their various classes and activities.

Tien hovered at the bedroom doorway of Yuen Qui while Dolly sat on the single chair, waiting for the doctor's exam to be finished. Dolly hadn't the heart to send Tien away, although the girl should have been in class.

So Tien heard every word the doctor said.

"Tuberculosis," the doctor said in a grave tone. "An advanced case, I'm afraid."

"Are you sure?" Dolly had to ask because she didn't want to believe her friend could be so sick.

"I'm sure, Miss Cameron." He slowly packed up his medical bag, then turned to look her square in the eyes. "And I am very sorry."

Dolly nodded, her eyes burning with tears. Yuen Qui had fallen into a restless sleep again, worn out by the examination. "How long?" Dolly whispered.

The doctor glanced at the doorway. Tien had disappeared.

"A couple of weeks at the most," the doctor said.

The diagnosis rocked through Dolly. Losing Yuen Qui would be painful, and it would devastate Tien. "Is there nothing to be done?"

The doctor shook his head, his eyes filled with sorrow, but Dolly took no comfort in commiserating.

The doctor rested his hand briefly on Dolly's shoulder. "I will inform Miss Thompson, then show myself out."

She nodded, but she couldn't meet his gaze. Her eyes were trained on the sleeping form in the bed. Had Yuen Qui comprehended what the doctor said? The minutes passed, and Dolly wasn't sure how long she sat in the chair across the room, trying to absorb the doctor's news. As the sounds of the house hummed about her while the residents went about their day, all that Dolly could focus on was the stilted breathing of Yuen Qui.

It seemed that loss surrounded her at every turn. First, Miss Culbertson had died. Ah Cheng had married and moved. Mrs. Field had quit. Mrs. Browne had retired. Now sweet and lovely Yuen Qui was on her deathbed.

"Please, Lord," Dolly whispered, "give me strength." She rose to her feet and crossed to Yuen Qui's bedside, where she knelt and clasped the sleeping woman's hand.

Yuen Qui stirred but didn't open her eyes.

There was nothing left to do but pray.

That, and find the grieving Tien. She would suffer deeply. Another, more acute fear had taken root inside Dolly. In the Chinese culture, grieving wives would often take their own lives after a husband died. Although there was no marriage here, Tien loved Yuen Qui like a mother.

But when Dolly went in search of her, Tien had barricaded herself in her room, and no cajoling would bring her out. Defeat stole through Dolly's whole being, and she slid to the floor outside the bedroom and leaned against the wall, hoping and praying that Tien would eventually let her in.

"What is it?" Frances Thompson asked, joining Dolly in the hallway.

"Tien refuses to open her door," Dolly said.

Frances looked from the closed door to Dolly. "Perhaps she needs to work out her grief on her own."

Dolly exhaled. "But I'm afraid she'll see no way out of her grief except following Yuen Qui into the afterlife."

Frances's brows lifted, but she understood Dolly's meaning. "I'll speak to the others," Frances said. "We'll all rally around her."

It was all they could do, and Dolly knew it. But that didn't make this any easier. Yuen Qui had received a death sentence, and Dolly hoped it wouldn't be the same for Tien.

Over the next three weeks, Dolly spent every spare moment by Yuen Qui's bedside. Despite the doctor's prediction of two weeks, she hung on for another week, painfully hovering between life and death as the symptoms of tuberculosis wracked her increasingly thinning and frail body.

Dolly and Frances took turns treating her fevers, night sweats, chest pain, and coughing. Each morning, Dolly would find Tien curled up on Yuen Qui's floor, asleep.

When Dolly tried to speak to Tien, the girl would turn away or leave the room.

One morning at the end of the third week, Dolly once again arrived at Yuen Qui's bedroom. Frances had been on duty to check in on her throughout the night. But when Dolly opened the door, she found only Tien inside, standing next to the bed, gazing down upon her friend.

Something was different about the room. The atmosphere was too quiet, too still. Dolly approached the bed and saw what she dreaded most.

The lovely Yuen Qui had died.

Despite having known for weeks that this day, this moment, would come, Dolly felt like the world had been stripped of color. Yuen Qui's face was beautiful, ethereal, yet so very pale and still. Absent were her light and smile. And in their place, emptiness.

Dolly's heart felt like a vase that had shattered on a tiled floor, the broken shards too numerous to count. Her knees gave way, and she sank onto the bed beside her beloved interpreter. She had no control over the sobs that wracked her body and the pain that lanced hot through her limbs.

Yuen Qui was too young to suffer as she had. She should have lived a good number of years more. She was desperately needed by the mission home, by the girls, by Tien. By Dolly.

She and Yuen Qui had traveled the bowels of the underworld of San Francisco together, leading girls from the darkness into the light. And now . . . she was gone.

"No, no, no," Dolly repeated over and over. Her prayers had been in vain. Yuen Qui's sacrifices had brought her only grief. How could a woman so good, so full of purpose, and with so much more to give, be taken from the earth?

Someone patted Dolly's shoulder, but she had no strength to rise.

"*Lo Mo,*" Tien said.

When Dolly didn't, couldn't, respond, Tien spoke again. "*Lo Mo,* I will help you. Don't cry."

It was the first time Tien had called Dolly *Lo Mo.* In this torturous moment of dear Yuen Qui's departing, she had left behind a miracle after all.

"I will help you with the rescues, *Lo Mo,*" Tien said. "I won't be afraid, and I will work harder than anyone." The girl sniffled, and Dolly brushed at the tears on her own cheeks and turned to Tien.

The young teenager fell into Dolly's embrace and wrapped her sturdy arms about Dolly's neck.

Dolly squeezed her eyes shut as she held Tien. The Chinese girl trembled as if she stood barefoot in a winter storm. The two clung to each other in their shared grief and sorrow, while something that neither of them could define sprouted. A seed that had a future of its own. The light of Yuen Qui lived on.

CHAPTER TWENTY

*"A picture of their early homes may shock your sensibilities, yet
I want you to realize the life from which our innocents come.
Ah Yoke's home in Chinatown was a house of vice on Spofford
Alley. Her mistress, Foon Ying, one of the cruelest, most
depraved women of the underworld, vented her anger on this
helpless child every time her evil nature asserted itself."*

—DONALDINA CAMERON, PLEA TO THE BOARD TO START
A HOME FOR THE YOUNGER GIRLS

1904

One night, Huan Sun had told her. But a full month had passed now, and Mei Lien had yet to go outside. Someone could be waiting; someone could be watching. The fear of the ever-present unknown had carved a hollow into her stomach. This morning, the shop had yet to open. The rain outside made it seem earlier in the morning than it actually was. And Mei Lien felt every bit of the gloomy mist as if it had seeped inside her very soul.

She couldn't complain, though. Huan Sun had put her to work sewing and repairing clothing that came into his shop. He had also insisted that she sleep on the only cot in the back room. Where Huan Sun slept, she wasn't sure. He was awake long after she went to sleep and before she arose in the morning.

Mei Lien was grateful for every moment that she spent in this place, but every moment also seemed another moment closer to . . . what? She didn't know, and her mind conjured up all sorts of images. At least for now, there was no Ah-Peen Oie to beat her, no Zhang Wei to beckon her, no days without water or food. No temptation of opium, although the sweet smell wafted in from the shop window now and again.

Mei Lien had gone through withdrawals the first week at the shop, but they were a small price to pay for her escape. Now, she only felt nauseous. Huan Sun's meals were sparse, but regular, so it wasn't because she was hungry. And although she slept a full night each night, she always craved more rest.

Mei Lien knew the cause of these symptoms, but she wouldn't let herself think about it for fear her thoughts would make her situation into reality.

And she was determined to earn her keep for as long as Huan Sun tolerated her presence.

Now, Huan Sun walked into the main part of the shop where she worked. "Someone's coming,"

He didn't need to say anything more. Mei Lien turned and scurried past him to the back room. She moved into the narrow closet to her usual hiding place. When patrons entered the shop, it was her job to disappear. At the back of the closet, Huan Sun had constructed a false door, and she drew it open, then squeezed into the small space.

She closed her eyes as she steadied her breathing. Closing her eyes helped calm her. Huan Sun sometimes sensed things before they happened. The fact that he had discovered her in the middle of the night had been remarkable. And now, he knew someone was coming to the shop before the doorknob was even turned.

Voices sounded inside the main shop, and Mei Lien held her breath to listen. *Men.* At least two of them, their voices higher pitched than Huan Sun's lower, more mellow tone. When she heard her name spoken, all the warmth drained from her body.

"She very pretty," one of the men said. "You knew her at Ah-Peen Oie's."

"I visited many women there," Huan Sun said, his tone remarkably even and calm.

"Ah-Peen Oie says you have not returned since visiting Mei Lien," the man continued.

"My shop was robbed, and I had no money." Huan Sun's explanation was the truth, but the men in the shop weren't satisfied.

"Every Chinese man is poor," the man said. "Yet, every Chinese man visits the brothels."

Huan Sun's reply was muffled.

Then something banged. Mei Lien's breath hitched.

"Don't move," one of the men growled. The order must have been directed at Huan Sun.

Mei Lien hardly dared to breathe, and she feared that her thudding heartbeat would be loud enough to give her away. Sounds of banging and clanking told her they were searching the place . . . for her.

Footsteps entered the back room, and even through the false door, Mei Lien knew the man was heading straight for the closet. The door clicked open, and he banged on the walls. Mei Lien nearly yelped, but she bit down hard on her lip, stifling a scream.

The next bang on the closet was right above her head. Panic lurched through her body. Her stomach roiled, and bile burned her throat as she squeezed her eyes shut, willing herself not to cry out.

Someone called to the man in the closet, and he suddenly left. Mei Lien didn't know what was happening, but new voices came from the front of the shop. A patron must have come in.

She could only wait and pray that Huan Sun would be all right, and that the tong would leave. The wait was agonizing, and Mei Lien had no idea how much time had passed. But when Huan Sun finally opened the false door, she ran past him to the latrine bucket. Falling to the floor, she vomited.

When her body had completely spent itself, she curled up on the floor next to the bucket.

Huan Sun crouched next to her and touched her forehead.

Mei Lien peered at the man through bleary eyes. He had a growing bruise below his eye, and his bottom lip had been split. "You're hurt," she whispered.

"It could be worse." There was no censure, no anger in his expression.

His injuries both incensed her and made her want to cry. "Why are you protecting me?"

Huan Sun didn't answer. Instead, he gently took her arm and helped her stand. Then he led her to the cot.

"Rest."

"But I should help you clean up the damage," she said, even as she sank onto the cot. "How much did they—"

"Hush," Huan Sun said. "They could have done much worse. I will clean up. You rest."

"I shouldn't be resting." She knew her voice was hysterical, but she couldn't help it. "You're the one who got beaten."

"You're pale," he cut in. "And you have been sick."

Mei Lien looked away then. She'd been sick, yes, but it wasn't just because of the tong's visit.

"What is it?" he asked, his voice gentler.

She couldn't pretend anymore. Huan Sun would notice soon enough. She looked down at her body, then placed her hands on the new tightness of her belly. "I am pregnant."

Huan Sun didn't move, didn't speak for a moment. Then he sat on the cot next to her with a sigh. There had been no relations between them since she had arrived, but he had not been the only man she'd been with.

"Zhang Wei?" The name cut a path into her soul.

"I don't know," she whispered. "He was only one night. And you . . ." Her words faded into the bleak room.

Huan Sun nodded.

He wasn't looking at her, and she didn't blame him. She was in a shameful state. Being a courtesan had not been the low point of her life, she realized now. Having a fatherless baby was unforgivable. Without a husband and without money to feed the child, she was helpless.

"You cannot stay here," he said.

She knew that, but hearing him say so widened the crack in her heart. "I don't want to get rid of my baby. No matter who the father is, this child is *mine*."

"It is not because of the baby," Huan Sun said. "The tong will be back. After following whatever other leads they might have, they'll circle back because I am the last one who had a contract with you."

Mei Lien's breath hitched at this. "Where will I go?"

He exhaled. "I hoped to find a better place, but we are now out of time. There is a laundry business down the street, and the owner said she would take you in. You would have to work for free, and . . . I'd have to pay her as well."

"But you're still recovering from your own losses—"

Huan Sun grasped her hand, which silenced her immediately. "I can't let you fend for yourself on the streets. Especially now that there's a baby on the way—a child who might be mine."

She bit her lip as her eyes welled with tears. "I have put you through enough."

But Huan Sun didn't let her go; he didn't turn her away. Instead, he wrapped his arm around her and pulled her close.

"I care about you, Mei Lien," he said in a quiet voice. "I know that our relationship has been unconventional, but despite everything, I'm fond of you."

Mei Lien couldn't have been more surprised. Her imaginations about Huan Sun had always been in her mind only. His arm around her now, and his sincere words, told her that perhaps her future could be different.

She wished she and Huan Sun could move far away from San Francisco and the tong.

Resting her head against his shoulder, she wrapped her arms about his waist. He was warm and solid, and when he kissed the top of her head, she closed her eyes. And held on. She would have to leave him in order to keep him from getting assaulted by the tong again.

"Mei Lien," he murmured against her hair. "You need to leave tonight. We cannot wait a single day."

Tears pooled in her eyes. "All right. I will be ready."

He drew away and gazed at her. She scanned the bruising in his face, the dried blood upon his lip. Gently, she placed a hand on the uninjured side of his face. "I am sorry, Huan Sun, very sorry. I did not mean to bring all of this upon you."

He placed a hand over hers. "You are a beautiful young woman, Mei Lien. It is not your fault that you've drawn the attention of the powerful tong. They are responsible for their own actions, and I will do whatever it takes to protect you."

Mei Lien could not stop the tears that fell. Oh, how she wished she did not have to leave this man. He was a pearl among the filth of her life.

"You should not say such things to me unless you want me to fall in love with you," she whispered.

The edges of his mouth lifted, and then he leaned forward and kissed her. Gently. The kiss was over before anything could deepen. "Fate has brought us together for a reason, and it will be my honor to get you to safety. Although it means we will have to say good-bye."

Mei Lien choked back a sob. He was right. They had already tempted fate too much. "I don't want to say good-bye."

His smile was sad. "If circumstances were different, then perhaps we could have found our own happiness. But you are a wanted fugitive, and I am at the mercy of my debts." He drew away slowly and released her. Then he rose to his feet. "I need to put the shop in order. You stay in this room and don't make a sound. We can't take any chances. The tong might be paying someone to spy on me. When dark falls, we will leave."

Mei Lien wanted to step into his arms again, feel his physical comfort. But he was right. There was no future for them, and there was no way she could remain in his shop for even one day longer.

The day passed agonizingly slowly. Every sound, every patron, made her heart stutter with fear. She tried to concentrate on her sewing, but the sound of the shop door opening sent her into the closet more times than not as patrons came in to deliver or pick up orders.

When the setting sun cast the back room into a gold light, Mei Lien felt anxious for a different reason. Soon, she would be at the mercy of another person. Again. She had no worries about working for her keep, but where would she sleep? On the floor? And would she be able to go outside anytime soon?

Shadows crept into the room, and Mei Lien finished her current sewing task so that by the time Huan Sun closed the shop, she had a finished cushion to present to him.

"You are talented," Huan Sun said, taking the embroidered cushion cover and examining the neat and close stitches. "This is beautiful. Everything you've made has sold within a day in my shop."

The compliment warmed her through. If only she could stay.

Then Huan Sun set down the embroidery, and his gaze connected with hers. Without him speaking a word, she knew it was time.

She reached for the bundle she had created with the few clothing items Huan Sun had given her. She wore his mother's pearl bracelet high up on her arm, concealed beneath her clothing. It was the only thing she owned.

Huan Sun reached for her hand, and she slipped it into his warm fingers. She would miss this man, his touch, his presence. Perhaps if she were a good worker for the laundry woman, and perhaps if Huan Sun could get out of debt, they might cross paths again—long after the tong gave up on finding her.

She stepped outside with Huan Sun. He released her hand, but she stayed close to him as they hurried along the street through the cool night air. The foul scent of the soiled streets assailed Mei Lien, which only propelled her faster. They rushed past dark alleys, and even darker doorways, spoiled with the stench of opium and urine.

"Almost there," Huan Sun whispered.

A strong hand snaked around Mei Lien's upper arm, and she might have thought it was Huan Sun, but he was on her left side. Then the hand tugged her back so hard that she lost her balance. Before she could scream, someone clamped a hand over her mouth.

She twisted with every bit of strength she had, but there were now two people holding onto her. She bit the hand over her mouth and yelled, "Huan Sun!"

Someone slapped her. Hard. The hot sting traveled the length of her body.

Then she heard him. Huan Sun was arguing with someone; then his yelling turned to cries of pain.

"No!" Mei Lien gasped. "Leave him alone!" But her words were again cut off as she was hauled over a man's shoulder and carried into a nearby alley. She hit the man's back until he stopped and set her on the ground. Instead of releasing her, he wrapped his strong hand around her neck.

She stared at the man looming over her. *Zhang Wei.*

"Quiet." His bulging eyes locked her in place. "If you want Huan Sun to live, you will do as I say."

CHAPTER TWENTY-ONE

"Little Yute Ho Ji . . . made her debut into public life a few weeks ago when she appeared before the Grand Jury of this city to bear witness to the fact that even tiny children are brought into this country as slaves. She made such an impression upon that august body that several members soon visited the Mission to see for themselves what was being done in the way of rescue work."

—Donaldina Cameron, mission home report

1901

"You must come for a visit," Jessie told Dolly over the telephone. "If only for a day or two. A weekend. You can see Reverend Ben Bazatas. Remember, I wrote to you about him."

Dolly laughed at her sister's antics, even though the last thing she felt like doing was laughing. The death of Yuen Qui still tore at her soul, and although Dolly had tried to put on a happy face around the residents of the mission home, in truth, she ached every day. Deeply.

"You know I love you, Doll," Jessie continued. "But I also worry about you. You're in your thirties. Don't you think it's time to consider your own future? Yes, you're a godsend to those little girls, but . . ."

Dolly had heard the arguments and persuasions from her sister before. But the truth was, Dolly would love a short break. The responsibilities of running the mission home, the constant pressure and legal troubles from the tong, in addition to the crippling emotional weight she was sagging beneath, made her less present than she should be. Plus, she missed her darling niece, Caroline.

"All right, Jessie," Dolly said. "I'll come next weekend. Tell Caroline to expect a hundred kisses from Aunt Dowey."

Dolly wasn't even sure her sister heard that last part because she was squealing so loudly. Dolly laughed, and this time it was genuine. She would have just enough time to make Caroline a present. Perhaps a summer dress—she had recently acquired some beautiful white organdy.

She set down the phone receiver, and the door to the office cracked open. Dolly knew instinctively that it was Tien. The young woman rarely knocked, and she continued in her habits of listening to everything going on in the mission home. Which Dolly had found quite useful now that they were working together. Tien reported on happenings that Frances missed—when a girl hadn't come out of her room all day, or when an argument broke out or someone stole from another person in the house, or even when one young woman had tried to harm herself last week.

Tien immediately brought any and all news to Dolly, and she was ever grateful for it.

"You are leaving?" Tien hovered in the doorway, her gaze unsure, her shoulders hunched.

"Only for a few days," Dolly said. "I'm going to visit my sister Jessie and her family."

Tien nodded, but Dolly didn't miss the longing in her eyes. She still wasn't quite used to this new side of Tien.

"Miss Thompson will watch over things while I'm gone," Dolly continued, hoping to reassure. Who would have thought the young woman would miss her? "And I'll give her Jessie's telephone number. If you need something, you can call me."

Tien's gaze dropped as if she were embarrassed to be so needy.

Dolly walked around the desk and crossed to her. She rested a hand on Tien's shoulder. "Can you be my eyes and ears while I'm gone?"

Tien's dark eyes flitted upward, and she nodded.

"Thank you," Dolly said.

With Frances Thompson's fervent promise that all would be well, Dolly packed for her weekend visit to the small town of Alhambra, near Pasadena. As she packed, she thought of the changes in Tien since Yuen Qui's death.

Tien had done an almost 180-degree turn in her personality. She had become like a shadow to Dolly, much as she'd been to Yuen Qui. Tien had begged to join Dolly on a rescue and be the interpreter. Dolly had brought her on a rescue, then another, and another. Tien was proving to be clever and fierce. She had already persuaded more than one of the more reluctant rescued girls that Dolly wasn't a white devil who would bring generations of cursing upon their heads, but someone to be trusted.

Yet Dolly knew she needed a complete break from the mission home for a few days. So she would travel on her own.

Finally, the day arrived, and when the mountain peaks of the Sierra Madres came into view, Dolly felt some of the burdens lifted for the first time in months, perhaps years. She knew the break would be temporary, but for now, she would relish in the sweet balm.

The moment Dolly walked into Jessie's lovely home, Caroline ran to her.

"You came, Aunt Dowey." Caroline's bright eyes peered up at Dolly. "You really came."

"I'm here, sweetheart." Dolly stooped to pull the young girl into her arms. "I brought you a special present, too."

Caroline jumped up and down in Dolly's arms, and she laughed at the little girl's enthusiasm. "Come with me to my room, and I'll unpack it from my trunk."

Jessie followed with a wide smile, and everyone crowded around the bed as Dolly ceremoniously opened the trunk and produced a white organdy dress.

Caroline clapped her hands together, then threw her arms about Dolly. "Can I wear it to church tomorrow?"

"Of course," Dolly said.

When Caroline scampered off with the dress, Dolly turned to Jessie. She found her sister observing with a soft smile.

"Thank you for the dress," Jessie said. "It means the world to her, and I'm sure you made a lot of sacrifices to find the time to make it."

Dolly lifted a shoulder. "Love is always worth the time."

"Oh, Doll." Jessie stepped forward, and the two women embraced. When they drew apart, she added, "You also look tired. Do you want to rest before dinner?"

Jessie couldn't have said anything more perfect.

"I'd like that very much." Dolly spent the next couple of hours luxuriating in the quiet and peace, and when the smells of cooking dinner made her stomach grumble with impatience, only then did she venture out of the guest bedroom.

She found her brother-in-law Charlie in the front room with the newspaper. When he spotted Dolly, he immediately leapt to his feet and greeted her. "How was your journey, sis?"

"Excellent," Dolly answered. "Thank you for opening your home to me."

"Anytime." Charlie's brows pinched together. "And I truly mean it."

Dolly knew there was much more meaning behind those words. Her family members hadn't held back their concerns about her unending work at the mission home.

"Caroline is enchanted with your gift," Charlie added. "Have a seat. I am sure you're exhausted."

"I've been resting long enough," Dolly said. "I think I'll go see what I can help Jessie with."

Charlie shook his head, but his blue eyes were filled with warmth.

When Dolly joined her sister in the kitchen, she marveled at the meal Jessie had put together of baked chicken, vegetables, and rice. Dolly was used to mass food preparation, but here, in Jessie's home, the place seemed peaceful. A husband, a wife, a daughter. A quiet meal together in the evenings. And so much love.

Although the atmosphere at the mission home was different, love still reigned. The busyness and chaos might be ever-present, but Dolly loved the place. And right now, despite everything, she missed San Francisco. She put that out of her mind and decided to be a cheerful guest in her sister's home.

"Smells wonderful," Dolly said.

"You're up?" Jessie turned, her look expectant.

"I'm up, and thank you for the rest," Dolly said. "Now I need to get my lazy bones moving again. Give me an assignment."

Jessie laughed. Soon the two women had finished the meal preparations, and as Dolly and Caroline set the table and carried the food in, Jessie called for Charlie to join them.

Once they were seated around the abundant table, Charlie asked Dolly to say grace over the meal.

As Dolly prayed, her heart overflowed with gratitude. Despite her losses in life, she was still surrounded by love. Focusing on her blessings brought her the greater joy. Spending time with her family was wonderful and interacting with Caroline a delight. Dolly wished that every young person could grow up like Caroline, in a loving and safe home. Even now, as Dolly basked in her family, she worried about her Chinese daughters.

Partway through the meal, Jessie said, "We've been invited to the Bazatases' tomorrow night for dinner."

Dolly quirked her mouth. "Really. Why am I not surprised?"

"Ben's a wonderful man, Doll," Jessie said.

"That he is," Charlie added in a knowing tone.

"Why do I feel like I'm being ganged up on?" Dolly asked with a smile. She was over thirty now, well past the age most women married. And her sisters wouldn't let her forget it, subtle as they tried to be.

"I don't know why you feel that way." Jessie raised her very innocent brows. "It's only dinner."

Dolly laughed. "All right. Dinner never hurt anyone."

But when Dolly stepped into the church building the next morning with Caroline's small hand clutched in hers, Jessie and Charlie walking arm in arm a few feet ahead, Dolly sensed the speculation buzzing in people's minds. They didn't even need to say a word for Dolly to know that everyone was hoping she and Ben would come to a meeting of the hearts.

She saw him immediately, of course, at the head of the chapel. His dark hair and steady blue eyes were familiar to her, and she felt a fondness when their gazes connected. But there was no spark, no sense of urgency or beginnings of pining for more time and conversation with him.

Yes, Ben was a charming man, solid in his religious beliefs, who insisted on seeing the good in every situation. He was also a gentleman to the ladies, and he took care of his widowed mother and two younger sisters. Dolly took her seat with her family, settling in to hear the sermon. As Ben's rich baritone voice filled the chapel, the birds outside the open windows seemed to twitter in response.

She had the distinct impression that this town was Ben's domain, these people were his people, and any wife of his would be integrated into his world. Regardless, Dolly listened to the sermon with appreciation. But her life was not here in this small town. Her life, and her heart, were miles away in the mission home, surrounded by her Chinese daughters. To change her relationship with Ben into something more than friendship wasn't something she could desire.

The peaceful confirmation about her choices came slow and sweet as the sun's rays filled the chapel with soft light. The day couldn't have been more perfect, and of course Dolly wished that her Chinese girls could bask in such a beautiful building as well.

Once church services ended, Dolly became caught up in chatting with several of the ladies. Some she had met before, and some she had only heard of through Jessie. Soon, the family headed to the Bazatas home for dinner.

At the door of their home, Dolly embraced Mrs. Bazatas. Dolly didn't know her well, but Jessie had shared many stories of the family. Each time Dolly visited Jessie, she encountered Mrs. Bazatas at least once and had a nice visit.

"It's wonderful to see you again, Donaldina," Mrs. Bazatas said, her usual knot of worry between her brows.

It was as if Dolly could feel the hope running through the older woman.

Dinner was served, and, not surprisingly, Dolly found herself seated next to Ben. "How are you, Ben?"

Ben grinned his friendly smile, his light eyes a contrast to his darker hair. He had aged a little since the last time she'd seen him, as she had herself. A few silver hairs graced his temples, and his jawline had softened. "Excellent. It's great to see you, Donaldina."

His smile did nothing to Dolly's heart. He felt more like a brother than a potential beau. He was always kind, always cheerful, always friendly. But it was the same for every person he interacted with.

"I enjoyed your sermon," she said. "Especially the part of—"

"Charles!" Mrs. Bazatas said.

Dolly looked over at the dining room entrance to see a tall, broad-shouldered man. He swept off his hat, revealing wavy, blond hair. As he smoothed his fingers through his hair, Dolly decided that although his blond hair was in sharp contrast to Ben's darker hair, there was no question that the two men were related. This must be his brother. Her mind raced to piece together any information she had heard about Charles before. All she could recall was that he had played football at the Occidental College in Los Angeles.

The two Bazatas sisters, Anna and Aloisia, rose from their places to greet Charles with enthusiastic hugs. Charles laughed as he squeezed his sisters tightly. Next came his mother. Then the two brothers embraced, pounding each other's backs.

"We didn't know you were coming," his mother gushed. "Have a seat, and I'll bring in an extra plate."

"Thank you." Charles scanned the faces about the dining table. "I must admit, I'm starving."

His mother gave him a doting wink, then hurried from the room.

"Charles," Ben said, "I'd like you to meet the Bailey family, and their sister who is visiting, Donaldina Cameron."

When Charles's green eyes landed on Dolly, she smiled, if only to cover the sudden fluttering inside her stomach. She didn't even know much about this man; he could be married, for all she knew. But his very persona had caught her full attention.

Charles came around the table and shook Dolly's hand.

How were his eyes so impossibly green? They reminded her of the leaves of a young apple tree. And his warm, strong handshake could be felt long after he'd moved on to greet her sister and brother-in-law.

"Nice to meet you all." Charles's voice wasn't quite as deep as his brother's, but it had a nice low tone all the same.

His smile was rather beautiful too. The man's athletic grace and skilled conversation kept Dolly mesmerized the rest of the meal. When he turned his attention to her, it was as if she couldn't look away from the depth of his dark green eyes. She wanted to ask him so many questions. She wanted to know everything about him. Charles Bazatas was wholly unexpected.

Following dinner, the family moved onto the wide front porch to enjoy the cooling weather and the scented breeze coming off the apple orchard. Dolly wandered to the porch railing and gazed across the front yard. The setting sun's rays had turned the sprawling grass and neat road leading away from the house a rich golden color.

"I had never thought I would have the privilege to meet you, Donaldina." Charles joined her at the railing. His smile was easy, his voice mellow. "My brother has shared more than one story about 'Miss Cameron from San Francisco.'"

Ben had talked about *her* to his brother? Her neck warmed, and it wasn't only because of what he'd said—it was the way he studied her. As if he were truly interested in what she had to say, and as if they weren't surrounded by other family members who could very well hear every word spoken.

"Call me Dolly." She rested her hands on the rail. "Everyone calls me that—well, at least most people."

"Most people?"

How did he pick up on every single nuance? Charles was standing close to her—very close—or was she just that aware of him? And was he wearing cologne, or did he naturally smell like sunshine and leather combined?

"The girls at the mission home call me *Lo Mo*." The warmth of her neck spread upward, flushing her cheeks. She wondered if it would be rude to head inside the house for another glass of iced lemonade.

"What does that mean?" Charles pressed.

"Directly translated it means 'old mother.'"

Charles grinned. "Really?"

She laughed at his reaction, and the warmth continued through her body, nearly reaching her heart. "It's an endearment."

"To be sure." Charles rested his hip against the porch railing so that they could see each other eye to eye. Folding his arms, he said, "You're doing remarkable work, Dolly. Puts the rest of us to shame."

The way he'd said her name sent a new thrill through her. She really should call it a night and tell her sister she was ready to return home. But speaking to Charles felt so easy and natural that she found herself telling him stories of the Chinese girls along with women of other nationalities the mission had helped. Charles's expression appeared truly intent, and he listened to every word.

When she looked across the porch, it seemed that everyone had disappeared. Had she and Charles really been so involved in their conversation that she hadn't seen the others leaving? Voices and laughter trickled from the house. Maybe they were having dessert? Charles noticed the same thing.

"Looks like we wore everyone else out," he teased.

Dolly swung her gaze back to his and found his green eyes had darkened in the fading light of the evening. "They're tired of hearing my stories, I suppose."

Charles chuckled and lowered his arms, setting his hands on the railing. He crossed his legs. Dolly tried not to look at his elongated form and kept her gaze on the trees in the yard.

"I doubt that anyone could tire of your stories," Charles said, his voice lower and softer than before. "From what I've observed, every word you speak is interesting."

Dolly turned toward Charles, if only to add some distance between their bodies. Was he . . . flirting with her? Or was he usually this complimentary toward others?

"And I'm sure you could fill pages and pages with your experiences, Dolly," he continued. "I don't profess to know a lot, but news of your mission home has reached even the corners of Los Angeles. Everyone knows about the Palo Alto case."

Dolly exhaled. "Yes, it was a nightmare." Memories arose like shards in her mind. At the mention of the case against Kum Quai, her blood still simmered. She stepped away from Charles and walked to the top of the porch steps.

Charles followed in a heartbeat, and he joined her at the top of the steps. Slipping his hands into his pockets, he rocked back on his heels. "I'm sorry for bringing it up."

She blinked back the stinging in her eyes. "It's all right," she said. "When everything was happening, I wasn't really considering any consequences, I was just determined to protect Kum Quai. I don't mind talking about it, truly. In fact, the more it's discussed and reported on, the better chance we have at changing the system and stopping more abductions."

"I agree." Charles hesitated. "If you had known what the outcome would be, would you have gone through it again? I mean, you spent a night in jail, and you went up against dangerous men."

" Of course." Dolly cast him a small smile. "Kum Quai hadn't been with us ver   when those men came to fetch her, but all of those girls are like da g   I have chased after any of them."

          e a low histle. "You're out there fighting for justice for helpless wo   n and children. You're walking into danger every day, while the rest of us are . . . sitting at desks and listening to stuffy professors."

Dolly stilled. She didn't want accolades. Rescuing those girls wasn't about *her* and never would be. She kept her gaze on the ragged silhouette of the Sierra Madres because she didn't want to see the awe in Charles's eyes. She'd seen it in others, and it just didn't feel right. Yes, she was a conduit, but the work was made possible by the work of many faithful women, loyal police officers, honorable lawyers, and generous donations from people all over the nation.

"There is nothing else I'd rather be doing," she said at last. "It's truly been a privilege to work at the mission home."

Charles was quiet for several moments; then he said, "My brother is saving souls, you are saving souls *and* lives, and I . . ."

At his pause, she finally turned to look at him. His blond hair was no longer bright since the sun had set, but that didn't diminish his charisma or the warmth of his eyes in the least.

When their gazes caught, he finished with a half smile, "When you began working at the mission home, I was pushing men around a football field and chasing after pigskin."

"If you love the sport, there's nothing wrong with that."

Charles placed a hand over his heart. "I do declare, Miss Cameron, that you flatter this old heart." He leaned close, and Dolly tried not to let her thoughts scatter. "I'll hold onto that small compliment, but believe me, your courage and stamina are the true wonders."

Dolly didn't look away from his green eyes this time. She saw admiration, yes, but more importantly, sincerity. "Nothing I've done in my life has been entirely thought out and deliberate," she said. "One thing after another happened, and somehow events fell into place."

Charles's stare was incredulous. "Do you think that if any other woman had started working at the mission home, all of the miracles would have still taken place?"

With no hesitation, Dolly said, "Of course."

Charles didn't speak for a moment, which was making her more nervous than anything.

Then he grasped her hand. If Dolly had thought she'd felt fluttery around him before, his fingers wrapped around hers created a sensation like a flock of birds startling from a grove.

"No, Dolly," Charles said, his tone insistent. "*You* are the difference. I can hear the love and enthusiasm in your voice. This is not merely a job for you. Those Chinese girls call you *Lo Mo* for one reason only. You're like a mother to them."

Dolly wanted to refute his bold statement, but she couldn't speak over the sudden tightness of her throat. And with his hand still holding hers, she was feeling things that she wasn't sure how to identify. It was as if their connection had been almost instant, and it only grew stronger by the moment.

"What are you doing tomorrow?" Charles asked. "I want to spend time with you. We could go for a ride. Or a walk. Or go to a restaurant and have lunch or dinner."

Dolly's heart pressed into her throat. "I return to San Francisco tomorrow. I can't stay away too long."

He squeezed her hand gently. "Of course you can't. What about next weekend? Would you turn away a visitor if he showed up on your doorstep?"

Dolly's smile bloomed. "I would not turn away such a visitor."

The front door to the house creaked open, and Charles released her hand.

She looked over at Mrs. Bazatas. If she had noticed they'd been holding hands, she didn't comment on it.

"Dessert is served," Mrs. Bazatas said, her tone cheerful. "Ben said it's your favorite, Dolly."

Dolly felt Charles's gaze on her, and guilt pinged her heart. Ben. It wasn't as if they had any sort of understanding. There had been only friendship between them. But now, after meeting Charles, Dolly could never imagine herself with Ben. And surely Ben had noticed.

"Thank you," Dolly told Mrs. Bazatas.

Half an hour later, Dolly walked with her sister's family back to their home in the darkness. The temperature was mild, and the cooling breeze felt nice on Dolly's still heated cheeks. Caroline was being carried by her father, and her head bobbed against his shoulder as she slept.

"You're quiet," Jessie said as they walked side by side.

Dolly exhaled slowly, choosing her words carefully. But she was positive that Jessie had already noticed enough.

"Charles is going to visit me in San Francisco."

Dolly felt the warmth of her sister's smile cross the distance between them. "You like him." It was a statement, not a question.

"I do," Dolly admitted. There was no use denying it. She liked Charles Bazatas, and that fact alone made her future look much different.

CHAPTER TWENTY-TWO

"[My owner] used to make me carry a big fat baby on my back and make
me to wash his diapers. And you know, to wash you have to stoop over,
and then he pulls you back, and cry and cry. Oh, I got desperate, I didn't
care what happened to me, I just pinched his cheek, his seat, you know,
just gave it to him. Then of course I got it back. She, his mother, went
and burned a red hot iron tong and burnt me on the arm."

—Tien Fu Wu

1901

Dolly ran a brush through her hair with a trembling hand. She was more than nervous, if she were to admit it. Charles Bazatas would be at the mission home in only a few minutes, and she had already delayed in her bedroom long enough. Quickly, she pinned her thick hair up, then rose to her feet and surveyed her appearance in the half mirror.

Would he notice the blush on her cheeks or her too-bright eyes?

No matter. The weather was warm, the clouds wispy, so she opted to forgo a shawl or jacket. And she wanted to be the one to open the front doors. The girls were already abuzz with the news. Despite herself, Dolly had been unable to keep it from her staff members, which now included Tien.

Dolly left her bedroom and found no fewer than a dozen girls waiting at the bottom of the stairs. Her cheeks flushed hotter now that she would have quite the audience when Charles arrived.

He was late by about twenty minutes, but the moment his knock sounded on the door, Dolly immediately forgave his tardiness. He grinned as she welcomed him into the foyer, and the Chinese girls suddenly became shy.

"Well, hello, everyone." Charles swept off his hat and dipped his chin into a nod.

"Hello," the girls chorused, and Dolly held back a laugh at their curious eyes.

Lonnie stepped forward first, holding out her hand as if she had all the confidence in the world. "I'm Yoke Lon."

"Nice to meet you, Yoke Lon," Charles said, giving her hand a very formal shake.

Then the other girls crowded around him, also wanting to shake his hand. The younger ones turned into instant chatterboxes, asking him where he was from, how tall he was, and Dong Ho asked in her sweet voice if he'd ever played the game *Tiu-u.*

"It's like dominos," Dong Ho said.

Charles chuckled. "I can't say that I have played your version, Dong Ho, but I'd sure like to learn some time."

Dong Ho's face bloomed red, and she scurried behind another girl.

Charles only winked at Dolly. "Well, if you ladies don't mind, Miss Cameron and I had better be going. We have reservations, you see."

The girls tittered, and even Tien smiled, although she stayed in the background.

Gallantly, Charles extended his arm, and Dolly slipped her hand around his forearm. Charles replaced his hat, and together they walked out the door to the waiting buggy.

Charles handed Dolly into the buggy, then turned to wave at the girls crowding the doorway. When he settled into the buggy and tapped the ceiling so that the driver would pull away, he looked over at Dolly. "That was something. It's plain they adore you."

His observation warmed Dolly to her toes. "They were certainly enamored of you, Mr. Bazatas," she said. "I don't think I've ever seen them quite this animated with a guest before."

Charles's dark green eyes hadn't left her since the buggy had started moving. "It's good to see you."

The sincerity in his voice made her pulse dance. "And it's good to see you. I hope your journey was uneventful."

Charles didn't answer right away because he was gazing at her quite intently. "Everything was fine. I only wish it hadn't taken me so long to come visit."

"You're busy," she said. "I'm busy. That's life." They had written letters, and he had even telephoned once. But until he knocked on the door of 920 Sacramento, she wasn't sure that what was happening between them was entirely real.

Yet here Charles Bazatas sat. Right across from her. In the flesh. His green eyes were just as she remembered, and his tousled blond hair practically begged for her to smooth it back.

He reached across the space between them and grasped her hand. "Did I tell you that it's good to see you?"

"You did." She loved his smile. The humor in his eyes. The energy that practically hummed from him. And now he was holding her hand, and she was enjoying it very much.

"I hope you're hungry," he said. "We're going to a nice restaurant for a five-course meal."

"It's the middle of the day." Her protest was weak even to her own ears.

"I want to keep you to myself as long as possible," he said. "Although I do wish I could stay another day."

Dolly was very much wishing he could stay longer too.

The afternoon sun had slanted against the buildings by the time they reached the restaurant.

True to his word, Charles ordered a five-course meal. There was no way Dolly could eat everything brought to her, but she at least tried each dish. Conversation with Charles was easy, and she found herself laughing most of the time at his stories of college, of his football team, but then the conversation turned sober when he asked her about the articles he had read.

"Tell me about Yute Ying," Charles asked.

Dolly set down her dessert fork. She could hardly eat another bite of the lemon cake anyway. "We rescued Yute Ying from a tenement house between Stockton and Dupont. The place is horrifically overcrowded. We found the ten-year-old preparing breakfast for her owners. Her appearance alone told us of the abuse and neglect she'd suffered."

Charles's forehead creased. "And now she's doing well?"

Dolly sighed and looked down at her plate. "Yes. We won the case." She met Charles's gaze. "Yute Ying was with us for a year. She thrived at the mission home. Her eyes became clear, her hands, cracked and bleeding hands from so much work, healed, and she learned to smile."

Charles reached for Dolly's hand across the table and squeezed.

Dolly took comfort in the warmth of his touch and the compassion in his eyes. "All kinds of Chinese relatives suddenly surfaced after Yute Ying's rescue. They pressed charges against me and the mission home."

"Unbelievable," Charles murmured.

"I'll never forget Yute Ying as she stood in front of the grand jury," Dolly said. "She was courageous as she testified of what she had experienced and suffered."

"It's hard to believe girls that young are brought from China for the slave trade," Charles said in a quiet voice.

"It's awful," Dolly said. "The stories of the younger girls are even more tragic, since they are kidnapped from their families, or desperate parents are lied to. We try to do everything in our power to rescue the younger girls before they age and are sold into prostitution. When the authorities visit the mission home, they are greeted with the true purpose of our mission and how much the girls are thriving. The girls become educated and gain employable skills with us."

Charles ran his thumb over her hand. "I can't imagine what you face each and every day. I'm glad the authorities are giving these girls a chance to testify for themselves."

Dolly took a sip of her drink. "Not all court appearances have a happy ending. Testifying can be traumatic for the girls, and some of them shut down."

"They won't speak?"

"Correct," Dolly said. "One of our girls, Yoke Hay, was rescued from a Chinese doctor who owned her. He had already sold an older servant girl to a house of ill fame in Fresno. So I got a warrant for Yoke Hay, and she appeared before a judge."

Charles nodded for her to continue.

"Of course, in the courtroom, there sat the angry doctor and his wife, with all their friends." Dolly exhaled. "Yoke Hay froze. She refused to repeat the story that she had told us through our interpreter. The judge was forced to return her to the man who had falsely claimed to be her father."

Charles didn't say anything for a moment, and Dolly's emotions crept to the surface. Thankfully, the restaurant was nearly empty, and no one seemed to be paying them much attention.

"I'm sorry for Yoke Hay," Charles said at last. His gaze filled with admiration as he squeezed her hand. "But your work is truly saving and changing lives. It's amazing to think about, and it makes me want to do something different with my life. Something where I can be an instrument in helping other people."

Dolly gave him a small smile. She had heard him talk about this before in his letters, and she half expected him to move to San Francisco and join the board of the mission home. But what he said next couldn't have surprised her more.

"I've decided to enter the ministry like my brother," Charles said.

She could only stare at his beaming face. "You're leaving your job?"

"Yes, and I'll be entering the seminary at Princeton," he continued. "I received my acceptance letter yesterday."

Dolly opened her mouth, but she couldn't come up with a response.

Charles stood and extended his hand. "Come, I see I've shocked you. Perhaps we can walk for a bit and discuss it."

Heart in her throat, Dolly stood and took his offered hand. Her mind whirled at the thought of Charles leaving California and traveling all the way to New Jersey. They would be so far apart; all communication would have to be long distance.

Charles led her out of the restaurant after cheerfully bidding farewell to their waiter. Dolly didn't feel cheerful at all. Yes, she admired Charles for his decision, and she could tell that it filled him with a renewed purpose. But what would it mean for *them?* Was there even a *them* for her to mourn over?

They walked slowly toward the harbor, and Dolly tried to look on the positive side of things. Heaven only knew that was how she survived every day at the mission home. Focusing on the tender mercies and the smallest of triumphs allowed her to move forward one day at a time. Charles really wanted to find a way to serve, and this was a natural way to do it.

They rounded the block, and the bay came into sight. Up ahead, seagulls filled in the silence that had fallen between them. They continued onto the pier, their footsteps echoing on the wooden walkway. Charles stopped at the railing overlooking the marina. The wind was stiff, but the day was still warm. Regardless, Charles shrugged out of his jacket and set it across her shoulders.

The feel of his jacket was like being held by him, which only made her eyes burn.

"New Jersey sounds like a lifetime away," she said at last.

Charles turned to face her, his back against the railing—reminding her of that first night they had talked on his mother's porch. "Believe me, I've thought of it from all angles, and I decided to leave it in the Lord's hands. If I got accepted at the Presbyterian seminary, then I would go."

Dolly lifted her chin, gazing into his green eyes. Everything about Charles was so . . . alive and warm. And she would miss him, terribly. But who was she to stop him, to ask him to stay? "How long is the training?"

"A few years. I'm entering the ministry and obtaining a master's in divinity and theology." He lifted his hand to tuck some of her blowing hair behind her ear. "And it won't make me a rich man." His tone was light, and she wondered if he was keeping it that way for her benefit.

"Money isn't everything, right?" she said.

"I think we could be very happy without much of it, darling." His smile was soft as his gaze scanned hers, as if he were memorizing every detail of her face, and perhaps he was.

"It's only a few years, right?" she said. "It's not like I'd be pining for you anyway. I am very busy."

He chuckled. Then his expression grew more serious than she had ever seen it. "Donaldina Cameron, what will I do when I miss you?"

She gave him a half smile, although it felt like her heart was cracking bit by bit. "Write to me?"

He nodded, then leaned forward.

She hadn't expected him to kiss her, especially in the middle of the day, and in public, no less. But it seemed that Charles had no such qualms. His hands settled at her waist and pulled her close. His kiss was warm, brief, and over within a moment.

But Dolly knew she would never forget it.

When he released her, he slid his fingers into hers. "We'll see each other soon; you'll see. I'm already saving my pennies."

Dolly doubted he had many pennies to begin with, but she smiled anyway. She wanted to enjoy every last second and minute with this man before she had to say good-bye.

"When are you leaving?"

"Three weeks," he said.

Dolly's heart twinged. She exhaled slowly, then smiled. "You will help many people."

"I can only hope."

They continued to walk along the pier, and Dolly felt the weight of each passing moment, counting down to their final farewell.

When Charles helped Dolly down from the buggy in front of the mission home, he pulled her into an embrace. She held onto him, her pulse throbbing, her heart aching, and hoped that this separation would somehow be bearable. When he drew away, his gaze was tender, and his words only for her. "You have my heart, Donaldina Cameron. And I will miss you every day."

Dolly didn't want to let him go, but she could never ask him to give up his dream. Even now, the purpose and confidence in his eyes bore into her. She didn't want to hold him back or watch him regret anything.

"I will miss you every day too, Charles," she whispered at last. Then she stepped away from the man who had brought so much light to a forgotten corner of her life.

Holding back her tears until she was inside the door, she hurried down the corridor to her office.

Finally, she was alone and could wrap her mind around all that had changed in her life and in her heart. She sat at her desk and gazed out the window into the deepening colors of the approaching evening. She hadn't given up on the idea of marriage, exactly, but over the last weeks, she had allowed hope to bloom as the idea of marrying Charles had formed into a possibility. No, she hadn't known how all the specifics would work. Perhaps she imagined serving on the board of the mission home and staying involved as much as possible.

She had ignored the deep ache that idea had brought to her soul because she'd fallen in love with Charles. But now . . . a small part of her was relieved. She would have more time with her daughters while Charles was in training.

Immediate decisions about her future would be delayed. She could continue in her work.

As if the heavens were agreeing, Tien cracked open the office door.

Dolly dried her tears and turned with a smile.

But Tien wasn't fooled. "You are sad."

Dolly's chest hitched. "Charles is . . . he's going back east to attend school."

Tien's brow wrinkled. "For how long?"

Dolly looked away. "Years," she whispered.

Tien entered the room and sat in the chair across from the desk. "He is a good man."

Dolly could only nod, and when their gazes connected again, she sensed that Tien understood things far beyond her years. Perhaps that was what happened when one's childhood was ripped away. The two didn't speak for a moment; it wasn't necessary. Dolly knew this melancholy would pass soon enough. Tomorrow would be a new day, and there would be challenges aplenty to distract her.

Tien held up a folded piece of paper. "This note arrived while you were gone."

She handed it over, and Dolly scanned the short message. It seemed that her few moments of feeling sorry for herself had already come to an end. "We need to leave immediately," she told Tien. "This girl's mistress is away from Chinatown for the day, and if we hurry, we can save her from more atrocities."

CHAPTER TWENTY-THREE

"While the world today is convulsed with war, our Home too has not been exempt from its share of exciting events . . . as some poor slave girl or abused child made her hasty and terrified flight . . . from her angry pursuers. Our warfare against the wickedness and cruelty . . . is sometimes a discouraging conflict, yet as we look back over the past year we are thankful to see that much good has been done, and many victories gained."

—DONALDINA CAMERON, MISSION HOME REPORT

1904

Mei Lien didn't know exactly where she was, but it wasn't San Francisco. Despite the numb stupor she'd been in for days, she remembered the smell of the ocean, the sting of the salt, the cry of the gulls, then finally the motion of a boat. She had been taken on a boat, or a ferry, and now she sat in a small, windowless room.

How many days had passed, she wasn't sure. In the small room she now existed in, she'd been fed and allowed water, so she knew they didn't want her dead . . . yet.

Zhang Wei. He was behind all of this. Did that mean Ah-Peen Oie was involved too? Of course she was. It was the only thing that made sense.

The slave owners would get their investment from Mei Lien yet. Keep her fed, keep her strong, then either sell her again or force her into the trade at a new location.

Footsteps sounded on the hardwood floor outside her room, and she tensed as the door unlocked, then opened. It was Wang Foo, the man who had first sold her to Ah-Peen Oie. She cringed at the sight of his wide-set eyes and stocky face.

The hardness in his eyes made her stomach flip. He carried no food, and she could only guess what his purpose was. Likely the same purpose of other men who had visited her small room. Or was he here to punish her in a different way?

"Get up," he said. "We need to hide you. *Fahn Quai* is here, looking for any paper daughters."

Mei Lien scrambled to the far corner and drew herself into a tight ball.

Wang Foo grunted, then entered the room.

"No," Mei Lien whispered in a hoarse voice. "I'd rather face the white devil than go anywhere with you."

"You have no choice." Wang Foo grasped both her arms and wrenched her to her feet.

Yes, Mei Lien had been fed in this prison, but she was also weak and exhausted. Wang Foo had an easy time of it carrying her from the room. She didn't try to get away, she didn't scream, she didn't yell.

Wang Foo carried her along a narrow corridor with other doors. The dimness was broken only by a light at the end of the hallway. He paused before a door, then fumbled with the lock before getting the door open. The room's stale atmosphere made Mei Lien's throat feel scratchy. It was as if years of dust had accumulated and been trapped in here.

"Don't make a sound," Wang Foo said. "If the devil gets ahold of you, she will use you to cast spells, and then your ancestors will return from the dead and haunt you until you die a terrible death. Then Zhang Wei will send orders across the ocean to have your mother pay in your name."

The threat was old, but it never failed to wedge Mei Lien's fear even deeper into her soul. She crouched without a word of protest and moved inside the cupboard Wang Foo held open.

He shut the door and latched it closed.

In the new darkness, Mei Lien didn't even bother to look around. She couldn't see anything anyway. Beneath her hands, small pellets indicated the presence of mice. Old or new, she didn't know. The space was warm and musty, and she held back more than one sneeze.

Listening, she could hear voices, doors opening, footsteps echoing.

She guessed there to be more than one person with the white devil. How many devils were there? The footsteps grew louder, then an argument broke out.

Wang Foo said, "There's no one in there."

"You should dust more, sir," a woman said in Chinese.

Another woman spoke in English, but Mei Lien didn't recognize any of the words.

The door opened, and footsteps grew closer.

Mei Lien couldn't be any quieter or make herself any smaller. She hoped they wouldn't open the cupboard because she had no doubt that Wang Foo would tell Zhang Wei it was her fault she had been discovered.

The creak of the latch on the cupboard caused the hairs on her arms to raise, and suddenly, the air shifted and cooled.

Candlelight flickered, and Mei Lien had to close her eyes against the brightness.

"Mei Lien?" the woman's voice was soft, spoken in an accent.

Then another woman spoke in Chinese. "Mei Lien. We are from the mission home. We are here to take you to safety."

No one touched her, but the light remained.

Slowly, she opened her eyes to find two women crouched before her, their gazes upon her. One woman was Chinese. Her face was clean, her black hair looked soft, and her eyes were intelligent. She couldn't be much older than

Mei Lien. The other woman had lighter eyes, pale skin, and she seemed oh-so-tall, even though she too was crouched before the cupboard.

"No, no! *Fahn Quai*!" Mei Lien burst out.

Neither woman looked startled. In fact, the pale woman smiled. She spoke in a soft but firm voice, and the Chinese woman translated, "Miss Cameron says she's been called much worse."

Wang Foo yelled something from the corridor. He hadn't even come into the room?

"My name is Tien Fu Wu, and we are here to rescue you from the men who hold you captive."

The pale woman scanned every inch of Mei Lien.

"Come with us," the Chinese woman continued. "We will clean you up, feed you, and give you an education. You will be free to find your own path—"

"I cannot," Mei Lien said, her voice trembling. "They will make my mother pay."

Wang Foo echoed this sentiment from the hallway.

The pale woman who was called Miss Cameron gave a soft smile. "They have no power to harm your mother. I will make sure of it." She held out her hand. "Come, you will see."

Mei Lien shrank away. Wang Foo was still hollering in the hallway, spitting out threats about Zhang Wei hunting her down, and how her mother would be beaten, and how Mei Lien would be swallowed up by demons. Hot tears scaled her cheeks, and her chest felt like it would crack in two.

The two women looked at each other, then the pale woman nodded.

The Chinese woman named Tien Fu Wu leaned close and whispered, "Huan Sun sent us. He wants you safe, Mei Lien. He visited us last night and told us he sold his shop to get money. Huan Sun tried to give us all his money so that we could come find you."

Mei Lien stared at the crouching women. Could this be true?

"We told him to keep his money," Miss Cameron said through her interpreter. Her eyes also filled with tears, which Mei Lien found remarkable. Why was she crying?

"We told him that we would find the woman he cares about and that we would take care of her."

"Why?" Mei Lien whispered.

"We will show you why," the pale woman said. "But first we must get you to safety."

Mei Lien raised a shaky hand and put it into Miss Cameron's out-stretched one. "Huan Sun really sold his shop?"

"Yes." Miss Cameron's eyes were kind, and in them Mei Lien saw compassion. Understanding, perhaps.

"Then I will come with you," Mei Lien said.

She let the women help her out of the cupboard. Mei Lien's limbs felt as if she'd been folded into a paper decoration. The women urged her to hurry, and she ran with them past the cursing Wang Foo. She followed the women down the corridor, then around a corner.

They descended a set of steps, and Mei Lien's legs burned. She wasn't used to much running, but she pressed on. Someone shouted from within the house, and instead of heading out a front door, as she expected, the women leading her turned another direction. They reached the kitchen, moved around the table, and Tien Fu Wu opened the kitchen door.

"Through here," she said.

When Mei Lien stumbled against the edge of a chair, Miss Cameron grasped her arm. She murmured something Mei Lien didn't understand, and Tien Fu Wu didn't take the time to translate.

No matter, because the moment Mei Lien stepped outside into the cool night air, nothing else signified. She wanted to be free more than she had ever wanted it in her life.

A buggy was waiting, and the two women ushered Mei Lien inside just as two men came out the same back door, shouting for them to stop. But the driver of the buggy had already whipped the horses into a frenzy, and the buggy lurched forward.

Mei Lien realized she had been gripping Miss Cameron's arm so tightly that her fingers ached. She could only imagine the bruises she'd left. The horse continued to move forward, drawing Mei Lien farther and farther away from her place of captivity.

The women in the buggy with her wasted no time in unwrapping a basket of food and drink.

Miss Cameron draped a thick blanket over Mei Lien. She hadn't noticed the cold as they were fleeing the house, but now she was shivering. Then Tien Fu Wu handed over the food, and Mei Lien took a bite of a wonton. It was cold, but it was perhaps the best thing she'd ever tasted—a dish like her mother would have made on one of their holidays. After all that had happened and all that she'd gone through, this bit of food brought tears to her eyes.

"Thank you," Mei Lien told both women.

Miss Cameron could understand that much, and she nodded, then placed a hand on Mei Lien's shoulder. Through Tien Fu Wu, Miss Cameron said, "You will soon have plenty to eat. A bed to sleep in. A chance to learn skills to prepare you for a full life."

Mei Lien nodded, although she wasn't entirely sure she believed this woman's words. What if this were some delightful dream from which she would soon awake, only to find that the *Fahn Quai* had come to drag her to *Diyu*—a dark hell?

When Tien Fu Wu said, "No one is following us," Mei Lien found herself starting to relax.

And she was so very tired. "We lost them?" She hardly dared believe they could escape men in the tong.

"We've lost them," Tien Fu Wu said.

Mei Lien noted the hesitation in her voice, but her exhaustion won out, and she allowed her eyes to close. The warmth of the blanket along with the motion of the buggy soon lulled her to sleep.

A tap on her shoulder sometime later awakened Mei Lien, and for a moment she froze, wondering who had entered her locked room and what they would ask of her. But then the memories of her rescue flowed into her mind. She cracked her eyes open to find that it was still dark outside, and Miss Cameron was smiling at her.

Mei Lien saw Tien Fu Wu's face as well. Her eyes were warm, so unlike Ah-Peen Oie's eyes filled with distrust and hatred.

"We're at 920," Tien Fu Wu said.

Mei Lien straightened and looked out the window. They were in a small alley, one with brick buildings on both sides. Looking up, she could see the sliver of a cloudy night sky.

"This is your new home," Tien Fu Wu said. "But we need to enter through a tunnel in case any of the tong are watching."

At the mention of the tong, it felt like needles scraped her skin.

But Tien Fu Wu grasped her hand. "I will come with you while Miss Cameron enters the front of the building. No one will see us go in."

Mei Lien nodded. "All right," she said in a voice thick with sleep.

The door to the buggy opened, and the driver motioned for Tien Fu Wu and Mei Lien to hurry.

Mei Lien needed no prodding to climb out of the buggy. She winced at the aches that shot through her body, but she moved quickly and followed Tien Fu Wu. The woman led her along the alley, then stopped at a grate that covered a window. Instead of moving the grate, though, she lifted a heavy board on the ground.

"Down here," Tien Fu Wu said. "Hurry. Feel for the ladder."

Mei Lien stared into the blackness as cold rushed over her. "I cannot."

Tien Fu Wu grasped her hand. "You must. There are no evil spirits inside. I have been through many times."

Still, Mei Lien couldn't climb in. She scanned the dark alley. The stench reminded her of the streets where she had tried to flee but had only been captured again. "Is there no other way in?"

"The tong went to great lengths to recapture you," Tien Fu Wu said in a matter-of-fact voice. "Huan Sun told us what happened. They will try to find you again. You need to go through this tunnel, or I cannot protect you."

Mei Lien squeezed her eyes shut and thought of Huan Sun. The last time she had seen him, his face was bruised and his lip split open. "I will go." She swallowed back her fear, then knelt on the ground. She felt around until she touched the top of a ladder. Then she turned and descended into the darkness.

Tien Fu Wu came after her and pulled the board back into place, sending the two of them into utter black.

"Go slowly and feel your way," Tien Fu Wu said quietly, her voice sounding hollow in the narrow space.

"How far down do we go?" Mei Lien asked.

"We're halfway there," Tien Fu Wu's voice returned. "Keep moving."

Mei Lien tried not to let the darkness steal her breath. When her feet reached the bottom, she still couldn't see anything. She felt along the wall and stepped carefully to one side to give Tien Fu Wu room to step down.

"Now we have to crawl." The woman's warm breath rushed over Mei Lien's face as she spoke. "Hold onto me and let me guide you."

Mei Lien grasped the woman's clothing, then knelt. The tunnel was not much larger than what anyone could crawl through. There was no way to stand, and Mei Lien tried not to think about how she was beneath a street. Her damp palms slipped against the ground more than once as she crawled. The air was cool and damp, and frequent chills raced through her.

Tien Fu Wu didn't speak, but Mei Lien could hear her breathing, and it gave her courage to keep moving even though the very air around her seemed to be pressing her into the ground. The darkness of the tunnel reminded her of the feeling of helplessness she had when Ah-Peen Oie had locked her in. Then the tunnel curved upward, and bits of dirt and rock slid past her as Tien Fu Wu led the way.

"We're here," Tien Fu Wu said.

Mei Lien wiped at the tears on her cheeks as Tien Fu Wu rose to her feet. Then she grasped Mei Lien's hand and helped her rise. The area was still underground, and the darkness still surrounded them, but at least Mei Lien could stand.

"Come." Tien Fu Wu clasped Mei Lien's arm. "Miss Cameron will be waiting for us."

Mei Lien walked on shaky legs through the underground room; then they headed up narrow stairs made of creaking wood. Tien Fu Wu opened a door, and there it was.

Light.

Miss Cameron stood with a burning candle in hand, waiting for them in a narrow corridor. "You are safe now, Mei Lien."

CHAPTER TWENTY-FOUR

"We planned our raid carefully in advance. 'But how can we get in without chopping down the doors?' Miss Cameron asked me. An eighteen-year-old slave girl named Yum Gue was held prisoner, Miss Cameron had heard from a very much frightened Chinese girl, and she was afraid they would escape by means of some secret exit.

"I recalled that there was a skylight in the roof of the house that was left open during the day. I believed that it only dropped closed and was not locked during night time, so we planned to try to get through that."

—Sergeant John Manion, Women and Missions magazine, 1932

1904

Mei Lien gazed out the narrow window of her bedroom in the mission home. Outside, the sun shone, the people walked along the street, the trees swayed in the wind, and the clouds raced across the sky. But it was not her life. The outside belonged to others.

She did not leave her room. She did not speak to the other girls. When Tien Fu Wu came to visit, Mei Lien listened to the young woman's advice, but she could not bring herself to go to the dining room. Or to enter the kitchen. When Miss Cameron invited her to church services for her Christian God, Mei Lien could not betray her mother and ancestors.

Mei Lien's soul was black. The stain of her sins could never be washed away, no matter what Miss Cameron told her.

Mei Lien might have survived, but she was not alive.

Beyond the window, she watched a woman holding the hand of a young girl as they walked along the street at a brisk pace. They were not Chinese, and Mei Lien had never seen them before, but she could almost feel the connection between the mother and daughter.

Mei Lien did not expect to see her mother ever again. Perhaps she had believed at one time that it might be a possibility. Her husband would send money and bring her mother to San Francisco. Or she and her husband, along with their two small sons, would visit Hong Kong.

But there was no husband. No future.

And she didn't know if the child growing in her belly would be a boy, but he would be born to a mother who had nothing. Who *was* nothing.

Hot tears pricked her eyes, and Mei Lien was surprised yet again that she could cry anymore. She turned from the window. Today it was hard to even look at the life beyond, a life she would never have. She sank onto her bed and pulled her knees up to her chest until she was as small as she could possibly be. Beneath her mattress, she had hidden the pearls from Huan Sun. Right now, she did not feel worthy enough to wear them.

She had brought punishment to her mother. Surely the tong had already acted. And Huan Sun. He'd helped her, and now who knew what had happened to him?

A tear slipped down her cheek as she thought about her child. Soon enough, her belly would grow, and she could no longer keep it a secret. Soon enough, her rescuers would realize how far Mei Lien had truly fallen. How much of a burden she was.

Mei Lien closed her eyes, hoping for sleep to numb her. The sounds of young girls sweetly singing rose from one of the lower floors. She hadn't wanted to see any of the other rooms in the house. After her bath that first night, Mei Lien had stayed in this small space of a room, which wasn't much larger than the storage room where she'd been kept imprisoned. But this room wasn't a physical prison. The window let in the sunlight. The door was never locked from the outside. She didn't have to entertain any men.

This room was a different prison—one in which she had plenty of time to remember. The darkness. The hopelessness. And what might have been if only she and her mother had turned away the emigration agent. Yes, she and her mother had been poor, hungry, tired. Now, that seemed such a small thing. Now, Mei Lien knew that life could be much, much worse.

The melody of the singing below pushed its way into her room, tried to enter her soul and soften the hardness there. Dispel the darkness. But Mei Lien pushed back. She didn't want to feel happiness. She didn't want to accept the light. Somehow she knew that once she comprehended all that she had lost and all that she'd endured, the pain would be too much to bear.

"Mei Lien?" a quiet voice said outside her door.

She didn't answer. Perhaps if Miss Cameron thought she was asleep, she would be left alone. But the woman was persistent, as usual, and the next thing Mei Lien knew, Miss Cameron had turned the doorknob and walked into the bedroom.

Her smile was soft, her footsteps sure, and behind her was a Chinese girl who gazed at her with wide, curious eyes.

Don't stare at me, Mei Lien wanted to say, but she found that she was curious too. The girl settled on the bed only a short distance away.

"This is Yoke Lon," Miss Cameron said in stilted Chinese, sitting on the single chair in the room.

"Lonnie," the girl said immediately.

Miss Cameron chuckled softly.

"Lonnie is my English name." The girl nodded vigorously, causing her two braids to bounce along her shoulders. "Thank you for letting me in your room."

Mei Lien didn't remember "letting" anyone inside her room, but she said nothing. Lonnie acted as if coming into her room were a perfectly natural thing.

"When *Lo Mo* grew tired of my many questions about you, she said it was time for me to ask you myself." Lonnie smiled at Miss Cameron, then crossed her ankles and folded her hands in her lap.

Lo Mo . . . Mei Lien had heard the name spoken from the corridor about Miss Cameron. Mei Lien supposed the woman was like a mother to some of the younger girls, and the affection and respect in Lonnie's tone were unmistakable.

"Can I ask you questions?" Lonnie pressed.

No, Mei Lien thought. *I do not want to answer questions. I do not want to tell anyone what has happened to me.* She shook her head, and again, Lonnie wasn't bothered.

"All right, if I can't ask questions, I will tell you about myself. I came to *Lo Mo*'s when I was about six," Lonnie continued. "My parents were very poor, and they were promised that I would have a good home and a full belly if they let me come to America. My new mistress was very cruel."

Lonnie rose from the bed and crossed to the window. She peered out and released a sigh. "Sometimes I look out the window and wonder why I went through the things I did. Why can't I be like those people out there?"

Mei Lien found herself nodding.

"But then I remember my old life," Lonnie continued in a quiet voice. "I remember the beatings and being hungry all the time. If Miss Culbertson hadn't rescued me, where would I be now?"

Mei Lien's eyes burned with tears. She knew the answer.

Lonnie turned from the window, her own eyes shining with tears. "I would be dead. I am sure of it." Her face glowed with a smile that was both sad and triumphant. "To my very bones, I know that if I had not been rescued when I was, I would have joined my ancestors. But I am here. I'm alive, and I have a second chance to become something that never would have been possible."

Mei Lien returned her gaze to her clasped hands. Lonnie's words reverberated inside her chest. She knew that all the girls staying in this house must have come from somewhere and must have been through experiences similar to hers. But hearing Lonnie speak of her past so openly had made Mei Lien feel less . . . different.

She met Lonnie's brown eyes. In them, she saw the warmth, the acceptance, the nonjudgment.

"They lied to me, too," Mei Lien said in a quiet voice, the first words she had spoken since Miss Cameron and Lonnie entered. "From the first promise to my mother, they lied. They offered her money for her sacrifice of giving me up. They promised that I would be married to a wealthy man looking for a wife."

Mei Lien didn't realize tears were falling until Miss Cameron handed over a handkerchief. Mei Lien pressed the cloth against her cheeks.

Lonnie sat next to her on the bed again, this time closer. When Lonnie rested a hand on her shoulder, Mei Lien felt something she had never felt before in her life. This was what it must be to have a sister.

Mei Lien told her story in bits and pieces, stringing the events of the last several months together as best she could. She left out some of the harder, darker things, but there was no need to explain those in detail. By the knowledge in Lonnie's eyes, and the understanding and compassion in Miss Cameron's, Mei Lien knew both women heard all the words she couldn't speak.

"You have a second chance here," Miss Cameron said at last when Mei Lien had explained how Zhang Wei had caught up with her in the end, just when she thought she could escape and work for the laundry woman. "There are many things to learn, and no one will ever think less of you because of what you've been through."

Mei Lien had heard these words from Tien Fu Wu and Miss Cameron before, but with Lonnie sharing her story, slowly Mei Lien allowed herself to believe.

"I am grateful . . ." Her voice cracked, and she tried again. "I am grateful for the risks you've taken for me."

"It was our honor," Miss Cameron said. "You will be a wonderful asset to the mission home."

Mei Lien didn't know how. But she was tired of being tired. Tired of the heavy weight upon her chest and the deep ache in her stomach. For a few moments, with Lonnie here, she had felt lighter somehow. Less alone.

"Come to the kitchen," Lonnie said. "I'll show you how to make almond cookies. They're my favorite."

Mei Lien had only had almond cookies a few times in her life. They were a luxury her mother couldn't afford very often. Ah-Peen Oie had served them at the banquets, and Mei Lien had tried them there. "Is there a special occasion?" *Will there be a lot of people coming?* was her real question.

"No," Lonnie said. "The housekeeper allows us to bake anytime as long as we don't have class and we clean up after ourselves."

Mei Lien looked over at Miss Cameron for confirmation, and she nodded.

"Are there a lot of other residents down there?" The thought of leaving the confines of this room, of being around many others in a bigger space, still made her want to lock her bedroom door.

"Everyone is at their lessons," Lonnie said. "We will be the only ones in the kitchen. If I can bake, then so can you. When I was a slave, my mistress used to burn me if she thought I was lazy. It took me a long time to go into the mission home kitchen, and even longer to attempt any baking."

Mei Lien stared at the girl. It was hard to believe this cheerful, frank girl had once been too afraid to walk into a kitchen. Mei Lien bit her lip, battling with her physical reaction of walking down those stairs into the unknown. Could she do it? She knew her answer; she had to be strong enough to follow through. "All right," she said at last.

Lonnie wrapped her arms about Mei Lien, surprising her. She couldn't remember the last time she'd been hugged by another woman. Not since her mother's farewell, she was sure.

When Mei Lien hugged Lonnie back, the girl laughed. Mei Lien felt a small smile push its way to the surface. "We should go now, before I change my mind."

Lonnie drew back, her eyes shining. "Then let's hurry." She grasped Mei Lien's hand and practically pulled her off the bed with her.

Miss Cameron rose with them and opened the bedroom door. She gave Mei Lien an encouraging smile as they moved into the corridor. The house was abuzz with life and energy and voices, but no one was in the hallway.

So, tugged by Lonnie, Mei Lien descended the front staircase. When she had been brought to the house, they had used the back stairs—the stairs they'd told her she would have to go back down if there was a house raid. This front staircase was a thing of beauty, made from dark wood and winding from the top floors to the main level.

Each step brought her farther away from the sanctity of her bedroom; each step brought her closer to something different, something unknown.

When she hesitated on the last three steps, Lonnie turned and said, "Don't worry, Mei Lien. You'll never have to be alone again."

CHAPTER TWENTY-FIVE

*"It was necessary . . . in a way to break the letter of the law
though not the spirit of the law when we rescued a Chinese
child for there was no written law to uphold us in entering
a house and carrying off a child—then, too, before it was
possible to carry out guardianship proceedings."*

—Donaldina Cameron, mission home report

1904

The letter folded easily, its creases well-worn due to the number of times that Dolly had read Charles's words. He was thriving at the seminary in New Jersey, and his letter was full of enthusiasm and purpose, yet Dolly hadn't written him back. She missed him terribly, and she was afraid that her melancholy would bleed onto the pages.

No matter, it was late at night, and she should get some rest. This morning, she had accompanied little Mae Tao to the courthouse, where her hearing had been a farce. The judge had turned her over to her "uncle," and she was dragged out of the courthouse crying. The experience had left Dolly feeling as if her stomach had turned to stone.

There had also been a plague scare on the next street over. It turned out that the man was sick with something else, but it had been enough to send the entire neighborhood into a panic. The plague had spread despite the city officials' efforts to barricade neighborhoods, and more than a hundred people had died.

Tomorrow, Dolly would go to court with Yuen Ho's husband, who'd been shot by a highbinder after he helped his wife escape. Dolly doubted the highbinder would be caught and punished, but filing the charges would have to do for now. Her thoughts shifted to the young man who had delivered a message years before and had then been shot in the street moments after. Even with the passing years, the danger continued, and the stakes only seemed higher.

Dolly yearned for an outsider's point of view. She longed to discuss these events with Charles. But in truth, after recording the events in the mission home ledger, she was often too emotionally exhausted to repeat them in a letter—although Charles was always interested in hearing about her work. In fact, her work had been what had inspired him to find a higher calling in his life.

Dolly didn't miss the irony of the number of miles that now separated her from the man she hoped to marry. Yes, that hope was something she could admit to herself now that he was living across the country. She was trying to be understanding and brave and to continue to do her own work while she waited. . . .

Charles might be far away, but Dolly had plenty to be grateful for, especially, at the moment, the progress that Mei Lien was making. Lonnie had taken it upon herself to be Mei Lien's young friend, and the woman was spending more and more time each day outside of her bedroom. She had even joined in with the sewing class the other day. It turned out that Mei Lien was highly skilled in embroidery. Dolly had complimented her and was gratified to see a smile from the young woman.

Soon, Mei Lien would learn to trust again. She would learn to accept her own healing. And she would tell Dolly about the child she carried in her belly. The sadness in Mei Lien's eyes was unmistakable and unfortunately all too common in Dolly's experience in rescuing paper daughters.

After turning off the lamp, she walked out of her office. The house was silent, and Dolly double-checked to make sure the lights were off downstairs, save one, before she headed up to her bedroom. Since becoming director, Dolly had made no pretenses and had moved into one of the smaller rooms at the top of the house. Her closet might be tiny and fit no more than two pairs of shoes in width, but Dolly cherished the view she had of the city through the windows. She could see the comings and goings and watch the pulse of the neighborhood below.

A loud rap at the double front doors made Dolly pause as she neared the first staircase landing.

A knock at the door at this time of night had never brought good news. Despite her own exhaustion, Dolly's mind immediately went on alert. Was there another rescue? She hurried down the stairs and strode to the doors. Looking out the paned windows of the top half of the doors, Dolly saw two men on the front stoop. A few paces behind them stood four or five other men.

No. She felt as if she had been physically pushed back by an ocean wave. Dolly reached for the gong that would alert the girls upstairs. The newer girls had all been trained to head down the back stairs, all the way to the bottom basement. Tien would see to it. Dolly prayed that Mei Lien would be among them, because it was unusual to have so many men on her doorstep.

It appeared that Zhang Wei wanted his slave back.

Dolly started at the top of the door, turning the first lock. She had installed multiple locks scaling the door from top to bottom, allowing her to take more time to get the door open. And allowing the girls more time to escape the back way.

She slid the second lock open, then the third. She continued slowly, even though she could practically feel the impatience of the men on the porch oozing through the door. When the final lock was turned, she opened the door a crack.

"May I help you?"

A thick hand rested on the open door.

But Dolly didn't draw back. She straightened her spine and gazed at the men. All but two were Chinese. She recognized Attorney Abe Ruef and Officer Cook. Both she and the officer had aged over the years, and Cook's hair was generously peppered with gray beneath his hat. Their gazes connected briefly, and Dolly knew he wished he could have stopped this night raid.

"I have a warrant for Mei Lien's arrest," the lawyer announced.

"*Who?*" Dolly asked.

Ruef's face darkened a shade. "Mei Lien. You heard me."

Dolly pretended to consider the name while Ruef shuffled his feet impatiently. She had no qualms about stalling. She had put him through these paces multiple times, but he deserved it. She hated that Ruef now took money from the tong to represent them in these cases.

"May I see the warrant?" Dolly said.

Ruef promptly handed it over, and Dolly ever-so-slowly read through each word. "She stole a necklace from Mr. Zhang Wei?" Dolly looked up and scanned the Chinese men. "Where is Mr. Zhang Wei?" She very well knew what he looked like, but she made a show of studying them anyway.

"He's not here," Ruef said in a clipped tone.

"Oh?" Dolly looked past him again. "He is not one of these five Chinese men you have with you? Who are *these* men, then?"

"They are here to help us search your house if you do not produce Mei Lien immediately."

Dolly merely pursed her lips, then turned toward Tien, who by practiced agreement had come to the front door after ushering the new girls to the basement. "Tien, have you heard of a girl named Mei Lien? These gentlemen are looking for her."

"Mei Lien?" Tien's forehead pinched. "I have not heard of her." Her English might be stilted, but it was perfectly understandable to everyone on the porch. "Did they try the next house? Maybe the girl is there."

"She's *not* there," Ruef growled, pushing on the door. "Let us in. We will search for ourselves if you refuse to bring her to us."

Still Dolly didn't budge from her place. "Do you have a search warrant for these premises, Officer Cook?"

He gave a stiff nod, and Dolly knew he hated to be on this errand. "We do, Miss Cameron." He took his time fishing it out of his jacket pocket, then handed it over.

Dolly grasped the search warrant and again took her time reading every single word.

"Well, Tien, it appears we must let these gentlemen inside to search." Dolly sighed. "Please be quiet. Most of our residents are asleep, and some of them are young babies. Abandoned, you know, by their Chinese fathers."

Ruef moved past Dolly, bumping her shoulder and offering no apology. The instant he crossed the threshold of the mission home, it was as if someone had cracked a horse whip. Six men were suddenly inside the house; two of them headed toward the kitchen, while the other four pounded up the staircase to the higher floors.

Officer Cook remained by the door, his hands on his hips, a scowl on his face.

So much for keeping any semblance of quiet. Not that any of the Chinese girls were sleeping. Still, Dolly prayed that Mei Lien's hiding place in the basement would keep her safe. Hopefully these men held the usual Chinese beliefs that evil spirits lived below ground, which suited Dolly just fine.

She and Tien followed the men up the stairs in order to make sure they didn't disturb too much. All the girls knew to tell any man who asked after another girl to claim they didn't know her.

Dolly walked into the bedrooms the men had left, quickly reassuring each girl that everyone was fine, everyone was safe.

When she stopped by Lonnie's room, the girl wrapped her arms about Dolly's waist. "Will they find her?"

"Hush," Dolly whispered. "Everyone is safe."

Lonnie nodded vigorously, her eyes welling with tears.

Dolly bent and kissed the top of the girl's head. "Don't cry. We must be strong and have faith."

Another nod, and Dolly had to move on. There were many more girls and women to check on and offer comfort to. And all the while, she listened to the men going through each room, searching. It seemed hours had passed before they left, but it had been only a half hour. When they reached the lowest level above ground, they peered into the dark basement below.

Dolly watched from the top of the corridor, holding her breath, as she waited to see whether they would enter. Their murmured voices were indistinguishable, but Tien joined Dolly and whispered, "They think that is where you leave the girls you poison."

Dolly might have laughed if the situation weren't so grave. The men were literally feet away from stepping into the same space where Mei Lien was hiding. Dolly clasped her hands behind her, clutching her fingers together.

Tien, with her astute observance, said, "They will not go down there. They are more afraid of what might be lurking in the dark basement than of any punishment they might receive from Zhang Wei."

Sure enough, the men eventually left without going into the basement. The moment Dolly had clicked the last lock on the tall, double doors, she turned and rushed to the door leading to the basement. There, she found Tien already inside, with her hand in Mei Lien's.

The trembling young woman stepped out of the darkness and into the dimly lit corridor. Tears stained her face, and her skin was as white as a goose egg.

"Was it Zhang Wei?" Mei Lien whispered.

"It was the men who work for him." Dolly stepped to the woman's side and rested an arm about her shoulders. With Tien translating, Dolly said, "They found nothing, and no one gave you away. You are safe here, just as I told you."

Mei Lien nodded, then suddenly, she turned toward Dolly. Dolly pulled her close and held her as sobs racked her body. Tien simply stood and waited. Despite the lateness of the hour and the disruption to everyone's sleep, neither of them was in a hurry to get Mei Lien to bed.

After several moments, Mei Lien lifted her head and drew away. Dolly offered her a handkerchief. Mei Lien wiped at her face. Then she folded the damp cloth into a square, and folded it again. She continued twisting the handkerchief between her fingers as if she had something else plaguing her beyond the raid.

Finally, she whispered, "I am pregnant."

Tien translated, but Dolly already knew what the young woman had said. She grasped Mei Lien's hand. "We know, dear."

Mei Lien's eyes widened at that admission. "You know? How?"

"We have seen others in your situation," Dolly said.

Mei Lien asked, "Will you make me leave now?"

"No," Dolly said with a soft smile. "Your child is welcome here too. Have you seen our nursery yet?"

"I have walked past it," Mei Lien admitted.

"They are the babies and young children of other residents," Dolly said. "Of women who found themselves in your same situation."

Mei Lien stared at her. "You mean, they were pregnant when they were rescued, and you didn't send them away?"

Dolly nodded after Tien translated.

It seemed that once Mei Lien realized she wasn't going to be sent away due to her pregnancy, the tension that always surrounded her softened. Over the next few days, Mei Lien spent more and more time outside her bedroom. She joined in the classes and cooked in the kitchen with Lonnie.

Several evenings later, Dolly was working on returning overdue pieces of correspondence when someone knocked at the front door of the mission home. It was a quiet knock. A quick look at the clock told Dolly it was about an hour after dinner.

Of course, a knock any time of day could mean anything. It was with trepidation that she approached the front door. Through the glass she could see a Chinese man. He was alone, and Dolly recognized him immediately. He had visited her weeks ago with a desperate plea.

Something wasn't right. The expression on his face looked pained. She unlocked each of the bolts quickly, then opened the door. "Huan Sun, are you all right?"

The man staggered through the doorway, grasping his shoulder. He said something in a raspy voice, but it was all in Chinese.

When Dolly saw the blood, she called for Tien.

CHAPTER TWENTY-SIX

*"Let the first oath be recited. By this incense stick we swear to avenge
any wrong committed against any brother of this Tong. He who
violates this oath, let thunder from all points annihilate him. . . . He
who violates this oath, let him suffer death by a thousand knives. . . .
By this incense stick we swear to kill without mercy all who lift their
hands against any member of this Tong. He who fails to keep this oath
shall without fail die at the hands of the salaried assassin."*

—Ceremony of the Tong with the Exalted Master, the slave owner, the
secretary, the treasurer, and Six Honorable Elders in attendance

1904

"You must come. Now."

Mei Lien glanced up from her embroidery to see Tien Fu Wu in the sewing class, looking like she had bit into a sour lemon.

"What is it?" Mei Lien asked.

"There is a man," Tien Fu Wu said. "And he's been shot."

The rest of the girls in the class stilled. One of them gave a little cry. After a few seconds of silence, the room erupted into noise as the girls abandoned their work. Some fled the room; others crouched beneath tables.

Mei Lien stared at the young interpreter. Why had she been singled out?

261

"Who is this man?" Then she knew, without Tien Fu Wu telling her. Mei Lien scrambled from her chair and hurried into the hallway.

"It's Huan Sun, isn't it?" she demanded from Tien Fu Wu. "Was it the tong?"

"Yes," Tien Fu Wu said.

Mei Lien didn't waste another moment. She didn't ask if Huan Sun was still alive. She bolted into the corridor and hurried down the stairs. "Huan Sun!" she cried as she reached the main level. Where he was, she didn't know. She continued through each room until she found him on the couch in the Chinese parlor.

Miss Cameron hovered over him, and another staff member stood nearby. Huan Sun wasn't moving.

Mei Lien choked on a sob and moved to his side, searching his face for any sign of life. "Huan Sun," she whispered.

His eyes fluttered open, and Mei Lien started to cry. He was alive.

"Don't cry," Huan Sun said. "They missed my heart."

Mei Lien only cried harder. She grasped his hand and sank to his side. "Who did this to you?"

His voice was a whisper. "I don't know."

"It has to be Zhang Wei," she said.

Huan Sun's gaze was resigned, which told her he agreed. He grimaced as Miss Cameron undid his shirt. Mei Lien began to help remove the stained garment. She blinked through blurry vision when she saw the wound. The blood was not stopping.

"Where is the doctor?" she asked, but Miss Cameron couldn't know what she was saying, and neither did the other staff member.

"We need to get you to the hospital," Mei Lien told Huan Sun.

"No," he said in a faint voice. "They won't treat Chinese there. That is why I came here."

"What do you mean they will not treat Chinese there?"

Tien Fu Wu entered the room then, and Mei Lien peppered her with questions.

"The doctor is coming," Tien Fu Wu assured her. "You should sit down and not get overexcited."

Mei Lien shook her head. "I can't sit and do nothing. What do you need help with?"

"Watch for the doctor's arrival," Tien Fu Wu said. "As soon as he arrives, bring him in here."

This, Mei Lien could do. What she couldn't do was have a man who had just been shot for protecting her look at her with sympathy. She waited for what seemed like a hundred minutes, and when she saw a man approach the door, she called for Tien Fu Wu.

"That's him," Tien Fu Wu confirmed. "Let him in."

Mei Lien opened the door and ushered the doctor in. She locked the door behind him, then led him to the parlor. The doctor set to work immediately, and Mei Lien wished she spoke enough English to ask him questions.

First the doctor examined Huan Sun, speaking to Miss Cameron. Tien Fu Wu translated for Huan Sun. Then the doctor took out a bottle of liquid from his black satchel. After swabbing the wound with the red liquid, he poured something else into a handkerchief and held it to Huan Sun's nose.

His eyes slipped shut.

"What's happening?" Mei Lien asked, rising to her feet.

"He is only sleeping," Tien Fu Wu said. "The doctor said the bullet went through his arm, and it needs to be sewn closed."

Still, Mei Lien stayed on her feet, and only when the doctor prepared to stitch up the skin did she turn away.

When the doctor finished the repair work, Mei Lien's first question was, "Will he live?"

Tien Fu Wu smiled. "Yes, he'll live."

Mei Lien absorbed this good news, then fled from the parlor, her stomach churning. When she reached her room, she vomited into the washbasin.

Then she curled up on her bed, hating that she was weak. She also hated that anyone took punishment because of her, and she hated that her baby would be born in such a cruel world.

Eventually Mei Lien fell asleep from exhaustion, and when she awoke, it was sometime in the middle of the night. Shame washed over her as she thought of how she'd fled the scene of a little blood. Huan Sun had been the one who had been shot, not her. The least she could do was take care of him.

She rose from her bed and crept down the staircase. Outside the parlor, she paused, watching the patches of moonlight coming in from the high windows. Huan Sun was asleep on the couch. Across the room, Tien Fu Wu was sitting in a chair, asleep as well.

Not wanting to disturb either one, Mei Lien watched Huan Sun breathing from where she stood. Assured that he seemed to be doing well, she turned to leave.

"Mei Lien." His whispered voice stopped her.

Slowly, she faced him.

"Are you all right?"

Her throat burned with emotion. "I am all right. *You* are the one who was shot." She moved closer to him, keeping her voice low.

He raised up on an elbow, but then grimaced and lay back down.

"Don't move," she cautioned. "I don't want your stitches to pull out."

Huan Sun motioned with his good hand for her to come toward him. Carefully and quietly, she crept forward, then knelt next to the couch.

"You are feeling better?" she asked.

"I need to tell you what happened."

"If you are too tired . . ." Mei Lien glanced over at the sleeping Tien Fu Wu.

"Mei Lien." He grasped her hand and held on tight. "Zhang Wei will not stop. When I found out he sent the members of his tong to this house a few nights ago to search for you, I knew I had to do something more. I paid him the money of your contract from selling my shop. I told him I was going to marry you, and that I would not allow anyone to make you a slave again."

She stared at Huan Sun. Was this all true? He had paid off her contract? "Why?"

"Why?"

She nodded, tears forming in her eyes, then escaping onto her cheeks. "You have done too much. I could not live with myself if something else happened to you."

Huan Sun only tightened his hold on her hand. "I feel the same way, Mei Lien. I want to take you away from this place. We will marry, and we will live a good life. Away from San Francisco and men like Zhang Wei and women like Ah-Peen Oie."

Mei Lien drew in a breath. His words sounded like a dream—one she had never thought she could have. But the constant knot in her stomach reminded her of her added responsibility. She had more than one person to care for now. "Where would we go?"

"I don't know yet," he said. "I will find a place, and I will come back for you."

Mei Lien stared into the warm brown eyes of Huan Sun. "You would do that for me? You care that much for me?"

He ran his thumb over her wrist. "Have I not already proven it?"

Yes, he had. Many times. But Mei Lien, her hope shredded, had been too afraid to believe. To think that her life might truly change and become something good. Still, she worried. "What about the child I'm carrying? It might be Zhang Wei's."

Huan Sun brought her wrist to his lips and pressed a soft kiss on her skin. "It doesn't matter. From the moment I met you, I felt something between us. And I believe you felt the same."

"I did," Mei Lien whispered. "But I didn't recognize it. My life had changed so much. And you were the first . . ."

Huan Sun released her hand and ran the tips of his fingers alongside her face. "I need to leave before the sun rises. Miss Cameron doesn't want me here when the girls wake up."

"Take the pearls," she said. "They can buy your way."

"No, they are yours." He rested a hand on her shoulder. "I will find a way. I want to learn English and study the Bible. The mission ladies said I need to be Christian to marry you."

Mei Lien hadn't heard of this. "Why?"

"They are very strict about who they let their girls marry."

"Then I will leave."

"No," Huan Sun said. "I want you safe. Here. Wait for me, Mei Lien."

Mei Lien nodded, then wiped at the tears now coursing down her face. "I will wait."

And she did wait.

Weeks passed, and she still waited. Her belly grew with her child. And yet Huan Sun did not return. No word was sent—no letter, no message—and Mei Lien was left to wonder.

The days blended into endless weeks, and the weeks became one month, then two, then three. She worried about Huan Sun's safety. She worried the tong would return and kidnap her. Or perhaps they had found a way to punish her mother. What if they came when her child was born and stole him away?

The first labor pains began when Mei Lien was with Tien Fu Wu, working on her English. The low, deep pains in her back soon wrapped around to her stomach, spreading like a quick-burning flame.

"What is it?" Tien Fu Wu rose from the table, her expression already alert.

Mei Lien's eyes slid shut as the pain ebbed, bringing a sweet but temporary relief. "The baby . . . is coming."

Everything after that was a blur as Tien Fu Wu ran from the room shouting for help. Miss Cameron came. Other women in the house crowded around her, and people were giving orders in both Chinese and English.

Tears burned Mei Lien's eyes as her belly contracted and the pain elevated once again, getting stronger now. She wanted her mother. "*Ah Ma,*" she whispered over and over again, but her mother never came. Her mother would never know this grandchild of hers.

"It's a boy," someone said in Chinese, and then Tien Fu Wu was smoothing back her hair, a huge smile on her face. "He is healthy."

Miss Cameron's face came into view, and she presented to Mei Lien the smallest of bundles. A baby. Mei Lien's baby. Carefully, she took the warm bundle and pressed her lips against the baby's damp forehead. His hair was dark, his eyes closed, and his eyelashes a perfect row. *He* was perfect. No matter who his father might be, *she* was his mother.

"My son," she whispered because her voice was too raw to make a sound. She had never felt so elated or so miserable at the same time. Even as she gazed down at the beautiful child in her arms, she wished that Huan Sun could have been with her.

The girls of the mission home, who had become friends to her, filed into her room to gaze upon the tiny creature. It was only after everyone had left that Mei Lien broke down into tears. Labor pains had not brought such tears of despair, but knowing that this child might grow up fatherless was what broke through her bravery.

When Tien Fu Wu entered her room later that day, Mei Lien handed over the baby to her.

"I cannot do it," Mei Lien said, her voice choked. "This baby does not deserve such a weak mother. I have no father to give him. No income to provide for him."

Tien Fu Wu merely took the baby and walked the room, cradling him in her arms.

Mei Lien watched the young woman carrying the child. The calm manner. The soothing words. The guilt was crushing her like a boulder.

"Huan Sun still hasn't returned," Mei Lien said in a stilted voice. "What if he changed his mind? Or what if he's . . . dead?" She swallowed back a rising sob. "I should leave here. I don't deserve your care and goodness. I have nothing to offer in return. I am nothing."

Tien Fu Wu sat on the single chair in the room. Her dark eyes focused on Mei Lien. "I used to think I was nothing. But Miss Culbertson kept believing in me. Then Yuen Qui was always kind, no matter what. And finally, Miss Cameron trusted me. Because of that, I know that *you* have a home here. And your son will too. Once he's old enough for school, we will find a place to educate him. No matter who his father is, or if he never knows a father, he still has a mother and many, many aunties."

"Miss Cameron will not kick me out for having a son?"

"No." Tien Fu Wu's smile was soft. "You are both family here. If *Lo Mo* can put up with me, housing you is no problem."

Mei Lien watched the remarkable young woman holding her child—a baby Mei Lien already loved fiercely. Her love for the child was overwhelming, making her wish that her life had been different, that he'd been born into a marriage, and that she had the ability to give him the world.

"I don't want to leave," she admitted in a whisper.

Tien Fu Wu rose from her chair and settled next to Mei Lien on the bed. Together they gazed down at the sleeping baby.

"He will grow into a fine man," Tien Fu Wu said softly. "With a mother as devoted as you, he can't help but have a happy and productive life."

Mei Lien desperately wanted Tien Fu's words to be true.

"Now, you must rest. Miss Cameron's orders," Tien Fu Wu continued. "I will walk the corridors with your baby while you sleep. When he is hungry, I'll bring him back to you."

Mei Lien closed her eyes, and the last sound she heard before falling into a warm sleep was Tien Fu Wu humming softly to her little boy.

CHAPTER TWENTY-SEVEN

*"Kindness and peace had a soothing effect at first, but later brooding
over her sorrows and worries, and possessed by a fierce jealousy, fits
of despair seemed to possess [Chow Kum]. The climax came one day
when she tried to jump from a window with the little girl in her
arms. After that she had to be taken away from the Home."*

—DONALDINA CAMERON, MISSION HOME REPORT ON CHOW KUM

1904

Dolly stepped off the train into the midmorning sunlight of a hot August day. She had arrived in Philadelphia at last, nearly a week late. Today she would see Charles Bazatas. She could hardly believe it had been nearly four years since she had seen the man with whom she hoped to build a future.

The weeks and months and years had passed, one after the other, and still they were living on opposite ends of the United States. Anticipation simmered in Dolly as she thought about what it might be like to see Charles after all this time. She was older, he was older, they were both wiser. Perhaps.

Charles's letters were always full of enthusiasm for his work, and Dolly replied in kind with briefer summaries of hers. In truth, the last few years had been hard. She thought of the girls and women who had left the mission home—some of their own accord, others by a judge's ruling to return to their "uncles" or "grandfathers," still others being deported.

Girls moving on, girls arriving, babies being born, and still . . . Mei Lien waiting for Huan Sun to return. Her baby boy was now a few months old, and he was a delightful child. Just thinking about him brought a smile to Dolly's face.

And Tien . . . Dolly already missed the young woman who had grown from a defiant child to a clever woman. Dolly depended on her more and more, and Tien was up to the task, acting as a staunch defender of victims and a willing aide to Dolly. Tien now went on all the rescues, and it was because of her skills that Dolly felt she could take a sabbatical.

Dolly was thirty-five years old now and had been at the mission home for nine years. She had never taken more than a short vacation. Her work was her life, and she loved it, but exhaustion had set in of late. She couldn't forget how Miss Culbertson had never taken a break and had quite literally died days after a forced retirement. With the board's permission and encouragement, Dolly was on furlough to travel to the East, then to visit Scotland and see her sister she had never met. Her parents had left her oldest sister in Scotland to offer their grandmother some comfort when they moved the rest of the family to New Zealand.

After seeing her sister, Dolly would finally travel to China for the first time. She had been assured that the mission home would be in good hands under the direction of Wilmina Wheeler as temporary director, housekeeper Frances Thompson, and of course their young and fierce interpreter Tien.

This journey back east was sorely needed. Not only did Dolly need the break, but she knew that she had to see Charles and decide on their future once and for all. Yet her heart was now divided between relief from setting aside the demands of the mission home and loneliness from missing her daughters.

She had visited one of her Chinese daughters in Minnesota, followed by a visit with a friend to the mission cause who convinced Dolly to stay several extra days at her lodge on Lake Minnetonka. It was a lovely and peaceful time, and she felt more than prepared to finally see Charles again.

The Philadelphia train platform was busy with people coming and going, finding their luggage, calling out to friends and family, and sorting out their transportation.

Dolly didn't know where to look first, so she headed for the porter to retrieve her modest trunk. Once she had it in hand, she hefted it toward the ticket office. She should have been more specific as to *where* to meet Charles. He could be only feet away from her, but it was hard to pick out anyone in such a thick crowd.

"Donaldina Cameron!" a voice called.

His voice seemed to lift her feet from the ground with elation. She turned and searched for any sight of him. At first, she didn't see him, but then a tall, blond man came into view as a family shuffled past with a crying baby.

Charles was the same, yet different, too. Even though he had a hat on, she could see that his hair was much shorter. Gone were the waves. Had he grown taller, too? Or had she forgotten what it was like to look up into his deep green eyes?

His smile was broad, and warmth swelled her heart. She laughed as he drew her into a tight hug in front of everyone on the platform. It had been so long since she'd felt his arms about her that she was sure she was dreaming. The best dream imaginable.

She closed her eyes, the echo of her heartbeat the only thing she could hear now as she breathed in everything that was Charles. He smelled of sunshine and musk and leather.

When he drew away, an inexplicable sense of sadness descended upon her. That didn't make sense. She had been waiting forever for this day, and she should feel only joy. Yet, it was as if a fierce battle was going on inside her heart as pure happiness warred with piercing sorrow.

Dolly pushed back her confusing emotions and smiled at Charles. "You found me."

His grin nearly split his face. "I found you." As his eyes scanned her features, she felt self-conscious. It had been nearly four years. Of course, she had changed. The silver through her hair had multiplied, and the fine lines about her mouth and eyes had deepened.

Charles himself looked thinner, his face more angular, but he was still a beautiful man. Full of light and cheer.

"I can't believe you're here." Charles grasped her hand. "In my city."

Her heart pinged at the way he said "my city" so easily. Did he now consider Philadelphia his permanent home? "I'm sorry for the delay," she said. "I had really planned to spend more time here with you, but my ship for Liverpool leaves tonight."

"I understand," he said, and although she saw the flicker of disappointment in his eyes, his smile didn't falter. "You will have a wonderful reunion with your sister. I can't believe you've never met her."

Dolly nodded. "I suppose my parents didn't want to leave my grandmother completely without a grandchild when they took the entire family to New Zealand."

He squeezed her hand. "I can't wait to hear all about it." He looked down at the trunk next to her. "Now, is this your only trunk?"

"Yes, I packed light," she said. "Although I might have to purchase a carpetbag once I'm overseas, since I'll be buying souvenirs."

"I wouldn't expect anything less." Charles picked up the trunk with ease. "Are you hungry?"

"Yes," Dolly admitted. "The train fare was slim." She didn't add that she'd been too anxious to eat.

"Great," he said with a wink. "We'll take your trunk to the pier and leave it with the office."

"All right." She was already regretting that she had less than a day to spend with Charles after being apart for so long.

"Then we'll go eat at a place nearby before I take you on the grand tour," he continued.

"The grand tour, hmm?" Dolly said, unable to stop her smile.

It was refreshing to be with Charles and to bask in his cheerfulness. His letters had been wonderful, but they were not nearly the same as speaking to him in person.

Charles hailed a buggy, and soon they arrived at the wharf, where they deposited her trunk at the harbor office.

Dolly took the opportunity to visit the powder room there. She gazed in the mirror for several long seconds. Charles was surely growing impatient, though she couldn't imagine him doing so. He was the definition of patience, as proven by his tenure in the seminary here. How could she jump into his life for such a short time, then leave him behind again?

She touched her cheeks. Her eyes were too bright, her lips a hesitant line, her pulse rapid. Why was she feeling this conflicted? Why couldn't she go outside and spend a carefree day with him? But the questions plagued her mind. What were his intentions toward her? Did they have a future together? Would he ask her to marry him, to move out here? Would he return to California?

Would she say *yes*?

Dolly dropped her hands, then turned away from the mirror. She had delayed long enough. It was time to be with Charles, and she could only hope that the answers would come while she was there. She exited the powder room and walked down the corridor that led past the office where they'd checked in her trunk to go aboard the steamer *Merion*.

When she stepped outside the office, she saw Charles speaking to the porter. Charles didn't see her at first. He had no trouble chatting with anyone whom he happened to cross paths with. When he turned, the smile that lit his face made her doubts flee.

At that moment, if she hadn't completely understood before, she knew that Charles Bazatas was in love with her. He was at her side in a few strides, and he offered his arm like the perfect gentleman that he was.

"Hello, darling," he said. "Are you ready?"

"Yes." She returned his smile. She could do this; she could be happy.

Dolly felt like she was floating as they walked along the street. The heart of Philadelphia was charming. The architecture of the towering buildings was beautiful, and the wide streets gave buggies, wagons, and horses plenty of room to navigate. Compared to San Francisco, the lack of Chinese population was noticeable.

They walked a short distance to a charming Italian café. It appeared that Charles was a regular here, because the waiter made a big deal out of his bringing a date, calling Dolly "Charlie's special woman."

After they placed their orders, Charles leaned across the table. "Did you hear what he said? You're my special woman."

"I heard," Dolly said. "Does that mean I'm the first woman you've brought here?" She meant it as a tease, but his brows pulled together.

"You're the only woman I would take anywhere, Dolly," he said. "Do you think I'm seeing other women?"

"No." A slow burn spread across her cheeks. "And even if you were, it's not as if . . . I mean, we haven't seen each other in years."

Charles's frown remained. "I thought I made myself clear before I left San Francisco."

Dolly could only nod. He'd said some sweet things, yes, and now she felt guilty about being petty. He had never given her cause to believe he wasn't completely loyal to her. Except . . . for the years and space that divided them. Perhaps the distance had bothered her more than she'd allowed herself to admit. Or perhaps the emotional buildup to this time and place of being with him again had made her thoughts unreasonable.

"Dolly." He reached across the table for her hand.

She let him take it, and the warmth of his fingers was like a gentle caress to her troubled heart.

"You are everything to me, darling."

And she believed him because she didn't think his green eyes could lie, and in them, she saw only earnest truth. Yet, shouldn't being "everything" to someone mean that they lived in the same city, or at least the same state? Didn't it mean that vows would be made and lives fully shared?

She had to ask; she was ready to ask. "So how much longer will we be apart?"

"Two years at the most," he said. "Then I'll be fully qualified."

She tried not to let her disappointment show or her eyes swim with tears. She took a sip of her water to keep the trembling in her heart at bay. It didn't work.

"Look," he continued. "After our meal, I want to show you something, and I think you'll enjoy the walk."

What else could she do but agree? He hadn't proposed or anything, but perhaps this was the best he could do right now, under their circumstances.

The waiter brought their steaming pasta, and they spent the next several moments enjoying their meals. Dolly was soon full, and while she waited for Charles to finish, she told him of the latest events at the mission home. His attention was rapt, as usual, and he asked many questions about the rescued girls.

Despite the heavy disappointment of his *two years* pronouncement, she loved discussing events with Charles. He was always so interested and complimentary. She couldn't deny that she enjoyed the appreciative gleam in his eyes when she told him of her more daring rescues and close calls with court cases.

Once Charles had paid the bill, they walked out of the restaurant. He placed her hand on his arm, and they headed along the wide sidewalk. A soft breeze had kicked up, and clouds meandered across the vast blue sky. They walked along Market Street, and the bustle of the citizens and various shops was a distraction for a while. Philadelphia felt open and wide compared to San Francisco. She caught sight of a couple of Chinese men walking briskly on the other side of the street.

Charles noticed her diverted attention. "We have a Chinatown here, much smaller than in San Francisco, you know. We could visit?"

"No," Dolly said immediately. She couldn't allow any attachments to form here, more than she already had in Charles. Her plans were set, starting with the steamer departure tonight. But it did give her more to consider.

Living in Philadelphia wouldn't mean she would have to be cut off from a Chinese community. It just wouldn't be *her* community.

After leaving Market Street, they walked along a quieter road until they reached an apartment building that was three stories high. The dark red brick was elegant, the rows of windows tall and stately, and the building was topped by soaring flags that seemed to rise to the sky.

Charles brought her to a gentle stop and peered up at the upper stories. "What do you think?"

"It's a beautiful building," Dolly said. "Do you live here?"

"Not yet." He glanced down at her. "But I'd like to. The apartments have two to three rooms, large enough for a family starting out."

Dolly met his gaze, and he smiled that smile that always tugged her heart.

She should have been warmed through, but instead, the clouds seemed to darken overhead, casting a temporary shadow upon them.

"Surely you know that I intend to marry you, Dolly," Charles said. "We both have callings in life, but I believe we can be even stronger together." He squeezed her hand as it rested on his arm.

Yes. This was what she wanted: his declaration. Although it hadn't exactly been a proposal, his intentions were clear. Did this mean that in two years they would marry?

"How is your family?" he asked, and she welcomed the change of subject.

She told him about her siblings, their spouses, and their children.

Next, he talked about his family who lived close to Jessie. Yet, as they spoke of their families, she felt another pang in her heart. In two years, she would be thirty-seven. Would she ever have a family like they were speaking of?

Dolly fully considered the Chinese girls at 920 Sacramento Street her daughters, and even now, she missed them with a longing she hadn't expected.

They walked for hours, and Charles pointed out his favorite restaurants and places to visit. Dolly appreciated the charm of the place, and she could hear the affection in Charles's voice as he continued their tour. Yet his affection didn't override the gnawing in her stomach, which had nothing to do with hunger. The more enthusiasm he expressed, the more Dolly longed for her own corner of the world.

They stopped at another café as the sun was setting, splashing orange and pink across the elegant buildings of Philadelphia. Dolly ate slowly, savoring each bite. She couldn't explain it, but she knew she wouldn't be returning to Philadelphia. She didn't know if she had the right to ask Charles to move to California, or if he would even want to. For her. Surely he could find happiness and fulfillment anywhere? If that were true, then so could she.

But she couldn't think of anyplace she would rather work and serve than Chinatown in San Francisco. Even the thought of leaving all her girls behind created an anxiety within her that she couldn't tamp down until she thought of the alternative—letting Charles go. Not for two more years, or three, but forever.

Would she have to choose?

After they finished their meal, Charles walked her slowly to the pier through the emerging twilight. The pier was a hive of activity as the seamen prepared the vessel for sail. They hadn't called for passengers to board yet, so Charles led her along the wooden planks.

Every few moments, they stopped to watch an incoming sea vessel. Activity bustled about them, but Dolly felt that she and Charles were somehow separate from it all. They were both quiet, and although it wasn't as if they had run out of conversation, it seemed that words couldn't quite convey her emotions.

As the shadows lengthened and night fell, the salty breeze lessened, becoming a blanket of warmth. The gulls quieted as they found alcoves and hovels in which to roost.

When Charles drew her to a stop, she looked up into his eyes. Behind him, the glittering stars in the sky acted as a backdrop.

"Dolly . . ." he whispered. "I don't want to let you go."

She smiled, but her heart was already hurting with their impending good-bye.

Charles leaned down and brushed his lips against hers. Here they were, on a dock again, kissing. Just like their first kiss.

Something urgent rose up in Dolly, and she slid her arms about his neck, pulling him closer. Charles didn't hesitate, and wrapped his arms about her more fully. He kissed her again, this time deeper, and it was as if their hearts were in total communion. She could feel his tenderness and love toward her in this kiss. And she knew she would never kiss another man with so much of her heart.

When Charles broke off the kiss and rested his forehead against hers, she felt different. Her pulse raced, and her heart wept with the knowledge of what she had to ask. Because it mattered. Greatly.

"When?" Dolly whispered in the damp night air. "When do you think you'll be in a position to marry me?"

Charles lifted his head. "I'll work for a pittance at first, but within a year, I'll have enough to put money down on the apartment I showed you." He smiled at her, his fingers pressing against her waist.

The two years had now turned into three.

He must have noticed the consternation in her expression because he added, "We've survived four years already; a little longer will be bearable, darling."

The warm, salty breeze, the creak of the sea vessels, the thousands of bright stars . . . all of it created a moment that could have been romantic, even magical.

But only sorrow filled her heart. She knew without a doubt that Charles was completely loyal and devoted to her. Given her age, her childbearing years would be at an end soon. This moment was perhaps the first time Dolly truly realized she would not bear her own children.

Charles already had a piece of her heart, yet it would never come back to her, not in the form of marriage, at least. *I have dozens of daughters,* Dolly thought, *all of whom need me. And I need them.*

"I cannot leave them, Charles." Dolly did not need to explain who "they" were. "They are my daughters. I never want to leave California. I want to be close to those I've worked for, served, loved, and rescued for the past nine years."

Charles's smile faded at the serious tone in her voice. He didn't answer right away. Finally he said, "I will come to California, then."

But she had seen and heard the hesitation. She placed a hand on his beloved cheek. His skin pulsed warm beneath her fingers. Oh, how she would miss him. "You would not be happy," she said. "Your work is here. The light in your eyes when you speak of it cannot be denied."

Except now Charles's eyes had filled with tears. "I will find something. I could help the mission home. I could—"

"Charles." She rested her hand on his chest. "You've told me multiple times that God has called you to this place. You've felt confirmations more than once that you're here for a reason."

He clasped her hand. "Yes, but I can work anywhere."

It was a concession, and they both knew it. They had just spent several hours together, and most of the discussion had been about his work in Philadelphia and his future plans.

"I love you, Charles Bazatas." Her own tears burned now. "But God has called us to different missions. You *belong* here. I belong with my daughters in California."

Charles rubbed his face with one hand, then looked past her, staring at something unseen for several moments. His jaw tightened, and when he again met her gaze, she saw the resolve and determination there, edged with sorrow.

"If you ever change your mind, my darling, you know where to find me," he said in a fierce whisper.

She nodded, tears making a trail along her cheeks.

Then he cradled her face with his hands and kissed her one last time.

CHAPTER TWENTY-EIGHT

"We must pass now . . . to the no less important . . . stories of the young Japanese women who have been helped and protected during the year, fourteen in number. The three under our care at present are Yorki, Roe and Asa, all bright, interesting girls, helpful and willing about the house work and their studies. Asa . . . only fifteen . . . was brought to San Francisco by an agent of the notorious ring of Japanese men, who make a business of importing these young girls."

—Donaldina Cameron, mission home report

JULY 1905

The moment Dolly caught sight of the shores of California was the completion of healing her heart that had been broken nearly a year before in Philadelphia. She gripped the rail as the steamship journeyed toward land. The sights, the smells, and the sounds enveloped her; even the fog was like its own welcoming committee. And Dolly relished every bit of it.

Yes, she'd loved her year-long furlough, but only weeks into it, she had dearly missed her Chinese daughters and her devoted staff. Yet she knew that her soul needed this journey. After her tearful good-bye to Charles, she spent the next ten days on a steamer across the Atlantic. The high seas were thankfully mostly calm, and she spent a lot of time on deck basking in the fresh air and sunshine. She was met in Liverpool by a friend of her family who guided her to the train that took her to Inverness, Scotland.

There she finally met her oldest sister, Isabella, along with Aunt Catherine, her mother's sister. In Scotland, Dolly was no longer Miss Cameron, but a sister and a niece. She couldn't believe how instantly she and Isabella connected. They spent their days together exploring the glens and walking the moors. Dolly's heart sang as she visited the land of her ancestors. Bit by bit, the healing from leaving Charles began to take hold, although he was never far from her thoughts.

Dolly enjoyed visiting castles and cathedrals alike. The best part was meeting cousins and family friends and hearing the old family stories. The memories she made in Scotland would be cherished for the rest of her life, and she only wished that her other siblings could have accompanied her.

On the first week of January, 1905, she boarded the *Mombasa* steamer, captained by a MacKenzie family friend, Captain Stephenson. Dolly's next stops included Spain, the Near East, Calcutta, Rangoon, and finally, Hong Kong. The rush of anticipation that skipped along her skin at this last stop was hard to put into words. The docks teemed with Chinese, and everywhere she looked, she spied resemblances of those she loved back home.

On mainland China, she made it a point to visit the Canton province, from which many of her girls had come. She was guided along the streets by a woman who was a former teacher of Chinese in San Francisco. They traveled the crowded streets of the cities and visited the smaller villages with their thatched roofs and sprawling rice fields. A major highlight included being reunited with N'gun Ho, one of the rescued slaves from San Francisco who had returned to China and married. In China, N'gun Ho had struggled with her in-laws accepting her Christian views, but she had eventually won over her mother-in-law. At every school and every mission home Dolly visited, she shared her message of stopping the sale of girls and women.

The final leg of the voyage home to America was long and arduous, but worth every passing hour. Dolly would never forget China or its people and beauty.

But San Francisco was home. As the steamer neared the harbor, her heart swelled at least two sizes. A crowd had gathered to await the arrival of the ship.

Set apart from the main crowd was a smaller group. Dolly recognized her sisters and her niece, Caroline, along with several of the dark-haired girls who called her *Lo Mo.*

Her daughters.

Dolly wiped at the tears that were falling too fast for the wind to help dry them. She was home, and she laughed as a couple of the Chinese girls began jumping up and down, pointing at her. Lifting her hand high, she waved at the girls, then placed her hand over her heart. Her gaze soaked in their features: Lonnie, Dong Ho, Jiao, and Leung, all young women now. And of course, Tien was among the group. Her smile was full of light, and Dolly's heart soared at the sight of her beloved daughters. As soon as Dolly was allowed, she walked off the steamship, right into the arms of her dearest loved ones.

After hugging all the Chinese girls, Dolly next embraced Caroline and Jessie, as well as two of her other sisters, Katherine and Helen. She had sent them letters about Isabella and a quick note about how things had ended with Charles Bazatas.

When Jessie drew away, she pinpointed Dolly with her gaze. "Are you all right?"

Dolly knew she was referring to the breakup with Charles. That day spent with him in Philadelphia seemed ages ago. In the past year, Dolly had traveled the world, met so many people, and refocused her goals in life.

"I am home with my daughters, and this is where I want to be."

Jessie studied her for a moment, then nodded. "Very well."

But Dolly didn't miss the wistfulness in her sister's eyes, the lost hope Jessie clearly felt, thinking her sister had turned down an opportunity to marry. Perhaps the last one. But with all the time Dolly had had to consider her relationship with Charles, both before and after seeing him in Philadelphia, she had come to realize their callings in life would always conflict.

Even now, her Chinese daughters tugged her hand, each waiting impatiently for her turn to speak to Dolly next.

"Thank you for coming," Dolly told Jessie after giving Caroline another squeeze. "Come up to the mission home any time you are able."

On the buggy ride to the mission home, her daughters competed for conversation, giving her news and updates, while Tien sat silently beside her. Dolly looked forward to learning all that Tien had been up to, but it might be a while before they were alone.

The first few hours at the mission home were filled with hugs and the girls taking turns telling her their stories. When Mei Lien stepped forward with her one-year-old son to embrace Dolly, Mei Lien whispered, "I still haven't heard from him."

Dolly knew that the "him" she was referring to was Huan Sun. She wished she knew what had happened to him. For better or for worse, knowing would ease the pang in all their hearts. "We will keep praying," she said.

Dolly was introduced to several girls and young women who were new arrivals over the past year. Now wasn't the time to learn their stories, but she hoped to soon.

As the excitement and news updating slowed down, and bedtime approached, Dolly met with Wilmina Wheeler and Frances Thompson in the office. Tien joined them as well, since she'd been the primary interpreter on the rescues.

"How has everything gone?" Dolly asked Frances.

The woman had aged, but her eyes were bright, her smile genuine. "We've had an eventful year, as you can imagine."

Dolly had heard very little news, since she wasn't able to receive letters as she traveled to so many places.

"We spent most of the year defending the girls who are already here," Frances continued. "Plenty of tong members came to the mission home, trying by any means possible to get their slaves back."

Dolly was dismayed, but not surprised. They never allowed the girls to go outside alone, and whenever they had visitors, they were careful to vet them.

"A merchant asked after Kum Ying," Frances said. "He said he wanted to marry her. He brought in an American lawyer and justice of the peace, along with a marriage license. Wilmina phoned the marshal, and we found out that the papers were fraudulent."

Dolly shook her head. "They are getting bolder."

"That's not all." Frances clasped her hands together. "We had a slave owner ask to see his former slave girl one more time. We didn't let him, but we found out later that he had planned to abduct her and sell her again."

Frances and Wilmina continued with more stories, and Dolly listened intently, marveling at all she had missed—all she used to handle herself. Tien remained silent throughout most of the conversation.

By the time Frances had finished sharing the bigger events, the hour had grown late.

"Thank you for protecting the girls," Dolly said in a quiet voice. Her time away from San Francisco had been much needed, but it made her ill to know how the mission home continued to be a target. "And those new girls, who are they? Some of them are Japanese, correct?"

"Yes," Wilmina confirmed. "We rescued nine Chinese girls and eight Japanese girls in the past year. We've also had more than thirty come to us for help in that time."

"We're a beacon for the hopeless," Frances said, "and a target for the ruthless."

Dolly couldn't have agreed more. As long as there was corruption on all levels and among all races, the mission home's work would never be finished.

"And how is Mei Lien doing?" Dolly asked. "No word from Huan Sun yet?"

"Nothing," Frances said. "Although Zhang Wei and Ah-Peen Oie are still controlling parts of the slave trade, I've heard there was a falling out between the two."

"Perhaps one of them will leave Chinatown, then," Dolly said. "Make it safer for Huan Sun to return." She could relate to Mei Lien more now than ever. With Dolly's failed relationship with Charles, her expectations dashed, she had a glimpse of what Mei Lien must be feeling.

Tien remained behind after the other two women left the office. At last they could speak alone. Dolly looked over at her, so happy to see the young woman's familiar face again.

"How have you been, dear Tien?" she asked in a quiet voice.

Tien's smile was soft. "I've been busy."

Maybe it was because Dolly was completely exhausted, but she burst out laughing. "I'm sure you've been very busy. I'm sorry I wasn't here to help."

"You were in the right place," Tien said, her smile widening. "We were all more than happy to work extra in your absence. It was an honor."

One minute she'd been laughing, and now Dolly felt like crying. "You have been a blessing to the mission home."

Tien's gaze dropped then, and Dolly wondered if she'd said something wrong. She waited, though.

Tien's voice was hesitant when she spoke. "I want to learn more," she said. "I know a lot, but I don't have a good education."

Dolly frowned. "Your English is very good, and you do well in every class here."

"That's not what I mean." Tien released a sigh. "I want to be educated in a college. And then I will return to the mission home and help how I should be helping."

Dolly stared at the young woman. "You want to go to college?"

Tien nodded. "I know if I study very hard, I can get into college in a few years."

Dolly thought of the complications of a Chinese woman attending college in San Francisco. "It would have to be back east."

"I know," Tien whispered.

And in that whisper, Dolly understood the hesitancy in her friend's voice. They would be separated for years. Tien, who had known only the mission home since she was a young girl, would be going into another world—possibly in two to three years, when she was eighteen or nineteen.

Dolly smiled, although emotion had started to surface. "I believe you'll be wonderful in college. And *if* you return here, we'll be happy to have you. But if another opportunity were to arise with your new education, we would support that as well."

Tien's gaze turned fierce. "I won't be like Charles. I *will* come back, *Lo Mo*. This is my home."

This Chinese young woman was years away from that decision, but Dolly knew that if anyone could make a promise about the future, it was Tien.

"Now, you are tired," Tien said. "You sleep as long as you want and I will take care of things until you awake."

Dolly didn't know how she had been so blessed in her life to have so many who cared about her. She moved forward and embraced Tien. "It is so good to be back, and I can't thank you enough for all your help."

"It's easy to help people who are grateful," Tien said.

Over the next few weeks, Dolly slept in snatches as she spent hours catching up with all that she had missed, reacquainting herself with her daughters, and working hand in hand with the staff. Frances had been right. The mission home was often put on the defense, and Dolly spent a good deal of her time preparing for court cases, then testifying on behalf of the newer residents of 920. They also kept the doors and lower windows securely locked, and they stayed vigilant on who was allowed to enter the mission home.

Following each rescue, the Chinatown squad would patrol the neighborhood for several nights and days.

She continued to work with her lawyer, Henry Monroe, who aided her in many cases. The girls at the mission home called him "our Abraham Lincoln," and it was fitting. Monroe aided Dolly in proposing an amendment to state law that would empower a judge to assign her temporary guardianship of a child until the hearing. When the bill reached the governor, he vetoed it.

Dolly was devastated when Monroe called with the news.

"What do you want to do, Miss Cameron?" he asked next.

She gripped the receiver, trying to hold her emotions together. "I don't know."

"We can make a few adjustments and resubmit."

Dolly found herself smiling. "What are you waiting for? My permission?"

Monroe chuckled.

A few weeks later, Monroe called with the astounding news. "My presentation with the legislature went quite well."

Again, Dolly gripped the receiver she held. "How well?"

"Governor Pardee signed the bill this afternoon."

Dolly might have shouted into the phone, and by the time she hung up with the lawyer, he was still laughing. By all accounts, this was a major victory because now she could offer more protection and not worry about being arrested for being in contempt of court. Not only did the rescue of Chinese girls continue, but the highbinders had brought over Japanese girls as well as other nationalities, peddling their same old lies to desperate women and families.

But when a typewritten note arrived one evening at the mission home, and Dolly saw the plea for help along with the address off Commercial Street, she prepared herself for the worst. It was the same location where Mei Lien had been taken after her arrival in San Francisco. The same brothel where the slave mistress Ah-Peen Oie lived. There was a good chance that Zhang Wei would be there.

"Tien," Dolly said, knocking on her bedroom door, then opening it.

The young woman rarely locked her door anymore, and now she was sitting on her bed cross-legged, with English textbooks spread about her. When she saw the paper in Dolly's hand, she immediately scrambled off the bed.

"Where is it?"

"Commercial Street," Dolly said.

"Oh no," Tien said, knowing the significance of the location. "Should we tell Mei Lien?"

"Not yet," Dolly said. "But she might know whoever it is that is asking for a rescue. They probably both worked under Ah-Peen Oie." Which also meant that the girl would be severely traumatized.

"We will need several policemen," Tien said, grabbing the oversized jacket that she wore on rescues. Often she transferred it to the shoulders of the starving, shivering slave girl.

"I've already called and let Cook know of the location."

Officers Cook, Farrell, and Green met Dolly and Tien at the bottom of the hill on Sacramento Street less than an hour later. Walking along the roads of Chinatown late at night brought back myriad memories of all the years Dolly had gone on rescues. She was extra nervous tonight; it was the first rescue since her return from her sabbatical. And she worried that this could be a trap.

"Welcome home, Miss Cameron," Officer Cook said as they took a side road to avoid being seen by some of the main brothel owners.

"Thank you," Dolly said. The night air was cool, and she pulled her cloak closer to her body. "All has been well with you?"

Cook tapped his sledgehammer against his leg. "As you've probably heard, the tong have people in place among the lawyers and even some on the police force. The only level I don't think the corruption has reached is the judiciary members."

Dolly hoped that no judges would accept bribes. "What can be done?"

"Keep fighting each battle as it comes," Cook said. "After tonight, Chinatown will know that you've returned."

She swallowed. "For better or for worse."

"Definitely for better." He slowed his step for a moment as he lit a cigarette.

She noticed the slight limp as he walked. "Were you injured?"

Cook drew in a puff of his cigarette, then glanced down at his leg. "Not every encounter has gone smoothly." And he left it at that.

They approached the house, which was unusually quiet and dark. Dolly didn't know if that was a good thing or a bad thing. She knew about the banquets that took place here, and the opium den in the basement. Cook pinched his cigarette out and dropped it in the road.

Farrell knocked on the door, and Dolly found herself holding her breath. No one answered, as expected.

Then, surprisingly, the door swung open. The slave owner Ah-Peen Oie herself stood there.

Dolly's pulse jumped. The officers immediately took a step back, and Tien grasped Dolly's arm. Every slave girl in Chinatown knew who Ah-Peen Oie was, and everyone at the mission home knew what she had done to Mei Lien.

The slave owner wore a beautiful teal-colored silk cheongsam, and even in the compromised light of evening streetlights, her hair shimmered down her back. Her eyes were large and luminous, and her features were painted with makeup for emphasis. Dolly wasn't fooled by the woman's seemingly vulnerable beauty, though.

Cook stepped forward, resting the sledgehammer on his shoulder. "We received a note from this address," he said. "Stand aside."

Dolly sensed he was bracing himself for an argument or a door slammed in his face. It wouldn't be the first time, and it wouldn't be the last.

But instead of acting defiantly, Ah-Peen Oie nodded and stepped back as if she were allowing the police officer to enter.

Were there tong members inside, in the dark, waiting to attack?

Cook and Farrell entered, but Green hung back, keeping guard over Dolly and Tien in case there was a planned retaliation.

"What do we do?" Tien asked.

They could no longer see Ah-Peen Oie. A faint glimmer of light came from inside, probably from a single lamp.

"Let's go in." Dolly nodded to Green, and the three of them walked into the room.

Only Ah-Peen Oie was inside, and she sat on a chair. The place was like a ghost town of its former self. All the other furniture was gone, and only remnants of its previous glory remained. A few beads were scattered about the floor, beads that had once been part of the hanging décor. A crumpled fish-skin lantern lay in one corner, discarded and forgotten.

"Where is everyone?" Cook asked, and Tien translated.

Dolly definitely didn't expect Ah-Peen Oie to answer, but the woman continued to sit calmly in the chair. It was strange, almost eerie. This house was notorious for banquets and opium dens . . . yet, the place seemed empty now.

"No one is here," Ah-Peen Oie said through Tien's translation.

Cook nodded at Farrell. "Go look upstairs. See if there are any girls up there."

While Green and Cook remained on the main floor, they listened as Farrell's footsteps pounded on the steps, then moved across the floor above.

Ah-Peen Oie remained in her chair, her elegant hands folded upon her lap.

Moments later Farrell returned. "Everyone's gone. Furniture, beds, tables . . . all cleared out. Only the rats are still here."

Ah-Peen Oie spoke in a voice so quiet that Tien asked the slave owner to repeat herself.

"I wrote the note," Ah-Peen Oie said. "I want to take refuge at the mission home."

Dolly frowned at Tien after the translation. "Are you sure that's what she said?"

The translator's nod confirmed Ah-Peen Oie's claim. What an elaborate ploy. Frances had told Dolly of other antics by tong members to retrieve their slave girls. Now, Ah-Peen Oie was using her own cunning.

Dolly folded her arms. "Tell her we're leaving and to never contact us again."

When Tien translated, Ah-Peen Oie leapt to her feet, her hands clenched together. Oddly, they were trembling. It seemed as if the woman's composure had cracked. "No, please. I need to leave here. I've sold everything I can. Still, they want more. My former owner, Hip Chang, wants to sell me to Wong Dick for three thousand dollars. Hip Chang thinks that he still owns me—that because I lost Mei Lien, and Zhang Wei lost her too, I have to pay for all the money she would have earned."

Tien was translating as fast as she could, but Dolly was becoming lost in the web of information. Ah-Peen Oie continued to explain how she owed money on an opium consignment, and this debt was in the thousands of dollars too.

"I cannot pay them both," Ah-Peen Oie finished. "I sold everything, but even then, I cannot pay enough."

Dolly took a step closer to the door. It sounded as if Ah-Peen Oie was on the blacklist of the most powerful Chinese tong in the city. Housing her would only bring more trouble to the mission home.

Besides, this beautiful, composed woman had beaten Mei Lien, and countless other girls, and stripped them of their dignity. The mistress had inflicted terror and control on innocent people. Forced them into addictions so then they would be under her power.

Her deeds went too deep and were too black.

"We don't help slave owners get out of debt." Dolly cut her gaze to Tien. "Come. We have no rescue here." She nodded at the officers. With a final scan of the room, they followed her to the doorway.

Before Dolly could cross the threshold, Ah-Peen Oie cried out, "Please wait! Take me with you. I beg of you."

Her English was broken, but Dolly understood well enough. She turned, ready to deliver another, final set down. She would not let this woman coerce her, just as she must have so many others before.

Then Ah-Peen Oie threw herself to the ground next to Dolly and grasped the hem of her skirt. The woman's broken English was interspersed with tears as she pled. "You do not understand. You rescue girls in captivity, yes?"

Dolly didn't move, didn't answer.

"But where were the mission ladies when *I* was a girl?" She twisted Dolly's skirt as if she were holding onto a life preserver. "I was kidnapped from my family and sold to the powerful tong." Ah-Peen Oie's tears turned her makeup to dark rivulets running down her cheeks. "Where were you when they forced opium onto me until I would do anything for another dose? Including working with them to find more girls?"

The woman made a grievous argument, but how did Dolly know Ah-Peen Oie was speaking the truth? Had her greed and desperation for money brought her to another level of lying?

Ah-Peen Oie's voice dropped low, filled with anguish. "I was a rat in their cage. They poked me, and I did their bidding. They held out food and I grabbed it. They beat me and used me until I became a monster like them, inflicting the same pain upon once-innocent women like me." Her eyes slid shut, and she released Dolly's skirt.

Dolly bit her bottom lip to stop the threatening compassion. She would not feel sorry for this woman.

"I am nothing," Ah-Peen Oie whispered. "Less than nothing. I don't deserve anyone's kindness, and if there was any way I could make recompense to all those I robbed and hurt, I would." A sob broke, and she curled up on to the ground, covering her face as her shoulders shook.

Dolly could only stare in shock at the crumpled, sobbing woman. It could all be an act, a ploy, but the empty and desolate room beyond was a testament that the slave owner was at least telling the partial truth. Something pricked the edges of Dolly's heart, something she didn't want to acknowledge or feel. She looked at Tien, hoping she would have the answers.

But only confusion reflected in Tien's eyes.

Dolly released a sigh. There was no way she could take Ah-Peen Oie to

920. Not with Mei Lien there. Not with every girl in the house petrified of this woman. There was only one option she could think of. "We can offer you protection if you're willing to go to the city prison until we can come up with a place for you to stay." She didn't know if Ah-Peen Oie would balk or not.

The woman raised her tear-stained face. "Will I be safe?" she asked in a trembling voice.

"You will be safe there." Dolly scanned her silk clothing, now damp with tears and wrinkled from the floor. "You'll want to change your clothing, though."

Ah-Peen Oie nodded, then wiped at the ruined makeup on her face. With shaky legs, she rose to her feet. "I'll go and change."

CHAPTER TWENTY-NINE

*"Only last week Chow Ha was rescued and she is a truly
pathetic object-lesson in what this appalling system of Oriental
slavery can bring a young girl to in one or two years. Sorrow
and physical suffering combined with the use of opium have
made of Chow Ha a pitiful object. Such a sad, hopeless face I
have seldom seen. But when she said to me with a glimmer of a
smile lighting up her poor pale face, 'This is the best day I have
had for years [referring to the day she entered the mission] and
soon I will grow strong and well,' I knew there was hope for
Chow Ha, and when the good Physician lays His healing hand
upon her she will be healed of soul and body."*

—Donaldina Cameron, mission home record

1905

Mei Lien spent the first waking moments each morning watching her
little boy sleep. Most days, she convinced herself that he looked like Huan
Sun. On her worst days, she thought she saw a flash of Zhang Wei in the boy.
Today was a good day. Mei Lien was sure the tilt of her boy's lips was identical
to Huan Sun's.

Where he was, she could only guess. Over the past year, with so many
things changing at the mission home—Miss Cameron's absence, new girls

coming in, many girls leaving to continue their lives in education, marriages, and even some returning to their homelands—had left Mei Lien with a sense of displacement.

She would never see her mother again, that she knew. Even with the skills she was learning at the mission home, it would take years to save up enough for a ship's passage. And she didn't even know if her mother was still alive.

Oh, how her mother would love to know her grandchild. And in another world or existence, there would be no disappointment in how the child was conceived. Now, in the gray light of the morning, just a short time before the birds would begin their song, Mei Lien took out the paper that Miss Cameron allowed her to keep in her bedroom.

With a thick pencil, Mei Lien sketched out the characters she had learned over the past year at the mission home and wrote a note to Huan Sun. She told him about his son. She told him about how each day when the sun rose, she hoped that today was the day he would return. She wrote how she would be forever grateful for his kindness. The risk he took to save her. His sacrifice now. She told him that she missed him, that she prayed he was well and had found happiness in life.

Then she folded the note and moved to the side of her bed. Kneeling, she withdrew a small paper-covered box and lifted the lid. Inside were at least a hundred other notes, all written to Huan Sun. In the early notes, her words were much simpler, her characters roughly sketched. Placing the newest note on top of the others, Mei Lien felt a deep sense of satisfaction.

Writing gave her a way to move time forward, to propel her life into action, to begin each day with renewed hope. Soon, she would be writing her notes in English. She was determined to learn all she could while at the mission home, since she didn't know what life would bring her next. And she wanted to be prepared. Her son would eventually be too old to live in the mission home for girls, and she would need to find a place to live and a way to support him.

The soft knock at her door startled her because she hadn't heard footsteps in the corridor.

"Mei Lien," came the whispered call.

She scrambled to her feet and unlocked the door. Then she cracked it open, tamping down the nervous beat of her heart.

Tien stood there, the dim corridor making her look as if she were a dark figure. "Miss Cameron requests your presence in her office."

"So early? What is it?" Mei Lien said, both fear and hope colliding in her breast. Perhaps she would be forced to leave after all. Or perhaps . . . this had something to do with Huan Sun. Had he been found? Was he alive?

"Miss Cameron will tell you." Tien stepped back, giving Mei Lien room to exit.

She glanced at her sleeping son, but Tien said, "He will be fine for a short time. We must go immediately."

Mei Lien hurried out of her room then, and Tien followed behind. Down the staircase they went, the creak of some of the steps louder in the silence of the dawn. It was strange walking about the house when most everyone was asleep.

Miss Cameron's office door was open, and Mei Lien found herself holding her breath as she entered.

Miss Cameron turned from the window, and Mei Lien saw immediately that the woman had not likely slept all night. Miss Cameron's usually neat hair was falling out of its pins, and her blouse was wrinkled. "Have a seat, Mei Lien."

Blindly, Mei Lien sat down, not wanting to take her eyes away from the mission home director. Miss Cameron didn't sit. Instead, she rested her palms on the desk, as if to brace herself.

The hollowness in Mei Lien's stomach grew.

"Last night we went on a rescue," Miss Cameron said, and Tien translated.

Mei Lien straightened in her chair. This was not what she had expected to hear.

"We went to the house off Commercial Street," Miss Cameron continued.

At this, Mei Lien felt sick. Had they found another beaten and abused girl like her? Had Zhang Wei done something terrible? What about Ah-Peen Oie? Would Miss Cameron be forced to return Mei Lien to those slave owners' hands?

"The place has been cleared out," Miss Cameron said. "Sold off."

Mei Lien wrinkled her brow. "What happened?" she whispered.

Tien continued to translate, and Miss Cameron said, "Only one person was left inside the building. She was the one who sent the note for rescue."

Mei Lien thought of the girls she had known at the house. Had one of them found out about the mission home somehow and sent for help? Or . . . had it been a trap?

"Who?" she asked.

"Ah-Peen Oie sent the note for help—to rescue *herself*," Miss Cameron said.

Mei Lien stared at the director's tired eyes and disheveled hair. Surely what she was hearing couldn't be true. And surely Miss Cameron had seen through the ruse.

"Ah-Peen Oie said she was desperate. She owes thousands of dollars to two different men, and her original slave owner claims he still owns her." Miss Cameron moved around the desk until she was near the second chair in the office. She took a seat and grasped Mei Lien's hands. "I was about to leave, but she pleaded with me on her hands and knees."

"She's a liar," Mei Lien hissed, pulling her hands away. "She was never a slave."

Miss Cameron exhaled. "I spent half the night gathering information through my sources. She was a slave once, and she bought her freedom. She owes Sing Choy two thousand dollars. And Hip Chang is trying to sell her to Wong Dick for three thousand."

Mei Lien didn't care about Ah-Peen Oie's problems. She deserved them. "I hope you kicked her like a dog." The words were harsh, but since coming to the mission home, she had found other girls who had crossed paths with Ah-Peen Oie. No one had anything good to say about the demon woman.

Miss Cameron looked down at her hands for a moment, and when she again gazed at Mei Lien, there were tears in her eyes.

"I don't fully trust her either, Mei Lien," Miss Cameron said. "But I know desperation when I see it. Hundreds of times, I've seen desperation. And Ah-Peen Oie is desperate. Does that mean her heart has changed? That she is remorseful for all her crimes? I don't know yet."

Mei Lien's mouth opened, then shut. What could she say? It was unbelievable that Miss Cameron, of all people in San Francisco, could be duped by the devil woman.

"We've taken her to the city prison," Miss Cameron said. "I know the matron there, and she'll keep her through the rest of today. Then we're going to move Ah-Peen Oie to a schoolroom on Joice Street that's no longer used. She'll be kept under lock and key until we decide what to do with her."

Mei Lien's mind churned. This seemed beyond any compassion that Ah-Peen Oie deserved. "She owned other slave girls in this house. She abused them and forced them into prostitution."

"I know," Miss Cameron said, her tone soft, remorseful. "That is why she will *not* be brought here. We will keep her completely separate."

Mei Lien shook her head, unbelieving. Her gaze connected with Tien's, and in the translator's eyes, Mei Lien saw that she didn't agree with Miss Cameron's actions either.

"So, she'll live behind a locked door now," Mei Lien said with bitterness churning her stomach. "How fitting. I lived behind Ah-Peen Oie's locked door for months."

"Mei Lien," Miss Cameron said softly, urgently. "The girls in this home will always be my priority. *You* are my priority."

Mei Lien looked away, her eyes burning with emotion. Miss Cameron had changed her life. If it weren't for her, Mei Lien doubted she would be alive today. But if Miss Cameron believed in rescuing enslaved women, then how could she help their perpetrators?

"I do not know all the events that led Ah-Peen Oie to her actions of depravity," Miss Cameron continued. "But I have been reading from the Bible this past hour about how the Lord taught the sinners and the shunned. How he extended a merciful hand to them and gave them a chance to change. When the Lord visited the woman at the well in Samaria, she was living in sin, yet the Lord offered her the living waters. Will Ah-Peen Oie truly change? I don't know." She broke off, and silence surrounded them.

The first bird began to sing outside the office window, a faint, mournful tune.

Mei Lien sniffled as tears coursed down her cheeks. If Ah-Peen Oie had been a slave early in her life, then turned that around to become the mistress of her own fate, weren't they all in the same wretched cycle not of their own making? A cycle of greed, immoral appetites, and desperation?

Mei Lien had learned many of the Bible stories over her time at the mission home, and she was familiar with the story of the woman of Samaria. The staff had taught that they were all beggars beholden to a higher being.

Miss Cameron handed over her monogrammed handkerchief to Mei Lien, and she wiped her tears. Then she met the director's gaze. In Miss Cameron's green eyes, Mei Lien saw light and love, a sharp contrast to the harsh darkness of Ah-Peen Oie's. Miss Cameron had battled with this decision deeply. That much was clear.

If her faith had guided Miss Cameron through her rescues over the past decade in Chinatown, then perhaps this most recent rescue had a purpose as well.

"All right," Mei Lien said at last. "Thank you for telling me. Although I do not know if I will ever be able to look upon the woman again."

"I would never force you to do something you didn't want to," Miss Cameron said.

Mei Lien nodded and closed her eyes. "I know." She dropped her head into her hands, and her shoulders shook as she silently cried. She had been hoping to get news about Huan Sun. But perhaps the fall of Ah-Peen Oie was the first step in giving Huan Sun the chance to return to San Francisco. Fear and worry clashed in her chest. Worry for Huan Sun. Fear for the darkness that crept into the edges of her mind with the news about Ah-Peen Oie.

Miss Cameron wrapped an arm about Mei Lien's shoulders. "All will be well, dear Mei Lien," Miss Cameron said. "We must trust in that."

And Mei Lien tried.

Over the next few days, she carried the knowledge in her heart that her former slave owner was being kept under lock and key a few streets away. Tien and other staff helpers took food to the woman three times a day. They had informed the other residents at the mission home, but Mei Lien refused to talk to anyone about the woman who had mistreated her so badly.

When Miss Cameron told Mei Lien that Ah-Peen Oie was gravely ill and had been taken to Lane Hospital for an operation, Mei Lien didn't know how to react, what to feel. The thought of Ah-Peen Oie dying did odd things to Mei Lien's mind. It would be a relief, to be sure, but it would also be an added weight. Had Mei Lien willed the woman's fate toward such an end? Did that make Mei Lien herself no better than the slave owner?

But Ah-Peen Oie recovered, and, strangely, Mei Lien was relieved. She had heard reports from the staff members who fed the woman that she was a changed person. Mei Lien had yet to see for herself, and she wondered if that day would ever come—a day when Mei Lien could look upon her former slave owner again and hear her plea for forgiveness.

That day of testing came soon enough. Tien was the one to knock on her door one morning, and when Mei Lien opened it, she found Miss Cameron standing there too. By the looks on their faces, she knew they were there for an important reason.

"Mei Lien." Miss Cameron's voice was soft, and Tien translated. "We've come to ask if you would consider meeting with Ah-Peen Oie. We know this is a lot to ask, so if you aren't ready yet, we'll completely understand."

Mei Lien waited for the pain to lance through her body, to buckle her knees, to make her heart grow cold. But none of that happened. A bird began its song outside her window; one of the girls laughed in a distant room; someone ran down the stairs, their footsteps thumping along.

Life had moved on. Mei Lien had a baby boy now. She'd gained friends. She'd learned some English. She'd sung hymns and recited scripture. She had come to recognize that every morning and every evening was a gift—a gift of a new life.

She could very well understand another person wanting to change, to grow, and to become like new. Shed the old life. The darkness. The sins.

Just as Mei Lien had.

"I will come," she whispered, because she didn't trust her voice. Her eyes were already watering by the time she met Tien's gaze. "Can you stay here with my baby?"

"Of course," Tien said.

Then Mei Lien grasped Miss Cameron's hand, holding on as if she needed the support. "Where is she?"

"She is waiting in my office," Miss Cameron murmured.

Mei Lien walked along the corridor, her heart thumping louder than her footsteps. By the time they reached Miss Cameron's office, Mei Lien had changed her mind a dozen times. The only thing keeping her feet moving forward was her grip on Miss Cameron's steady hand.

Miss Cameron opened the door.

And there she was. Ah-Peen Oie was no longer wearing a silk dress. Her hair was not swept into an elegant style. She wore no makeup. Her hair had been cut short and now framed a face with aging lines. Her clothing was a simple white tunic over white trousers. She could have been anyone on the street, but there was no doubt it was the same slave owner. But the most significant change was that the woman's eyes had changed. Gone was the hatred from their dark depths.

The light in Ah-Peen Oie's eyes told Mei Lien that the slave owner's soul had changed too.

The woman sank to her knees and bowed her head. As Ah-Peen Oie whispered her plea, Mei Lien's tears dripped down her face. She realized she had *wanted* to forgive this woman; she *wanted* to be free of the burden of grief and heartache.

Instead of the sorrow or anger that Mei Lien had expected to feel toward the woman, she felt a strange kinship. And the very air seemed sweet with love.

"Ah-Peen Oie," Mei Lien whispered, kneeling next to the woman and grasping her trembling hands. "I forgive you, and I only wish you happiness and peace."

Ah-Peen Oie collapsed against Mei Lien, and the two women held each other, both crying. It was many moments before Mei Lien realized that Miss Cameron had left the room, giving them privacy to talk through their heartaches and hopes for the future.

After meeting with Ah-Peen Oie, Mei Lien hadn't expected another miracle. But it seemed her act of forgiveness had opened the floodgates. Another early morning, another sketching session, and Miss Cameron knocked on Mei Lien's door before the sun crested the neighboring eastern buildings. When Mei Lien answered, Miss Cameron whispered, "Come with me and bring your son."

Mei Lien hesitated, but the director looked like she had been crying. Mei Lien picked up her sleeping son from his bed. His dark head lolled against her shoulder, but as they walked down the corridor, he stirred awake.

Following Miss Cameron, they headed down the back stairs. To the basement? Had Zhang Wei come for her, then? Thankfully, her son was quiet and had laid his sleepy head on her shoulder. But Mei Lien's heart pounded loudly. At the ground level, Miss Cameron opened the door to the final staircase.

This couldn't be good, Mei Lien decided. She had brought nothing for her son. If they had to leave the mission home, they had only the clothing they were wearing. Once they reached the final step with Miss Cameron, Mei Lien saw that there was a light on. The room was full of shadows, but the wan light was enough to reveal the man standing there.

Mei Lien's breath hitched. She had been dreaming of Huan Sun's return for so long, and fearing Zhang Wei's appearance just as long, that it took her a moment to believe what her eyes were seeing.

"Huan Sun," she whispered.

He looked different, yet the same. His hair was shorter, and he had more lines about his eyes. But those warm brown eyes were the same, as well as the familiar curve of his mouth. He seemed taller than she remembered, yet there was a distinct sag to his shoulders. Had he been doing manual labor? The railroad, mining, or factory work?

Huan Sun smiled, and then he was walking toward her.

"Who is this?" Huan Sun asked, resting a hand on her son's shoulder.

Her son didn't flinch; he merely stared at the strange man.

Seeing the two together left no doubt in Mei Lien's mind. Huan Sun was the father of her child. They looked like replicas of each other. One had rounded cheeks and bright eyes, the other showed the lines of aging beginning—but their features were the same. The arch of their brows, the shape of their chins, the curve of their mouths. Even their ears were duplicating patterns of each other's.

"He is beautiful," Huan Sun said.

Mei Lien's eyes pricked at the sound of his voice. Memories shot through her, good and bad, but none of them mattered now. Huan Sun was here. He'd returned. To her.

"This is your son, Huan Sun," she said in a trembling voice.

He leaned forward and kissed the top of the boy's head.

"I still have the pearls." Slowly, she slid the bracelet from the upper part of her arm to her wrist.

Huan Sun smiled and lifted her wrist, then placed a tender kiss where the pearls met her skin. When he enfolded both her and the child in his arms, Mei Lien knew that at last, happiness might be possible.

CHAPTER THIRTY

*"We only aim to leave a few words of testimony to bear
witness in coming years to the kind care of a loving heavenly
Father, and also to the unselfish courage displayed by our
Chinese girls throughout the terrifying and distressing
experiences of the days in which our city and the Home we
loved were wiped out of existence."*

—DONALDINA CAMERON, COMBINED 1905–06
AND 1906–07 ANNUAL REPORT

APRIL 1906

The following year, Dolly's restlessness had driven her from sleep early in the morning. Today was the annual Occidental Board Meeting. The new housekeeper, Miss Minnie Ferree, and the girls had spent the past few days scrubbing the mission home from top to bottom. Everything from the attic to the basement had been swept, polished, and cleaned. The floors shone, the windows sparkled, and all the woodwork gleamed with a new luster. When Frances Thompson had resigned last December, Dolly had worried about replacing such a faithful and efficient woman. But Miss Ferree had proved very capable.

Last night, before retiring to bed, Dolly and Tien had double-checked the preparations. Not a thing had been left undone. A couple of women from the board had stayed the night and had also remarked on the cleanliness and order.

Miss Ferree had pulled the younger girls into a final rehearsal of their sweet song and recitations. Everyone was ready, everything was in place, yet Dolly couldn't sleep.

She gazed up at the ceiling and watched the dark of the night fade to the dove gray of morning. She had been the director now for over six years, and every year had had its challenges. Some nights, Dolly dropped into bed exhausted, unable to do one more thing or even think one more thought. Other nights, she didn't sleep at all, only to go on another rescue.

Over the past few months, death threats had arrived at the mission home. This was nothing new, but these threats were specifically aimed at Tien. As a budding young woman, her scars had faded and she was pretty in her own right. The threats alternated between capturing her to warning her to stop betraying her own people . . . or else.

Officer Cook had taken the threats seriously and had made a few of his own threats toward the higher ranks of the tong. He hoped the message would trickle down, yet on the weekends, when most activity seemed to take place, he frequently posted an officer to keep an eye on the mission home through the night.

Tien didn't seem fazed. She kept going on rescues, even as she was preparing for college. Dolly deeply admired her for this, but she also wanted the young interpreter to be safe.

The mission home was no longer a fable or a whispered secret in Chinatown. Unlike during the first years she had worked there, now it seemed more girls and women showed up at the mission home for help. They were no longer afraid of the missionary women. Even babies were dropped off on their doorstep. There were currently three babies at 920. These babies and younger girls were hard to manage in a household of women who had been through extreme trauma and weren't always on their best behavior.

Dolly mulled over one of the requests she wanted to make to the board about opening a second home for the younger children. This way, the younger children's needs could be fully met, and they wouldn't be exposed to some of the language or stories that came with mixing all the ages. She planned to involve Mei Lien, who was now married to Huan Sun. They lived in Oakland and ran a tailoring shop there. Mei Lien was pregnant again, and Dolly loved the idea of including the young woman in the organization of the new home for babies.

Mei Lien's forgiveness of Ah-Peen Oie had been perhaps the most tender moment Dolly had ever witnessed. The former slave owner had recovered from her surgery, then had declared that she wanted to study Christianity. Dolly remained skeptical for months and kept Ah-Peen Oie separated from the girls at the mission home. It wasn't until an acquaintance had agreed to tutor Ah-Peen Oie that Dolly began to fully trust in the woman's change of heart.

The weeks had turned into months, and Ah-Peen Oie became one of the most devoted women Dolly had ever met. She was humble, she was a hard worker, and she made it her new mission to serve others. Perhaps it had been a leap of faith to let her begin working on the looms in the industrial department, but Ah-Peen Oie continued to prove herself over and over. She went from being a hard worker at the looms to being suggested by Tien to fill in a vacancy at the mission home kitchen.

After Ah-Peen Oie sought and gained forgiveness from Mei Lien, the former slave owner had repeated her plea for forgiveness to each and every girl in the mission home who had been afflicted by her. For some of the girls, their healing finally became complete as they were able to forgive their former slave owner.

Ah-Peen Oie worked in the kitchen, serving those who had once been her slaves. She had married a Christian Chinese man three weeks ago, but she still came several mornings a week to the mission home to help prepare breakfast.

The soft glow of dawn finally dispelled the gray in her room, and Dolly's memories faded like a fine mist. She heard a few sounds coming from below, likely in the kitchen. She wouldn't be surprised if Tien was awake and already ordering breakfast to be started, with Ah-Peen Oie at her side fulfilling those orders.

Dolly stifled a yawn. She looked forward to this evening, when much would be accomplished, and she hoped that meant she would be able to tumble into bed with a satisfied heart. After today, she would be able to help with the upcoming wedding for Yuen Kum, one of their residents whose life had undergone a remarkable change. In three days' time, she would be marrying her sweetheart. The glow about the young woman after escaping her life of abuse was such a joy to see. Dolly's heart could only be full at such a time as this.

A deep rumble interrupted her thoughts. If Dolly had lived closer to the train station, she might have thought the sound was an approaching train—it was too deep for it to be an early morning streetcar. Then her bedroom seemed to shift, and Dolly's stomach dropped like a stone. Before she could comprehend what was happening, she had tumbled off her bed and smacked into the dresser.

Earthquake!

She scrambled to her feet, her nightgown in disarray, her hair spilling over her shoulders. The room had stopped moving, but every part of her was shaking. An eerie silence descended.

It seemed the entire house was holding its breath.

Then the first cry came, a child's cry, followed by another.

The girls.

Dolly snatched her robe with trembling hands and hurried out of her room. Other girls had left their rooms, wandering the hallways or staring about in dismay. Some were crying, others were stunned, and a few held onto younger girls, comforting them. As Dolly made her way through fallen plaster, shattered glass, and broken debris, she checked each room, verifying that no one was harmed.

"Take the little ones downstairs immediately," she said over and over after doling out hugs and reassurances. She met Tien at the top of the stairs. The young woman's eyes were round with fear.

"Are you all right?" Dolly asked.

"Yes," Tien said in a rush. "But look outside."

Dolly moved past her to look out one of the cracked windows. The buildings surrounding them had suffered significant damage, and fallen bricks littered the ground. People were congregating in the middle of the street in the early morning light. Down the hill, wisps of white smoke climbed the sky like a ladder.

"There's fire," Tien said in an awed voice.

Dolly released a breath as she watched the smoke climb higher and turn darker. Right now it was far enough away that there was no threat to their building. But what would time and wind do? She turned and surveyed the walls of the mission home. Nothing significant had fallen or caved. Yet . . . "We might need to move the girls."

"Where?" Tien asked.

"I don't know." Dolly's thoughts were too scattered for her to think of a solution. "We'll speak with the board members who spent the night." As she descended the stairs, she stopped on each level to check on the girls who were trying to make sense of what had happened. She ushered them downstairs to the main parlor where everyone was gathered.

Her heart broke a little when she saw the shattered ornaments, the overturned plants, and the kitchen in complete disarray. Things could be replaced, though; everyone was safe and alive, which was what mattered.

As Dolly stood before them, wide eyes and dusty faces peered back. "Let's account for everyone first," she said. They went around the room, verifying that every person was in attendance, except for Miss Ferree.

"Where is she?" Dolly asked.

Lonnie pointed toward the front door. "She went to get bread."

"Bread?" Dolly turned just as Miss Ferree entered the front door, carrying a large basket of food.

"I found bread for our breakfast," Miss Ferree said in a triumphant voice. "I got to the bakery before the rush. When I left with the bread, others were starting to argue over the remaining food."

Dolly was incredulous, but Miss Ferree acted as if it were a regular morning. With the help of a couple of girls, she set out the bread. Tien and Lonnie scrounged up apples for everyone, and after setting the tables and chairs to rights, they all sat down to eat.

"Miss Cameron," Ah-Peen Oie said in her soft voice, "might I go and check on my husband?"

"Of course," Dolly said, meeting the woman's gaze. The worry ran deep in her eyes, and Dolly didn't blame her. "We'll be fine here. You take care of your home and husband."

Ah-Peen Oie clasped her hands together. "Thank you."

After she left, Dolly ate a bit of bread, but her stomach wouldn't allow anything more. While everyone else ate and discussed the earthquake, she returned to the windows that looked over the street and kept a vigilant watch. The white wisps of smoke had turned darker, and now thicker smoke billowed from the lower levels of San Francisco. She couldn't imagine what was going on in those lower neighborhoods.

Sacramento Street had become a viewing spot. People had climbed the hill to watch the approaching smoke, and as the spectators filled in, so did others who weren't exactly watching the destruction below. Some of them seemed to be scanning the people instead, looking for opportunities in the uncertainty. The unpredictable crowds were making Dolly nervous. She knew that people took advantage of destruction by looting. Might that extend to recovering their slave girls as well? With the chaos of the neighborhoods, all of her girls would be more exposed, and would Officer Cook even have time or the forethought to think of the death threats against Tien?

"What are we going to do with all these girls?" Mrs. Meyers, one of the board members who had stayed the night, asked, joining Dolly at the window. She released a small gasp. "Look at that smoke."

310

Dolly nodded, transfixed. Then her attention was diverted by a group of cavalry on a lower street, crossing Sacramento.

"Martial law," Mrs. Meyers whispered.

"The damage must be significant," Dolly said. It also meant that violence and looting had already started. A man across the street looked toward the mission home, and in the light of the rising sun, Dolly recognized him. A member of the tong—a slave owner who had come to their mission home just a few months ago, insisting on seeing one of the girls. Tien and Dolly had turned him away, but not before he spat at Tien's feet. This, of course, was reported to Officer Cook.

Now, martial law and desperation meant that the Chinese girls might soon have no protection at all. If the police force were compromised, the slave owners would no longer fear being apprehended for an attempted break-in. What was to stop all the tong from Chinatown from descending on this mission home and recapturing the girls?

"What about the First Presbyterian Church?" Mrs. Meyers said in a quiet voice. "It's eight blocks farther up from Chinatown." Dolly knew the one she referred to, on Van Ness Street.

Just then another aftershock raked through San Francisco. Dolly moved away from the window, grasping onto Mrs. Meyers.

Some of the girls started to cry again, and many of them hid under the breakfast tables.

"We need to leave," Dolly whispered, and Mrs. Meyers nodded.

Dolly clapped her hands together and spoke above the cries and whimpers. "Girls, we need to stay calm. Until we know that we are safe, we are going to the First Presbyterian Church to take refuge. We must take only what is necessary, and only what we can carry."

No more orders were needed from Dolly as the other staff members jumped into action, organizing and helping the girls prepare to leave. Hearts were heavy, eyes were wet with tears, but everyone focused, and soon they had all assembled in the foyer.

Dolly motioned for Tien to join her, and they both gave out instructions, in English and Chinese, for the girls to stay together at all costs. The adults were to keep everyone corralled and keep a watchful eye. All were instructed not to stop and speak to anyone. They would travel as quickly as possible, and everyone would do her part. Even the smallest child, five-year-old Hung Mui, carried two dozen eggs.

Dolly unlocked the doors of the mission home, wondering if this was the last time she would stand within these walls. She led the way out of the double doors into the now-bright sunlight. The calm and sunny weather mocked the devastation surrounding them. Buildings on both sides of the street had tumbled-down walls, collapsed roofs, and floors exposed to the elements. It was like peering into a destroyed life-sized dollhouse to see beds and tables and chairs in a jumble with no surrounding walls. Rubble of brick and glass littered the streets, intermixed with clothing and shoes and various items of trash. Yet when Dolly looked back at the mission home from a half block above it, she marveled that only the chimney had collapsed.

There was no doubt a higher power had watched over them. As their group of girls and women passed by crumbled mansions on Nob Hill, bricks and stones were scattered like twigs and leaves. Dolly felt humbled at the blessing her daughters had received.

Inside the First Presbyterian Church, the coolness of the dim interior was immediately calming. The church had received minimal damage and felt much safer than 920. The threat of fire was farther away, and no tong members had followed them.

Mrs. Meyers's eagle eyes picked out the immediate tasks to be done. "Why don't we use the church pew cushions for beds?" she suggested. "We can take them to the basement area and begin setting things up. That way, the younger girls and babies can take naps."

Dolly knew the girls might be nervous about sleeping in the basement, so she went downstairs in advance to make sure all the lights were turned on. By the time the girls came down with their makeshift pallets, everything was as bright as possible.

The day crept slowly by as the staff members made multiple trips outside to watch the events in the city below. The dark, billowing smoke took up the entire skyline now. When evening approached, instead of fog rolling in, as might be the case on an early summer night, it was smoke.

As Dolly stood with Tien, smoke stung their eyes even at this distance. All around, ash littered the streets, floating from the sky like snowflakes.

"What is happening to the world?" Tien said, her tone full of disbelief. "Has the end come?"

Some of the sermons they had heard in church discussed the last days, the end of times, and the destruction the earth would go through before the second coming of the Lord. Dolly could understand how Tien would ask such a question. As Dolly now had a firsthand view of her beloved city disintegrating before her very eyes, it made her wonder too. Was this the wrath of God?

A shiver trailed its way along her spine. So much destruction had already happened, and now the fires. She couldn't imagine the chaos taking place in the areas where the fire was surely driving out human and animal alike. Where would everyone go? One part of her wanted to head down the hill, to find out how she could help. Perhaps people needed rescuing. Perhaps it was a good time to find more slave girls whose owners would be more concerned about their own lives than about their "property" in the face of such devastation.

She placed a hand on Tien's shoulder. "I don't know the answer, dear Tien, but I do know this is larger than all of us. May God have mercy on San Francisco."

Throughout the day, more people arrived to take refuge at the First Presbyterian Church, and Mrs. Meyers and Dolly evaluated each arrival to make sure they didn't have a dual agenda. Despite anyone else's misfortune, her priority was the safety of the girls of 920. She could only guess at the looting and increased desperation that might be taking place below in Chinatown as people competed for shelter, for food, for water, and for refuge.

As the sun finally set on the awful day, the smoke had filled the air with a bitter tang. Orange flames created a glow in the area of Chinatown, and Dolly's stomach turned to lead at the thought of the many businesses and livelihoods destroyed. Where would all the Chinese people go?

Officer Cook showed up at the church. He wore no suit coat or hat, but instead looked as if he had spent all day working on a railroad, with his sweat-stained shirt and rolled-up sleeves. "Are all the girls all right?" he asked as Dolly led him into the cool interior of the church.

"Yes, no injuries," Dolly said. "And the mission home is fine, only minor damage."

"I passed by there," Cook said. "One of the neighbors told me where you'd gone. Some people are refusing to abandon their homes and seek shelter."

It worried Dolly a bit that people knew where they had fled.

"What about you, Miss Cameron?" Cook asked next. "How are you faring?"

"As well as can be expected," she said. "But you look like you need a dunk in the bay."

Cook chuckled and scrubbed a hand through his hair. Ash floated down. "Sorry, I'm making a mess."

"I think a little ash is the least of our problems."

His brows pulled together. "You're right. It's been a long day, and the night will be even longer. Keep the girls and women inside and the church doors locked. Looting has already started, and—" He broke off. "Where's Tien?"

"She's in the basement with the others," Dolly said. "It takes some effort to convince them that there aren't demons lurking beneath the basement floor."

Cook grimaced. "As if they haven't been through enough." He exhaled. "Tien might be in more danger than before."

"I saw some tong members on Sacramento Street before we left." Dolly folded her arms. "Is that what you're referring to?"

"Exactly. They're taking advantage of this situation," Cook said. "You'll need to relocate soon. Tomorrow, if possible. I'm afraid that the entire infrastructure of San Francisco and Chinatown has collapsed."

"I understand," Dolly said. "We have some options we're looking into."

Cook seemed satisfied with that. "I'll stop by again tomorrow."

After Officer Cook left, Dolly paced the foyer of the church, questions plaguing her mind. They needed to leave, and then what? How long would they be gone? When could they return? As darkness settled over the city, the flames of the massive fire created a surreal orange glow over the streets and shattered buildings. It was only a matter of time before the fires continued their climb up Sacramento Street. There was no doubt that, like so many other buildings, the mission home would burn.

But where could she relocate more than fifty women and girls?

The night dragged by minute by minute, and finally Dolly drifted to sleep on a pallet she had positioned closest to the basement steps, only to wake up a few hours later with dread squeezing her chest. All was silent, and there was no reason she should have awakened. But the pounding of adrenaline would not subside. And then she remembered.

The papers—the guardianship papers—were at the mission home. If they burned, the tong could claim that Dolly held no legal rights to her Chinese daughters. What other papers might be lost or burned in the fires? Surely the legal system would be thrown into chaos. Yet, if Dolly had those guardianship papers, then no one could contest any of the cases that she had won.

She rose from her pallet and felt around in the dimness for her shawl. She didn't need it for warmth but to keep from inhaling too much smoke. Without waking a soul, she crept up the basement steps and through the main part of the church. Keeping as quiet as possible so as not to disturb others who had taken refuge in the building, she let herself out of the side door.

The night air boiled with ash and smoke, and Dolly's eyes immediately burned. She wrapped her shawl about her shoulders, then positioned it to cover her mouth. Continuing to the middle of the street where the debris littered the ground, she hurried toward the smoke and flames.

The closer she got to 920 and Chinatown, the heavier the devastation. Blockades had been set up, and guards had been stationed to prevent people from returning to destroyed neighborhoods. The night echoed with cries of desperation. Shouts. Men fighting.

Death. Rats. Smoke. Cruel heat.

She skirted around crumbled buildings and destroyed alleys until she was stopped on Sacramento Street by an armed guard.

"No one is allowed on this street," he said, peering at her. The guard was shorter than she was, but his shoulders were broad, his body stocky.

"I'm Donaldina Cameron, and I must return to the mission home to fetch important documents."

The guard scoffed. "Sorry, ma'am. The fires are nearly to that street, and we don't have the manpower to pull everyone out." He shrugged. "Letting it burn, they are. The fire brigades are busy with Nob Hill. The officials have decided to let Chinatown burn."

Chinatown was dispensable, it seemed. Dolly didn't have time to be incensed. Her girls came first in all matters. "Please, sir. The documents are guardianship papers I have for the slaves and prostitutes that came to us for protection. Without those papers, their slave owners can claim I'm harboring them illegally."

The guard studied her. "Where on Sacramento Street are you going?"

"The Occidental Mission Home at 920. It's the large building on the corner. It was barely damaged in the earthquake."

"It won't escape the fire," the guard warned.

"I know," Dolly said, although she hoped it wouldn't be the case, "and that is why I need to go now, tonight. Tomorrow will be too late."

Perhaps it was because Dolly had made her case, or maybe the guard was just as exhausted as everyone else in the city, but he waved her through. "Go ahead, then, ma'am. Be quick about it. I won't have your death upon my conscience."

She didn't give him a chance to reconsider. Dolly hurried along the street, running now while keeping an eye out for obstacles that might trip her. She ignored the crumpled form of a body in the middle of the street, and, as she passed by, the rats scattered.

Dolly's heart lifted when she reached Powell Street and could see the dome of 920. The building still stood, tall and proud and as yet unburned. She continued along the final half block, then started up the steps, when someone behind her shouted, "Halt!"

She stilled, then turned.

Another guard approached. "This street is closed." He motioned for her to move back down the stairs. "No one goes into these buildings."

Dolly said a silent prayer, then explained who she was and what she needed. "If I don't get those papers, dozens of Chinese girls will be in danger. Officer Jesse Cook can vouch for me."

"I don't care who you know, lady. I have an order to shoot anyone who tries to enter these houses."

She weighed her options. She had come this far, and she refused to turn back empty-handed. Her life's work was tied to the legality of protecting her daughters. "You'll have to shoot me, then." She turned away from the guard's harsh gaze and hurried up the steps.

He hadn't tried to shoot her yet, so she pushed open the doors and entered the dark foyer, lit only by the orange glow coming in through the windows.

Dolly heard the footsteps of the guard coming up the stairs. Would he forcibly make her leave? But he didn't grab her as he entered the foyer. He only said, "Hurry, you have seconds, then you need to get out—"

The ground shuddered beneath her, and the building felt like it had cracked in two. Another earthquake? Dolly sank to her knees and covered her head as plaster fell about her. The guard gripped her arm and hauled her to her feet.

"Hurry! They're dynamiting the next block," he said. "By creating a fire break, they hope to protect the upper homes and neighborhoods."

"Chinatown," Dolly whispered. "They're destroying Chinatown."

"Get those papers and get out."

She moved quickly, yet it seemed she was barely moving at all. Her ears rang from the explosion, and her mouth and throat burned with dust and smoke. She hurried into the office where she had spent hours and years running the mission home, praying for her daughters, and planning rescues.

She grabbed the ledger and the document folders that held the paperwork of her daughters' lives. Clutching them to her chest, she followed the guard out of the building. There was no time for a final look at the rooms. There was no time for farewells to the memories within.

For the last time, she left 920, and, after thanking the guard, she began the steep trek up Sacramento Street. If possible, the smoke had thickened and the fires seemed even closer. Another boom from the direction of Chinatown ricocheted through Dolly's entire body. Her legs trembled and her breathing skipped, but she pushed forward.

She didn't know how much more her heart could stand when she finally arrived at the First Presbyterian Church. She entered the side entrance again. Once inside, she took deep, cleansing breaths of the sweeter air. She had done it. She'd saved the guardianship papers and the years of written records of the events at 920.

When Dolly lay on her pallet again, she finally slept. Tomorrow, she would be facing another mountain to climb, but she'd at least successfully climbed one tonight.

CHAPTER THIRTY-ONE

"It was a thankful though a completely exhausted company
that sank down amid bundles and babies on the lower deck
of the steamer, too weary to walk to the saloon. But tired and
homeless, knowing not where that night we were to lay our
heads, our only feeling was one of gratitude for deliverance as
we looked over the group of more than sixty young faces and
realized how God had cared for His children."

—Donaldina Cameron, report of events
following the 1906 earthquake

1906

What should have been a beautiful, clear spring day in San Francisco
was in fact obscured by thick clouds of smoke, smoldering buildings, and
thousands of homeless people. Dolly surveyed her group of women and girls
and babies as they walked together, two days after the earthquake, skirting
low-burning fires and ash-filled neighborhoods. A messenger had brought
word that the women from 920 had been offered accommodations in Marin
County.

The challenge was to make it there with a group as large as theirs.
Preparations had been hectic. Several of the girls bemoaned the items they'd
left at the mission home, but mostly the girls and women were in good spirits

and willing to help where needed. One young woman, Yuen Kum, who was engaged to be married, had carried a large box of letters from her suitor to the church. And she was still carrying it now.

Dolly marveled at the determination of these girls and women who had already been through so much and now had to endure once again. Tien had taken it upon herself to issue orders about who would carry what. Lonnie, Dong Ho, and Leung were all given assignments to watch over the younger girls. Jiao walked with little Hung Mui, who had insisted on carrying something as they trekked toward the ferry building.

It was gratifying to see Kum Quai moving among the women, helping and encouraging where she could. She offered to carry one of the young babies.

Dolly motioned Tien over. "Stay in the middle of the group with Kum Quai. We don't know who might be watching or following us, but Officer Cook says that the tong have not evacuated the city yet."

"I will watch over Kum Quai," Tien said.

"*You* are in danger as well," Dolly added. "Do not risk anything."

Tien simply nodded, a determined look in her eyes, then joined the traveling pack.

By the time the troupe reached Embarcadero Street, they had become footsore, but everyone was still determined. They needed to cross the bay into Marin County, and there, Dolly hoped they could begin to stitch together their fractured lives. Other women joined their procession—women displaced by the tragedy and seeking shelter. By the time Dolly spied the Ferry Building, she worried they wouldn't be able to travel across the waters together as a single group.

She entered the Ferry Building to inquire about the availability. The employee there was nonplussed and simply said, "The incoming ferry is empty. You've just missed the main crowd." He cast his blue-eyed gaze over the women and children carrying a mishmash of luggage, items, and bundles. "There is room for you all, ma'am."

Dolly's knees felt weak with relief. They were getting out of San Francisco. They would be safe. After boarding the boat, she moved to the rail and gripped the top as they pulled away from the shore. The view of San Francisco was hard to fathom. Smoke filled the sky like a dense quilt, and buildings were ghosts of their former selves. Everything she saw broke her heart for her beloved city.

She sank onto a nearby bundle, needing to rest her legs. Dolly didn't know where they would end up sleeping tonight, but at least they were away from the choking smoke, the crumbling memories, and the searching eyes of the tong.

In Sausalito, the group was met by friends of the board and taken to San Anselmo. The barn they were led to was lacking in comfort, but considering their situation and the size of their group, this was the only option for now. They would make do. When ladies from the Relief Committee brought in food, it was likely a bit of a shock for them to see so many Chinese women together under Dolly's leadership.

When she explained how the mission home operated, one of the relief women pulled Dolly aside and said, "We've seen other Chinese coming through our town because of the earthquake. Where are they all going?"

"To whoever will take them in," Dolly said, her mind reeling. Which Chinese? Families? Tong members? She blew out a breath. "Most are fleeing destroyed and burned homes. It will take years to rebuild what was lost."

The woman's eyes widened. Dolly supposed some might find the sudden influx of Chinese from Chinatown bothersome. She could only hope that the slave owners would not recover anytime soon and that they would either scatter or stay far away.

But Dolly's hope was in vain. Only a handful of days later, while she and Miss Ferree were coming out of the nearby Presbyterian orphanage where they'd been given clothing to share with the girls, Dolly saw a man she recognized as a tong member, the one who had spat at Tien's feet. And with him was a woman Dolly had encountered at a previous rescue. This woman had refused to let Dolly enter her house.

When she and Miss Ferree returned to the drafty barn, Dolly immediately found Tien. "I need to speak to you in private."

They went outside behind the barn where they only had the trees and buzzing insects for company. "The tong are here," Dolly said. "The man who spat at you, and another woman who despises me. They might be the ones behind the death threats."

Tien folded her hands in front of her. For a long moment, she didn't say anything. "You've had plenty of death threats too, yet you continue to work."

"That's different," Dolly said.

"How?"

"I'm not Chinese, and I'm not young like you."

Tien shook her head, lines appearing between her brows. "You think you're replaceable, Miss Cameron?"

Dolly sighed. "Be careful, my friend. Be vigilant. Don't go anywhere alone."

"If the tong are here, then I am not the only one in danger," Tien said. "And I can't hide for the rest of my life."

"I know."

"We must call a meeting and tell everyone," Tien said. "San Francisco isn't the only place there is danger. As long as the tong exist, the war continues."

"You're right," Dolly said.

With all the older girls and women gathered, Dolly explained about the sighting with the help of Tien translating. Dolly hated to bring more fear into the hearts of these women who had been through so much, but she would never overlook the presence of slave owners, who were now more desperate than ever.

She surveyed the ragtag group of girls and women, their rumpled clothing, their scant bedding, with only a few saucepans and tin plates between them, and now Dolly had to deliver that bad news. "Miss Ferree and I were in town today, and we have brought back a warning." She watched the worry take over the expressions on her dear ones' faces, but she had to inform them. After explaining about whom they had seen, she added, "No one can be outside alone. We must always be in groups, and you must have a staff member with you. Do not leave without permission."

"Did they follow us from San Francisco?" Jiao asked in her little voice.

Dolly hesitated. She had no true confirmation, but the irony was that out of all the towns to flee to, they had chosen this one. "Yes," she said. "I believe they've followed us." She raised a hand before any commotion could arise. "We must have faith, like we always do, and be diligent. We've been blessed and protected this far."

As it was, Dolly used every influence and effort she could until they were granted a house for rent in San Rafael. The day they walked to their new sanctuary was one that Dolly would never forget. The house was a bit run-down, but it was serviceable, and more important, it was warm and offered greater protection. The late spring had produced blooming roses and acacia that edged the driveway leading up to the house, and even the towering trees had budded, creating a divine scent full of promise and warmth.

More than ever, Dolly was on alert. Gone were the San Francisco police squad and lawyers and judges. In San Rafael, the women were on their own, watching out for each other.

And then word began to arrive about the influx of Chinese into Oakland, about two hours' travel time from Dolly. The Chinese tong were making inroads into new areas by transferring their slave trade to Oakland, starting up their brothels and dens.

One morning, Tien hurried into the room that served as both office and bedroom to Dolly. Tien's face was flushed, and her lips were pressed tight. She said nothing, but handed over a sweat-stained note.

"What's this?" Dolly's heart thumped as she unfolded the note once, then once again. The words in the note sent a rush of anxiety through her. They might be miles from San Francisco, but her location had been found out.

"Excuse me," Dolly said, unable to have Tien's observant gaze upon her at this moment.

Dolly walked out of the large house and stood on the porch. She read the words of the note again as the scent of blooming flowers floated around her.

The words were written in childlike English, but they were clear enough. *Help me. Husband cruel. I cannot live here. Come to Oakland. My name is Li Na. Help me please.*

Below the words, a small map had been drawn of a row of houses, with one of the houses circled.

Here, while Dolly stood in this beautiful Garden of Eden, women were out there, desperate and in pain. Dolly might have once thought her work rested primarily in San Francisco, but now she realized it would continue no matter where she lived. And as long as there were women and children in need, she would do what she could.

Dolly released a sigh. Legally married or not, paper daughter or true daughter, no human deserved the abuse of another. She pocketed the note and walked inside the house. She rejoined Tien in the office.

The young woman stood straight, hands folded, dark eyes resolute, as she waited for Dolly to tell her about the note.

"Li Na lives in Oakland," Dolly said. "She's the wife of a cruel husband and wants to escape his abuse."

"I will come," Tien said.

With Tien exposed to the streets, she might be in danger yet again, but Dolly knew the young woman wouldn't be dissuaded.

An hour later, they were heading to Oakland. With the influx of the tong into the nooks and crevasses of surrounding cities, Dolly suspected that in the months ahead, more pleas for rescue would come.

When they reached Oakland, they made quick work of locating the address.

"Is this the right house?" Tien asked in a doubtful voice as they approached a stately house set back from the road. The grass and foliage were well kept, and all seemed peaceful and beautiful.

"Perhaps she's a maid or cook?" Dolly suggested.

Tien frowned. "And her husband takes care of the horses?"

Dolly adjusted her hat. "I guess we'll go find out." They walked to the wrought-iron gate and, finding it unlocked, swung it open.

As they headed up the short drive, no one tried to stop them, but Dolly sensed they were being watched—whether from the windows of the second floor or from the house across the street, she did not know.

Dolly knocked on the front door, fully expecting a maid to answer. Instead, the woman who opened the door was dressed in a beautiful long skirt, a Western-style blouse pleated with ruffles, and a prim waistcoat. She was also Chinese.

Her eyes rounded, and she stepped out onto the porch and raised a finger to her lips. "Do not speak yet," she whispered in Chinese.

Just then, the door opened wider right behind her, and a tall man stepped out. Tall Chinese men were rare, and this one towered over Dolly. Although she guessed him to be in his forties, there was nothing aging about him.

"Are you going to invite your guests in?" the man said in perfect English.

"They are here from the sewing club," the woman told the man in much less perfect English.

"We can't stay long," Dolly said in a sugary voice, giving the man a matter-of-fact smile.

He looked from Dolly to Tien. "Well, I must be on my way. I'll see you later, wife."

She nodded and gave him a brief smile that didn't reach her eyes.

The three women watched the Chinese man make his way down the driveway, then turn onto the sidewalk. When he disappeared from view, Tien asked, "Are you Li Na?"

"Yes." The woman grasped both Dolly and Tien's hands and pulled them into her house. The place was polished from floor to ceiling, and it smelled of flowers and lemon.

With another finger to her lips, she motioned them to follow her into a parlor, where she shut the double doors. Then she turned to them and began to unbutton her blouse.

Dolly held up her hand. "You don't need to show us anything."

Li Na stopped her progress, and it was then that Dolly noticed the woman's trembling fingers. Li Na closed her eyes, and a single tear dripped onto her cheek.

Dolly took the woman's hands in hers. "If you come with us, you might have to testify in court against your husband, should he come after you."

Tien softly translated.

Li Na nodded. "I will come with you, and if I have to testify, then so be it."

"Do you have any children?"

Tears again formed in Li Na's eyes. "I had a son, but he died. My husband told me I was a disgrace."

Dolly knew there was more to the story behind the woman's sad words. But if they were to leave with this woman, wasn't the sooner they left the better?

"Have you packed some things to take with you?" Dolly asked.

"Yes, my trunk is hidden beneath my bed. Wait here while I dismiss the servants. I'll give them the rest of the day off."

Dolly and Tien waited in the pretty parlor room, filled with elegant Chinese decorations.

When Li Na returned, she reported that her servants had all left. "But we can't let my neighbors or anyone see."

That wasn't a problem. "Wear your most sturdy shoes, and we will make our way through the hills until we get parallel with the train station. There, we can cut to the depot and catch the next train in the direction of San Rafael."

"Oh, thank you," the woman said. "You do not know what this means to me."

Yes, I do, Dolly wanted to say. She very well knew that a rescue meant a woman would have a second chance at living a fulfilling life. A chance of happiness.

Soon they left the house through the kitchen and hurried through groves of trees, around bushes, and skirting the hillsides until they could head unobserved to the train depot.

"I'll go first, then give you a signal that all is clear." But the moment Dolly arrived on the platform, she saw that she had company. Three Chinese men were waiting for the next train. Under normal circumstances, she would have thought nothing about it. But circumstances weren't normal. Besides, the men took turns casting looks in her direction. They were also dressed in full suits, and nothing about them suggested they were laborers. Rather, they appeared to be men who profited off of others for a living.

Dolly had no suitcase or traveling bag to occupy herself. And she couldn't very well run back toward the trees where Tien was waiting with their charge. So Dolly took a seat on a bench, folded her hands, and kept her gaze upon her lap as if she were in deep contemplation.

The men didn't speak to her, but she felt their eyes upon her more than once. If they had never seen her in person, they apparently had at least heard of her enough to know who she was.

The next train came, and, thankfully, the men boarded. Dolly's shoulders sagged as their departing train gained speed and eventually disappeared.

Dolly rose to her feet, crossed the platform, and waved toward the trees. It wasn't long before a disheveled Tien emerged, leading Li Na. They waited over an hour for the next train to arrive, and Dolly was a bundle of nerves until they were settled on the train in their own private compartment.

Only then did Li Na begin to tell her story. She told how her marriage had been arranged from China between her father and the man who was now her husband. She had come over to America with hope, but only a few weeks into the marriage, her new husband began to abuse her. Nothing she did was ever good enough. Nothing she could say would please him. Her husband only hurt her where others wouldn't notice marks or bruising.

"I heard my maid talking about Miss Cameron," Li Na admitted. "How she rescues women from brothels. And I thought . . ."

"You did the right thing," Dolly assured her.

Despite the many rescues that Dolly had been a part of, and despite the many stories she'd heard, it never failed to pain her heart when she listened to a victim share her story of trafficking and abuse. She moved to sit right next to Li Na and grasped her hand. Li Na clung to her fingers, and Dolly could only hope that Li Na would have enough courage to make a statement before a judge if her husband decided to pursue her.

When they climbed off the train and headed toward the house, Dolly went on alert when she saw a buggy leaving the house with no passengers inside.

"Who's here?" Tien said immediately.

Dolly hoped Miss Ferree had been wise in whom she let into the house. But once they stepped inside, Dolly smiled at the jubilant activity going on. It seemed wedding preparations were under way, and Miss Ferree hurried to Dolly. "Yuen Kum's beau has tracked us down."

The planned wedding day in San Francisco had come and gone with the events of the earthquake changing everyone's lives, but now Henry Lai had tracked down his bride-to-be.

Dolly looked over to where Henry Lai sat in the shabby parlor, a brilliant smile on his face. When he saw Dolly, he promptly rose to his feet and bowed. Then he explained how he had been desperately searching for them.

Dolly was smiling by the time he finished. "And Yuen Kum still wants to marry you?"

He laughed, knowing she was teasing. "She does, and we will be married tonight. Miss Ferree has already notified the minister, Dr. Landon, and he will marry us in the chapel at San Anselmo."

"Wonderful," Dolly said, elated for the couple. "I wish the two of you every happiness."

She was well aware of Li Na listening into the conversation, and Dolly's heart ached for the woman's shattered heart and broken past right now.

Dolly had only to look at Tien, who nodded and said, "I will find Li Na a place to sleep and spend some quiet time."

"Thank you," Dolly said. She left the groom-to-be in the parlor, still grinning, and went to find Yuen Kum.

She was dressed in a simple dress of linen, since she had been unable to bring her white wedding dress. Yuen Kum rushed to Dolly and embraced her. "Can you believe he found me?"

Dolly laughed softly. "You are a blessed woman."

Yuen Kum drew away, her smile as bright as the sun. "It's like you said, the Lord has watched out for us."

And the Lord wanted Dolly here, in San Rafael. Today had confirmed that.

CHAPTER THIRTY-TWO

We lay for women's rapid education
This cornerstone of everlasting foundation;
For our religious widening and civilization progressing
And peace of East and West we pray.

—Poem by Imperial Chinese Consul-General Huang Zunxian in
San Francisco, translated by J. H. Laughlin, cornerstone
ceremony for new mission home, August 1907

APRIL 1908

Tien cracked open the office door at their home in Oakland, interrupting Dolly's thoughts as she finished an entry in the mission home ledger. "The buggies are here."

Dolly looked up from the ledger, where she had just entered the sixtieth record of a rescued slave girl during their time outside of San Francisco. The thick ledger was the same one she had rescued from 920 before the fire swept through Sacramento Street two years before. She'd left a few blank spaces between some of the entries, hoping to add successful endings to the failed rescue attempts.

"All right, I'm coming." She rose and closed the ledger, then packed it into a satchel on the already cleared-off desk.

"I can carry it," Tien said. "You'll sit in the first buggy with Li Na and

Kum Quai." The two former brides had become close friends over the past two years.

Dolly nodded, but her mind was wrapped up in the words she had just penned: "We heard of this unfortunate slave girl, and we tried to rescue her. But the owner of the den was warned. You see, even away from San Francisco, they know who *Fahn Quai* is. By the time we arrived, she'd been spirited away, and we couldn't find her. This blank space below will hopefully be filled with news of her eventual recovery."

After living in San Rafael, Dolly had again moved the Chinese girls and women to Oakland, to a rented house. Requests for rescues continued to trickle in. For some of them, her team traveled hundreds of miles, reaching such places as Oroville, Marysville, Pacific Grove, Bakersfield, Oakland, and back to San Francisco. The highbinders had found new locations to set up their dens and revive human trafficking.

Tien picked up the satchel and moved to the doorway, then paused. "Will you miss Oakland?"

Today was their final morning in that city. They had spent the last week sorting and packing for their sojourn back to San Francisco and 920 Sacramento Street, where the mission home had been rebuilt.

So much had happened during the two years since the earthquake, yet it seemed to Dolly as if she'd just blinked her eyes. "I'll miss it, but I can't wait to get back home," she replied, and she meant it. "And you have college to look forward to. I can't believe the time has come."

Tien would be leaving at the end of the summer to attend college back east at a private girls' school, Stevens School, in Philadelphia. Her sponsor, Horace C. Coleman, had offered to pay for her schooling. "Soon, I'll return to you, and you'll see a new Tien," she said.

Dolly joined Tien in the doorway and wrapped an arm about her shoulders. "Don't change too much, my friend."

By the time they stepped off the ferry in San Francisco, Dolly felt as if they had been gone from the city for a decade. As they traveled up the hill, new construction dominated every street.

Chinatown had been rebuilt—risen again out of its own ashes. She'd read in the newspapers that the city of San Francisco had tried to curb the reclaiming of the land by the Chinese, hoping to avoid the infiltration of the tong. Despite those efforts, the Chinese still owned one-third of Chinatown. And the remaining two-thirds had been rented out by landlords to the Chinese.

When their hired buggy reached the base of Sacramento Street, Dolly told the driver she wanted to walk the rest of the way. He stopped, and she and Tien stepped out. Dolly had been sent sketches of the new mission home, but this was the first time she would see it in person. Her breath stalled as she gazed up the hill.

Right in the same location, on the same corner, a five-story square building had been constructed.

"That's it," Dolly breathed. "Home."

Gone was the elegant structure of the former mission home, replaced by the boxy architecture of the new home. The brown brick building rose from the former destruction, majestic in its own way. Many of the original bricks had been used, and their singed and partly melted edges speckled the building like battle scars.

The girls and women in the other buggies reached the building. After climbing out and unloading their belongings, they waited for Dolly to catch up.

"Miss Cameron," a voice boomed behind her.

She turned to see a police officer striding toward her.

"I thought you were arriving today," Officer Cook said. He was the same, yet different. His mustache was grayer, his shoulders leaner, and his limp more pronounced. He tossed his cigarette away.

Dolly grinned. "Officer Cook, you're still here."

He stopped in front of her and smiled. The lines about his eyes were deeper, but his expression was as intense and knowledgeable as it had ever been. "I'll always be here." His gaze shifted. "And how are you, Tien Fu Wu?"

She dropped her eyes, but said, "I am fine, thank you."

"What do you think of the new place?" Cook turned to look up the hill. "Quite a sight."

"Yes," Dolly agreed. "I would have thought you had retired, with the tong relocating to other cities."

Cook cut his eyes to hers, and his jovial mood sobered. "It's true that the earthquake destroyed much, Miss Cameron. You could say it laid wide open the underbelly of Chinatown. The destruction and fires uncovered passageways and tunnels of the opium dens and prostitution cribs, some of them three stories beneath the ground." He took off his hat, scrubbed at his hair, then replaced his hat. "All of this was laid out for the city officials to witness. No one could brush the problems of Chinatown under the table any longer."

Dolly remained very still, listening to every word.

"Chinatown has been rebuilt." He paused. "In full. With both the good and the bad."

"The war continues," she whispered.

"I'm afraid so." He lit another cigarette, and Dolly noticed the tremble in his hand. "We might live in the land of the free, but none of us are truly free as long as slavery exists in our society."

A whistle sounded farther down the street, and Cook glanced over, then took a step back. "Call the station with anything you need. Anything at all." He tipped his hat. Then, before striding away, he added, "Welcome home, my friends."

Dolly watched after him until Tien linked her arm through hers.

"Let's go," Tien said in a determined voice. "Everyone is waiting for the director to unlock the front door."

Dolly's throat felt tight with unanswered questions she had for Officer Cook. "All right. I'm ready," she told Tien.

Together they walked up the last part of the hill. The group of women and girls parted as Dolly moved to the front door. The board members were waiting for her, and, with smiles, they presented her with the key. Dolly and her daughters finally had their own place again, at the same beloved location—a place that would continue to be a beacon of light and hope to all who sought refuge and healing.

The board had been able to save the original double doors, so it was with nostalgia that Dolly fit the key into the lock and turned it. The last time she had stepped through these doors was on the night of the earthquake, when she'd rescued the guardianship papers. As she walked inside, the scent of new wood and fresh paint greeted her. Miss Ferree followed, then soon the rest. The chatter among the girls faded as everyone looked around. The place was well built and beautiful in its own way. It was a different home now, but one that would soon become beloved, Dolly was sure. An elegant staircase of dark wood rose from the main level, winding up to the top of the house. Wood-paneled walls were broken up by windows that looked out onto the street and brought in plenty of light.

It was plain that loving care and time had been poured into the interior. The wooden floors gleamed, and the place had been decorated with Chinese bronzes, embroideries, intricate carvings, a porcelain elephant, and brass ornaments. Other Christian organizations had donated elegant furnishings, rugs, and draperies.

Jiao's and Lonnie's excited voices raised above the rest, combined with Leung's and Dong Ho's footsteps as they pounded up the staircase in search of the best bedrooms. Dolly let them bask in their joy. She had no desire to curb the girls' enthusiasm, even if alterations in bedroom assignments might have to be made later.

Dolly walked through the house at a much slower pace, admiring the final touches and feeling overwhelmed with gratitude for the combined effort of rebuilding and decorating. A brand-new oak table sat in the parlor, where Dolly could meet with visitors and interview potential grooms. She made her way to the set of stairs in the back of the house, which went from the top floor to the basement. She took a few minutes to examine the basement, satisfied that the tunnel was still in place. A secret way out if needed.

Officer Cook's warning had been clear. Dolly's daughters would still need to be protected.

She climbed the back stairs, pausing on each level, then walked the floors. The scents of newness permeated the air, from fresh linens on the beds, to the new pine wall paneling, to the calcimine whitewash on the walls and ceilings. Once she reached the top floor, she walked through a bedroom connecting to a rooftop alcove.

Outside, Dolly turned in a slow circle, taking in the whole of San Francisco, much of it under construction. She was home at last. Finally, they could move forward with plans that had been put on hold for the past couple of years, such as raising funds for the babies' home and finding more sponsors for the older girls to attend college.

For just a moment, Dolly reflected on Charles Bazatas. There had been scant communication between them since Dolly had left Philadelphia four years ago. And that was how it should be. She had her work, and he had his. Today wasn't a day to reflect on the past and what might have been, but to look toward the future and enjoy the blessings of the present.

Dolly took one last look over the sloping city of San Francisco. The entire landscape had changed. Gone were the burned-out hulls of buildings, replaced by newer structures. Streets had been cleared of rubble, and there was no sign of the ash that had once covered every surface. It was as if the city had been given a new beginning. As Dolly stood on the rooftop alcove, she made a resolve to begin the next chapter of her life with renewed hope for a better future. There was no need to dwell on the losses and failures of the past. With an open heart, she would follow the Lord's guidance.

CHAPTER THIRTY-THREE

"Dozens of bright-eyed Chinese girls patter gaily about
in their black blouse-and-trouser costumes, playing at
housework, or working at their play with childish absorption,
laughing, romping, singing, full of the joy of life and the
blessing of freedom . . . they are happy. It takes only a few
minutes' walk through the Home to see that the Mission's
work of rescuing these girls from slavery has lit the light
of gratitude in all their eyes, and that they all, who were
friendless, have found in Miss Cameron a friend."

—E. French Strother, The California Weekly, February 26, 1909

APRIL 14, 1908

Dolly opened the double doors of the Occidental Mission Home to those she and the board had invited to Dedication Day. The spring weather had cooperated, and only a few clouds trailed across the sky. All morning, well wishes had been delivered by telegram and letters from friends too far away to attend.

Since returning to San Francisco, the girls and women had put their time to good use. They had sewed cushions, made curtains for the upper rooms, prepared desserts for the guests, and decorated with vines and flowers the chapel room where the annual board meeting would be held for the first time in this building.

As the chapel began to fill, Dolly noted that every board member was in attendance, as well as Dr. and Mrs. Condit, the founder of the home's original board. Other notables such as the Chinese and Japanese consuls attended, along with Chung Sai Yut Po, the editor of a Chinese newspaper.

But the most esteemed guests in Dolly's mind were the former residents of the mission home. Dolly greeted Mei Lien with a warm hug. She'd brought her husband, Huan Sun, and their two children.

"It's good to see you, *Lo Mo*," Mei Lien whispered in her ear.

The affectionate title made Dolly smile. Being on the receiving end of Mei Lien's respect was truly an honor.

When they withdrew from their embrace, Dolly took the youngest child into her arms. "She's growing so fast." The child grabbed for the brooch on Dolly's blouse, and she laughed.

Mei Lien smiled. "She thinks everything is hers."

"Of course. I wore this just for her," Dolly said with a wink.

"My husband says I can work here once a week," Mei Lien said. "I will help with anything you ask of me."

"Thank you," Dolly said. "We'd love to have you."

Not long after Mei Lien entered, Ah-Peen Oie walked in with her husband and her adopted baby, a child who had been abandoned at the mission home. Ah-Peen Oie had been quick to take over the care of the child. Dolly watched the interaction between Mei Lien and Ah-Peen Oie as they exclaimed over each other's children.

Dolly couldn't help but smile at the sight of the two women interacting. She knew that only by the grace of God had the former slave and slave owner been able to discover their paths of forgiveness.

Among all the speeches, the Chinese girls sang two of Dolly's favorite songs: "Just One Touch" and "That Man of Calvary."

In response to the spoken and sung accolades, Dolly concluded with,

"As we begin to enumerate our blessings they appear to multiply. There are so many bright and hopeful things in this work we should never be discouraged. With God all things are possible."

With the dedication over, Dolly spent the next days and weeks helping Tien prepare to travel to Philadelphia for her college education. Tien had promised over and over she would return to the mission home. Dolly could only pray that her dear young friend would. Time marched forward, and the moment of farewell had arrived as Dolly and Mei Lien faced Tien on the train platform where she would begin the first leg of her journey. Miss Ferree would travel across the country with Tien, then return to the mission home.

Dolly hugged Miss Ferree and said, "Thank you for taking her, and I will see you in a few weeks."

Next, Mei Lien and Tien embraced. "You have been a light in my life," Mei Lien told the young interpreter. "If only I can be like you someday."

Tien beamed a smile, then wiped at the tears on her face. "Don't let your babies forget Auntie Wu."

"I won't," Mei Lien said.

Next Tien turned to Dolly and grasped her hands. "I will return. You will see."

Dolly smiled, although the tears had already started. "I am so proud of you. From the first moment I met you, I knew there would be no stopping your ambitions."

"I gave you such a hard time," Tien mused, her expression contrite.

"You were a child," Dolly said. "A child who'd been crushed in body, but never in spirit."

And then the two women were embracing and crying. Dolly had been through many emotional upheavals in her life, but this one was the most bittersweet. She was so happy for Tien, yet her heart already ached with the many years that would pass before they were reunited.

Tien drew away first, her dark eyes flashing with determination. "I will pray for you every day, *Lo Mo*."

And Dolly knew she would. "We will all be praying for our dear Tien."

Dolly stood arm in arm with Mei Lien as the two of them watched Tien walk toward the waiting train. Just before she boarded, she turned and waved. Her countenance glowed with new opportunity and the fortitude she'd been born with.

Mei Lien, patient as always, waited with Dolly as the train pulled out of the station and the crowds disappeared. Only when they were the last ones on the platform did Dolly turn. One step forward, and then another. It was all she could do—all she could ever do. But her heart brimmed with happiness for Tien.

Her step paused when she saw Officer Cook standing near the train office. Smoke trailed from his cigarette, and his expression was grim. Was he here by coincidence? Or had he come to see Tien off? If so, he'd just missed her.

Dolly led Mei Lien to where Cook waited.

"We have an urgent situation," he said in a low voice, his gaze moving from Dolly to Mei Lien.

"You can speak in front of Mei Lien," Dolly said. "She is a volunteer at the mission home now."

Officer Cook's brows furrowed. "Can she interpret?"

"I speak English well enough," Mei Lien said. "I can help."

Dolly snapped her gaze to Mei Lien. "You don't have to—this is far different from teaching music or—"

"I want to help," Mei Lien insisted. Her luminous eyes focused on Dolly. "Please."

Dolly still hesitated.

But Cook had no such reservations. "The tong rivals are fighting over a girl," he said. "They are in negotiations right now. Whatever happens, whoever comes out on top, the girl will lose."

Dolly nodded, her jaw clenched. "Take us there."

"We will need backup," Cook said. "And I don't know how safe the rescue mission will be."

"If you're still in the war, then so am I." Dolly nodded to Mei Lien. "We already have our interpreter."

"Very well." Cook stubbed out his cigarette. "We'll take a buggy to the Hall of Justice, and I'll get a few men to come with us for backup."

Dolly and Mei Lien next found themselves in the buggy with Cook traveling to the newly built Hall of Justice on Washington and Kearny Streets. Officers Green and Riordan joined them, and soon the Chinatown squad walked together along the newly built streets.

Cook moved alongside Dolly and said, "The Chinese girl, Sai Mui, was brought from China as a paper daughter and forced into prostitution some months ago."

Dolly nodded, keeping her chin lifted, although her stomach had plummeted. So Sai Mui had already suffered terror and abuse.

"She escaped the slave owner who made her work on May Fong Alley," Cook continued, lighting another cigarette. "But she chose the wrong place to take refuge."

"Not the mission home," Dolly said in a quiet voice.

"*Not* the mission home," Cook confirmed. "A rival tong group got ahold of her. Sai Mui's slave owner demanded her back, but the rival tong refused, so the slave owner agreed to settle on a price for the girl." He inhaled on his cigarette, then tossed it into the gutter. "The meeting should be taking place now . . . bartering over the price of a human."

The disgust in his voice echoed that in Dolly's mind.

Her step slowed as they approached the building. Officer Riordan skipped any knocking or shouting and instead tried the door first. It was locked, but he made quick work of opening it with a single strike of his sledgehammer.

The main level was empty, and they climbed two flights of stairs as silently as possible. Before they reached the top of the landing, Dolly put up a hand to tell everyone to wait. Moving up another step or two, she spotted a guard standing before a heavy door, tightly shut.

Dolly turned to Mei Lien. "Go up there and ask him to open the door. Tell him you have an important errand." She could see that the brand-new interpreter was nervous, but Mei Lien stepped forward.

After a short conversation, the guard opened the door for her. Dolly hurried up the last few stairs with the policemen, and they pushed through the unlocked door.

"Stop there," the doorkeeper called, but there was nothing one man could do against the five of them. So he shouted a warning to whoever could hear him in the building.

On the floor above, something crashed, and it sounded like furniture was being dragged around. Panicked voices rose. Dolly and her group pounded up the last set of steps, and Officer Cook banged on the door with his fist. "Open up! Or we'll break this door down!"

The bolts slid open, and Dolly entered the sparse room.

More than a dozen Chinese men stared back at her, most of them sitting with folded arms.

"Where is Sai Mui?" she asked immediately, and Mei Lien translated in a trembling but determined voice. Dolly had no doubt that Mei Lien knew some of the men in this room.

"There are no girls here," one of the tong said in a smooth voice.

Behind the man, the window was open; on instinct, Dolly rushed to it. Peering out, she saw a man below, looking up. When their gazes connected, he pointed upward. Had Sai Mui gone through the skylight? And the only place to go from there was to the next house.

She withdrew from the window and told Mei Lien and the policemen, "Follow me."

They hurried out of the house and into the next, bypassing a guard who didn't give their group any trouble. They searched every room but found no Sai Mui.

Dolly and Mei Lien checked in every closet and beneath each bed, calling for the young woman. The policemen rumbled through the house, moving furniture and tapping on walls.

Finally, Dolly stopped before a cupboard pushed against the bedroom wall at an angle. She wrenched the heavy piece from the wall and found a young woman crouched behind it like a mouse hiding from a cat. The young woman's eyes were dark, her skin sallow with illness, and her lips were chapped and sore.

Dolly stooped and held out her hand. "Come with us, and you will be safe."

When Mei Lien repeated the words in Chinese, Sai Mui nodded and grasped Dolly's hand.

Dolly pulled the trembling girl to her feet, and the women flanked her as they walked out of the room and down the stairs. "We found her!" Dolly called out so the policemen could hear.

She didn't miss Mei Lien's tears of relief—and perhaps of remembered trauma. Dolly knew her own tears would come eventually.

When Officer Cook appeared at the base of the stairs the women were descending, his expression held stark relief. He did a quick scan of the girl, who seemed to be walking fine; then he nodded.

"Let's go," he ordered the other officers. "Riordan, you take the rear. There's a crowd outside."

Dolly kept hold of one of Sai Mui's arms as they stepped outside. Sure enough, a crowd had gathered. Would they be yelled at? Would Sai Mui be forced from their grasp?

One look at Officer Cook's tense shoulders and tight grip on his sledge-hammer told her this could turn into a terrible brawl, should the crowd turn aggressive.

"Cross the street," Cook commanded, guiding their group to the other side so they avoided walking past the original building where the tong had been in their meeting.

Four of the tong men stood in front of the doorway, arms folded, eyes narrowed. Above, leaning out the second-floor window, were the other tong men, watching every movement.

Dolly's mouth felt as dry as a desert, and her heart was nearly pounding out of her chest. She expected a fight to break out at any moment. There were simply too many people to maneuver around. But the crowd of Chinese on-lookers didn't try to recapture Sai Mui. Instead, they parted, making way for their group.

Then, a woman shouted, "Save our girls!"

"Let them through!" a man called out.

More joined in until everyone in the street was calling out encourage-ment. Chanting began as the people cheered for the rescue.

Dolly was stunned. The clapping, cheering, and support took her breath away and made her feel like she was walking a foot above the earth.

Here she was, walking through the newly built Chinatown, which held the same secrets, the same depravity, the same lost souls . . . yet light had crept in and taken hold. The Chinese people were taking a stand against the cor-ruption that had plagued their corner of the world.

It was then that Dolly knew slavery would come to an end.

Not that day, or that year.

But the tong were outnumbered. The slave girls no longer feared *Fahn Quai*.

Dolly's group pushed forward, walking through neighborhood after neighborhood, leading a sort of impromptu procession. As they traveled, more Chinese came out of their homes and their businesses, curious. When they saw what was happening, they joined in the cheering. The celebration. Mei Lien beamed, tears streaking her face, and Dolly knew this moment was a triumph for them all.

She had been thanked countless times and shown gratitude in many ways, but not until today had she understood the impact of her work upon future generations. There was no separating Donaldina Cameron from her calling to help rescue and serve her Chinese daughters. And no matter what might face her, or what might come, she planned to embrace the future.

With her whole heart.

By the time the policemen had finished escorting Dolly, Mei Lien, and Sai Mui to the mission home, humble tears streamed down Dolly's cheeks.

"We are here," Dolly told Sai Mui as they stepped up to the double doors of the mission home.

"Will I be safe here?" Sai Mui whispered in her native tongue, keeping a tight hold on Dolly's hand.

Dolly understood the simple question and replied in kind. "Yes. You are home, dear Sai Mui. You are home."

AFTERWORD

Donaldina Cameron continued as the director of the mission home until her retirement in 1934, after thirty-nine years with the mission. In 1942, the mission home was renamed the Cameron House. When the numbers of girls being rescued decreased throughout the late 1930s, and the Chinese Exclusion Act was repealed in 1943, the needs of the Chinatown community shifted. The Cameron House began to focus on expanding its offerings to social services for women and faith-based programs for youth (CameronHouse.org).

In the early 1900s, Nathaniel Tooker attended one of the general assemblies at the mission home with his two sisters, Mary and Gertrude (Martin, *Chinatown's Angry Angel,* 74). Over the years, Nathaniel was an advocate of the rescue work, crossing paths with Donaldina many times. They attended fundraising functions together, and soon Nathaniel proposed. Donaldina accepted (Martin, *Chinatown's Angry Angel,* 143–47). But she received hard news in July 1911, informing her by telegram that Nathaniel had died (Martin, *Chinatown's Angry Angel,* 152). Another setback for Donaldina, to be sure.

Donaldina dreamed of a home for the Chinese boys, and another home for the younger Chinese girls, primarily so that they wouldn't be influenced by the difficulties and sometimes harsh habits of the women who had come from brothels and abusive situations. Donaldina also wanted the children to be able to play outdoors in a safe environment. By 1912, there were some seventy residents at the mission home (Martin, *Chinatown's Angry Angel,* 157).

The mission board worked tirelessly raising funds, and on Donaldina's visit back east to her beloved friends Mary and Gertrude Tooker, they surprised her with a $2,000 donation. More fundraising continued, and the Tooker sisters donated another $5,000. At 953 East Eleventh Street, Donaldina located a large Victorian home with a fenced yard. Named the Nathaniel Tooker Presbyterian Home for the Chinese, in honor of Nathaniel, soon the place was home to thirty-two children, with Miss Nora Banks as director and Ida Lee as assistant (Martin, *Chinatown's Angry Angel,* 163–65).

Donaldina also founded the Ming Quong Home for Chinese girls. It was built in 1925, and Donaldina served as the superintendent until 1930, after which Ethel Higgins took over. In addition, Donaldina spearheaded the Chung Mei Home for homeless and orphaned Chinese boys. The Chung Mei Home was first located in an old wooden building in Berkeley, but eventually it moved to a larger location.

True to her promise, Tien Fu Wu returned to the mission home after six years of education in Pennsylvania and Canada. Tien had no problem jumping right into service and shared in Donaldina's burdens (Martin, *Chinatown's Angry Angel,* 153). In 1916, Tien traveled to China to fulfill her lifelong dream of finding the family she had been abducted from. Unfortunately, the search was futile (Martin, *Chinatown's Angry Angel,* 176). Tien worked faithfully at Donaldina's side, and she was affectionately called Auntie Wu by the girls at the mission home. When Tien retired in 1952, she moved into a cottage across from Donaldina's home (Martin, *Chinatown's Angry Angel,* 283). On January 4, 1968, Donaldina took her last breath after being in the hospital. Her Chinese daughter, dear Tien, was at her side (Martin, *Chinatown's Angry Angel,* 293).

Today, the Cameron House continues serving the needs of immigrant Asian families in San Francisco. Services offered include counseling, domestic violence intervention, food distribution, support groups, youth after-school and summer programs, adult ESL and computer classes, leadership

development, and volunteer opportunities. See the website, CameronHouse
.org, for ways to give, donate, volunteer, or get involved.

The National Human Trafficking website defines human trafficking as:
"the business of stealing freedom for profit. In some cases, traffickers trick,
defraud or physically force victims into providing commercial sex. In others,
victims are lied to, assaulted, threatened or manipulated into working under
inhumane, illegal or otherwise unacceptable conditions. It is a multi-billion
dollar criminal industry that denies freedom to 24.9 million people around
the world" (HumanTraffickingHotline.org).

How prevalent is human trafficking in the United States? "In 2017,
Polaris worked on 8,759 cases of human trafficking reported to the Polaris-
operated National Human Trafficking Hotline and BeFree Textline. These
cases involved 10,615 individual victims; nearly 5,000 potential traffickers
and 1,698 trafficking businesses" (https://humantraffickinghotline.org/
what-human-trafficking).

What can you do to stem the tide and become aware of needs in your
community? There are various organizations hard at work fighting this terrible
blight on our society. Awareness, education, and support are all imperative.
One organization to which I personally donate is Operation Underground
Railroad: OurRescue.org.

ACKNOWLEDGMENTS

When Heidi Taylor and Lisa Mangum sent me this story idea in the fall of 2018, I had no notion of the breathtaking journey I would undertake through researching the life of Donaldina Cameron. I had never heard specifically about Miss Cameron or her contribution toward thwarting the slave trade of Chinatown, but each day—in fact, every hour—I was drawn deeper into the unforgettable experiences of a woman, and the remarkable staff members and volunteers at the mission home, who personified a life of sacrifice and brought hope to so many downtrodden women and girls of San Francisco.

I knew the scope of this project would require carefully selected readers in advance of submitting the manuscript to my publisher. First, I'm grateful to my agent, Ann Leslie Tuttle, who went through the manuscript more than once and sent me significant insights that deepened pivotal scenes. Many thanks to my beta readers, which included Allison Hong Merrill and Angela Sng, both of whom offered needed perceptions into the Chinese culture and traditions.

Thank you to Taffy Lovell and Julie Wright, who read the manuscript under a tight deadline. And after revision work, Julie agreed to read it again. Extra thanks to Jen Geigle Johnson, who read the manuscript on another tight deadline to offer a fresh perspective.

Many thanks to Heidi Taylor and Lisa Mangum for the brainstorming sessions. Heidi also read the manuscript more than once, giving me in-depth notes and heartfelt encouragement. Special thanks goes to Chris Schoebinger of Shadow Mountain, champion of the project. I'm deeply grateful for editor Emily Watts, whose careful attention to detail built the bridge from my hands to yours. I'm blessed to work with such a talented group of people at Shadow Mountain throughout the entire publishing process.

Part of my research included traveling to San Francisco and visiting the Occidental Mission Home, which is now called the Cameron House and is still in operation, offering community and counseling services. Associate Director Cody Lee gave my daughter Kara and me the grand tour, which only drove home the remarkable work of Miss Cameron and her constituents. Kara and I also spent time walking the streets of Chinatown and visiting the places significant to the story. Thanks as well to David Pon, Marketing and Communications Director of the Cameron House, who kindly helped me with many questions.

My family has been my foundation in my writing career, and I'm grateful for their continued support. Thanks to my husband, Chris, and my children, Kaelin, Kara, Dana, and Rose. My parents, Kent and Gayle Brown, and my father-in-law, Lester Moore, have been my number-one fans.

And finally, thank you to my readers who have joined me on many journeys into history. The life of Donaldina Cameron has touched me deeply, and I hope that you will feel as moved as I have been while studying her life.

DISCUSSION QUESTIONS

1. Why do you think Donaldina Cameron and the mission home employees didn't have the prejudices or racial biases against the Chinese people that so many people of their era did?

2. What do you think about the contrast of Mei Lien arriving in San Francisco to start a new life, only to have it go so horribly wrong, with Donaldina's arrival in San Francisco and her expectations of working at the mission home for only one year?

3. Have you, in your life, made a prayerful decision, only to be faced with extreme challenges because of it? What sort of decisions did Donaldina make that led her to experiences she had never imagined being a part of?

4. Considering the era in which this story takes place, when marriage was deemed a pinnacle achievement in life, it might be surprising that Donaldina called off her engagement to Charles. Why do you think she did so?

5. Despite the mission home having other capable employees, why do you think it was so hard for Donaldina to take a vacation or time for herself?

6. It's heartbreaking to think that some of the rescued girls and women didn't accept the help of the mission home. Why do you think some people have a hard time giving up what they know is hurting them?

7. How did Donaldina reconcile herself to a life that had so many unexpected events and dangers, versus the traditional path that her sisters and friends took into marriage and bearing children?

8. Do you think Donaldina did the right thing by teaching the Chinese

girls and women English and requiring that they study the Bible, instead of letting them carry on their Chinese religious traditions?

9. Today, women enjoy freedoms only dreamed of in the early 1900s. What are some of the freedoms that you find significantly valuable?

10. Does it surprise you that even with all the work Donaldina Cameron and others in her sphere did to fight human trafficking, it is still so prevalent today?

CHAPTER NOTES

CHAPTER ONE

Epigraph citation: Will Irvin, quoted in *Woman's Work,* June 1916, vol. XXXI, no. 6, 143.

The Occidental Mission Home for Girls was founded in 1874 by the Presbyterian Church. The mission home's purpose was to offer refuge to the young Asian immigrants who had been caught in the corrupt "yellow slave trade," and soon the 1882 Chinese Exclusion Act escalated the smuggling efforts (CameronHouse.org).

Margaret Culbertson was the superintendent of the mission home from 1877 to 1897. For twenty years, she worked tirelessly, often through the night, in rescue work. Culbertson was a champion against prostitution and focused her life's work on establishing female morality and rescuing women and children from abuse (Yung, *Unbound Feet,* 34–35).

When Donaldina Cameron arrived in San Francisco in 1895 to work at the mission home, Sacramento Street was named China Street. I've kept the name as Sacramento Street throughout the story for consistency (Wilson, *Chinatown Quest,* 12). The conversation between Donaldina Cameron and Mary Ann Browne is referenced in Wilson, *Chinatown Quest,* 6–7.

Lorna E. Logan, staff member of the mission home, explains that the rescued girls were educated in English and Chinese, as well as sewing, maintaining a home, and Bible study. As their only opportunity for education, the mission home provided a service not found anywhere else in San Francisco (Logan, *Ventures in Mission,* 10).

CHAPTER TWO

Epigraph citation: B. E. Lloyd, *Lights and Shades in San Francisco,* 219.

Yuen Qui's full name is Leung Yuen Qui, but I refer to her as Yuen Qui in this book so as not to confuse her with Leung Kum Ching. In addition, Tien Fuh Wu, the precocious little girl in this chapter, was called Teen Fook or Tai Choie before her rescue. The record from the mission home reads: "Jan. 17/94. Tai Choie alias Teen Fook was rescued by Miss Houseworth, Miss Florence Worley and some police officers from her inhuman mistress who lived on Jackson St. near Stockton St. The child had been very cruelly treated—her flesh pinched and twisted till her face was scarred. Another method of torture was to dip lighted candlewicking in oil and burn her arms with it. Teen Fook is a pretty child of about ten years old, rosy cheeked and fair complexion" (Martin, *Chinatown's Angry Angel,* 46). Cody Lee, associate director of the Cameron House, said, "Miss Cameron called her Tien, the girls called her Auntie Wu. At Cameron House, we usually refer to her by her whole name or Auntie Wu" (conversation with author).

The Chinatown squad consisted of the policer officers who aided Margaret Culbertson: Jesse B. Cook, John T. Green, George Riordan, James Farrell, George W. Wittman, George Patrick O'Connor, and T. P. Andrews. These men used break-in tools such as wedges, hatchets, crowbars, and sledge-hammers (Martin, *Chinatown's Angry Angel,* 48–49).

CHAPTER THREE

Epigraph citation: Ban Zhao, *Lessons for Women.* 80 CE. Reference found: Sun Jiahui, ed., "Ancient China's 'Virtuous' Women: Three Obediences and Four Virtues." 风流中国, 21 Aug. 2017, https://culture.followcn.com/2017/08/21/ancient-chinas-virtuous-women-three-obediences-four-virtues/.

The character Wang Foo is based on Wong See Duck, a notorious slave owner who arrived in San Francisco in 1908. Wong See Duck was part of a major smuggling ring with Kung Shee, Jew Gwai Ha, and Yee Mar. The four of them were deported after the 1935 Broken Blossoms court case was won, indicting them for illegal importation for immoral purposes (Edward Wong, "The 1935 Broken Blossoms Case").

Mei Lien is a character created by the author, but her experiences are based on actual events that happened to the Chinese girls and women rescued by Donaldina Cameron and her associates.

CHAPTER FOUR

Epigraph citation: Annual Reports of the Mission Home (quoted in Martin, *Chinatown's Angry Angel*, 44).

Hong Leen and her husband Woo Hip both met tragic ends, yet their children, raised at the mission home, continued their parents' legacies. It was Hong Leen's greatest wish for her daughter to become a medical missionary and her son a minister (Wilson, *Chinatown Quest*, 13). I was not able to uncover the names of these children, thus *Kang* and *Jiao* are fictitious.

The detention shed that was used to detain Chinese people immigrating to America was in operation until 1908. Conditions were rough, and the immigrants were treated as prisoners while awaiting for their papers to be processed (*San Francisco Call*, vol. 104, no. 64, 3 August 1908).

The rescue story of Sing Leen is based on the rescue story of Sing Ho that took place on August 15, 1892. Heartbreakingly enough, not all the rescued women remained at the mission home, due to the power of addiction, trauma, or fears that came from believing the tong's threats and promises of curses (Martin, *Chinatown's Angry Angel*, 44).

CHAPTER FIVE

Epigraph citation: *Forty Seventh Congress*. Sess. I. Ch. 126. Chinese Exclusion Act, approved May 6, 1882, 61.

The criminal tong member names are fictional in this chapter, but their actions are patterned after deeds done by tong members Wong See Duck, his wife, Kung She Wong, moneylender Fong She, and procuress Kwai Ying (Martin, *Chinatown's Angry Angel,* 256–57).

Chinese girls and women brought over under false papers were taken to a slave market of sorts, which amounted to standing on a table or chair where they could be inspected by prospective buyers. They were made to undress so that the buyers could assess their overall health and appeal to the purposes they would be forced into, whether it was for domestic chores or prostitution (Yung, *Unbound Feet,* 27).

CHAPTER SIX

Epigraph citation: Annual Reports of the Mission Home.

Donaldina's clothing in the board meeting scene is described by author Mildred Martin, as well as the names of the Presbyterian Women's Occidental Board of Foreign Missions, which included Mrs. P. D. Browne, Mrs. E. V. Robbins, Mrs. Sara B. Cooper, and Mrs. Phoebe Apperson Hearst (*Chinatown's Angry Angel,* 51).

The case of the missing apples and Tien's tearful confession is based on an incident in the mission home that demonstrates that although the young residents had their needs provided for, they often resorted to survival tactics learned on the streets of Chinatown (Martin, *Chinatown's Angry Angel,* 45–46).

With Miss Culbertson's retirement and the changing of the guard, so to speak, Donaldina began to receive more threats and warnings than usual, and they became a constant nuisance. But Donaldina didn't cower. She believed that if someone truly meant her violent harm, they wouldn't send a warning in advance. Threats included the incident of finding a hanging effigy of herself in a room when she was tricked into following a note's direction to rescue a girl (Martin, *Chinatown's Angry Angel,* 53–54).

Even when Donaldina was sent directions to a rescue, others were in place to thwart her, including police officers who were bribed and watchmen and informers hired by the slave owners. The informers would warn the brothels of impending raids, and Donaldina's team would then have to outsmart them.

Another challenge came in the form of the legal system, which was faulty. Tong members paid corrupt lawyers to file false claims and obtain warrants for the slave girls' arrests, accusing them of theft. Of course, if a girl was recovered after a raid on the mission home, the girl would be transported out of San Francisco and never seen again (Martin, *Chinatown's Angry Angel,* 54).

The scripture quote from the Apostle Paul was particularly dear to Donaldina, as she relied on her religious beliefs, prayer, and scriptures to give her courage and strength (Wilson, *Chinatown Quest,* 26).

The record of Dong Ho and how she showed up at the mission house with her bundle of treasures is recorded in Martin, *Chinatown's Angry Angel,* 53.

CHAPTER SEVEN

Epigraph citation: Asbury, *Barbary Coast,* 176.

Ah-Peen Oie Kum was a beautiful courtesan who began to deal opium in order to buy her freedom back. She was clever and considered the "toast of Chinatown." She worked closely with the tong and became part owner of other girls. She became a feared leader in a system that she had once been a victim of. Her brothel was raided multiple times by Donaldina's team, and there was no love lost between the two women (Martin, *Chinatown's Angry Angel,* 238–39).

CHAPTER EIGHT

Epigraph citation: Annual Reports of the Mission Home.

Donaldina also dealt with challenges from the leadership in the mission home. Mary H. Field was not as devoted to the betterment of the Chinese women and girls. Her reading of Kipling's new poem was only a slice of her attitude toward them. She lumped them together by claiming that "Mongolian women presented a harder problem—'more conscienceless, more suspicious, more fiery and voluble, more utterly bereft of reason—half-devil and half-child'" (Wilson, *Chinatown Quest,* 17).

Jean Ying's parents were contacted about her survival in San Francisco.

They sent money for Jean Ying's passage home, and she traveled with a group of associates connected with the mission home in order to secure her safety. Many weeks later, Donaldina received word from Canton that Jean Ying had been reunited with her overjoyed parents (Wilson, *Chinatown Quest,* 18–19).

CHAPTER NINE

Epigraph citation: Frank Moore, ed., "The Chinese to the President," *Record of the Year, Volume 1* (New York: G. W. Carleton & Co., Publishers, 1876), 601.

The character of Huan Sun is based on the true story of Sin Kee. Sin Kee fell in love with a woman he met at a brothel on Mah Fong Alley. The woman confided how she must earn enough money each month for her expenses plus pay back three hundred dollars to her owner. Sin Kee helped her escape, but then the tong captured her and demanded one thousand dollars from Sin Kee. It was then that Sin Kee went to Donaldina Cameron for help (Wilson, *Chinatown Quest,* 37–38).

CHAPTER TEN

Epigraph citation: Rev. Ira M. Condit, *The Chinaman as We See Him: And Fifty Years of Work for Him* (Chicago, New York, Toronto: Fleming H. Revell Company, 1900), 140–41.

Chinese slave owners, especially members of the criminal tong groups, used the legal system to fight back against Donaldina Cameron and the mission home. When the Chinese owners arrived with an accompanying police officer or lawyer, Donaldina took her time opening the many deadbolts on the mission home door. A brass gong was rung to signal that a search was about to be performed on the house, giving the girls warning (Wilson, *Chinatown Quest,* 19).

There is some discrepancy in the accounts of how Kum Quai arrived at 920 Sacramento Street. Author Carol Wilson said that she came of her own accord, escaped from her master (*Chinatown Quest,* 19). Author Mildred Martin, who called her Kum Qui, said that she was rescued from Baker Alley and rushed to the mission home through a heckling crowd (*Chinatown's Angry Angel*, 55).

CHAPTER ELEVEN

Epigraph citation: Women's Foreign Missionary Society of the Presbyterian Church, *Annual Report*, 1902, 38.

Few of the Chinese women smuggled into San Francisco could read or write, which meant they signed their contracts with their slave owners with an X or a thumbprint. The typical contract included the money owed for passage across the ocean, the number of years to be worked (four to six), and a stipulation that if the woman was sick for more than ten days, she had to make up an extra month of work (Yung, *Unbound Feet,* 27). These contracts were often extended indefinitely because days not worked due to menstrual cycles, illnesses, or pregnancy were counted against the women. As Judy Yung pointed out, "Most Chinese prostitutes were subjected to such physical and mental abuse that few could outlive their contract terms of four to six years" (*Unbound Feet,* 28).

CHAPTER TWELVE

Epigraph citation: *San Francisco Chronicle*, April 3, 1900 (as quoted by Wilson in *Chinatown Quest*, 22).

When Kum Quai calls Donaldina "*Lo Mo,*" it's meant as an affectionate term that bonds two women together, or a child to her mother. Although the technical translation is "old mama" or "old mother," in Donaldina's case, it was adopted with love throughout Chinatown (Martin, *Chinatown's Angry Angel,* 61).

CHAPTER THIRTEEN

Epigraph citation: *San Francisco Call*, 1898 (quoted in Asbury, *Barbary Coast*, 181).

Judy Yung writes, "Whereas the majority of white prostitutes came to San Francisco as independent professionals and worked for wages in brothels, Chinese prostitutes were almost always kidnapped, lured, or purchased from poor parents by procurers in China for as little as $50 and then resold in America for as much as $1,000 in the 1870s" (*Unbound Feet*, 27). By the 1920s, the price reached from $6,000 to $10,000 in gold (Martin, *Chinatown's Angry Angel*, 239).

CHAPTER FOURTEEN

Epigraph citation: "Palo Alto Resolution," *San Francisco Chronicle*, April 3, 1900.

Attorney Henry E. Monroe spent over thirty years working in behalf of the mission home. And no matter where his career took him, he continued to donate countless hours to legal work that benefited the mission home residents. He led an honorable career and earned a high reputation (Wilson, *Chinatown Quest*, 49).

When Kum Quai was abducted from the mission home in March 1900, Donaldina would not back down. These events led to the fiasco of Kum Quai and Donaldina spending the night in jail, only to have Kum Quai abducted again and tried in the middle of the night on the roadside. Public upheaval led to indictments of the justice of the peace, the deputy constable, and the two Chinese abductors Chung Bow and Wong Fong (Wilson, *Chinatown Quest*, 19–25; Martin, *Chinatown's Angry Angel*, 55–57).

CHAPTER FIFTEEN

Epigraph citation: "A Science Odyssey: People and Discoveries: Bubonic Plague Hits San Francisco," *PBS*, Public Broadcasting Service, https://www .pbs.org/wgbh/aso/databank/entries/dm00bu.html.

In March 1900, Chinatown was put under quarantine against the bubonic plague. The upheaval in the city was immediate, with travel restricted for those living on both sides of the barriers. Leung Kum Ching (later called

Ah Ching) knocked on the mission home door when she was nine years old, crying about her dying sister. Her sister had been cast onto the street, as per pagan custom, during the bubonic plague. Since Chinatown was under quarantine, Donaldina had to go through skylights and cross rooftops in order to pass the barriers. Unfortunately, the sister died of appendicitis after the rescue (Wilson, *Chinatown Quest,* 29–30). Leung Kum Ching continued to live at the mission home, and when she was older she aided in more rescues (Wilson, *Chinatown Quest,* 38; Martin, *Chinatown's Angry Angel,* 77). Many Chinese were skeptical of the inoculations against the plague, and one girl in the mission home panicked, jumped out of the second-story window, and broke her ankle, all to avoid the shot (Martin, *Chinatown's Angry Angel,* 78).

CHAPTER SIXTEEN

Epigraph citation: M. G. C. Edholm, "A Stain on the Flag," *Californian Illustrated Magazine,* February 1892, 162.

Not only were the paper daughters exploited for their bodies, many of them succumbed to venereal diseases. "Once hopelessly diseased, they were discarded on the street or locked in a room to die alone" (Yung, *Unbound Feet,* 29).

CHAPTER SEVENTEEN

Epigraph citation: Martin, *Chinatown's Angry Angel,* 65 (quoted from California Historical Society with Donaldina Cameron House, 1931).

Dolly was called Mama by many of the Chinese girls in the mission home. The scene in this chapter where Dolly is questioned by another woman on the ferry truly happened. Part of the conversation was documented by author Mildred Martin. Dolly later said of the incident, "I hope my Creator will forgive me. But I told the legal truth, you know. Can't you imagine the head shaking that went on when those easterners took home their tale about cosmopolitan San Francisco?" (*Chinatown's Angry Angel,* 60).

CHAPTER EIGHTEEN

Epigraph citation: Asbury, *Barbary Coast*, 179.

Herbert Asbury informs us that the two types of brothels in San Francisco's Chinatown included the parlor house and the crib. The parlor houses were upscale and limited in number. They attracted wealthier patrons and were furnished in relative luxury. The women dressed in expensive and alluring clothing. Cribs littered the streets of Chinatown, sometimes lining both sides of an alley. The crib was meagerly furnished and consisted of a "small, one-storey shack some twelve feet wide and fourteen feet deep, divided into two rooms by heavy curtains of coarse material" (*Barbary Coast*, 175–76).

CHAPTER NINETEEN

Epigraph citation: Donaldina Cameron, quoting the Apostle Paul, Philippians 4:13 (cited by Wilson, *Chinatown Quest*, 26).

When President William McKinley visited the mission home late one night, he brought his wife, Ida, with him. Ida had been ill, and so their trip had been delayed. In Mildred Martin's book, she lists the president as President Theodore Roosevelt (*Chinatown's Angry Angel*, 62–63). But Julia Siler corrects the information in her publication, *The White Devil's Daughters* (167–68).

Several interpreters assisted at the mission home over the years. Yuen Qui had a close bond with Tien, and when Yuen Qui died, everyone grieved. When Tien saw how much Donaldina grieved, it put the director in a more human light, and Tien's heart began to soften (Martin, *Chinatown's Angry Angel*, 66–67).

CHAPTER TWENTY

Epigraph citation: Annual Reports of the Mission Home.

Women working in brothels did not get to keep their babies. Frequently, the babies were stolen so that they could become part of a human trafficking ring. Other times, the poor health of the mother prevented a live birth. Babies were left on the doorstep of the mission home because the mothers knew it was a safe place. Babies were also kidnapped in China and brought over to San Francisco, as was the case with an elderly woman who purchased a baby in Hong Kong for ten dollars, then tried to pass it off as a grandchild. Donaldina was called by Colonel Jackson to come take that baby (Wilson, *Chinatown Quest,* 30). Another tragic case centered on Yoke Wan, who had her baby snatched away from her and sold to a woman slaver. Despite Donaldina and her legal team helping Yoke Wan in a total of forty-seven court appearances, spanning a year and a half, Yoke Wan was never granted parental rights (Wilson, *Chinatown Quest,* 50–52).

CHAPTER TWENTY-ONE

Epigraph citation: Annual Reports of the Mission Home.

Although not highlighted much in this book, Donaldina's siblings were a great support to her, writing letters and exchanging visits. When she met and fell in love with Charles, it was her siblings' hope that she had fully recovered from the heartbreak of her first broken engagement. Author Mildred Martin shares the sweetness of the courtship between Donaldina and Charles in *Chinatown's Angry Angel* (72–76).

CHAPTER TWENTY-TWO

Epigraph citation: Nee and de Bary, *Longtime Californ',* 83–90.

In this chapter, Donaldina shares with Charles the success story of Yute Ying's courageous testimony in front of the grand jury. But not every court appearance had a favorable outcome. Yoke Hay was rescued from being sold to a brothel, and as Donaldina and her rescue team drove Yoke Hay to court, she told them how her owners were not her parents, as they claimed to be. But when she stood before the judge, her angry master and his group of Chinese friends intimidated her, so she refused to tell the true story. The judge ruled that Yoke Hay had to return to her "father" (Wilson, *Chinatown Quest*, 31).

CHAPTER TWENTY-THREE

Epigraph citation: Annual Reports of the Mission Home.

In one of Donaldina's darkest moments, she wrote: "The Chinese themselves will never abolish the hateful practice of buying and selling their women like so much merchandise. . . . Enactment by law does not reach this evil as it is impossible to get any Chinese evidence into court on account of the danger of life and property involved by incurring the enmity of the powerful and revengeful Highbinder Tongs" (Martin, *Chinatown's Angry Angel*, 85). Thus, Donaldina felt she was justified in her seizure and holding of minors until the legal system could make a decision.

CHAPTER TWENTY-FOUR

Epigraph citation: Inspector John J. Manion, "'Lo Mo,' Mother of Chinatown," *Women and Missions*, January 1932.

Not every rescued woman accepted her good fortune or new way of life. Their traumas ran deep, and women and girls arrived with addictions and ingrained behavior. In some cases, the rescued girls refused to leave their lives of squalor and abuse. The former slaves had been threatened by their owners with death or punishment if they tried to escape, and many times those threats became reality. Other women, such as courtesans accustomed to luxury clothing and accommodations, refused to dress in basic cotton dresses, eat the simple meals, or study and do chores (Martin, *Chinatown's Angry Angel*, 44).

CHAPTER TWENTY-FIVE

Epigraph citation: Annual Reports of the Mission Home.

Donaldina spent an immense amount of time dealing with the courts.

Some of the judgments that were handed down infuriated her, and she was held in contempt of court more than once. Her determination led to a new bill being passed by the state legislature that enabled a temporary guardianship of a child until a hearing—this Donaldina used to its full effect (Wilson, *Chinatown Quest*, 86).

CHAPTER TWENTY-SIX

Epigraph citation: Charles Shepherd, *The Ways of Ah Sin: Composite Narrative of Things as They Are* (Old Tappan, NJ: Fleming H. Revell, 1923), 87.

In 1880, California's civil code was amended to prohibit marriage between a white person and a "Negro, Mulatto, or Mongolian," which meant many Chinese immigrants were without a way to marry. As a result, the trafficking of Chinese women became hugely profitable (Yung, *Unbound Feet*, 29–30).

The incident in this chapter of Huan Sun being shot by the tong is based on the true story of Foon Hing, who was targeted by the tong because he brought his cousin to the mission home. Foon Hing had been followed by a highbinder, and as soon as he left the mission, he was shot on the sidewalk (Wilson, *Chinatown Quest*, 37).

CHAPTER TWENTY-SEVEN

Epigraph citation: Annual Reports of the Mission Home.

Donaldina took a year-long furlough after working at the mission home for nine years, four of them as the director. With the assurance that the mission home would be in good hands under the direction of temporary director Wilmina Wheeler and housekeeper Frances Thompson, Donaldina set off. She traveled across the United States, visiting former residents of the home, met Charles Bazatas in Pennsylvania, visited her sister Isabella for the first time in Scotland, then finally visited China (Martin, *Chinatown's Angry Angel*, 74–76, 88–95).

CHAPTER TWENTY-EIGHT

Epigraph citation: Annual Reports of the Mission Home.

During Donaldina's absence from the mission home, Miss Wheeler and Miss Thompson fended off the usual shenanigans of intruders. A slave owner pretended that he was an upstanding citizen and wanted to marry Kum Ying, then had a false marriage license created. In another situation, slave owners acted as devoted parents who had lost their child and showed up at the mission home asking for her. Although the power of the criminal tong groups was stronger than ever, Miss Wheeler was able to rescue nine Chinese girls and eight Japanese in addition to harboring thirty more women (Martin, *Chinatown's Angry Angel*, 95–96).

When Donaldina returned from her year-long travels, she was elated to see her Chinese daughters again—daughters who would go on to become influential women. Tiny, or Tye Leung, became the first Chinese woman to work at the US Immigration Service as the Chinese matron on Angel Island. Margaret would attend the University of Arizona in Tucson, and Lonnie would become the first Chinese nurse at the Presbyterian Hospital in Philadelphia (Martin, *Chinatown's Angry Angel*, 156).

CHAPTER TWENTY-NINE

Epigraph Citation: Annual Reports of the Mission Home.

Ah-Peen Oie bought her own freedom from slavery from her original owner through opium sales. But she was blamed for the loss of a slave girl, which meant she now owed that price to the tong leaders (Wilson, *Chinatown Quest*, 110–11). After Ah-Peen Oie asked Donaldina for help, she changed her name to Amy and began the process of renouncing her former ways. She underwent a true conversion to Christianity (Martin, *Chinatown's Angry Angel*, 238–39).

CHAPTER THIRTY

Epigraph citation: Annual Reports of the Mission Home.

After the 1906 San Francisco earthquake, transporting such a large group of girls and women was an ordeal for Donaldina and the mission home employees. Not only did they have to seek shelter and provide food, but danger still lurked, with opportunists looking to capitalize on misfortune.

CHAPTER THIRTY-ONE

Epigraph citation: Donaldina Cameron, report of events following the 1906 earthquake (quoted in Wilson, *Chinatown Quest*, 78).

Miracle after miracle happened to get the girls out of San Francisco, and Donaldina's ragtag group finally secured passage at the Ferry Building. In her own words: "It was a thankful, though a completely exhausted company that sank down amid bundles and babies on the lower deck of the steamer, too weary to walk to the saloon. . . . But tired and homeless, knowing not where that night we were to lay our heads, our only feeling was one of gratitude for deliverance as we looked over the group of more than sixty young faces and realized how God had cared for His Children" (quoted in Martin, *Chinatown's Angry Angel*, 107).

Donaldina told the story of Yuen Kum and Henry Lai in her own words, a remarkable event considering the devastation of the earthquake: "Long before the eighteenth of April the cards were out for a wedding at the Home. Yuen Kum, a clear, bright girl who had been with us several years, was to be the bride of Mr. Henry Lai of Cleveland, Ohio. The date set for the wedding was April twenty-first. And to prove the truth of the old adage 'Love will find a way' let me tell you that the wedding did take place on that very date! The ceremony was performed by Dr. [Warren H.] Landon in the beautiful, ivy-covered chapel at San Anselmo, and notwithstanding all the difficulties the young man had gone through in finding his fiancée, on his arrival from the East the day of the earthquake, and all the trying experiences through which Yuen Kum had passed, they were a happy couple as they received the congratulations of those present. Just after the wedding, Mr. and Mrs. Henry Lai started for their home in Cleveland amidst showers of California roses and the best wishes of their many friends. So romance with its magic touch helped us for a time to forget our great losses" (SFMuseum.net).

CHAPTER THIRTY-TWO

Epigraph citation: Poem by Imperial Chinese Consul-General Huang Zunxian in San Francisco, translated by J. H. Laughlin, cornerstone ceremony for new mission home, August 1907. Poetry collection found in J. D. Schmidt, *Within the Human Realm: The Poetry of Huang Zunxian, 1848–1905* (Cambridge Studies in Chinese History, Literature and Institutions, Cambridge University Press, 1994).

The need for rescue work continued even when Donaldina left San Francisco after the earthquake. The underground slave trade of women and girls unfortunately shifted from San Francisco to surrounding communities. Donaldina went on rescues not only in the cities she lived in, but in other locations as well. During her two years living in Oakland and San Rafael, she helped to rescue sixty more women. Some of them were losses, and in those cases Donaldina left blank spaces below ledger entries, with the hope that a later rescue would prove successful (Martin, *Chinatown's Angry Angel*, 114).

Joyous was the day when Donaldina and her daughters entered the rebuilt mission home on 920 Sacramento Street. The Presbyterian Foreign Mission Board had been allotted $11,000 toward the new structure, and all other funds were raised through donations (Martin, *Chinatown's Angry Angel*, 111).

An article in *Woman's Work* magazine described the interior of the newly finished mission home: "The whole furnishing of the Home is eloquent with love. . . . Each dormitory is a memorial gift either in the memory of those 'gone before,' or to the zeal and love of auxiliaries and young people's societies. Chinese friends have lavished bronzes, brass ornaments, embroideries, carvings. . . . Oh, that dear friends everywhere might catch an echo of the laughter and song that floated down the halls, or see the happy faces of these jewels of great price rescued from the filth of sin! Then would you know that your gifts have not been in vain" (quoted in Martin, *Chinatown's Angry Angel,* 118–19. Original reference: *Woman's Work* magazine, vol. XXIII, 168).

CHAPTER THIRTY-THREE

Epigraph citation: E. French Strother, "Setting Chinese Slave Girls Free," *The California Weekly,* February 26, 1909, 213, 216.

The dedication of the new mission home at 920 Sacramento Street took place on April 14, 1908. Well wishes came from all over the country in the form of telegrams and letters. The chapel filled with guests, and reporters eagerly took notes for their articles (Martin, *Chinatown's Angry Angel,* 121), and the portion of Donaldina's speech is recorded by Martin (*Chinatown's Angry Angel,* 122). Although the day was filled with celebration and visiting dignitaries, the rescue work was far from over. The rebuilding of Chinatown included the reestablishment of human trafficking.

Sai Mui, a paper daughter forced into prostitution, ran away from her captors, only to run into rival tong men. Donaldina's interference was both courageous and dangerous. With the help of the police and her interpreter, Donaldina was able to secure the girl. To Donaldina's surprise, she was cheered in the streets as they hurried to the mission home. The victory was sweet, but the journey was far from over for Donaldina. Children, teenagers, and women were still being trafficked, and Donaldina felt the need to be ready to aid where she could (Martin, *Chinatown's Angry Angel,* 125–27).

Tien's education sponsor was Horace C. Coleman, who paid for all six years of her schooling. She attended four years in Germantown, Pennsylvania, and two years at the Bible Training School in Toronto, Canada. Tien kept her promise to Donaldina and returned to the mission home, playing an integral role in guiding the work forward (Martin, *Chinatown's Angry Angel,* 153).

SELECTED BIBLIOGRAPHY
AND RECOMMENDED READING

Annual Reports of the Mission Home to the Woman's Occidental Board of Foreign Missions, written by Directors Sarah M. N. Cummings, Margaret Culbertson, Mary H. Field, and Donaldina M. Cameron, and their assistants, matrons, and housekeepers. San Anselmo, CA: San Francisco Theological Seminary, 1874–1920.

Asbury, Herbert. *The Barbary Coast: An Informal History of the San Francisco Underworld.* New York: Thunder's Mouth Press, 1933.

"Cameron House." *Cameron House*, https://cameronhouse.org/.

Donaldina Cameron's San Francisco Mission Home for Chinese Girls—1906, http://www.sfmuseum.net/1906/ew15.html.

Harris, Gloria G., and Hannah S. Cohen. *Women Trailblazers of California: Pioneers to the Present.* Charleston, SC: The History Press, 2012.

Lloyd, B. E. *Lights and Shades in San Francisco.* San Francisco: A. L. Bancroft & Company, 1876.

Logan, Lorna E. *Ventures in Mission: The Cameron House Story.* Wilson Creek, WA: Crawford Hobby Print Shop, 1976.

Martin, Mildred Crowl. *Chinatown's Angry Angel: The Story of Donaldina Cameron.* Palo Alto, CA: Pacific Books, 1977.

Nee, Victor, and Brett de Bary. *Longtime Californ': A Documentary Study of an American Chinatown.* New York: Pantheon Books, 1972.

New Era Magazine: Presbyterian Church in the U.S.A. General Assembly. New York [etc.]. February 1920, vol. 26, no. 2.

One Hundred Fourteenth Annual Report of the Board of Home Missions of the Presbyterian Church in the United States of America. New York: Presbyterian Building, 1916.

Pryor, Alton. *Fascinating Women in California History*. Roseville, CA: Stagecoach Publishing, 2003.

Siler, Julia Flynn. *The White Devil's Daughters: The Women Who Fought Slavery in San Francisco's Chinatown*. New York: Alfred A. Knopf, 2019.

Wilson, Carol Green. *Chinatown Quest: One Hundred Years of Donaldina Cameron House*. San Francisco: California Historical Society with Donaldina Cameron House, 1931.

Woman's Work magazine. Woman's Foreign Missionary Society of the Presbyterian Church. New York: Presbyterian Building, 1908.

Wong, Edward. "The 1935 Broken Blossoms Case—Four Chinese Women and Their Fight for Justice." *Atavist*, 23 July 2015. https://edwardwong .atavist.com/the-1935-broken-blossoms-case-four-chinese-women-and -their-fight-for-justice. See also https://www.archives.gov/files/publications /prologue/2016/spring/blossoms.pdf.

Wong, Kristin, and Kathryn Wong. *Fierce Compassion: The Life of Abolitionist Donaldina Cameron*. Saline, MI: New Earth Enterprises, 2012.

Yung, Judy. *Unbound Feet: A Social History of Chinese Women in San Francisco*. Berkeley and Los Angeles, CA: University of California Press, 1995.